The Monk Without Dharma

A NOVEL

THUKTEN YESHI

Published 2024
Printed in the United States of America
Print: 979-8-9903536-0-2
E-book: 979-8-9903536-1-9
Library of Congress Control Number: 2024908873

Cover art by Chimi R Namgyal
Cover design by Tenzin Tshering
Interior design by Tabitha Lahr

The Monk Without Dharma

THUKTEN YESHI holds a master's degree in filmmaking and a bachelor's degree in English literature. He began his career in media research and television before transitioning to film and fiction.

His love for and interest in film and fiction, both as a creator and consumer, are centred on mainstream stories. Therefore, he places significant importance on the art and craft intrinsic to mainstream storytelling.

Notably, this emphasis on art and craft extends to incorporating elements of tantric Buddhism that influence the trajectory of the characters' lives or affect the story world in some other ways into the toolkit of storytelling, so that the narrative form employed to tell the story can portray the depths of the Himalayan Buddhist story world.

Hailing from Dechheling in southeast Bhutan, he completed his undergraduate studies in the country and pursued his post-graduate education in Australia. He currently lives in Thimphu with his wife and two children.

www.facebook/thukteyeshi
www.twitter/thuktenyeshi

May this book illuminate the path of dharma for all in search of truth. May its words resonate with those in need of inspiration. With deep reverence, I offer this aspiration prayer that the light of dharma may reach and touch the lives of all sentient beings.

This book is a piece of art, not a scholarly work on Buddhism, history, culture, tradition, or any other subject. Anything stated herein is only to serve the narrative's purpose and not to make any assertion or claim on any matter.

ACKNOWLEDGMENTS

I would like to express my heartfelt gratitude to my beloved wife, Jangchu Choden, for her incredible support throughout the journey of writing this book. Her encouragement to persevere against all odds and her dedication to our family have been instrumental in bringing this novel to fruition at this level.

Next, I am profoundly thankful to Khenpo Tshulthrim Dorji for his invaluable assistance and guidance on matters of dharma. He patiently sat through several read-throughs of both the film script and the novel manuscript to ensure the correct portrayal of dharma.

I also extend my sincere appreciation to my two good friends in the film industry, Mila Tobgyel and Sherub Gyeltshen, for their expertise and assistance in the aspects of culture and tradition, as well as for their genuine goodwill, encouragement, support, and belief in me and my potential.

Furthermore, I wish to acknowledge translator Adam Pearcey of Lotsawa House for his generosity in permitting to use the English translation of the *Jangchub Sempe Chopa la Jukpa* text in the story. His dedication to preserving and disseminating important Buddhist texts has been invaluable to this book.

Finally, I would like to wholeheartedly thank Pema Choiden, a genuinely goodhearted person in New York known for assisting everyone in need, for facilitating all payments to the editor and the entire publishing team for the services they rendered.

To everyone mentioned above, and to the countless others who may have played a part in the creation of this novel, I once again offer my deepest gratitude. Your support and contributions have enriched this work beyond measure.

THE MONK WITHOUT DHARMA

PART ONE

CHAPTER 1

Tompo—a nine-year-old boy—stood in the harrowing stillness of his home, gripped by visceral fear, with his gaze locked in a helpless, vacant stare. Across the room, his parents lay on a thin mattress of threadbare cloth, succumbing to a deadly new disease that did not even have a name.

I'm only three years short of completing one astrological cycle, and that makes me nearly a man, he said to himself, to shore up his failing courage. For he had neither a sibling nor a relative to depend upon for help, and no other person would come near his house, as the killer disease was said to transmit even from a distance.

"Everything looked so certain, so promising," his father said, referring to the deal that he had struck with the village headman. "It was within my grasp." His eyes shone briefly underneath the wilting eyelids. "I was going to acquire that piece of land and make ourselves a landed family. But it was a fickle dream, beyond our merit, meant to lure us to our ruin. Instead of getting land, I lost all that we owned and left you in lifelong bondage."

"That is all right, Father," Tompo replied, hoping that his brave countenance would mask his concerns.

"But I didn't gamble our future away, as many say. Although the deal was highly skewed in favour of the headman, it provided us with a rare opportunity—the opportunity of a lifetime to obtain what was denied to us by our birth, the opportunity to begin a new life of dignity and honour, the opportunity gifted by the gods and the deities of the territory."

"Gifted by the gods and the deities of the territory?" Tompo repeated, his head jerking up in a mix of confusion and surprise.

"Yes, Son," his father affirmed unequivocally. "It may sound strange to you, but it is true. This is our family secret, going back to the time of our ancestors. I didn't tell you because you were a child. Of course, you are a child even now, and you may not understand, but since we are dying, there is no other choice but to tell you everything."

"Yes, Father," replied Tompo, his voice growing eager.

His father nodded. "Now, listen carefully. Although our ancestors were only tenant farmers, toiling for their landlords, they were profoundly sincere and truthful and wholeheartedly devoted and dedicated in their work. Over time, that way of working became a way of life for them, and those qualities their defining characteristics. These virtues pleased the gods and the deities to such an extent that Nature reciprocated."

"Nature reciprocated?" Tompo's eyes widened.

"Yes, Son. The gods and the deities are the lords of the land. They control all elements of Nature: wind, rain, clouds, rivers, and even pests, animals, and plants. That is why we pray to them for rain during drought, good harvest during famine, and for sunshine, wind, and clouds as well, depending on our needs. But this gift granted to our ancestors was different. It was not only rain and sun, but everything else given bountifully."

"What *everything*, Father?" Tompo bent forward, momentarily forgetting his fear.

"The entire climatic condition. It was not only made conducive for the healthy growth of the crops, but for our ancestors to work without being inconvenienced by bad weather. Also, the state of their fields never deteriorated. The soil remained soft and fertile all seasons. Then, the weeds didn't encroach upon their fields, and the pests and animals kept away from their crops."

Tompo stared in awe, fascinated.

"But these things were too significant to go unnoticed or left unquestioned if discovered by others. So, concerned that the others would find out and subject them to unnecessary scrutiny and hassle, they chose only those isolated farmlands far from the village. Thus, most of their fields were in rocky or steep areas that no other tenant farmers wanted. Yet, they had bumper crops year after year."

"Then what happened, Father?" Tompo pressed, his face animated and eyes gleaming with curiosity.

"They kept everything closely guarded and passed the secret gift down through the generations, from parents to children, as we do this day. That is why we are so sincere and truthful, and devoted and dedicated, not only in our farming work, but also in other aspects of our lives. This is also the reason why we have good crops in all the fields."

Tompo nodded, the weight of the revelation settling on his young shoulders. But he was still not able to fully comprehend the enormity of such an extraordinary thing, much less come to terms with it.

"So, you see, that was why I got into this deal. No matter how poor the soil was, we could have produced bumper harvests of all the crops, paid him every grain that was agreed upon, acquired that land, and changed our future forever." He paused briefly, his face falling, before continuing, "But no man can overcome his bad karma." He shook his head feebly. "Now, here we are, struck down by this illness. Of the eight of us who had been across the border to the accursed village of Jayul in the plains, only two of us contracted it."

"I don't understand, Father," said Tompo, his brow creasing.

His father offered a meek smile. "I think we might have had some good karma to be born into this ancient family of tenant farmers, and have Nature respond to us, but not enough to own lands and be our own masters. With adequate good karma, we might have been born into a family of landowners, but we were not, and now we are not able to change that. Everything must conform to karma, for it governs our very existence in this universe."

"But if the gods and the deities—"

"Even though they are powerful," his father interrupted, "the gods and the deities are only masters of the temporal world. They can protect us from some harm, heal us from some illnesses, clear some obstacles in our lives, and even control some aspects of Nature, but they cannot change our karma. For having not gained mastery over the true nature of existence, they themselves are subjected to karma. Lama Jar Tong Dargyel said that only the buddhas and the bodhisattvas at an advanced stage are freed from the shackles of karma."

Tompo nodded sadly.

"I had hoped to alter your fortune, but instead I have brought misfortune upon you." There was remorse in his voice. "Before long, you will have neither parents nor a home. You will be forced to endure a life akin to slavery, toiling for the headman and his family indefinitely, as a means to repay the debt incurred in this deal. It will be a life of utmost hardship, even compared to tenant farmers."

Again, Tompo heard his father's despair. "Father, I can work; I will do what I must."

"I know that, my son. In fact, you can work harder than all of us. You are far more wholehearted in your devotion and dedication than we are, and far more profound in your sincerity and truthfulness. I am sure the gods and the deities will be pleased with you even more, and will bless you with greater gifts."

"Yes, Father," Tompo replied, his young heart filling with hope.

"Now, remember this," his father continued, his voice so weak it was nearly a whisper. "Headman Thodak Zamba and his family must have accumulated great merit in their past lives to be born in this state of comfort and luxury, prominence and position. You must serve them well, not just to pay off the debt, but also to cleanse your bad karma and accrue good merit."

"I will, Father," Tompo promised.

"You must also be grateful for everything in this life, and continue to live a truthful life, as you do now. No matter what happens, no matter how much you suffer, you must never be dissatisfied with your life and feel miserable about it. Follow this and you may exhaust your bad karma and possibly have a better rebirth in your next life."

"Yes, Father." The boy looked at the man, unsure what more he could say.

"Finally, do not tell anyone about our family secret, not even your most trusted friend, for who would not want to have such a priceless gift for oneself? Some people may even get greedy and decide to kill you for it, without really knowing what it is that you possess."

"I will not tell anyone, Father."

His father nodded meekly and said nothing further, for he was completely exhausted.

Tompo stood and left the room, leaving his father to rest and regain his strength, but both his father and mother's condition deteriorated later that evening.

By early the next morning, one after the other, they died, leaving their son on his own, alone, scared, and weeping.

Chapter 2

Tompo, with an old bamboo basket filled with clothes, boots and a few personal items on his back, stood mesmerised, lost in the moment, forgetting even his sorrows and grief.

Before him lay the renowned Dungje mansion, straddling a hillock in all its grandeur. This three-storey structure had white stone walls, larger at the base, and slightly sloping inwards at the top, with embellished wooden windows jutting out from the second and third floors.

The village messenger, who had brought him there from his home, stood beside him. "I experience this astonishment every time I come here," said the man, with a sense of both pride and nostalgia in his voice. "This is not a building of stone and mud, but an object of beauty and joy that is not made anymore, in this day and age."

Tompo could not even nod.

"It was built three hundred years ago by one of Headman Thodak Zamba's ancestors, and it still stands today as it was before," continued the man, growing even more enthusiastic. "This is a testament to the greatness of the Dungje nobility and a reflection of the class and wealth that the family enjoyed when it was the ruling dynasty of the region."

Tompo turned and faced the messenger, his eyes dancing with eagerness.

"They had great power and authority, and they ruled over the whole region of Lrarong in those days." The man paused, twitching his lips. "Unfortunately, when the country changed politically over time, they lost their status and power." Seeing the confusion in the boy's eyes, he quickly added, "Of course, they are still wealthy and prominent, with their influence reaching the court of the governor at Lamja."

Nodding eagerly, Tompo turned back to the mansion and was struck again by its sheer scale and magnificence. The courtyard was twice as vast as his house, and the stone stairway rising to the second floor was stately and majestic.

As he stood gazing, an old servant came out of the ornate wooden door on the second floor. He looked nothing like anyone residing in such a grand mansion, as he stomped down the stone stairs, cursing and swearing at the top of his voice.

When he reached the courtyard, he did not even acknowledge the messenger's warm smile, but rudely gestured for Tompo to follow him and then walked away, heading straight towards the door leading into the ground floor.

Following him meekly through the door and thence a dark corridor, Tompo arrived at a tiny dingy bedroom at the far side of the building.

"I was certain you would also contract the disease," the old man finally spoke. His voice was as harsh and grating as his words, and his scaly lips twisted in an ugly way. "But you didn't," he added quickly, then giggled. "The headman had some luck. If you had also died, then the deal would have been all for nothing."

Taken aback, Tompo gaped at this grumpy old man.

"What are you gaping at, boy?" The man's face crinkled, and his brow furrowed. "Don't you expect any sympathy here. They will not even let you mourn, but will make you work from today. Those people have been reduced to the mere house of a village headman, yet they still live as if they were the ruling nobility with twenty servants." He paused and glared, stopping his hand movement and freezing his expression at the same time.

Tompo was unnerved by the man's stare. To break the silence, he quickly asked, "How many servants are there?" But his voice came out squeaky, revealing his fear even more.

"Just me . . . and now you," the man grumbled, his eyes narrowing. "There are some herdsmen in the cow camp, but they are not household servants, and they don't come here. So, get it in that thick head of yours, boy. It is just the two of us here, and there is so much work, both inside the mansion and outside in the barn and the garden."

Tompo flinched. "Yes, *Agay*," he muttered, addressing the man by the term reserved for grandfathers and old men.

"Who are you calling agay now?" The man pounced. "I'm neither your agay nor old enough for the term." When Tompo gaped again, he mellowed down slightly. "My name is Orop," he offered rather stiffly then. "Actually, it is not my name. I'm supposed to be from a village called Oro, and everyone here called me Orop."

"What is your real name then?" asked Tompo, still hesitant.

"I don't have one," the old man replied, somewhat tartly. "I was left here as a toddler, without even a name. But let us not act nice-nice here. We are neither related nor acquaintances. Come, now," he ordered. "I was told to show you around the mansion and to brief you about your work."

In one swift moment, Tompo swung the basket off his back and placed it in one corner. Orop was quite surprised by the boy's agility, but he did not say anything. Instead, he led the boy out and commenced their tour, going from room to room, explaining what and where everything was, while also detailing his responsibilities along the way.

Upon concluding their orientation, Orop stopped, turned around, and fixed his gaze on Tompo's eyes. "We will go and meet the headman and the *amala* now," he said with a stern demeanour. "Be careful how you conduct yourself. Always keep your head low, do not stare directly at them, and speak only when spoken to."

Tompo nodded, feeling a knot forming in his stomach.

"Of the two, watch out for the amala. She can find an edge on an egg and sniff your misadventure from a mile away. You can't let your guard down even for a moment. She manages the house with a lashing tongue and an iron fist."

I must be careful, thought Tompo, as Orop led him through a large door into the living room, but as soon as he was inside, he was awestruck by the grandness of the room. The floor was smooth and shiny, the windows were carved and painted, and swords and shields hung on the walls.

At the far side of the room, in the centre of the large middle wall, sat Headman Thodak Zamba and Amala Nangsa Dolkar in all their stateliness on a raised seat of silk brocade, with a magnificent *choedom* in front of them.

Tompo remembered his father mentioning this intricately carved and ornately decorated low table with great admiration upon his return from the mansion one time. *This must be the same choedom that Father told me about*, he thought as he bowed down fully in a customary greeting and then stood there with his head bent low.

The headman surveyed Tompo with narrowed eyes and seemed to be impressed at this first sight. But the amala eyed him with suspicion and hostility, sending chills up the boy's spine. He bent his head lower, reclining his torso from the midriff, and stood holding his breath.

The headman leaned forward. "I could not figure out what it was, but there was something in your father that made him stand out from the rest of your kind, boy. That was why I gave him that deal." He tipped his head, as if waiting for Tompo to speak, but then rushed ahead. "And you have that same something, even more than he did. I saw it at a glance. You carry yourself far too well for a landless youngling. But I guess it is in your blood. How old are you?"

Tompo deftly raised his right hand over his mouth to stop his spit and bad breath going towards the headman and the amala when he spoke, even though he was standing a good distance away from them. "I am nine years old, Headman." There was a slight shiver in his voice but no one detected it. *I must calm down*, he thought frantically.

"You are the same age as our son, Kathog. But the way you carry yourself, your manner and appearance, make you seem mature beyond your years. I think you are by Nature graceful and immaculate. Look at your *gho*," he added, gesturing towards Tompo's clothing that fell from his shoulders to his knees. "Even though it is old and worn, you wear it so neat and tidy that it lends you an impeccable look."

Not knowing how to respond, Tompo bowed.

"But I think you are not only smart, but also intelligent. So, if you get up early, work hard, and complete your tasks ahead of time, I could teach you to read and write with Kathog. You know what good education can do for a boy like you? It can open a world of opportunity and change your life for good . . . forever."

The amala turned abruptly to the headman, nearly spilling her tea. "Teach him to read and write?" She glared fiercely. "You must be out of your mind to even entertain such a thought. Why would anyone teach a bondservant to read and write? Everyone and everything has a place in the society, for a reason and a purpose."

The headman turned red. "When I say one thing, you have to say another thing. I told you Kathog needs a study partner, someone his age and intellectual level to engage and debate with."

The voice of a boy came from the adjoining room, reciting a verse in Chokë, and interrupted the headman. A moment later, a plump boy clad in a black brocade gho walked into the room, reading from a piece of paper. "Our thoughts are like seeds that are planted in the soil. Like wheat grows from a wheat seed and barley from a barley seed, we grow from our thoughts."

Tompo had never heard the classical language of dharma before, and he was fascinated by it. *The boy must be their son, Kathog,* he thought, his fascination masking some of his fear. However, even before the thought was fully formed in his mind, Orop nudged him and whispered in his ear, "Let us go now."

As both the headman and the amala's attention were drawn towards their son, who proudly continued to recite the verses that he had composed, Orop and Tompo made their departing bow and quietly left the room.

When they had crossed the corridor and reached the kitchen, Tompo was greatly relieved, but his hands and legs suddenly started shaking, causing the old man to burst into laughter.

"If we had remained inside a moment more, you would surely have wet yourself, boy. I told you about the amala. She is the mother of the devil himself. She can instil fear in anyone with one fierce look. But she doesn't just frighten you, she also throws scalding tea on your face."

Tompo flinched, his expression growing grimmer.

"But the headman seemed to be impressed with you," said Orop, his demeanour changing. "However, this is nothing to be happy about, but something to worry you. If the headman and the amala continue to hold differing views about you, they could continue to jab at each other over you, and this will not bode well for you. The amala is unforgiving and vindictive about such matters."

Tompo became even more frightened.

"But that will only be the case if you are as bright as the headman thinks you to be, and you excel at Kathog's level in study. The headman is a passionate scholar who becomes an entirely different person when it comes to dealing with the matters of education. He sees and treats everything differently. Otherwise, he is no better than his wife."

Tompo gaped, at a loss for words.

"I don't know what he saw in you in one glimpse to think you would be bright and intelligent," said Orop. "To me, you seem more like the dimwit of Risa village. But even if you are intelligent, I doubt you could be as good as Kathog. That boy is said to be so brilliant that he is unlike anyone we have seen or heard about."

Tompo gaped even more.

"Again, this is not just the headman saying it. Every official from the court of the governor who comes here says it, too." Orop became more dramatic as he spoke. "So, think about it, boy. There is no way you could be as bright as Kathog. If I were you, I would not get my hopes high. You will only find trouble. Regarding this, I see the demon before the divination."

"I don't want to study only," Tompo defiantly rebuffed.

"Don't you get it? This is not for you to decide, boy. In this mansion, you will do as you are told. You will not even think your own thoughts." Orop let the words sink in. Then he leaned forward, right onto Tompo's face. "If you want to survive here, you must be shrewd like me. If I like you, maybe I will teach you my tricks, and even help you. If not, you are on your own."

Tompo was dumbfounded. He had expected his life to be challenging, but he had not anticipated it to be this difficult and complex. Whether the headman liked him or the amala disliked him was immaterial to him. He also did not care one bit if he got an education. But for all that to become an issue was unthinkable.

And as if that were not enough, the old man deliberately frightened and taunted him for no reason.

As Tompo stood reeling, trying to make sense of his situation, something turned in his stomach, and a strong feeling of nausea shot up into his mouth. It tasted bitter and metallic, and he turned his head away in disapproval and disbelief.

CHAPTER 3

Beginning the following day, Tompo worked from dawn to dusk and sometimes even through the night. But like the old man had said, work in the mansion was never finished.

No matter how hard Tompo worked, the amala was never pleased. She scolded him for even the most trivial thing and often for no reason at all.

Though Tompo soldiered on through each day with gritting teeth, he sobbed every night in his bed. His life was not only hard and miserable, but also, without his parents, empty and joyless.

He also worried about them suffering in the bardo, which the village messenger had explained to him was the intermediate state between death and rebirth. According to the man, in that state, unaware that they had died, his parents' consciousness would wander formless, seeing and feeling everything, including hunger and thirst, but unable to interact with anyone or eat and drink anything.

The boy's concerns were even greater because he was not able to light any butter lamp, nor could he hoist a prayer flag for them, like the messenger had said he should, to ease their suffering in the bardo and help them acquire a better rebirth afterwards. Most importantly, he was not sure how the weekly rituals and rites for the dead were conducted.

Since no lamas or monks would come to his house, fearing the disease, the crazy lay monk, who wandered around inebriated, had come by and cremated the bodies of his parents. The man had also promised to conduct all the weekly rituals and rites until the forty-ninth day in the cave where he lived, somewhere high up in the mountains.

However, this lay monk was nowhere to be found, and no one seemed to know the location of his cave.

Then one night, after a long day of toiling in the mansion, Tompo dreamt of his parents. They told him not to worry about them, but to focus on his work, as they had passed through the intermediate state and were reborn in the northern *zhingkham* of Dewachen.

Even though it was only a dream, he was relieved and happy. He remembered his father telling him that everyone would be reborn in Dewachen Zhingkham, the pure land of Buddha Yoedpame, if one recited the Dewachen aspiration prayer with absolute devotion. He recalled how his parents had recited this aspiration prayer fervently day and night, as they lay dying on their bed.

Although only a bodhisattva could be reborn in a zhingkham, his father had said that anyone who prayed to Buddha Yoedpame with a true heart could be reborn in his pure land of Dewachen, because of the vow he had made before creating the pure land. Once reborn there, they would live for hundreds and hundreds of aeons, receive pure dharma teaching, and become fully enlightened.

Tompo also faintly recollected the crazy lay monk, who had been in what seemed a drunken state, mentioning something about his parents being reborn in a zhingkham, as the man cremated the bodies and conducted the ritual, drinking and barking orders at him to assist in performing this or that task.

As the dream vividly correlated with these actual events, he wondered if they could be reborn in the zhingkham of Dewachen. *If so, then it was good that they had died*, he said to himself, and he felt much better.

Tompo took what his parents had said to heart and worked harder, mustering his devotion and dedication even more, until one morning when he went to feed the pigs, he noticed the sty clean and the pigs unusually well behaved. They did not jump onto each other and fight for their shares, but took turns feeding without spilling much.

For the boy, this was a sign that the gods and the deities of the territory were pleased with him, and therefore were treating him most kindly. From that day on, everything around him became amicable and cooperative, easing his difficulties.

To his amazement, soon even his gho stayed in place as he wore it. Even more, it remained stainless and creaseless all the time, encouraging him to work even harder and further cultivate his traits of devotion, dedication, sincerity, and truthfulness. As a result, he became purer in his thoughts and more graceful in his movements.

Observing these remarkable transformations in him, the headman became convinced of Tompo's brilliance and intelligence. He realised that Tompo was the right person to study with Kathog, and so despite a strong objection from his wife, the headman decided to teach the boy.

With this new responsibility, Tompo had to awaken well before dawn and complete much of his work by noon, and then attend the class in the afternoon and resume work from sundown through the evening, and often late into the night. It was a rigorous schedule that tired him to the bone but also made him happy, for he had an inexplicable yearning to learn and acquire knowledge.

Thus, he took great enjoyment in his education.

However, the easy part lasted only until they came to the final lesson on the alphabet. From then on, beginning with vowel marks and their usages, and on through the building of consonant clusters using subscripts and superscripts, and then the nouns and their nominalizing suffixes, he became confused and could barely make sense of anything. Chokë was not only a new language for him, but it was also extremely difficult.

This left the headman dumbfounded, for his son, Kathog, had covered all of it in just one go.

Tompo was deeply embarrassed and shocked to discover he possessed no intelligence whatsoever. He was, as the headman had said, far below even the most below-average person. *How could this be possible?* he asked himself. He had always considered himself to be intelligent with a sound mind, but now he found himself unable to grasp even the simplest subject matters and lacking in memory to retain what he was taught.

Unable to believe or accept his situation, Tompo prayed to the gods and the deities to let his brain respond to these teachings, like everything else in Nature.

But his prayers were in vain.

No matter how hard he studied, he could not grasp anything. In a moment of reflection, he remembered what his father had said about karma and thought that perhaps he was not meant to study and better himself, much like his parents were not meant to own lands and become their own masters.

From then on, he did not want to study, and he said as much to the headman, but the man would not listen, saying Tompo had all the more reason to study, to nurture and enhance his intelligence.

However, Tompo suspected that the headman only wanted to teach him because he was the most dimwitted lad in the village, and his utter lack of intelligence a sharp contrast to Kathog's brilliance.

Tompo's suspicions turned out to be true. For the headman, employing this stark contrast between them, threaded their personal lives into a dominant story of the village, likening them—two boys born on the same day, in the same year, and in the same village—to day and night. One did not need illumination and the other could not be illuminated.

But Tompo did not mind how the headman exploited him, and in doing so how his image of a dimwit was popularised. Instead, he wholeheartedly accepted being a dimwit, and so lived his young life likewise, insignificant and unappreciated, but nevertheless content and happy.

This unexpected revelation greatly surprised Orop. Having fought for his survival and railed against his bad karma all his life, Tompo's selflessness and unconditional acceptance of his karma touched his heart in a way that rekindled the embers of love and affection within him and made him sympathetic towards the boy.

CHAPTER 4

A tall and trim young man went frolicking through the dark forest of Yarong, whistling a jubilant tune, with his *patang*, a short sword handy for all sorts of work, safely sheathed in its scabbard as it swayed from his waist in rhythm with his movement.

As if Nature bent at his will, nothing hindered him along the way. Not a speck of dirt jumped on his boots, a burr caught on his gho, or a branch nicked his hat.

He was Tompo, six years later.

A twig snapped faintly, somewhere behind him, startling him and disturbing the tranquillity of the woods. He stopped abruptly, turned around and thought he saw something. *Did someone dart behind a tree?* he asked himself. *Or was it my imagination?*

Uncertain, he shrugged and was about to continue on his way when a sturdy dried branch sticking out from a thicket of creepers beside the trail caught his eye.

Pondering whether there was a full tree hidden underneath the thicket, he pried open a wall of leaves and climbers and moved inside. His lips curved upwards, and his eyes sparkled as his face broke into a big, bright smile. *Yay, Agay Orop will die of joy*, he thought, almost saying it out aloud.

A large fallen poplar, all dried and ready to be chopped into firewood, lay with its branches spread across the forest floor. Happy that there was so much before him, and knowing that the agay's favourite smokeless wood would last for over a month, he went on his way, already thinking which branches to chop and take home when he returned later.

By then, he was almost at his destination, and so he soon came out into the wide-open space of the pastureland of Yalang—and how he loved it. The feeling of coming out of the dark woods into the openness of the grassland was liberating. No matter how many times he came here, he felt as if he were here for the first time.

Stopping at the edge, he took a long deep breath, looked around, and surveyed the area. The vast plain of green prairie, dotted with herds of cattle, spread into the distance, and the headman's cattle, perhaps a hundred heads, were all huddled in one corner at the far end of the pastureland and adjacent to the trail leading to the lake.

He wondered if he should fetch the luscious, broad green leaves from the lakeside for the milking cows, for whose extra feed he had been sent there, or simply drive them into the forest and cut branches from a tree.

Still mulling it over, he walked on, in the direction of the herd, and noticed another herd of about the same size behind a nearby mound.

Even though there were only a few herds that size, he did not know whose it was until he saw a slender young woman carrying a bag on her back. She was some distance away, ahead of him, walking towards the animals, having come from the village just before him. He recognised her at once.

Aerka Lhamo was not only pretty, but she also had a distinctly unique way of dressing and carrying herself, making her easily recognisable anywhere, whether she was seen from the back or even from a far-off distance. In fact, she had that distinctness in everything about her.

Since all the headman's cowhands had been ill from some

infectious diseases, and Tompo had been sent to the pastureland daily to assist the two new hired hands, he had seen Aerka Lhamo also coming regularly and wondered what could be bringing her here, among the stinking cowhands.

Her father, Landlord Jang Namdrol, employed some of the best cowhands in the village, so there was no need for her to be here. As a person, she was known for her no-nonsense attitude. She would not come here to idle away her time in frivolous pursuits.

There must be some other reasons, he thought.

He followed her through the grassland, steadily gaining the distance on her as, every now and then, she slowed down to pluck thistles out of her attire, until he caught up with her in front of her herd, where she was bent down, untangling the hem of her *kira,* a long dress that was clumped with burdock.

Tompo adjusted his pace and casually began to walk past her, and as he did so, he gave her a quick glance. Her boots were covered in dust, her jacket or *tego* perforated by prickles, and her hat smudged with tiny green spots.

But just as he was about to pass her, she turned and saw him. "How do you manage to come through that forest so clean?" she asked, her eyes scanning him from head to toe, filled with amazement.

Taken by surprise, Tompo's initial response was a nervous bow. She had never spoken to him before, even when they had passed each other this closely. It was as if, to her, he did not exist. Yet now, as she engaged him, her conversation directly veered towards his closely guarded family secret.

"Oh, I take extreme care not to get dirtied," he offered, his words carrying a faint quiver. "I hardly get time to clean myself," he added, his explanation hanging in the air, and hoping this addition would satisfy her curiosity.

"Good for you," she said with a nod. "I find that amazing."

Tompo returned the nod, and then nervously turned and went on his way. He wanted to respond but could think of nothing to say.

When he reached his herd, one of the hired hands was running after a playful calf straying towards the forest, and another man was frantically lashing at two bulls locked in a fierce fight, trying desperately to separate them.

Leaving them to their tasks, Tompo quickly gathered all the milking cows and drove them to the forest. There, he stopped by a giant alder tree, somewhere in the vicinity of the lake, and methodically cut down the leaves and the branches from one side of the base, doing so with much ease. Even the sturdier branches fell with only one swoop of his patang.

When the lower branches were cut down, he proceeded to tackle the higher ones. Among them, one particular branch with a big bunch of leaves was quite high up on the trunk, and when he jumped to reach it, a gust of wind blew out of nowhere, swaying the branch down, right into his grasp. "Yay, I got it!" he exclaimed, with no one nearby to hear him.

But no sooner had he cut off the branch and sheathed the patang back into the scabbard than he heard the rustling of leaves and the startled flapping of a bird, taking flight from a clump behind the adjacent tree. He turned around and looked at the dense creepers and bushes, ears pricked.

Aerka Lhamo appeared from the thicket, dusting her tego and kira, and walked towards him. "One of my cowhands saw a young aquilaria tree somewhere in this vicinity, but I can't find it," she said, shaking her head in disappointment. "My father badly needs some agarwood."

Tompo gaped at the young woman, a mix of confusion and suspicion freezing his expression. *Is she following me around and spying on me?* he asked. *Was it her in the Yarong forest earlier?*

"I presume you didn't see it, either," she went on.

"No, I didn't," he replied, his head shaking nervously.

But her attention had already moved to the large pile of branches and leaves heaped around the trunk of the tree. "That was fast," she remarked. "You must have just arrived here, for you were only beginning to gather the milking cows when I left my herd."

"Oh, not really," he answered promptly, his countenance displaying a nervous crinkle. "It is just that they are not stacked properly. There is not much there."

Again, she did not pay attention to his response, but shifted her gaze to a large branch that he had chopped off. "That was a neat one-swoop slice," she said. "Either you are really strong, or your patang is very sharp. I have not seen anyone cut a branch that big in a slice."

"This is a soft tree," he said, downplaying her compliment.

"Yes, alder is relatively soft compared to other hardwood," she agreed, "but it is still a hardwood. Not easy to be sliced so effortlessly." Her expression changed from a thoughtful frown to a flashing smile. "But, of course, you are different. You are known to work hard, and quite impeccably, too."

Tompo gaped at her again, his expression now marked by concern, unsure of what to say.

"And those are too high, even for your height." She pointed at the stubs of the branches he had cut on the trunk, high up on the tree. "But, again, you are agile and acrobatic. I have seen you leap like a grasshopper."

Tompo felt his face turn red with discomfort.

"You are a wonder, Tompo," she added quickly. "You work like you have magic in your hands, and there is nothing you cannot do. You know, I tell my parents that you are the most skilled and hardworking person, not only in Tamchu, but also in the whole of Lrarong."

"Oh, no, Aerka. I'm just like anyone."

Moments before Aerka was about to speak, a gentle wind swept through, causing the forest to murmur eerily. The cows stopped feeding, as if frightened, and moved about restlessly. A few even started to move in different directions.

Opening her mouth slightly and inhaling sharply, Aerka froze. "What is this wind?" She looked around at the trees, her eyes wide and her eyebrows raised, then at Tompo, suspicion in her expression. "I must go now." Quite frightened and spooked, she scurried away, without even waiting for Tompo to respond.

Tompo sprang into action, summoning the cows by their names and stopping them from breaking into a run, and soon managed to calm them down and get back to feeding.

But the wind continued to blow.

Where did this breeze come from so suddenly, stirring the forest to murmur like that? he thought. *I'm sure it didn't originate from the usual climate of the land. It was caused by something else. Could it be the spirit residing in that tree, angry at me for cutting down the branches? Or was it a local deity displeased with me for some other reason? Nothing like this has ever happened to me.*

As he stood mulling over the strange occurrence, a weird feeling came over him, and he wanted to leave. Not just the forest but also the pastureland, and go back to the village.

So, as soon as the cows had had enough to eat, he drove them back to the herd, gave his lunch and beverage to the two cowhands—as it was still too early for lunch—and left in a hurry.

CHAPTER 5

Still thinking about what had happened and feeling dismayed and anxious about it, Tompo hurried back through the forest of Yarong, without even taking a stack of firewood from the poplar tree that he had found earlier, and soon arrived at the village.

There were no children playing outside the houses or anybody working in the fields and the gardens. Except for a few animals wandering around, Tamchu was unusually quiet and deserted.

Wondering where everyone had gone, Tompo continued walking and arrived at the well-known four-way intersection that served as the central hub connecting all parts of the village.

The wooden cantilever bridge on the national pathway was festooned with brocades, cloths, and flags, and a makeshift shed of branches and leaves had been built on the grassy bank of the sparkling Yangchurung River.

Tompo, remembering someone had said a few days back that a renowned *trulku* would pass through the village and thinking that it was this day, hurried to the place and saw a large crowd of people in their finest costumes seated in rows, facing the shed.

But his gaze went straight to Kathog. The illustrious scholar and young scion of the Dungje nobility had donned a black brocade gho and sat majestically on a raised seat that bore a stately dragon-carved dais equivalent in height to that of the headman. His posture was upright with his chin lifted, his chest thrust out, his shoulders drawn back, and his hands resting on his cross-legged knees.

Kathog must have been given the privilege of sitting on a raised seat beside the headman in anticipation of his new post, thought Tompo.

Amazed by Kathog's brilliant mind and excellent education, the governor had recently asked the headman to appoint Kathog deputy headman of the village at an opportune occasion, fuelling speculation about the governor's plan to induct him into service in the court and train him as his potential successor.

But that is not all, thought Tompo, as his gaze shifted to Uma Dolma, sitting between her father, Landlord Kunzo Yebar, and her mother, La Azom. *Kathog is going to marry the village beauty and the daughter of its wealthiest landlord. This would solidify his position and status even more.*

Lost in his thoughts, Tompo had nearly forgotten about the trulku, when a deep and melodious voice spoke softly from inside the makeshift shed. "Even though I don't have much time, I will tell you something about the things that affect your life, so that you understand your life better, and live better."

The words hit Tompo in the deepest part of his being. He felt his hairs stand on end, and stood motionless for some time, as if paralysed. When he pulled himself back together, he realised that the trulku was speaking about karma.

"When we talk about karma," the trulku said, "we often refer to ourselves as a person of good karma or bad karma. We also attribute to our karma anything good or bad happening to us. Therefore, according to what we believe and say, karma is what defines us and determines our life. This is true, even from the dharma's point of view. Karma is all that we are now, in body and mind, as a result of all that we have done in the past."

"How true it is for me," muttered Tompo, clasping his two

hands together into one, in obeisance to the trulku. "I am my bad karma," he whispered.

"For this reason, we call our body the resultant aggregates of ripened karma," continued the trulku. "Speaking about it in this way, it may seem like our karma rules our lives. But this is not so. Our future is not set and predetermined, and we are not inescapably stuck in our karma. Far from it, we are free to act and determine our future, as we want it, not only in this life, but also in our next lives."

Feeling goosebumps rise first on his arms and then all over his body, Tompo tried to peer inside the shed. But having arrived at the gathering from the side of the structure, he could not see the trulku.

"You do good and good will come to you. This is the law of cause and effect. Causes determine results. In fact, everything in existence is brought about by certain causes and conditions aligning in a specific way. That is why it is important not only to do good, but also to do good the right way."

Turning around, Tompo moved towards the back of the crowd, but when he was halfway through it, he came upon a hedge of shrubs, and there was no way to continue because the people were sitting close to the hedge and blocking his path. But hearing the trulku's powerful words, he wanted to see the saint with an increasing urgency.

"That is, to create the right causes and conditions aligned the right way, to achieve the right outcome," went on the trulku. "This is called *tendrel*, the ceremony that we conduct before we begin any important work. Tendrel also refers to how things generally turn out for us. We say the tendrel is good or bad by the thing or the event that we encounter, depending on its nature and its state in relation to our situation and the goal we seek."

Not ready to give up, Tompo circled the hedge and arrived right behind the crowd, then again put his hands together in obeisance and looked inside the shed. But being far away, he could see only a hazy figure of a monk sitting on a throne. *I can't see from the back either,* he thought, his heart sinking.

"It also refers to the auspiciousness of an act, such as pouring a full cup of wine or taking something when you go to another person's new home. We say we do this or that for good tendrel. So, you see how important it is to do good and do it the right way if you are to accrue merit, have things work out for you, and have a better life."

With nowhere to go, Tompo went down onto his knees and remained like this, with his hands folded and pressed against his chest.

"But again, remember, no matter how many good deeds you do, how much good karma you create, you will still be trapped in the never-ending cycle of birth and death, from which the only way out is through dharma. So then, why not practise dharma and free yourself straightaway?"

"I want to practise dharma," muttered Tompo, in aspiration prayer. "May I have the merit for it. May the guardian deities of dharma bless me."

"But, of course, caught up in this great game of life, you will not realise the severity of your situation. At the prime of your life, even if you hear about the pain of death and the suffering of the bardo, you will not be moved. But when your end comes, you will find out that nothing can save you."

"I will not waste this life and be reborn again like this," continued Tompo, becoming more devotional. "I must go in the front and see the trulku, even if it is only a glimpse." He stood and surveyed the way to the front of the crowd, from the other side.

"Your wealth, family, friends, name, and fame—nothing will matter when death comes knocking on your door. Nothing can hold it off, even for a short time. Then, like a hair pulled out of butter, your consciousness will be severed from your body, and you will wander formless in the bardo, experiencing all forms of torments and sufferings that you cannot even fathom now."

"If we die now, we will be likewise," lamented someone nearby, as Tompo, in a trance-like state, moved towards the front of the crowd, crossing one line at a time.

"You cannot do anything then," explained the trulku. "You will slowly lose the sense of being a human being, and you will neither remember nor know anything. What becomes of you from there on will depend on your karma or, in other words, on what you do now. If you live a righteous life and do good deeds, you may be reborn as a human being. If not, you may be reborn as an insect or even a hungry ghost."

There was the sound of rustling, people shifting in discomfort, and then a woman said, "How frightening," as Tompo passed her row.

"But if you practise Buddha's dharma and gain mastery over the true nature of existence, then death and rebirth will be like leaving one room and entering another, changing only the clothes in between. With complete control, you will walk through these processes, even deciding where and when to be reborn."

The crowd broke into a loud sigh, with some expressing the gravity of life's situation and others conveying astonishment at what was possible, and these communal sounds filled the air with soft murmurs and the atmosphere with a sense of heaviness.

In that moment of finale, Tompo reached the front row and saw Riwang Trulku sitting resplendently on a lofty throne. A strikingly handsome young man sporting an orange shawl over a yellow shirt and a red robe, he looked like a celestial being.

Struck with awe and wonder, Tompo stood entranced, staring at the trulku.

And in that very moment, the trulku, having concluded the sermon, led the crowd in chanting the *guru mantra*, electrifying the atmosphere and intensifying Tompo's sensory experience.

A strong wave of devotion surged in Tompo from deep inside his being, and his body shuddered, as if an explosion had been set off within him. And then something limitless, exhilarating, and indescribable came over him, causing tears to flow unchecked down his cheeks.

Gripped by this overwhelming emotion, and in homage to the trulku, Tompo put his hands together yet again in obeisance and prayer and chanted the guru mantra fervently. In that moment, a rain of flowers fell, a halo encircled the sun, and a rainbow arched across the valley.

Seeing these sacred signs appear, Tompo dropped down and prostrated himself before the trulku. A moment later, a translucent image of a *dakini* appeared on a thin layer of papery white cloud in the cerulean sky.

Everyone, including the trulku's disciples and attendants, scrambled to their feet, chanting the mantra fervently, and prostrated themselves before the trulku in a spiritual frenzy. But even as they prostrated, the image slowly faded and disappeared.

Soon, the rain of flowers stopped, too.

But the halo around the sun and the rainbow above the valley remained, even after the trulku and his entourage left the village, and until the sun disappeared beyond the mountains.

CHAPTER 6

It was the first time that Tompo spent the afternoon without doing any work since he had moved into the mansion. After those moments with the trulku, he had been too affected to do anything. So, even after going home, he had remained seated by the fireplace in the kitchen, soaking in the spiritual experience of the day.

"What is it with you today, sitting down like your bottom has grown roots?" asked Orop, creasing his brow in consternation as he ran around the room, moving from one chore to another. "What if the amala comes in and sees you? You will get spanked unnecessarily."

Tompo didn't reply at first, but slowly looked up, his face so serious that it caught the old man's attention. "Something unusual happened to me today, Agay," he said in a heavy voice. "I felt great devotion for dharma from deep inside my heart, as if Buddha himself had appeared in front of me and touched my crown."

Orop's eyes opened wide in surprise.

"I have not felt anything like this before today. My whole body quaked, as if something exploded inside me. Then I felt a sense of limitlessness and exhilaration come over me, causing tears to flow down my cheeks, and I was helpless to stop them."

Orop's forehead creased, and his eyes squinted. "That is good, Tompo," he replied, enunciating on each word clearly, being careful of what he said. "You were fortunate to arrive there on time today. For a great saint like him, just being in his presence will prevent rebirth in the eighteen realms of hell for many lifetimes to come."

Tompo thought about those words for a moment before responding. "That may be so, Agay, but my devotion goes far beyond him and getting blessed. I don't know how to say it, but I yearn for dharma. I also feel something strong and gripping deep inside me, like a sadness. This is strange and unusual for me, Agay."

Orop looked deep into Tompo's eyes, and his face turned grave. He didn't know what he saw exactly, but it frightened him, so he said carefully, "Devotion for dharma is good, Tompo, but you must not let it affect you. You must have control over your feelings and emotions in all matters."

"You need not worry about it, Agay. I have decided to leave everything behind and pursue the path of dharma now. Of course, I don't have anything or anyone to leave behind. I am just a homeless orphan. I am only saying it as an expression of leaving the worldly life."

Orop was stunned. For a moment, he could not see or hear anything. Then his lips twitched and his face became grey, as he grew nauseated by the shock he was feeling.

As Orop struggled with his emotional reaction, Tompo, lost in his own thoughts and unaware of the old man's distress, stood up with purpose and left the kitchen. He crossed the corridor in a few steps and walked into the living room.

The headman and the amala, just returned from the trulku's reception, were engrossed in their conversation, their cups of butter tea untouched on the choedom. As they didn't notice him, Tompo stood at the doorway waiting. For no matter how spiritually charged he was, the mere sight of the amala evoked enough fear in him to remain silent.

"To manifest such remarkable miracles, he must truly be one of the greatest masters of our time," the amala proclaimed, folding her hands together in supplication to Riwang Trulku. "I have not heard of auspicious signs like that appearing anywhere."

"Rainbows, rain of flowers, and halos of the sun are common auspicious signs, and they appear on many religious occasions and in many places," replied the headman. "But a dakini doesn't appear in the sky just like that." He chanted a quick guru mantra. "This is a rare occurrence."

Before the amala could reply, Tompo cleared his throat, and the headman and the amala turned and stared at him curiously. He hesitated, and then could not say anything, infuriating the amala.

"What is it now, standing and staring like the fool that you are?" she demanded, glaring at him.

"Something profoundly spiritual happened to me today, Amala," Tompo stammered. "I experienced an overwhelming devotion for the trulku and dharma. It was not merely a mental feeling confined to my heart, but a tangible experience felt physically throughout my entire body. It was as if—"

"That is very good, Tompo," interrupted the headman, without giving any serious thought to this declaration. "We also felt profound devotion. Riwang Trulku is a great saint. He blessed our village and all of us here. So, we should consider ourselves fortunate."

"Thank you, Headman." Tompo put his hands together in gratitude to him. "I have made up my mind to pursue the path of dharma now. So, if it is not against the kind wishes of the headman and the amala, I would like to seek your blessing to go away from here and follow the path of dharma."

Taken by utter surprise, the headman and the amala sat gaping for a moment, and so Tompo went on. "Nothing else matters to me now; I have made my decision. From today onwards, dharma will be the only thing for me in my life."

The headman shook his head, recovering from the momentary loss of direction. "I know how you are feeling, Tompo. Everyone must be feeling the same right now. But this feeling is not permanent. If it were, then everyone would become monks and nuns and our villages would be empty."

"But my devotion is genuine, Headman."

"You leave that nonsense of yours and go from here before I throw this cup of hot tea on your stupid face," said the amala, glaring fiercely. "You are spoiling our spiritual moments and making us accrue negative karma."

Tompo wanted to explain and request more, but afraid of angering the amala further, he bowed and left the room, biting his lip and holding back his tears.

He found Orop waiting for him in the corridor. Without looking at the old man, Tompo brushed past him, and rushed into the kitchen sobbing.

The old man came marching after him, feeling both concerned and angry. "What devil got into you today, right after getting blessed by a trulku?" he scolded. "You could have gotten yourself spanked for no reason."

"But I'm serious, Agay," shot back Tompo, his eyes gleaming with determination through the tears. "I want to go and pursue the path of dharma, and I'm going . . . no matter what."

Orop felt an overwhelming surge of dread from deep inside, sickening and nauseating him. "But where do you want to go, Tompo? Dharma is not for everyone, and definitely not for you. It is not an easy path. You will only suffer more, much more than you suffer now."

"I don't know, Agay, but I will go, for I have to. I have no other choice. This is my destiny." Tompo's voice trembled with an unusual fervour. "If I don't go, then something bad will happen. But even if nothing should happen, I will die of sorrows."

Orop jerked slightly and stared wide-eyed in utter shock. Tompo's words were not the usual expressions of devotion that one would normally hear from people. And even less likely from a boy of fifteen. There was something distressful and foreboding about the way he put it. But Orop didn't know what it was. He had never seen Tompo like this before, and it both frightened and puzzled him.

Chapter 7

Kathog picked at his breakfast without much appetite. He was subdued and sombre, but both his parents were so lost in their own thoughts and engrossed in their breakfast that they didn't notice his changed demeanour.

However, that suited him just fine, for he didn't want his mother fretting about him or pestering him with endless silly questions.

More than anything, he didn't want her snooping into his thoughts, as she regularly did with uncanny success. For this time, his thoughts were on something else, something completely different.

He was thinking about dharma.

Riwang Trulku was truly awesome. The brilliance of his sermon, so simple yet so profound, the miracles he displayed, and the reverence people held for his extraordinary powers—these moved him greatly.

He could also achieve such greatness. He had the capability. But what would his parents say? He was the much-talked-about scion of the Dungje nobility, and he was expected to carry its lineage forward, whether the nobility was recognised or not.

Still, even on the path of dharma, he could marry and have a family, once he completed his studies and became a lama, if he chose to. However, that would not be the same. He would not be the Dungje nobleman serving as the village headman, a scholar, or a courtier.

He would, instead, be a lama in a monastery, somewhere far from home.

But beyond anything else, he was expected to become a governor someday and bring glory back to the mansion. All the hopes and dreams his father and mother had harboured for him for so long would shatter instantly.

To compound his troubles, even Tompo unexpectedly expressed his desire to go and practise dharma, as if the sacred path were something anyone could take on a whim, much to his father's dismay and his mother's frustration.

Just as he thought about the orphan, and as if on cue, Tompo burst into the room, startling him and his parents out of their reverie, and went down on his knees, his hands put together in a dramatic plea.

"Benevolent Headman and generous Amala," Tompo pleaded, tears flowing down his cheeks. "Please, take kindly to this unfortunate orphan who has no one and nothing in the world. Please, have pity on me and allow me to pursue the noble path of dharma. I can neither sleep nor eat in peace now."

Her face flushed with anger, eyes flashing with fury, and her mouth nearly frothing with agitation, the amala picked up her cup of butter tea and hurled the liquid at Tompo's face. "What is with you, you moron, not letting us finish our breakfast in peace?"

Exasperated by Tompo's nonsense, the headman pushed his plate aside and threw his hands in the air in frustration. "What on earth is wrong with you, Tompo? Have you lost your senses? Do you think dharma is a joke? The path of dharma is not for everyone, and certainly not for someone as foolish as you are."

Tompo quickly wiped the tea off his face with his sleeves, then turned to the headman with utmost respect. "You are right, noble headman. I am a dimwit, and I have no intelligence to study dharma, but even if it should take my entire life to learn one word of Buddha's teaching, I am willing to do it."

"Tompo, you don't know what you are saying," insisted the headman. "Speaking those words is easy. They may sound motivating and inspirational, but putting them into practice is altogether a different thing. You can't even learn the language and grammar of Chokë, so how do you expect to study volumes and volumes of dharma texts?"

"You don't owe him any explanation," the amala retorted, her gaze piercing the headman. Then she turned to Tompo, her gaze even fiercer. "You can go wherever you want, but after paying off your debt. Then you can go pursue the path of dharma, or jump into the Yangchurung River and die, for all I care."

Too stunned and petrified to say anything, Tompo stood there gawking stupidly, with his eyelids batting and his facial muscles twitching.

The way his lower jaw shifted, first one way and then the other, seemed to make the amala even more furious, but before she could burst out in yet another deadly rage, he came to his senses, quickly bowed, turned around, and left the room.

Orop was waiting in the corridor, his eyes filled with tears.

Tompo brushed past the old man into the kitchen, took his patang and bag, and left the mansion, quickening his pace through the corridor and breaking into a run as he went out the door.

He ran down the flight of stairs and sped across the courtyard without even taking his hat that still hung on the wall. He raced down the hill, across the village, and through the forest, all the way to the Yalang grassland.

When he came out of the woods into the open space of the grassland, he was heaving and panting, and his feet were aching. Yet, he continued, running nonstop across the large swath of the pastureland to the other side. Then he threw himself facedown on the ground and cried until the pain inside him subsided.

After some time, Tompo slowly lifted himself into a sitting position and was startled to find Aerka Lhamo seated next to him. He jolted backwards, nearly falling onto the ground, and then, without trying to regain his balance, scooted farther away until there was some distance between them.

Aerka remained calm, looking him in the eye with kindness and gentleness. "Whatever it is that is afflicting you, Tompo," she said, her voice filled with concern, "you don't deserve to suffer like this." She continued to stare until his uneasiness was assuaged and he was feeling comfortable. "I think you need a strong drink to pull yourself together. If you will come with me, I have such a liquor."

Not knowing what to say, Tompo nodded meekly.

Aerka nodded back, and then they both stood up and went to the large oak tree where she had left her bag hanging from a branch. After ushering him to sit under the shade of that tree, she opened the bag and poured him a cup of *ara*.

"Thank you, Aerka." Tompo bowed his head gratefully. "I pray that you gather merit from this act of kindness, and these merits, in turn, endow you with an even greater ability to perform more acts of kindness for the welfare of more unfortunate people."

"You need not feel that way, Tompo. I am happy to be of any help to you because I know about the hardship you face living with the headman. Without any of your own people, your life has been one of pain and sorrow. But the good thing is that you have managed to live a virtuous life without succumbing to your misfortune. Even then, a man can only take so much. There has to be a way out for you at some point in time."

Tompo was deeply touched, but as always, he was resistant to any thought that he lived a hard life with the headman. Yet, at the same time, he could not bring himself to contradict her. "It doesn't matter, Aerka," he said. "Whether it is good or bad, it is my karma. I will have to live with it and exhaust it."

"But you are a good person, Tompo, not deserving of anything like that, even if you have bad karma. You are also honest and hardworking. You know, I could talk to my parents and clear your debt," she said, her casual gaze resting on him, as if there were nothing unusual about her words.

Tompo jerked in utter surprise, nearly spilling his drink, and then stared at her wide-eyed, unable to believe what he had just heard.

She stared back, looking him in the eye encouragingly, and said, "Yes, Tompo, my parents can pay off your debt, and you can come live with us."

"Live with you?"

"Yes, but not as a bondservant," Aerka replied. "I have so much land and properties, and I am also hardworking like you. If we are together, we will prosper like Landlord Kunzo Yebar, or even more. Who knows? We may even become as wealthy as the headman."

Tompo could not believe his ears. He stood blinking for some time. Then his heart pounded loudly in his chest, and a mix of emotions—surprise, disbelief, and distress—surged through him. "What are you saying, Aerka?"

A faint grin flickered on her face. "Even though our situations are different, we are very much alike in many ways, making us a perfect match for each other. But, of course, we need not marry right away. As we are still young, we can afford to wait for a few years. But you can come and live with us right away. You will be free."

Tompo was both stunned and numbed by this offer. Unable to believe his ears, he stared at Aerka and she stared back, again looking him directly in the eye encouragingly. But in that instant, a deafening thunder blasted across the sky, quaking the ground under them and shattering the silence over the grassland.

The cattle, startled and frightened, ran in all directions, mooing and bellowing, as a blanket of dark clouds came swirling furiously towards them, spreading darkness over the fields.

A moment later, a strong wind swept through the area, howling eerily and spraying large drops of rain on their faces. Then more reverberating thunder rumbled through the deep hollowness of the sky, followed by sparkling lightning that came blasting through the dark clouds and struck the oak tree, just above them, sending them scrambling for safety. But no matter where they went, this was such a fierce storm that nowhere was safe.

Tompo and Aerka got separated in the scramble and found themselves among their own group of cow herders, hunkering down for shelter. As they remained there, the storm raged fiercely and unabated, lasting through the whole morning until, by midafternoon, they were forced to drive the herds back to the cow camps.

Battling the violent storm, Tompo forgot all his sorrows and pains. But when he reached home late that evening, he found himself physically exhausted and emotionally drained.

He had no appetite for dinner, so he went straight to bed without eating. But he could not fall asleep, not even after Orop came in late at night.

The storm also showed no sign of abating.

Then, just when Tompo believed this storm could not be more powerful, a violent gust of wind, shrieking like an angry woman, struck the mansion, shaking the floors and rattling the windows and their shutters.

The old man, in the throes of making up his bed, stopped abruptly, spooked by the force of this storm, and began to chant the guru mantra.

A moment later, the lamp flickered from the draught that entered the room through the gaps between the shutters. "I have not seen a storm like this in my sixty years, not even in the midst of summer," muttered Orop more to himself than to Tompo as he climbed into his bed. "And it is only the beginning of spring."

"The storm came suddenly out of nowhere, as if the guardian deities were angry," said Tompo, commenting on what the old man had said. He fell silent for a moment, and then added, "It was all my fault. I was in distress and Aerka Lhamo comforted me and offered to pay off my debt."

Orop bolted upright from his bed.

"I don't know what devil got into her," went on Tompo, with a trace of sadness in his voice, "she even proposed to marry me, saying we are both hardworking, and we would prosper like Landlord Kunzo Yebar and become as wealthy as the headman."

Orop was stunned. It seemed like the most unbelievable thing he had heard in a very long time, yet he knew it was true. Worried that Tompo might have turned down the proposal, but unable to ask directly, he skirted around the issue, "Why would the guardian deities be angry?"

"The moment she proposed to me, the thunder roared angrily, shaking the earth, and the gust came furiously, whipping through the air, while the lightning struck the very tree that we sat under. So, it was definitely her family's guardian deity being furious at what was happening and wanting to stop it then and there."

"But why would her family deity be angry?" Orop pressed, his heart pounding and his mind racing.

Tompo thought about this for a moment. "How could she marry a homeless orphan and a dimwit like me? Even suggesting it publicly could ruin her reputation and destroy her life. She is the daughter of a wealthy landlord, and her family has a high standing."

"You may be a homeless orphan and a dimwit, but you are

a very good human being, Tompo," insisted Orop, fighting to remain calm despite feeling nervous and jumpy. "And, like she said, you are sincere and hardworking as well. So, you are as good as any young man in Tamchu village. Aerka is a wise girl and she knows what is good for her."

"No, Agay, she was not herself. I think her windhorse had weakened, and some evil spirits were leading her astray in her thoughts and actions. That was why her family's guardian deity was protecting her, but I am sure she will come to her senses soon."

No, no, no, thought Orop, almost saying it aloud. And then, instantaneously thinking that Tompo would not be persuaded by anything he said, he turned his head away, closing his eyes, crinkling his face, and biting his lips. Yet, not ready to let the only person he cared about in the world make a colossal mistake like this, he drew a deep breath and composed himself.

"You should think before throwing away a good opportunity like that, Tompo," he said, his brow furrowing in concern. "This may be the only good thing coming your way, and your only chance to escape from here. You are a good person, and you deserve a better life, but if you push your good luck away, I am afraid you will end up like me, working for the headman all your life."

Tompo didn't say anything.

"You know," continued Orop, "that Aerka Lhamo is right. The two of you would prosper like Landlord Kunzo Yebar, or even more than him or the headman. You see, Tompo, I don't know if Kathog would become a governor someday, in a distant future, but I know you would become a very wealthy person and live a comfortable life immediately, if you accept her proposal."

Tompo still didn't respond.

Orop leaned forward and saw that Tompo had fallen asleep, looking innocent and pitiful in the pale-yellow light of the lamp. Feeling deeply sympathetic and concerned, he stared at his young friend for some time. Then, blowing out the lamp, he got into his bed and slept.

But no sooner had the old man fallen asleep than he was awakened by Tompo's loud and frightened rambling in his sleep. The storm had also turned fiercer.

Leaning over and looking closely, Orop noticed that Tompo was again having the nightmare of his parents dying, a repetition of that terrible dream from the previous night.

It is going to be another long night, he thought, and then pulled the covers snugly around his shoulders and went back to sleep.

CHAPTER 8

Tompo woke up before dawn with the remnants of the dream vivid in his mind and its ache pulsating in his heart. It had been more than six years since his parents had died, but with this dream replaying for the second consecutive night, resurrecting images that felt as real and poignant as ever, it made the event seem like only yesterday.

What could have triggered such a recurring dream? Was it my emotional state? he asked himself, but he had no time to muse about it. He swiftly arose, dressed, ground maize, pounded paddy, fed swine and horses, and completed all other chores before sunrise. Then, he washed up and went into the kitchen.

Orop was getting the breakfast ready to be taken into the living room for the headman and the family. Upon seeing Tompo, he stopped his task and turned to the young man with purpose. "Tompo, you listen to me," he said, pointing directly at his face, which was something he had never done before. "You leave this nonsense of pursuing the path of dharma. You will only suffer, suffer much more than you do now. You don't have anything. You don't know anyone. And you have not been anywhere beyond these mountains."

"I know your concern for me surpasses even that which you hold for yourself, Agay," Tompo replied, his voice earnest. "But you need not worry about me. Nothing untoward will happen to me." He paused briefly and stared at the old man with a reassuring expression. "Even if something were to happen, I am all right with it. I have already thought about this and come to terms with it," he said, nodding as if to affirm it. "This is my path; this is my destiny."

The old man shook his head. "What destiny can be there for people like you and me, burdened with karmic debts?" he snapped, fixing a penetrating gaze on Tompo. "Destiny is a luxury reserved for the fortunate. For people of unpurged karma such as us, life revolves around cleansing our bad karma from the day we are born until the day we die."

Tompo remained resolute. "Whatever force it may be that is pushing me on this path—whether it is destiny or negative karma—it will be what it is, Agay," he replied, his voice unwavering and his gaze steady. "And it doesn't matter what I decide, for there will be no escape from either of these. So don't inflict pain and suffering upon yourself by worrying about me in this matter."

"What have you become now, Tompo?" said Orop, gesturing in frustration. "Look at you, wearing that look of stubbornness, like you are under some spell of an evil spirit," he continued, shaking his head in utter disbelief. "You neither see reason nor listen to counsel. This is not you, but someone I don't know."

"It is not like that, Agay."

"Yes, it is. You have not only lost all sense of judgement, but you suffer nightmares throughout the night. You have been rambling and crying in your dreams these last two nights. That means your windhorse has weakened, and you are under the influence of evil forces."

"No, Agay. I had those dreams because I was upset."

"Whatever it is, please don't commit this grave mistake," Orop pleaded. "I was afraid that you would rot here like me, but you have received this heaven-sent opportunity from Aerka

Lhamo. This is a gift for you from Ugyen Guru Rinpoche himself for being a good person."

"No, Agay," Tompo said, shaking his head, "it is not a gift from anyone or anything good. Far from it, this is a strange thing spun by an evil spirit to confuse me in my decision-making and weaken me in my resolve. But I am clear about what I must do and I will not falter . . . even slightly."

Orop stared for some time at Tompo in exasperation and then, shaking his head, he walked out of the kitchen, carrying the steaming teapot stacked on top of the rice pot.

Tompo followed the old man, carrying utensils and crockeries.

"Don't come inside," ordered Orop. "The amala is not in a good mood."

Tompo nodded and returned to the kitchen, put the utensils and crockery back on the shelf, and then quickly ate his breakfast and left for Yalang right away.

He arrived early at the pastureland, and the headman's herd was not yet there, so he went to the lake beyond the knoll and collected ample loads of luscious green broad leaves, selected a good open space below the knoll, and led the milking cows to that spot when the herd arrived.

Leaving the cows to feed, he ascended to the top of the knoll and settled into a thoughtful sitting position, contemplating what he should do next.

Absorbed in his musings, he didn't see Aerka Lhamo coming up the knoll until she was upon him, extending a warm greeting in her charming voice.

Giving a meek nod, he didn't respond.

However, unaware of his emotional state, she sat down beside him and spread upon the ground the food and wine she had brought in her shoulder bag. "I told my parents about us last night," she said. "They were happy that I chose someone humble and hardworking, instead of someone noble and haughty . . . a person who would not lift a finger to do a thing."

Tompo shook his head, but he still didn't respond.

"So, your debt will be paid off and you will be free, anytime you want," she stated, her tone carrying a touch of haughtiness.

"Aerka." He turned and faced her. "I may be humble and hardworking, but I am also an orphan and a fool." There was a slight terseness in his voice. "I will only bring shame and dishonour to you and your family. People will mock and scorn you. They may even denounce and ostracise your parents." He paused, hesitating for a moment, and then continued. "It is not your true feelings that guide you, but some evil spirits leading you astray."

Aerka's face displayed confusion, and then her eyes flashed in anger. "No, Tompo, I know exactly what I am doing," she said, keeping her anger in check. "I have thought about this deeply. At first, everyone will be shocked beyond words, but when we are married and you are living like any wealthy man, they will forget everything. Even more, they will change their perception about you and may even begin to respect you."

"No, Aerka, no." Tompo shook his head strongly. "This is not only improper but also gravely wrong. A person of my social stature and mental ability cannot marry a person of your social stature and mental ability. Our marital union will not only upset the people of the village, but it will also displease the gods and the deities of this place. What is more, I will gather more negative karma."

Again, her eyes flashed, but Tompo could not tell if he was seeing anger or confusion.

"Who filled your head with such notions, Tompo?" Her face furrowed with bewilderment and anger.

"It is true, Aerka," Tompo affirmed. "Our amala says that everyone and everything has a place in the society for a reason and a purpose. It is all part of the scheme of things." He paused briefly, then added with emphasis, "I am a person of unpurged karma, so my place in the society is at the bottom, not at the top. If I don't heed this karmic law and choose to indulge in unmerited things, I will only go down, not up."

"Tompo—" Aerka responded, her expression challenging.

He raised a hand and interrupted her. "Aerka, I have also decided to leave this worldly life and follow the noble path of dharma for the rest of my life. So, please, I beg you not to pursue this matter of marriage any further, as it is really not you but some evil spirits leading you astray to create an obstacle along my way."

"You want to pursue the path of dharma?" she repeated, her voice rising in pitch.

"Yes, Aerka. Ever since I encountered Riwang Trulku, an overwhelming devotion and yearning for dharma awakened within me. I don't know if this is a good or a bad thing, but if I don't pursue this noble path of dharma, I will die of sorrow."

Greatly surprised, she peered into his eyes, studying his face, and observed an intense faith and devotion gripping him, accompanied by conviction and determination to pursue it.

Then a feeling of foolishness swept over her, which quickly transformed into fury. "I thought you would be grateful and overjoyed to marry me," she burst out, her voice quivering and her eyes blazing. "But it seems that is not the case! When you cannot even lead a normal life, how can you possibly study dharma texts and follow the path of dharma?"

Tompo was stunned by her outburst.

"You are not only a fool, but also a loser," she said, jabbing her finger at his nose. "You deserve everything that has befallen you so far, and everything that awaits you."

"I'm sorry, I didn't mean to offend you," he said quietly.

"Offend me? It is I who will offend you when I reveal your secret!"

"Secret? What secret?" A sense of dread rose in his chest.

"Do you think I don't know about it? You worship a demonic spirit of the land and the forest, and make it do your weird and strange bidding, all to make your work easier. I investigated you for months, Tompo, and I have seen with my own eyes everything that you did. I will tell everyone about it."

Demonic spirit? He gaped at her.

Aerka turned away from him and, with one swoop of her hand, she swept the food packages and the wine canisters off the ground and into the shoulder bag, then stood up and marched away, chiding and cursing him under her breath, incoherent but with undeniable anger.

With his heart pounding, he tried to go after her, but sat rooted as if unable to move. *Worshipping a demonic spirit? No! From where did she even get an idea like that? How could anyone worship a demonic spirit? But what should I do if she really told people about it?*

Chapter 9

Kathog sat, his body tense, puckering his lips and clenching his fists, unsure on which side his parents' argument would wind up regarding the day of his appointment, and knowing that their decisions could determine his next course of action, and possibly his future as well.

"This month's fifteenth day has just passed," asserted the amala, drawing a vexed face. "It will be a long wait until the next fifteenth day, nearly a month. We cannot wait that long. By then, it will also be mid-spring and everyone will be busy in the fields."

"But we must follow the astrology," countered the headman, his voice equally angry. "He cannot begin his career on a non-auspicious day, this possibly the most significant day of his life. So, we must create the best possible tendrel for a long and successful career. Remember what the trulku said about tendrel?"

"Yes, of course. It is just that I am worried about him. Something has happened to him." She looked around, as if seeking an answer. "He has become so lost since we came back from the trulku's reception. He has hardly said a word." She turned to Kathog. "What has happened to you? Are you ill or something?"

"No, Mother, I am all right."

"Then why do you look like your life force has been severed from you? You should be jumping with joy, instead of sitting here in gloom and doom. Are you not excited about this? I thought you were waiting for something like this to come your way all this while."

"Actually, I was thinking," Kathog stammered, his thoughts fumbling as he struggled to determine whether he should reveal his decision to pursue the path of dharma. He hesitated. Telling them about it now, while they debated his career, felt inappropriate. Yet, if they settled on a date and began making preparations for the ceremony, it might be too late to inform them. "I was thinking," he repeated, "I should learn more from Father."

The headman and the amala turned and stared at each other, bewildered. Then they turned back to Kathog and stared at him with a confounded look. But before any one of them could speak, Uma Dolma barged into the room, startling them.

Kathog instantly sat upright and smartened up, but the young woman seemed more interested in his parents than him, as she straightaway directed her attention towards them.

"Headman and Amala will not believe it," she exclaimed, her eyes wide with excitement. "Aerka Lhamo has proposed to marry orphan Tompo. She has even told her parents about it, and they agreed to it."

"What nonsense, Uma Dolma!" the amala blurted out, a mix of surprise and anger in her voice.

"It is true, Amala," Uma Dolma affirmed, her eyebrows rising even higher. "Metog overheard Aerka Lhamo and her mother talking in their house. The girl offered to pay off his debt immediately. I don't know what she was thinking. But for whatever reason she might have done it, this is insane and bizarre."

"Metog must have been joking, you fool," the amala said, her anger masked only by a semblance of civility.

"No, Amala." Uma Dolma shook her head so strongly that the jewellery on her chest clattered. "Metog saw Aerka Lhamo returning home from the Yalang pastureland this morning, muttering and cursing. So, becoming curious, she followed her to her house and peeped through the window and could hear her talking to her mother."

Since Aerka Lhamo was said to be frequenting the pastureland recently, the details of Metog's story lent more credence to the information, shocking the headman and the amala.

Even Kathog, who normally didn't bother about other people's personal affairs, came alive with his ears pricked up.

"But Tompo refused her, saying he wanted to pursue the path of dharma," Uma Dolma went on, her eyes gleaming. "This is even more insane and bizarre! It is unbelievable."

The headman, in utter disbelief, and the amala, flustered, turned and stared at each other.

"What will happen to Aerka now?" Animated, Uma Dolma lifted her hands in the air, shaking her head in disbelief. "She will probably wish she could vanish from the face of the earth." Then, remembering something, her expression froze briefly. "Oh, I must go and tell Jarsang about it." She bowed, turned around, and left, without even waiting for the headman and the amala to react, her mind so preoccupied.

"What on earth is this?" the headman erupted. "Aerka Lhamo wants to marry orphan Tompo, and her parents agreed? What were they thinking? This is madness, even by their level and standards. I know they will do anything for wealth, but marrying Tompo—" He shook his head in disbelief.

"So what?" snapped the amala, becoming angrier. "Whatever it is, there is no reason for you to get all excited. For all I care, and for all that matters, that moron of a dimwit and an orphan should have accepted and gotten married. All I want is my debt paid off."

"Yes, I know," he said, "but he refused her because he wants to pursue the path of dharma. I thought he was only looking for a reason to get away from here. Now I see that he was serious about it. He really wants to do this, but he doesn't have the intelligence for it."

The amala sighed loudly. "Whatever it is, leave such talk aside now."

"To study dharma," went on the headman, as if she had not spoken, "one must at least have average intelligence. The dharma texts are quite hard. Some are said to be extremely difficult, even for the brightest. So, if anyone should pursue the path of dharma at all, it should be our Kathog. He would understand any text easily, and then go on to become a lama in no time."

The amala shrugged and let out a dismissive sigh, then turned her head away and looked out the window.

However, Kathog, who had briefly drifted into contemplation, was jolted from his inertia by these words. Suddenly, his face shone, his eyes sparkled, and his body jerked, making crackling sounds. "Father, I also want to pursue the path of dharma," he declared.

The headman and the amala were stunned. Something seemed to buzz in their heads, and they were not sure what they had heard. They turned towards their son and simply stared for a moment. Kathog's eyes were dancing with excitement. "What did you say?" they asked in unison.

"I also want to pursue the path of dharma," Kathog reiterated, his face beaming. "I can understand any dharma text and teaching, like Father says, and I can achieve greatness like Riwang Trulku in no time."

His parents were shocked.

"How could you say such a thing?" his father asked, glaring fiercely. "Riwang Trulku is a great saint. You will accumulate bad karma even to think like that. And to compare yourself to him—" The man could not bring himself to complete the thought. "I believed you knew better than that."

"I know, Father," Kathog countered, "but I am sure he was also a normal, ordinary boy like me before he became a trulku. If I study hard and practise dharma diligently, I can become like him in the future. That is a real possibility, and was said categorically by none other than Lord Buddha himself. So, what is wrong with my saying it?"

For once, the headman and the amala were stumped.

But the amala soon gathered herself. "What are you saying now? And where did this notion even come from? You are appointed the deputy headman of Tamchu village. Also, you don't talk about dharma like that. I think that dimwit Tompo has poisoned your mind. That-good-for-nothing orphan!"

Tompo's light footsteps, familiar to everyone in this house, were heard coming through the corridor, as if on cue.

The amala's face contorted with fury. "Tompo, you come in here!" she shouted, her voice seething with anger. "Right now!"

"Yes, Amala," came Tompo's frightened reply, followed by a hurried movement. Moments later, he entered the room like a scared mouse, going pale upon seeing the amala's fierce glare.

"Where have you been all morning?" she demanded.

"I was at the pastureland, Amala," he told her.

"Don't lie to me. I heard you romanced with that girl Aerka Lhamo all morning. If my dairy production goes down, you will have to bear the loss. But I guess she will compensate me on your behalf. I heard she even offered to clear off your debt and marry you."

"No, it is not what you think, Amala," replied Tompo, his surprise evident that she knew about it. His concern deepened, fearing that it might become a village scandal. "She saw me unhappy yesterday and merely wanted to console me."

"What, she saw you unhappy and wanted to console you?" she mimicked him in fury. "When she had the courage to propose to you, you cannot even speak out about it? What are you scared of? That you will have to accept her proposal?" The ring of her voice hung in the air as she stared, freezing her expression of incredulity.

Tompo gaped, speechless.

The muscles on her face relaxed, but her expression changed to one of a sneer. "I suppose you didn't accept it because you wanted to pursue the path of dharma," she said, the derision in her voice slicing through the orphan's heart. Then her face became taut. "But what I don't understand is how you plan on leaving without paying off your debt."

Tompo saw a malevolent glint in her eyes in that instant, and he knew she would unleash her wrath without any restraint.

"Whatever it is, whether you pursue the path of dharma or marry Aerka Lhamo, you will go because I don't want you here anymore. Your negative karma is not only affecting us, but you are also a bad influence on Kathog. So, pay off your debt and leave."

Tompo's heart turned cold and his mind went blank.

"I said, you must now pay off the debt and leave," she repeated sharply, and then she scrambled to her feet, grabbed Tompo by the hair, and dragged him out of the room, still cursing and chiding.

Hearing the commotion, Orop emerged from the kitchen and pleaded on the orphan's behalf. However, the amala would not yield, but instead continued to drag him through the corridor all the way to the front door, and thrust him out onto the stairway landing.

CHAPTER 10

Kathog's declaration of his decision to embark on the noble path of dharma came as a significant surprise to everyone in Tamchu, effectively nipping Aerka Lhamo's brewing scandal in the bud.

The attention of the village immediately shifted to him and his prospective future spouse, Uma Dolma. Some believed he would excel in dharma studies and soon become a great lama; others speculated he would go astray. And a few even wondered about Uma Dolma's marital fate.

On his parents' part, the headman and the amala thought he was misguided in choosing to pursue the path of dharma, as he had neither interest nor aptitude for it. To them, he was a worldly person by all accounts, a young man with nothing but his intelligence and a firm command over the language of dharma.

However, no matter how much they tried discussing, debating, and arguing about it, day in and day out, he could not be persuaded to change his course. He steadfastly refused to see the reason or rationale behind doing so. As the month came to an end, his parents were left with no alternative but to give in.

"Very well, then," the headman stated firmly. "If you cannot be dissuaded by reason, you will not be stopped by force. But let me tell you this: the path of dharma is a lifelong commitment with dire consequences. Once you have taken it up, it cannot be abandoned."

"I know what I am getting into, Father," Kathog reassured him. "I have thought about it deeply. This is what I want to do with my life. I will not falter in my commitment or fail in my practice. You have my word on that."

The headman nodded. "We will not object anymore," he said. "But don't think that, because we tried to dissuade you and failed, we will withhold our support. No, we will support you wholeheartedly and with dedication. We are your parents, and we will stand by you."

His mother concurred. "Other than not having displayed any interest in dharma until now, you have been brilliant in your studies. If you don't go astray, you will complete your studies on time. And if you are diligent in your practice, you may soon become a lama."

Kathog breathed a sigh of relief, and the headman and the amala gestured to indicate there would be no more discussion on the matter. Yet, despite this decision, a slight feeling lingered somewhere in their hearts, nagging at them and making them feel they might be making a grave and irreversible mistake.

However, later that evening, when they had eaten and drunk freely, they were finally feeling contented and peaceful.

"This is good," remarked the headman, alluding to Kathog's decision to follow the path of dharma, as he and his wife were preparing to retire for the night.

"Yes, it is," agreed the amala. "Even if he struggles and suffers, it will be for about ten years. Then he will at least become a lama and live a good life. We will not have to worry about him anymore." She looked at her husband, her face relaxed, and a sense of tranquillity reflected in her eyes. "We can die in peace then."

The headman looked back at her. "This is the good thing about dharma," he replied, his expression thoughtful and his voice carrying a tone of agreement.

"To which monastery should we send him?" she asked, already thinking about the next step.

The headman's demeanour turned solemn. "We should send him to a highly learned lama," he said, his expression firm with conviction. "It must be someone who is extraordinarily brilliant. Otherwise, his potential will be wasted, studying under an ordinary and average lama."

"There are no such great lamas around here," his wife pointed out.

"Not one in the entire region," agreed the headman, his brow creased with concern. "But we will find one, even if it is someone living afar. I will enquire around, beginning tomorrow. You need not worry about it. Ours is a country of dharma. We will find one."

"Yes, we will," she agreed.

The headman and the amala said their prayers, feeling a sense of calm settle within them. Then he blew out the lamp, and they lay down to sleep, their hearts lighter, and their minds finally at peace.

CHAPTER 11

A week later, *Tshongpon* Samdrup's caravan of horses and men arrived at the mansion, bringing goods for trade. As usual, the trader laid out his baskets of clothes, tea, salt, and an enticing array of products in the spacious courtyard. The villagers, led by the amala, traded with him, buying or bartering.

"Tshongpon Samdrup," a deep voice resonated from the second-floor staircase landing, his words heard over the surrounding noises. The trader looked up and spotted the headman descending the stone stairs, his face lighting up with a broad smile. "You really can travel, my friend."

"Yes, Headman," the trader replied, bowing slightly in greeting, and then gesturing to the goods spread out before them, "I am here again." With that, he beckoned one of his men to come and take over his place, so he could step aside to meet with the headman. "Travelling is my livelihood, Headman. There can be no trade without travel. So, like it or not, I must keep travelling to keep the salt and butter flowing at home."

The headman smiled. "Yes, there can be no trade without travelling," he concurred with a nod, "but it is not you alone in this business of earning a livelihood, Tshongpon Samdrup. All of us are engaged in it. No matter who we are by position, we have to do the part that is laid out for us. Everyone has to work for his salt and butter."

"Rightly said, Headman." The trader smiled.

They stood for a moment and watched the bustling around them. "And talking about travelling," said the headman, "you could not have arrived here at a more opportune time, for we are in dire need of some information that only a person as widely travelled as you could provide. So, I am very pleased to see you here today, and as a person who sets great store by auspiciousness, I would not take your arrival here today as anything other than a good tendrel."

"If tendrel is good, all else is good, Headman."

"True, Tshongpon Samdrup. For good to come, good tendrel must be set. Now, travelling all across the country and being a man of strong religious faith, you must certainly know a good and accomplished lama somewhere."

"Of course, I do Headman," the trader nodded. "In fact, I know quite a few of them all across the country, but why do you need a lama? I am sure there are as many good and learned lamas around here as well."

"My son, Kathog, has decided to follow the noble path of dharma," replied the headman, his countenance taking on a solemn respect. "As he is quite bright with the potential to achieve something truly remarkable, I want him to study under a good lama, but there isn't anyone around here suitable for him."

"That is truly commendable, Headman," the trader beamed in surprise and admiration. "Dharma is the only thing that matters in the end. Ultimately, nothing is of any real value; nothing can save us from our karma." He paused briefly, his thoughts momentarily absorbed in his words. "So, which lama would be better? All the high-calibre ones are quite far away."

"We would prefer someone close by," said the amala, as she approached them carrying her basket of goods. "That is, in the vicinity to which we can conveniently travel. I am sure we will want to visit him often, for one thing or the other."

"Amala, I am afraid there isn't anyone of such high calibre in your regular travelling distance. The closest I can think of is Lama Zangchak of Aeling. Those lamas closer to you are what I would consider to be average. Some of them may be above average, but not in that top league that you and your son require."

"Lama Zangchak of Aeling?" The headman was unimpressed, but he was careful not to reveal it in his face or voice, lest it offend the trader. "I have not heard of him." He twitched his lips as he searched his memory.

"He is a renowned lama of a very high status, Headman, and he is known for brilliance in study of text and philosophy, as well as excellence in conducting ritual and divination. He is a master scholar and a master performer known for perfection."

"That is impressive," said the headman, his face now beaming.

"Yes, Headman," said the trader. "He is a strict disciplinarian, too."

"But which Aeling?" asked the headman. "Aeling village or Aeling province?"

"Aeling province, Headman. The village is Tsokar."

"Oh, that is quite far away," noted the headman, his forehead creasing.

"Yes, far and to the north," replied Tshongpon Samdrup. "Almost eleven days' journey from here," he added, shifting his glance to the amala. "I am afraid there are no renowned lamas like him anywhere nearer."

"That is all right," she replied. "Eleven days is not that far. Some travel for months and even years crossing snow-covered mountains and swollen rivers, encountering thieves and bandits from Bod to Jagar, to pursue dharma . . . even in this day and age."

"But how are we going to send him?" asked her husband in a challenging tone. "It will take twenty-two days just going and coming back. I can't afford to go away for that long. Not at this time of the year," he added, drawing a long face and looking worried.

"If you can't go yourself, you could send him with me," suggested the trader, his tone earnest. "I will be returning this way in about a week. I will be travelling through Tsokar all the way to the western end, and like the amala said, there is nothing to worry about."

The headman's face relaxed. "That is very kind of you."

"This is nothing, really, and of no inconvenience to me. I am travelling that way whether I am with or without him. But I am afraid I cannot accommodate his luggage anywhere. All my horses and men are already overloaded."

"That is all right, Tshongpon Samdrup," said the headman, waving away his apology. "We will send a packhorse and a riding horse. You can return them when you travel this way next time. We just need someone reliable, not only to send our son with, but also to hand him over to the lama properly."

"Yes, Headman, I assure you I will deliver your son safely, and I will bring your horses back. This is no trouble, not at all. The two of you need not worry. I will hand your son to the lama's chief attendant in person, and will certainly put in a good word for him."

"Thank you, Tshongpon Samdrup."

"I will be back here in exactly one week, Headman," said the trader as he summoned his men with a wave of his hand to begin packing the goods. "Be ready to move in the morning of the following day," he told them.

"Yes, we will be packed and ready," answered the headman.

The amala said a quick goodbye to Tshongpon Samdrup, picked up her basket of goods and hurried up the stone stairs, leaving her husband to see the trader off. As she walked into the house, she was already thinking of the preparations for Kathog's departure and getting excited about it.

However, later that evening, she was beset by mixed emotions. She was happy about finding Lama Zangchak, but worried about Kathog's ability to cope with the life in a monastery so far away from parents and home.

She discussed these worries with the headman, and despite his reassurances, she became even more convinced that her son would not be able to take care of himself, let alone cope with the harsh living conditions of the monastery.

He would have to sleep with other monks in the quarters, wash his clothes, gather firewood from the forest, fetch water from the nearby spring, cook and clean, and above all else, survive on the measly diet provided by the monastery.

Thinking about it made her so worked up that she decided to send Tompo along with him to provide a helping hand and any other support he would need.

Chapter 12

Tompo walked into the living room and sat down quietly, facing the headman and the amala. He saw their stoic expressions and wondered why he had been called in, especially after they had said nothing to him for more than a month.

The amala cleared her throat and stared at him for some time. "We thought you were making an excuse to leave," she said, her voice surprisingly soft and kind. "But I see this is not the case, and you were serious about your intentions. Even now, I am told that you are determined to leave, and nothing we say or do will change your mind."

She paused, letting a momentary silence hang in the air, and leaving the orphan in a dreadful suspense.

"Very well, then," she declared suddenly, "if you are really bent on pursuing the path of dharma, we will not hold you back. We will also not ask you for our money. But you must go with Kathog. You must study with him and take care of him in the monastery."

Tompo was greatly surprised. For a moment he felt lightheaded, almost faint. Then something erupted deep inside him and a searing hot sensation shot through his veins and spread throughout his body.

"Yes, indeed that is right, Tompo," added the headman, his voice filled with paternal warmth. "After careful consideration, we have decided to send you and Kathog to a great and renowned lama called Lama Zangchak, in Tsokar village, in Aeling province. It is an eleven-day journey from here, and the two of you will travel with Tshongpon Samdrup."

An overwhelming surge of emotion washed over Tompo from deep within, and he began to sob without restraint. Then, with profound gratitude in his heart, he put his hands together in a gesture of appreciation towards the headman and the amala. As his emotions built up further, he instinctively moved to a kneeling position, shut his eyes and, weeping even harder, mumbled a prayer of gratitude to the gods and the deities, the buddhas and the bodhisattvas.

"Now, don't cry, Tompo," consoled the amala gently.

"Yes, Tompo," added the headman. "If this is really what you want in your life, then you work hard and make something of it. Even though you don't possess the intelligence required to study dharma, you can still gain merit from pursuing the path. This is the power of our insider's dharma."

With an endless stream of emotions flowing, Tompo could not control his tears.

"Stop crying now, Tompo," urged the headman, his voice filled with genuine concern. "For better or for worse, our karma brought us together, and we, each of us, did our part as we saw fit. Now that we must part ways, we wholeheartedly wish you well. Our prayers are with you, Tompo."

Nodding his head repeatedly, Tompo rested his palms on the floor and bowed down fully, his forehead touching the floor as if in prostration to a lama or a trulku. Then he slowly stood up and left the room, wiping his tears. He went straight to the kitchen, sat by the fireside, and cried loudly and unrestrainedly until he had no more emotion to vent and no more tears to shed.

Soon, some people passing by stopped to enquire and confirm the news about Tompo accompanying Kathog to Tsokar. *The word has already spread around, so Agay Orop will soon hear about it and come home*, thought Tompo.

Sure enough, Orop returned home from the field shortly thereafter, feeling both happy and sad, and eagerly wanting to talk to Tompo, but they could not find any opportunity to talk due to the steady stream of visitors pouring into the mansion.

Orop then thought of talking to Tompo properly, and at great length, later that night. However, when they retired to their room, before he could begin the conversation, Tompo, exhausted physically and mentally, fell fast asleep as soon as he lay down on the bed.

As Tompo had not even made his bed, Orop tucked him in, his eyes fixated on the young man's peaceful expression. In that moment of tranquillity, Tompo seemed relieved and peaceful, yet innocent and vulnerable, evoking a complex interplay of emotions within the old man's heart: happiness mixed with sorrow, hope intermingled with fear.

As he continued to gaze upon the orphan's serene face, a flood of emotions again engulfed him. His weathered face twisted, and he broke down and wept in the silence of the night, by the flickering lamp.

CHAPTER 13

On the last day of Kathog and Tompo's stay, the Dungje mansion buzzed with a flurry of activities, both inside and out. People had gathered from all over the village, some to help with the last-minute tasks, and others to see Kathog off before he left early the following morning.

With so much help being offered, Tompo and Orop were relieved of their work for the day, giving them time to be together in their room. But having spent the last week talking and sharing everything they felt, they had little more to discuss. Yet, as the day progressed, the heaviness of their parting set in, and their emotions began to surface.

"You are like a son to me, Tompo," the old man said, his voice heavy with emotion. "I should be sad to see you leave. Instead, I am happy because this is what you want. Again, although I am happy, I am also worried, knowing that the path of dharma will not be easy for you." He paused and gazed at Tompo for a while. "When it becomes hard for you, do not lose hope and give up."

"No, Agay, I will not," Tompo declared with determination, his gaze heavy with melancholy. "I may grow old, my vision may dim, my hearing may fade, and my limbs may fail, but I will never lose heart and give up on dharma. Even if it is just one word, I will learn it and practise, because this is the vow I have made to myself."

"That is good, Tompo. You have my prayers and wishes for a successful journey on the path of dharma."

"Thank you, Agay, and you have my prayers and wishes for a long and healthy life. Since it was our karma that brought us together like father and son, I make this aspiration prayer that we meet again in this life, even if it is in death, and that I am able to do something for you and fulfil my responsibility as a son."

"I am very old, Tompo." Orop's voice was weighed down by solemnity. "But I will not die soon, not so easily." He shook his head. "I will live for many more years. However, when I finally die, I will wander the bardo, suffer much, and be reborn in the animal realm. That is because I didn't live a righteous life like you, and I didn't say a word of prayer unless I was frightened of something."

"No, Agay, no. Don't say this."

"Yet I have no regret about it, Tompo, for it was a conscious choice that I made as a way to retaliate against my bad karma," the old man said defiantly, showing no fear. "You will study hard, learn valuable lessons, and say some prayers for me. This way, I may get some respite when I am suffering in the bardo and in my next life."

"You may not have lived a righteous life," Tompo gently acknowledged, "and your actions may not have been virtuous to everyone. Still, you are a good human being deep down in your heart, and you have also been good to me. I will never forget what you have done for me. No matter where life takes me, I will always keep you in my heart and in my prayers."

A tear rolled down Orop's cheek, but before he could respond, someone rapped on the door and announced that the amala wanted Tompo in the family room.

Leaving Orop to struggle with his emotions, Tompo went to the third floor and entered the grand family room. Kathog sat by the window and looked out impatiently, while the amala sifted through a pile of things on the floor.

But Tompo's gaze went straight to a large cane basket packed with Kathog's luggage. *It must be one full horse load*, he thought, and a shadow of concern passed over his face as he contemplated whether he could manage to carry it that far.

The amala noticed the scowl on Tompo's face. "What is it now?" she asked sternly. "A grim face like that on the eve of departure is bad for tendrel. Don't you want to go? If not, speak now, and I will find an alternative arrangement. There are many others who would happily take your place."

"No, Amala, I will go," Tompo replied hastily, his concern for the load replaced by the fear of the amala changing her mind to send him.

"The basket may be sizeable, but the things are light," she explained, as if having to provide a rationale. "So why send a pack-horse unnecessarily? You don't know when Tshongpon Samdrup will come; it may be months or even a year. That is too long a time to send two horses away, travelling all around the country, risking strain and injury."

"Yes, Amala," Tompo affirmed.

"What luggage do you have?" she enquired.

"Just my clothes, and sheets for sleeping," Tompo replied.

"Pack them in this," she instructed, handing him a thick piece of cloth equipped with two long straps for binding. "Hang it from the back of the basket. But don't place it on top. There are some things inside that are sacred. Also, don't soil this cloth. I don't want anything unclean and unsightly hanging from that basket."

"I understand, Amala," said Tompo.

"Go and pack now."

"Yes, Amala." Tompo bowed and left.

"Can I also go down now?" asked Kathog, eager to go meet the guests who had come to see him off.

"Yes, we are done here."

Kathog hurried down to the main living room on the second floor and joined his father, who was entertaining guests. By then, everyone close to the family had arrived and were eating and drinking, and Uma Dolma, concealing her sorrow from the others, had secretly cried in every corner of the mansion.

Kathog, being familiar with her emotions, immediately recognised the weight of her sorrow, and so his heart went out to her, feeling a deep sense of sympathy and guilt for the sadness she was experiencing.

But, later in the afternoon, when Tshongpon Samdrup and his caravan of horses and men arrived, and the actual farewell for him with feasts, singing, and dancing began, Kathog completely forgot about Uma Dolma's misery and suffering and thoroughly enjoyed the attention lavished upon him, with praise for his greatness and conviction of his future successes.

However, when everyone had left the mansion, and he retired to his bed later at night, a feeling of desolation began to set in. He realised that, come morning, nothing would be the same for him, not ever again.

Lying in the dark, Kathog wondered what the orphan Tompo was feeling. In the middle of his thoughts, he fell into a dreamless slumber, the weight of the impending journey and what might lie in store for him heavy on his mind.

CHAPTER 14

As the last remnants of darkness dissolved into the growing daylight of dawn, revealing thick white fluffs of morning mists, some floating in the air and some resting on the earth's surface, Tshongpon Samdrup's caravan of horses and men, travelling in a single file, left the mansion.

Tshongpon Samdrup, with a small leather bag slung sideways across his chest, led the way on foot, with Kathog following closely behind on horseback. Bringing up the rear, with some of the trader's sturdiest men, all carrying heavy loads, was Tompo, bearing the massive cane basket on his back.

Although Tompo's load was voluminous, it was surprisingly light, just as the amala had reassured him. He didn't buckle under the weight, as he had feared he would. Instead, managing to carry it without difficulty, he kept up with the rest of the caravan, and they soon went past the last house of the village and reached the nine *chortens*, built in honour of the guardian deities of Tamchu, at the periphery of the village.

By then, the sun was peeking over the mountains, turning the eastern sky crimson and shooting warm golden rays at them.

Although Tompo was starting to feel the load become heavier, he found the strength to pluck fresh leaves and flowers and offer them at the chortens, invoking the gods and the deities of the territory and thanking them for blessing him and his family for generations. Then bidding them goodbye and praying for a safe and fruitful journey, he hurried after the caravan.

The valley ended some distance from there, at the base of a steep mountain, and the path circled that base until they reached another similar mountain. From there on, they were forced to climb one mountain after another, always heading northwards, with each new mountain appearing taller and steeper than the previous one.

It felt like a never-ending climb. By midafternoon, Tompo had developed painful sores on his foot, and by sundown, he was struggling to take even one step forward.

However, he was not the only one battling the journey. Kathog was having difficulty sitting straight in the saddle. The insides of his thighs were painful, his back had gone stiff, and his buttocks hurt like hell.

But the caravan pushed on. Left with no choice, the two young men toughed it out until they reached a tiny spring at dusk and stopped to camp for the night.

Tompo helped the trader's men set up the camp. Then, he bathed his sore foot in the cool spring water and padded the wound with mashed artemisia leaves. This gave him some relief, but as night fell and the chill descended upon them, the cold pierced through his thin cotton clothes and stung his skin.

By then, everyone else had changed into warm woollen clothes, but since he had none, he invoked the gods and the deities of the area to tweak the weather a bit to warm him. However, nothing of the sort happened.

Perhaps the gods and the deities of the area don't know me, and so are not responding, he thought, and considered layering another cotton gho over the one he was already wearing, when one of the men, Namso Gyalwa, came to him and gave him an old and thick woollen gho.

Having not received anything from anyone, let alone a warm woollen gho on a cold night, Tompo felt so grateful to Namso Gyalwa that he dined with this kind horseman from the high mountains and later bedded by his side under a huge old tree.

It was a beautiful starry night, and one of the trader's men nicknamed Kalapingka, after the melodic bird, played his stringed instrument and sang songs by the campfire, late into the night.

Cradled by this harmonious serenade, Tompo gently drifted off to sleep, feeling free and truly happy in a long time. But come morning, the agony of the journey began again.

Tompo's sores became bigger and more painful, and Kathog's back ached even more. Yet, the trader pushed them on relentlessly, driving them higher up the mountains until, around noon, they finally reached Chugpo village, the land of the wealthy, located in a beautiful canyon at the base of twin mountains.

The village was visibly prosperous, with grand houses and well-built people who greeted and crowded around them. But the trader and his men had no time to talk to anyone. As soon as they picked up the goods they had traded, they were on their way, pushing even harder, and arrived at the next campsite before nightfall.

The spot was a large picturesque meadow, by the side of a *dangrim* chorten, on the belly of a slumbering hill. A silver stream meandered through it on the far side, filled with wildflowers of all sorts.

Kathog sat down where he dismounted, but Tompo had to help the men offload the packs from the horses, set up camp, build the fire, and fetch water and firewood.

Most importantly, he had to tend to his sores, but that evening he had his newfound friend, Namso Gyalwa, to help him. The man bathed his sores in warm water, padded them with mashed medicinal leaves that he had gathered from the nearby forest, and bound them with a cloth bandage.

Tompo didn't know what medicinal leaves Namso Gyalwa had used, but they stung him throughout the night and were healing his sores by the following morning.

However, no sooner had his foot begun to heal when another sore appeared on his shoulder, right on the spot where the handle of the basket chafed against his skin. This sore worsened quickly, and the excruciating pain slowed him down.

Kathog also, bending his torso in all directions to ease his increasing backache, fell behind. As they were slowing down the caravan, the trader left them behind with Namso Gyalwa to accompany them. But without the caravan to maintain pressure on them to keep moving, they trudged at a snail's pace and didn't reach the campsite until dinnertime.

Kathog collapsed onto a mat by the fireside straight from his horse and immediately fell asleep, while Tompo prepared to tend to his sores. But, as the new one was on his shoulder and particularly severe, requiring assistance and proper medication, the trader himself came with a bag of personal ointments and medicines and attended to him.

The medication worked fast, and Tompo felt instantly relieved. But as the night wore on and his body cooled down, the pain intensified, and then his body became feverish and hot. He tossed and turned in pain the whole night, sleeping very little.

When he awoke from a short sleep in the morning, he was not only feverish but also drowsy and fatigued. And when the journey resumed, the handle of the basket chafed his wounds again, exacerbating his pain and discomfort.

From that day onwards, there was no relief for either of the two young men. Kathog's back was permanently stiff, and Tompo's shoulder continued to fester and bleed. They were both in immense pain, whether resting or moving.

However, the last day, which was a descent into the valley, was more torturous for Tompo. As the descent was sharp, the load came down on his shoulders with all its weight, rubbing hard on his wound.

Unable to bear the pain, he sobbed several times and dearly wished that they could reach the valley soon. But they could not even see the valley, no matter how far they descended. Then, when he had given up hope of seeing it anytime soon, the caravan came upon a tiny crest overlooking a picturesque valley of farmlands and scattered houses.

Tshongpon Samdrup slowed his pace and let Kathog's horse come abreast of him, and then pointed. "The cluster of houses on that hillock on the far side of the valley is Lama Zangchak's monastery."

Kathog nodded meekly, without even looking properly, for he was in no condition to feel anything, much less speak.

But Tompo, overcome with joy, walked over to the edge, put his hands together, and said his aspiration prayer, asking that his pursuit of the path be fruitful.

From then on, Tompo, immersed in joy, didn't feel pain or exhaustion but was energised and recharged. He went ahead of Kathog and Namso Gyalwa and kept pace with the caravan until they pulled in at the monastery's ornate wooden gate at around sundown.

A young monk boy was sweeping the courtyard outside. On hearing the caravan, he glanced towards the gate and his face lit up on seeing Tshongpon Samdrup. Then, setting the broom against the wall, he sprinted towards the gate, calling out, "Tshongpon Samdrup!"

"You have grown taller," teased the trader, with a playful glint in his eye.

"Have I really?" asked the boy, his face lighting up with a mix of curiosity and excitement.

"Yes, you have," the trader nodded, his expression a blend of playfulness and seriousness. "How old are you now?"

"I am nine years now," the boy replied with a hint of pride.

"You are almost a man then." The trader smiled, his expression warm and caring.

"I will complete one astrological cycle soon," the boy added, his voice filled with a sense of anticipation and accomplishment.

Tshongpon Samdrup reached into his bag, retrieved a ball of sweet made from sugarcane juice, and gave it to the boy, whose face shone with immense joy.

Tompo and Kathog, who had observed the man to be thrifty, were surprised at his generosity towards the boy.

At that moment, a tall and hefty middle-aged monk walked out of the monastery. Seeing the caravan, he sauntered towards the gate, breaking into a broad smile, yet looking quite solemn, owing to his inherent nature.

Seeing him coming, the young monk quickly bowed at Tshongpon Samdrup and scurried away from the gate, clutching his precious sweet.

The trader took off his hat and smiled at the sturdy monk.

"Where did you come from this time, Tshongpon Samdrup?" the monk asked.

"A good question, Chief Attendant," replied the trader, laughing. "I have travelled all over the country, but I suppose I can say I came from Tamchu, from the foothills, for I have brought these two young men from there to study with you."

The chief attendant turned and stared at Kathog, who stood by his horse, holding the rein, and at Tompo, who was slumped under a heavy load. His mouth twitched and his head shook a bit in a subtle disapproval, but he didn't say anything. Instead, he turned back to the trader. "But are you not going to halt the night here?"

"No, Chief Attendant, I must depart," the trader stated firmly, but with a touch of apology in his voice. "I will meet the lama on another occasion." Then, pointing to Kathog, he continued, "Kathog is the son of Headman Thodak Zamba, a nobleman and a renowned scholar. I am sure you have heard of him." Then he gestured towards Tompo. "Tompo is a bondservant living with them. I will leave them here with you, Chief Attendant, if that is all right."

"Yes, of course, but it is already sunset," the chief attendant interjected, his expression reflecting practical concern. "You will not make it beyond the Azamgang plain. Why don't you stay the night here and leave early tomorrow?"

"Thank you, Chief Attendant, but I am running behind schedule to meet a trader coming from Bod tomorrow at the Gangzo ridge," the trader explained, his tone filled with a sense of urgency. "So, I intend to travel by moonlight tonight and arrive there by early morning."

"Oh, yes, I understand," replied the chief attendant.

"Sorry to come and go like this," the trader said, his expression apologetic.

"That is all right," said the monk, his voice understanding and accepting.

Bidding goodbye, Tshongpon Samdrup left, again leading his long caravan down the hill.

The chief attendant turned to Kathog and Tompo with a stern expression. "You must forget your old relationships from now onwards. This is a monastery, and there will be no differentiation of any sort."

"Yes, Teacher," replied Kathog and Tompo in unison.

"Good, then come along." The chief attendant began to shuffle away, but abruptly stopped and turned to Tompo. "Those sores of yours have festered badly. They need immediate attention.

Aren't they painful? Even a horse would not have made it this far in that condition."

Unsure how to respond, Tompo simply bowed his head.

The chief attendant sighed in concern and dismay, then turned and walked away, leaving Kathog and Tompo to follow him in silence.

Part Two

CHAPTER 15

The sun emerged from behind the Rewochen mountain range, casting its warm golden rays over Lama Zangchak's monastery, abuzz with morning activities.

Kathog, clad in a new red robe, and Tompo, still wearing one of his old faded cotton ghos, stepped out of the monks' quarters, built alongside and attached to the kitchen. They walked across the cobblestone courtyard, up the stone stairs, and into the monastery building.

Deychok, a senior student monk, received them from the entrance door and led them into a modest waiting room adjacent to the main shrine room. The chief attendant was waiting for them, and his gaze went straight to Tompo. "Where is your red robe?" he asked, with a look of surprise on his face.

"I don't have a red robe, Teacher," Tompo responded, his face taking on a sombre hue, and his ears turning red.

Noticing Tompo's unease, the chief attendant thought about it and nodded. "I think it will be fine for now. I will apprise the lama about it." He was about to turn away from Tompo, but stopped. "I have one new robe, a bit narrow for me, but it should fit you fine. I will give it to you after the audience." Then, shifting his attention to both Kathog and Tompo, he asked, "Where is your gift offering for the lama? What did you bring?"

Kathog lifted the shawl and unveiled an old gold-coated statue of Gautama Buddha resting in the palm of his left hand, with a folded ceremonial scarf held between his fingers. "My father sent this statue from our shrine. He said that it was cast by a master craftsman from Balyul specifically for our great-great grandfather."

The chief attendant's admiration for the exquisite gold statue was evident as he marvelled at the sacred gift. "An old sacred gold statue of Buddha. This is truly a remarkable tendrel, an auspicious alignment of causes and conditions. The lama will be very pleased. He sets great store by tendrel." Then he turned to Tompo. "Where is yours? What did you bring?"

Tompo shuffled his feet nervously and looked down, his voice softening as he admitted, "I don't have anything, Teacher."

The chief attendant's eyes widened, eyebrows raised, and mouth opened. "You didn't bring a gift offering for the lama?" His shock was palpable. "This cannot be. It is acceptable to arrive without a red robe, something you can always acquire here and there, but you must have an offering, specifically carried as a gift for the lama."

Tompo gaped at the chief attendant, perspiration appearing on his forehead.

"Didn't anyone tell you?" the chief attendant went on, his brow creased into a furrow. "It need not be a statue or anything significant, but certainly something respectable enough to honour the lama. It can even be something as small as a needle, but a new one. The objective is to create an auspicious bond between the lama and the disciple."

"I'm sorry, Teacher, I didn't know about this." Tompo's voice trembled. "But even if I had known, I still would have had nothing to offer. I possess nothing of value, nothing worthy to be offered to the lama. All I own are a few old clothes to wear and some old sheets for sleeping."

The chief attendant's expression softened, but remained firm. "I understand your predicament, and I empathise with your situation," he said sincerely. "However, I can't take you in without a gift offering. Our lama is very particular about tendrel. He will not accept you but reprimand both of us severely."

Tompo's emotions engulfed him in an instant, and tears welled up in his eyes and cascaded down his cheeks uncontrollably.

The chief attendant looked at Tompo with deep sympathy, feeling the pain in the young man's heart and understanding the gravity of the situation, yet aware that he had limited power and authority to alter the circumstances.

"Tompo, you must know that tendrel is very important in sowing the seed of the lama–disciple relationship in dharma," the chief attendant explained, his tone soft. "This is sacred and fundamental to the path. The bond between the lama and the disciple will determine everything, from the spiritual progress of the disciple to the flourishing of the lama's lineage."

But his words had no consoling effect whatsoever on Tompo.

"I understand that this is difficult for you," the chief attendant went on, his tone compassionate yet resolute, "but there is no way around it. This is an essential matter that determines the lama's suitability for a disciple." He paused and pursed his lips. "Compatibility, not on a personal level, but on a spiritual level involving destiny."

Tompo nodded, but kept crying.

"I think your destiny for dharma is not with our lama. However, this doesn't mean that it is the end of the path for you, for you can always go to another lama. It is said that if one lama is not suitable for you, another lama will be destined for you."

With his chest heaving and tears flooding down his cheeks, Tompo sobbed even harder, the mix of emotions overwhelming him.

"I am not turning you away from here, Tompo," said the chief attendant compassionately, his voice beginning to crack a bit. "Since you are an orphan without anyone to go back to, you are welcome to stay here and help with the monastery's work. You can stay as long as you want, even a lifetime."

Tompo was too devastated to be consoled, but he did not want to make it difficult for the chief attendant, so he forced himself to stop crying.

"It is all right, Tompo," the chief attendant reassured, but his voice was still filled with both concern and guilt. "This happens with many people, not just you."

"Thank you, Teacher," replied Tompo, still working to control his emotions. As his body calmed, he said, "And thank you for your kindness. I'm sorry for causing you trouble."

"Tompo, there was no trouble. You should not take it so hard. This is how things happen in dharma. You are not the first person encountering an obstacle like this. You can go for now. I will tell you what to do later."

Nodding with a bow, Tompo turned and left, his shoulders drooping.

The chief attendant stared after him for some time, his expression sombre and thoughtful. Then he shook his head and turned to Kathog, his face now serious.

"Our lama is particular about discipline and standards, so observe Deychok closely and follow his cues. Nothing should go wrong, as this audience will determine everything about your relationship with the lama, including its tendrel."

Kathog nodded, his face growing a shade grimmer.

The chief attendant's demeanour softened, his concern for the young man evident. "Give the statue to Deychok; you cannot prostrate holding it."

Kathog quickly handed the statue to Deychok.

The chief attendant rose from his seat and departed, prompting the two disciples to hasten after him, nearly running to match his giant strides. He led them out of the room, across the corridor, and into the sacred shrine room. There, he bowed to the lama, moved to the side, and stood waiting.

Kathog stood at the doorway, his eyes wide with awe and wonder. The walls adorned with fine frescoes, the intricately carved and painted beams and ceiling, and the polished wooden floor all left him mesmerised.

At the centre of it sat Lama Zangchak, portly and commanding, atop a grand throne exuding power and authority. His majestic presence at once captured Kathog's admiration.

When Deychok nudged him, he quickly pulled himself together and prostrated to the lama. He received the statue from Deychok, then walked to the throne and offered the ceremonial scarf and the statue to the lama.

The lama put the scarf back on Kathog's neck but took the statue in his hands, held it above his head, and mumbled a short prayer.

Kathog took the two ends of the scarf, neatly tucked them inside his shawl, and retraced his steps back to his earlier position beside Deychok.

"Our tendrel is auspicious," declared the lama, his voice resonating with significance. "A few days ago, I dreamt of an ancient gold statue of Lord Buddha being brought here, carried on the back of a great bodhisattva," continued the lama, sharing a remarkable revelation. "And this morning you offer me this old Buddha statue as a gift offering."

Kathog's eyes sparkled and his face shone.

"The causes and conditions have aligned, and our sacred bond has been established." The lama paused briefly and stared at Kathog. For a moment, a flicker of warmth appeared in his eyes. "I offer my ardent aspiration prayer for your swift and successful journey on the noble path of dharma."

"Thank you, Lama," said Kathog, his heart filled with gratitude and relief.

"You will join seven other monks studying the language and grammar in the foundation group," the lama instructed him. "Since they are all children of ages about five to seven, and they started only a few months back, you will be able to catch up with them soon without any problem."

Kathog's face turned grim, worried that he would have to study this again. "I have already studied the language and grammar with my father, Lama," he interjected hastily. "I come from the Dungje nobility of Tamchu village in Lrarong province, and my father is the renowned nobleman and scholar, Thodak Zamba."

The lama turned red. "If your father was a renowned nobleman and scholar, you could have also learnt dharma from him, and you need not have come here," he snapped, his fierce glare locking onto Kathog. "If he could teach you the language and grammar required at the level of dharma, I am sure he could have taught you dharma itself."

Kathog stood there, stunned and gripped by fear, as the lama's voice hung in the air, its weight bearing down on him.

"I don't like those who think they know everything," continued the lama in a thundering voice. "They are like a cup filled to the brim. Any more wine poured into it would just flow out."

Kathog quickly gathered himself. "I apologise, Lama," he offered humbly in a stammering voice. "Becoming anxious and nervous about having to start my studies from the very beginning, I expressed myself poorly. What I learnt from my father is far from the level of studies required for dharma, even by our village lama's standard."

The lama's anger subsided, and he listened attentively.

"And certainly not up to the lama's standards," added Kathog. "Although my father is highly regarded as a scholar in the layman's world, he acknowledges that he lacks knowledge of dharma and doesn't pretend otherwise. In fact, it is his passion for learning and admiration for the lama's profound wisdom that brought me all the way here from the foothills."

The lama nodded, his demeanour now pacified and content. "The language and grammar form the very foundation of dharma studies," he explained. "As a monk, your path doesn't involve clerical work, but delving into the profound texts of dharma, some of which are intricate and complex. If your grasp of the language and grammar is not robust, you risk losing your way in the depths of these teachings."

Kathog nodded meekly, feeling awkward about it.

"That is precisely why I don't permit even the chief attendant to conduct such instruction here. I uphold a stringent standard in these matters. However, don't be misguided into thinking that the chief attendant lacks the qualification to teach. On the contrary, he is more than qualified to teach any text, and in certain villages he could even be enthroned a lama."

"Yes, Lama." Kathog nodded.

"In that case," the lama continued, referring to Kathog's claim of having studied the language and grammar from his father, "if you really have studied these, then you may join another group that is about to begin the study of texts. However, I hope you are thorough in the subject and know things that you are expected to know, for your own benefit."

Uncertain how to interpret the lama's comment, Kathog mumbled a vague thank-you, accompanied by a slight bow of his head. Feeling Deychok tug at his robe, he quickly made his departing prostrations, bowed down, and left the room.

CHAPTER 16

Tompo sat on the bare ground behind the monastery, his back against the wall, his knees raised, and his head resting on them. He was sobbing again in heaves and gasps.

After a time, he fell silent and raised his head, exhausted from his emotions. His mind was blank. He looked around and saw a forest of weeds all dried up but strongly rooted into the ground and encroaching into the drain. He remembered the chief attendant saying he could stay and help with the work.

He walked over to the weeds and began to uproot them, but as he did so, his emotions welled up again. *I must work hard and suffer much more, if I want to exhaust my bad karma*, he thought, and so he uprooted those weeds even more forcefully and in large sheaves until his hands were bruised.

He worked on, putting increased effort into the work, without taking any rest, and by noon he had cleared almost the entire area behind the monastery. His hands were nearly bleeding and his body dripping with sweat, yet he would not rest, not even for a moment.

After some time, the chief attendant appeared from the corner of the monastery. He was on his way to his quarter at the far end of the campus and spotted Tompo toiling away with an almost frenzied intensity, as if under the influence of an evil spirit.

"Who instructed you to undertake this task?" enquired the big man, unnerved by what he saw.

"Teacher said I could stay here and help," Tompo replied with a hint of uncertainty, his voice faltering slightly, and his gaze shifting between the chief attendant and the task at hand.

"I told you to help with some work like sweeping, cleaning, cooking, and doing dishes, not pulling weeds with your bare hands. This crabgrass has grown deep into the hard ground for years. This is madness, Tompo, going far beyond the state of penance."

"I thought I had so much negative karma that if I didn't work hard and merely stayed here consuming and living off the monastery's provisions, I would accumulate even more negative karma, and suffer even more. That is why I am working hard to cleanse my bad karma."

Touched and, even more, surprised, the chief attendant was at a momentary loss for words. Then, feeling both anger and helplessness, he said in a scolding voice, "Go have your meal now. Then rest afterwards. Your body must still be feeling the strain from that gruelling journey. If you wish to live long and practise dharma, you must learn to care for your body and prioritise your health."

"Yes, Teacher." Tompo bowed, turned around, and started walking away, but before he turned the corner of the building, he paused and glanced back. He saw the chief attendant staring after him, his expression a mix of guilt, concern, and disbelief. Taken aback by this intense stare, Tompo swiftly rounded the corner and hurried across the courtyard.

When he reached the kitchen, lunch was over and no one was there, so he served himself some corn grains and bean curry, but he could not muster an appetite, still feeling devastated for not having been ordained as a monk.

As he sat mulling over his uneaten meal, the cook, Lalung Zang, walked in, heaving and panting under the weight of a *palang* of water.

"Where have you been?" the cook demanded, his potbelly of a stomach rising up and down inside his gho with every uttered word. "You should be on time for meals, or the chief attendant will have your hide. You know, the big fellow is stricter than the lama when it comes to timing."

"I was cleaning the area behind the monastery."

"Yes, I heard you didn't get the lama's audience," said Lalung Zang, his voice softening. "Tendrel means everything to this lama. He interprets the goodness of all things through it, and he will also not undertake any venture, no matter how small, without divining or reading the astrological charts. And he is very good at all of this."

Tompo nodded, his interest piqued.

"But then, he is brilliant at all things. He is a master of text, ritual, astrology, divination, therapy, medicine, and everything in the domain of dharma and religion. He can treat any illness, concoct any medicine, and divine with remarkable accuracy about any subject, whether predicting a patient's fate or locating a stray cow."

"That is amazing!" Tompo exclaimed, his face shining and his eyes sparkling. "If his divination is that accurate, it is like possessing profound insight into all things. You know, I have never had any divination done on me, and I wonder what the future holds for me in my pursuit of the path of dharma."

"Really? Then you should seek out the old astrologer Naku. Even he can reveal both your past and future correctly. Finish your lunch quickly and we will go and see if he is in his quarter. You can ask him about anything you wish to know."

His eyes gleaming and his heart racing fast, Tompo gobbled up his meal in just a few handfuls and stood to leave. But as he followed Lalung Zang, waddling out of the door, he became anxious, pondering what might be in store for him.

They turned left from the stairs and walked across the shaggy lawn beside the kitchen, went past the woodshed, then followed a trail leading towards the canyon, and arrived at a small, ramshackle cabin in the woods. But the old astrologer was not in. "Ah," exclaimed Lalung Zang, turning his head away in dismay, "the old man must have gone to the village to drink again. He always wanders around, inebriated."

Tompo shared in this disappointment. "When might he be back?"

"No one can tell. There is no certainty in old Naku."

Something rustled from behind the cabin, attracting their attention, and a monk appeared with a sheaf of small branches with leaves, neatly chopped off from different plants, in one hand and a knife in the other.

"Oh, it is you, Jarpa," the cook said. "We thought it was the old astrologer. What is it for?"

"The lama is conducting a ritual tomorrow in his residence," the monk replied. "Are you looking for the astrologer? Didn't you know he left? His younger brother came and took him back to their village."

"When?"

"Last week. He was led away from the village." With that, Jarpa turned and walked away.

Tompo and Lalung Zang returned to the kitchen. Initially, Tompo was disappointed and quiet, but as they spent the afternoon together, preparing dinner, the cook once again regaled him with endless stories of Lama Zangchak's greatness, drawing him into the conversation.

In the process, Tompo bonded with Lalung Zang and gradually settled down, his sorrows fading into the background. But towards sundown, Lalung Zang was suddenly sent off to the village to accompany the physician into the nearby forest to gather certain herbal leaves in the auspicious full-moon night, leaving Tompo to deal with all the kitchen work.

That evening, as Tompo was serving the monks their dinner, a wealthy trader and his wife arrived and gifted a new woollen blanket to each of the monks, but not to him.

Tompo didn't mind not getting one of those blankets, but it served to exacerbate his pain of not receiving the lama's audience and being ordained as a monk.

A strong feeling of disappointment hit him first, then the realisation that it might not be appropriate for him to sleep among the monks in their quarters. After mulling about it for a while, he quietly picked up his belongings and left the room.

As no monk had sought his friendship, and he had largely kept to himself, his departure went unnoticed. In fact, not one person glanced his way or enquired about his destination, but as he always preferred remaining insignificant and invisible, this suited him just fine.

Tompo returned to the kitchen and made his bed in one corner, but it was too early to sleep, and he had no one with whom to engage in conversation, so he swept the floor and started to clean each and every item one by one, using a piece of cloth.

As most of them had been left untouched for years, they were shrouded in a thick layer of soot, dust, and grease. Cleaning them meticulously, he became engrossed and did not hear the heavy footsteps approaching the kitchen until the door was flung wide and the chief attendant stood at the threshold.

"What are you doing?" the big man demanded, looking surprised.

Startled out of his reverie, Tompo jumped to his feet. "I'm sorry, Teacher. It was too early to go to bed, and I had nothing to do, so I thought of cleaning the kitchen and sorting everything."

"But it is far past your bedtime," the chief attendant said, his brow creased as he glanced out of the window and into the night.

"I got lost in my work and didn't realise the time," Tompo replied, his eyes briefly darting towards the window.

The chief attendant shook his head. "Go to bed now."

Nodding with a bow, Tompo quickly dropped the cloth into the corner, put everything back where it belonged, and then picked up the oil lamp and hurried away to his bed in the corner of the room.

The chief attendant was utterly surprised to find Tompo's bed set up in that spot. "Are you planning to sleep here?" he enquired with astonishment.

"Yes, Teacher."

"Why?"

"Since I am not a monk, I believe it may not be appropriate for me to share their sleeping quarters. I fear that my impure presence may defile their sacred space and potentially lead to accumulating negative karma. It might also displease the gods and the guardian deities of dharma, and possibly bring misfortune upon everyone here."

"What nonsense is this, Tompo?" The chief attendant frowned, turned his head away and sighed loudly. "Who told you such a thing?"

"It is my own thinking, Teacher," Tompo responded earnestly.

"None of this is true, Tompo." He gestured towards the door. "Go and sleep inside."

As he was about to leave, he noticed Tompo's meagre sleeping arrangements, consisting of only a few old thin sheets. "This is all you have?" His concern was unmistakable. "It is cold here in Tsokar, not like in your Tamchu. But it is not just the cold that is concerning. With only these thin sheets, the floor will be hard."

"I use all my ghos, Teacher."

The chief attendant shook his head in disapproval. "Leave your things here and come with me," he said, gesturing with his hand, then turned around and left the kitchen.

Tompo followed him out of the kitchen, across the courtyard, past the monastery building, and to the man's own quarter on the far side of the campus. It was a small and cosy house, with one small living room and one bedroom.

Asking Tompo to wait in the living room, the chief attendant went into the bedroom. Tompo, pacing around in the room, looked out the window and saw the kitchen lamps burning brightly. *The chief attendant must have seen the lights and came to check them*, he thought.

"Here, you take these," said the chief attendant from behind.

Tompo turned around and saw the big man coming out of the door, carrying a thick mattress, a woollen blanket, and a set of red robe, shirt, and shawl neatly folded and stacked in a pile. "These are all new. The robe was sewn narrower and slightly shorter for me by mistake."

"Thank you, Teacher." Tompo received it, bending in gratitude. "Even though I have so much of bad karma, I am fortunate to have met you, for you are truly kind and generous, giving more than I deserve. I will never forget this kindness but cherish it gratefully as long as I live, and as long as I can remember."

"You need not feel that way, Tompo," replied the chief attendant with an edge of emotion in his voice. "Everyone deserves equally. No one is better than the other in any way. As human beings, and more so as monks practising Buddha's dharma, we need to share what we have with others."

Tompo gave him a heartfelt nod, bowed down most gratefully, and then turned and humbly walked out of the door, taking care to move sideways, so he would not turn his back on the chief attendant.

The large man stood there shaking his head and staring after Tompo, his expression filled with mixed emotions.

CHAPTER 17

Kathog sat on the floor on a mat of threadbare cloth. Coarse and hard, it was a long way from the soft silk mats he had been accustomed to at home. *I should have brought one along like Mother suggested*, he thought. *But even if I had done so, how could I carry it around the monastery without making a fool of myself?*

He shook his head and shifted his attention away from the mat to the six monks seated in silence. Two of them were his age, but the others were little boys of about eight years old. That both embarrassed him and hurt his pride. He stared at the youngest one intently and thought, *Are these boys as bright as I was when I was their age? Well, we will see.* He nodded in response to his thoughts and then glanced around to survey the room.

The classroom was plain, devoid of any decorative elements on the walls or the ceiling, in stark contrast to the grand shrine room that had left him in awe. Even the throne was basic in its structure and modest in its design.

Yet, despite its simplicity, everything exuded elegance, and the throne in particular emitted the profound sense of knowledge and authority that Lama Zangchak embodied.

Kathog's wandering mind stopped, and he froze, feeling the lama's eyes fixed on him, a palpable gaze that seemed to penetrate his consciousness.

"Everything in here is plain, simple, and basic," said the lama, as if he had indeed read Kathog's mind. "This is in keeping with the simplicity, plainness, and the foundational nature of Buddha's dharma at its core."

"Yes, Lama," replied Kathog, with a nervous bow.

The lama settled into a comfortable position and looked around the room, preparing to commence the class. "We will begin the study of dharma scripture with a popular text called *Jangchub Sempe Chopa la Jukpa* or *Chönjuk,*" he said, his gaze encompassing everyone, as he gently unfurled the silk cloth covering of the text. "It is written by one of the greatest Mahayana Buddhist scholars of its time, Gyalse Zhiwala."

Kathog felt a warmth stir in his gut and spread to other parts of his body, finally reaching his ears. *I have not been this eager and excited before*, he thought, as he straightened his back until he was sitting upright and listening with intense concentration.

The others seemed less interested, less intent on catching every word.

"I will tell you about the practice of vows, implementing the verses of the text that you study in your daily lives, and other related things later," continued the lama. "But before that, allow me to read through the entire text to generate merit for us and to ensure our successful completion of this endeavour."

The monks mumbled agreement in unison, bowing respectfully. The lama then flipped open the text and began reading.

With devotion I pay homage to the buddhas gone to bliss,
To their Dharma body, noble heirs and all worthy of respect
In accordance with scriptures, I shall now in brief describe
The way to adopt the discipline of all the buddhas' heirs.

Lama Zangchak's reading was unlike anything Kathog had heard before. Each syllable was enunciated clearly, pauses flowed naturally without strain, the rhythm was succinct, and the intonation glided smoothly, creating a mesmerising cadence.

Kathog was enthralled, and his respect and admiration for the lama grew immensely. With his face beaming, his eyes sparkling, his posture erect, and his heart fluttering with excitement and awe, he listened to the reading.

This free and favoured human form is difficult to obtain.
Now we have the chance to realise the full human potential,
If we don't make good use of this opportunity,
How could we possibly expect to have such a chance again?

Tompo was clearing the drain filled with soil and overgrown with hard roots behind the monastery. He moved a few steps forward and unexpectedly found himself in front of the windows of the study room. There, he heard the lama reading the text with such enchantment in his voice.

Like a flash of lightning on a dark and cloudy night,
Which, for just a single instant, sheds brilliant light,
Rarely through the Buddha's power,
A mind of virtue arises, briefly, to the people of the world.

Tompo's body shuddered violently. Then he felt immense devotion well up in him from the deep recess of his being. "The lama's sweet voice carries the words of Buddha's dharma!" he exclaimed.

All ordinary virtues therefore are forever feeble,
Whilst negativity is strong and difficult to bear—

But for the mind intent on perfect buddhahood,
What other virtue could ever overcome?

He dropped the spade and clasped his hands together, closing his eyes in prayer. "May all my defilements be purged! May all my bad karma be exhausted! May Ugyen Guru Rinpoche bless me, and may I receive all of Buddha's teachings in this lifetime." With that, he picked up the spade and began to strike hard at the roots with much more vigour and fervour.

Contemplating wisely throughout the ages,
The mighty buddhas have seen its great benefits:
That it helps the boundless multitude of beings
Easily to gain the highest states of bliss.

Continuing to listen to the verses, Tompo became even more devotional, and as he did so, he struck the spade with even greater force, exerting himself and drenching in sweat.

Tompo remained deeply immersed in that heightened state of spirituality and continued to toil in the same manner, even after moving away from the windows where he was no longer able to hear the lama's voice. As a result, he was completely exhausted when he stopped his work and made his way to the kitchen for dinner in the evening.

The chief attendant, who had been occupied the entire day and remained unaware of what Tompo had been up to, was about to break into a tirade, but upon seeing a strange expression on Tompo's face, the big man restrained himself and decided to wait until dinner was over and everybody had left, before he addressed the matter.

"What happened to you, Tompo?" he enquired later, his approach gentle and concerned.

"Nothing, Teacher," replied Tompo, his response brief and subdued.

"Tompo, you should learn to share your problems. It would lighten your heart." He paused and stared at Tompo. "Keeping everything buried inside you will only make them seem worse, and may even make you ill. Now, tell me about it," urged the chief attendant, his tone filled with genuine concern.

"I was cleaning the drain behind the monastery this morning when I heard the lama teaching from the window. I felt immense devotion well up from deep inside my being, sending a strong wave of emotion through my body." Tompo's hands went to his chest, as if he felt it even now.

The chief attendant was taken aback, his eyes widening in surprise.

"Then I made an aspiration prayer that all my defilements be purged," continued Tompo, clasping his hands together into one, "my negative karma be exhausted, and that I be blessed and receive all the teachings of Buddha. And then, thinking I had accumulated too much bad karma, I worked even harder, Teacher," he gestured, explaining how he worked.

The man's countenance softened, his surprise mingling with a sense of deep compassion. "You have an astounding devotion for dharma, Tompo, but you cannot blame everything on your bad karma and be hard on yourself," he said, his tone gently disagreeing. "You don't even know if you have bad karma. Really, who told you that you have so much of negative karma?"

"No one told me, Teacher," Tompo responded, his head tilting slightly, "but must anyone tell me? Every facet of it is evident in my life."

The chief attendant was stumped momentarily, but he swiftly regained his composure. "I know your life has been hard, Tompo," he acknowledged, "but that doesn't automatically imply that you bear an excessive burden of negative karma, more so than everyone else."

"It may be, Teacher," Tompo replied.

"It is, Tompo," asserted the man. "Things in life don't happen like that. Just because your tendrel with Lama Zangchak was not good does not mean that you have bad karma." He stared hard at Tompo to make his point. "You don't know what is in store for you in your destiny. Who knows, you may meet a greater lama, or perhaps even a trulku or a rinpoche."

Tompo gave a slight nod, but remained silent.

The man stepped a bit closer. "You are a good person, Tompo, so I ask you to have faith in your goodness and wait for whatever will come to you. Let your good karma ripen; don't be hard on yourself. Don't punish yourself with this kind of penance."

Tompo nodded again, only this time he said, "Yes, Teacher, I understand."

The man sighed in relief, and his countenance softened into one of gentleness and warmth. "Go and rest now," he said kindly.

"Thank you, Teacher," Tompo nodded with a bow and walked away.

The chief attendant stood there, staring after Tompo, feeling concerned and wondering what could really be in store for this strange and unusual young man in his destiny.

CHAPTER 18

As Lama Zangchak and his spouse, *Ani* Choni, savoured their breakfast in the serene ambience of their living room within the lama's residence, they were greeted by the arrival of the chief attendant, appearing notably upbeat and excited.

"I have come to apprise the lama of the activities planned for the monks today," he said, his face glowing with enthusiasm.

The lama nodded curiously, wondering what could be causing his chief attendant's excitement.

"There is no need for cleaning, Lama," the chief attendant submitted a bit hastily. "The monastery is immaculately neat and clean, both inside and outside. Tompo has been working hard, doing everything from assisting with kitchen work to weeding and cleaning."

"That is good," the lama nodded, still curious about the chief attendant's buoyant demeanour.

"Also, quite strangely, the winds have ceased blowing leaves and dust into the campus," the chief attendant added, with a hint of hesitation in his voice. "And we are not seeing much grass growing either, although it is already summer."

"Maybe it is because the orphan cleans every day that you don't notice the winds blowing leaves and dust into the campus, or see the weeds growing," the lama replied with a casual tone, without giving any serious thought to it.

"Yes, indeed, Lama," the chief attendant replied, his face falling in a slight disappointment.

"So, what do you want the monks to do then?" the lama enquired.

"I am thinking of sending all of them to gather firewood, Lama," the chief attendant responded.

"Very well, but keep Kathog behind and have him make a copy of the *Chönjuk* text." Seeing the surprised look on the chief attendant's face, he explained, "His handwriting is impeccable, even better than mine. He is also amazing with spelling and grammar. I suppose he was right to speak with confidence that day."

"Indeed, Lama."

The lama nodded, concluding their conversation, and the chief attendant bowed respectfully and took his leave.

Contemplating how the other monks would react to Kathog being kept behind, he headed straight to the monks' quarters, and maintaining a straight and innocent face, instructed Kathog to stay back and make a copy of the *Chönjuk* text, while directing the others to go into the forest and gather firewood.

As he had anticipated, he noticed the senior monks' expressions turn sour, clearly displeased about choosing the newcomer, Kathog, over them for the task, but he refrained from saying anything, opting instead to pretend not to notice their dissatisfaction.

As for Kathog, their jealousy only fueled his pride, but not wishing to create any disharmony among the ranks, he didn't show any joy. Instead, maintaining a nonchalant expression, he followed the chief attendant into the monastery, took the writing materials and the lama's original copy of the text, and went into the study room.

There, he began working diligently and meticulously without taking any rest, that by late afternoon, when the lama walked into the room unannounced—entering so quietly that he had not even heard the heavy footsteps—he was in the third quarter of the text.

"I see you have completed much already," the lama observed, his surprise evident on his face. "That was remarkably fast, even by my pace," he added, with his concern growing apparent. "I hope you didn't make any mistakes. This paper is of the finest quality, brought all the way from Naro Tsam."

"No, Lama, I was careful."

The lama picked up the deck of folios and quickly skimmed through some of the pages. As he did so, his expression slowly turned into astonishment. "You have done well, Kathog," he said, looking up with admiration. "I forgot to mention the spelling mistakes in the text, but I see you have noticed them and made the corrections. Your attention to detail is commendable."

"Yes, Lama."

"You are even better than I thought, Kathog," the lama went on, beaming even more. "Now, let me see if you have grasped the essence of the text. Can you tell me the general theme or the gist of it?" he asked, eager to assess Kathog's understanding.

Kathog was taken aback for a moment, but he quickly pulled himself together. "It is a guide to the bodhisattva's way of life, Lama, and it is designed to cultivate bodhicitta or the mind of enlightenment, through the practice of six perfections."

The lama's eyes shimmered with delight. "Yes, that is correct. I could not have summed it up any better myself," he praised Kathog. "Now, how many chapters does this text contain?" he asked eagerly. "Let us see if your memory serves you well, as memory power is one of the most crucial qualities required in a monk in the study of dharma."

"There are ten chapters, Lama," Kathog replied with assurance, and then proceeded to name them confidently, flawlessly reciting each one from the first to the last. His delivery was smooth and precise, as if he were reading directly from the text, without even the slightest glitch or mispronunciation.

"Your memory is amazing; you are truly exceptional," the lama said in one breath. "I have never had a pupil quite like you. Starting from tomorrow, you need not study with the others. I will tutor you one-on-one in the morning and the evening. You also need not do any other work," he declared with a sense of pride and confidence in his new pupil's abilities.

"Thank you, Lama." Kathog felt his heart flutter with excitement, and despite his best efforts to maintain a composed demeanour, the pride and joy inside him surged to the surface, and his face shone with an unusual luminosity.

The lama returned the deck of folios to Kathog and began to walk away, but having a second thought, he turned back. "Stop at sundown and come to my house," he said nonchalantly, but his words carried a sense of purpose. Then without waiting for Kathog to respond, he walked away.

Kathog first felt a blend of subdued surprise and curiosity in response to the unexpected invitation, then an overwhelming sense of eagerness and excitement. This surge of feelings provided him with a newfound reserve of energy, propelling him to work even harder than before and completing the third quarter of the text by sundown.

He stopped his work there as the lama had instructed, replaced everything in the storage room, and went out. The monks were gathering outside the kitchen for dinner. However, mindful of exacerbating the senior monks' feelings of bitterness and resentment towards him, he quietly made his way to the lama's residence.

Kathog had only seen the lama's dwelling from a distance and had never been inside. The one-storey stone-and-mud house was simple and unpretentious, featuring only essential designs.

Yet, the structure exuded some sense of magnificence, infused with a mix of serenity and spirituality.

He paused briefly in the front yard, feeling both fear and nervousness stirring within him. Then he walked up the front steps and gently pushed open the cypress door. Lama Zangchak and Ani Choni were eagerly waiting for him in the living room, putting him at ease.

They greeted him warmly, served butter tea and snacks, and, to his surprise and joy, invited him to dine with them. To his even greater astonishment and delight, it turned out to be no ordinary dinner, but a special meal personally prepared by the ani herself, exclusively for him.

Although he had missed such delicious food for a long time, he cherished the profound significance of the lama having the ani personally prepare a feast for him as much as he appreciated the feast itself. He not only ate heartily, but also conversed openly with the lama and the ani, sharing every detail of his family and home.

In a reciprocal gesture, the lama and the ani also opened up to Kathog, sharing details about their own lives and families, creating a warm and welcoming atmosphere that made him truly happy, as if he were home.

However, later that night, as he departed from the lama's residence, making his way back to his quarters, his thoughts turned to his parents and home. A wave of homesickness washed over him, and he yearned for the warm embrace and familiar comforts of his family.

Engulfed in his emotions, Kathog did not immediately notice the absence of lights in the monks' quarters until he reached the door. Puzzled by the unusual darkness, he glanced around and spotted the kitchen door left ajar. Then he heard the chief attendant rebuking someone inside the kitchen.

He tiptoed to the door and peered into the kitchen. Tompo was standing at the doorway, his back weighed down by a hefty basket of grains, as the chief attendant berated him for not heeding his advice to work in moderation.

How strange it is that Tompo used to be scolded and, at times, even spanked, for not doing enough work back home, thought Kathog, *and how he is now being chided for working too much.* He let out a quiet chortle in the darkness, feeling bemused and bewildered.

Shaking his head, he scanned the room further. The monks crowded along the walls, their faces sullen, their demeanour gloomy, and their impatient eyes angrily fixed on Lalung Zang, who frantically stirred the pot on the hearth, sweat dripping down his brow and his potbelly jiggling inside his gho.

How could dinner be this delayed on the day the monks were sent to gather firewood? Kathog's brow creased, feeling for the monks. *How tired and hungry everyone must be. They had been waiting outside the kitchen at sundown.*

Thinking about their plight, he walked away, feeling relieved to have already eaten. Simultaneously, as he remembered he would no longer have to do any work, he felt immensely gratified. Then his homesickness suddenly disappeared, and he was back to his old self again.

CHAPTER 19

Time flew by swiftly, and before Kathog knew it, a year had passed. In that span, he had made remarkable progress in his studies, surpassing several groups of senior monks, and becoming a celebrated dharma prodigy. His reputation extended not only throughout Tsokar, but also across the entire region of Aeling.

Lama Zangchak, as such, continued to mentor him during the mornings and evenings, entrusting him with the task of copying texts during the daytime. This provided him with an access to a wide array of writings and ignited a profound love for the intricacies of advanced philosophies.

As a result, he became a great admirer and devoted follower of dharma philosophy, delving deep into such texts as *Uma la Jukpa* and *Uma Tsawa Sherab,* until he mastered them and could elucidate with expertise even the most complex of the ideas and concepts.

Therefore, as the philosophies were at an exceedingly advanced level and were extremely challenging, several senior monks started coming to him, seeking clarification on certain subjects or for supplementary explanations, and he gladly obliged them, recognising the need to guide them and to fulfil his own thirst for knowledge and learning.

Gradually, more monks joined, and soon he was teaching almost all the monks in the monastery. He taught anyone who came to him, regardless of the time or place, and he explained any chapter, concept, verse, line by line and word by word, always with great interest and at great length.

When the crowd around him became too large, he explained even a simple verse with passion and gusto. His fervour was such that those brilliant senior monks, who had been jealous of him in the beginning, became his admirers and followers, hanging around him and even performing his bidding at times.

Tompo also listened discreetly to Kathog's teaching with great interest and devotion whenever he found the opportunity, even though he did not understand a word of it. Ignored and left to himself by the monks, he had quietly settled into the daily routine of his work, primarily involving cleaning and assisting the cook, and at times washing the lama's clothes.

However, despite staying fully engaged, Tompo's yearning for dharma teachings persisted fiercely within him, unwavering and unabated. But apart from the chief attendant, who genuinely empathised with him, nobody seemed to notice his profound devotion for dharma. It appeared as though everyone had forgotten that he had come to be ordained a monk and study dharma.

Several years passed swiftly in this manner, yet Tompo did not lose heart. Instead, he worked even harder, wholeheartedly putting his effort into whatever he did. It was then that Ani Choni began to notice him and feel genuine sympathy for his situation.

One day, around that time, Tompo was washing Lama Zangchak's clothes at the bamboo water pipe outside the kitchen when Ani Choni saw him, a young man alone in the tranquillity of the day, diligently washing clothes while everyone else was inside the monastery, engrossed in studying, learning ritual instruments, or attending to other tasks.

Struck by his profound sincerity and devotion, Ani Choni stood there, watching him for some time, before leaving her work and walking over to him.

"Is there anything to be done, Ani?" he asked, eagerly scrambling to offer his assistance.

"Nothing, Tompo," she said, shaking her head. "I came to tell you that you are serving the lama and the monastery more than all the other monks, yet you are not receiving any teachings from the lama. This is unfair and unjust by any standard," she lamented.

"Please, don't think of it that way, Ani." Tompo put aside the shawl that he was washing, turned, and faced her, his expression changing into one of guilt. "It was all my fault. I could not establish a good tendrel with the lama. But even though I am not a monk, I am allowed to eat and live here," he explained, voicing the complex emotions that burdened his heart.

"It is not as you think, Tompo," said Ani Choni, shaking her head with warmth and sincerity. "You work far more than you eat, and to tell you straightforwardly, no one works as diligently as you do. So, it is not you who should feel obliged to us, but we who should feel deeply obliged to you."

"It is all right, Ani," Tompo replied, his voice gentle and appreciative, playing down the hardships that he faced.

"No, it is not all right, Tompo," she countered pointedly, her objection ringing in her tone. "You also came here to be ordained a monk and study dharma, and you have been here for several years now. I will request the lama to give you teachings on your behalf," Ani Choni declared firmly, determination showing in her eyes.

Utterly surprised, Tompo froze for a moment. Then, he came alive, clasping his hands together in immense gratitude. "Thank you very much, Ani," he said, with a feeling of joy surging through him. "Even if I get to hear just one word of dharma from the lama's mouth, it will mean heaven and earth to me," he added with heartfelt appreciation. "I will consider it a great blessing."

Ani Choni's heart melted right then and there. Overcome with compassion for Tompo and unable to contain her emotions any longer, she gripped his shoulders firmly and gazed into his pleading eyes as she spoke. "I have not encountered anyone with such remarkable devotion as you, Tompo, so let me tell you this: even if your tendrel with the lama may not be as you had hoped, and you do not receive essential teachings from him, I pray that you receive the highest dharma teaching capable of liberating you from samsara in this very lifetime."

"Thank you, Ani." His face reflected as much joy as it did wonder.

Ani Choni nodded emotionally, cradled his head in both of her hands, gently placed her forehead against his, and muttered an aspiration prayer. Then, patting his shoulder once, she turned and walked away, leaving him emotionally touched.

CHAPTER 20

Ani Choni anxiously waited for the lama to return from the monastery, thinking how best to approach him about Tompo's issue, since she had never involved herself in the affairs of this sacred institution.

However, the lama was held up with some pressing matters and could not come until after sunset, and then he did not arrive alone but was accompanied by the chief attendant and a worried villager whose spouse had fallen ill after returning from the lakeside.

Her anxiety increased as she waited for them to leave. Fortunately, both the astrological chart reading and the divination that the lama did for the villager yielded positive outcomes, determining that his spouse had been harmed by the lake's deity for cutting down a tree in the area and that she would recover in a day or two. That is, if he performed a deity-propitiation ritual and hoisted a few windhorse prayer flags.

The man was greatly relieved, and even the lama was visibly pleased.

Seeing a moment to act, Ani Choni swiftly seized the opportunity and spoke to the chief attendant, just as he was leading the man out the door. "I have to apprise the lama about something. If you don't have anything important to tend to, I would like you to stay."

Lama Zangchak gave her a surprised look.

Even the chief attendant was taken aback, as Ani Choni had never involved him in anything personal, whether it concerned her or the lama, and whatever she had in mind did not appear to be anything official or related to the affairs of the monastery. Nevertheless, he nodded and sat down, intrigued by what she had to share and wondering about the nature of her concerns.

She took a deep breath. "Lama, that orphan, Tompo, has been working very hard for all these years." Her tone blended formality with a personal touch. "Until now, no one has served the lama and the monastery with a truer heart." She paused briefly to assess the lama's reaction before continuing. "He also has great devotion for dharma," she said, emphasising her point. Then, turning to the chief attendant, she asked, "Isn't this right, Chief Attendant?"

The chief attendant came alive like never before. "Yes, Lama, he is sincere and hardworking, and his devotion for dharma is truly astounding. I have never spoken of anyone like this, but I have not seen anybody so pure in heart. He possesses no vices or negativities of any sort."

The ani beamed with hope and determination. "Lama, it is not my place to say this, but he has also come here to become a monk, to receive your teachings, and to follow the path of dharma like all other monks. It has been several years since he arrived, yet he has not heard a word of dharma from you. So, even if it is not the norm of the monastery, Lama may kindly reconsider his case."

"What should we do?" Lama Zangchak's brow furrowed as he pondered the situation. "The foundation group is far ahead, and the mornings and evenings are reserved for Kathog. There is no empty slot at any time of the day."

"I know Lama is hard-pressed for time," Ani Choni acknowledged, "but Lama must find some ways to teach him, even if it is just a word or two, for it would mean so much to him. He mentioned that even hearing one word of Buddha's dharma from Lama's mouth would be a great blessing."

Lama Zangchak stood, his mind deep in contemplation, and then decisively spoke. "Yes, I will teach him, but there will be no set timing for him. I will teach whenever I am free. If he is a quick learner, he will catch up with the foundation group. Yes, he should be able to catch up, if he studies like he works."

"He will study hard, Lama," said the chief attendant, offering his unsolicited opinion for the first time. "I am sure of that. He is eager to hear the words of dharma with all his heart. He also mentioned something about learning to read and write from Kathog's father."

"That is good. He can go directly into the study of text like Kathog," said the lama in one breath, relief coming over his face. "Give him a copy of *Chönjuk* and tell him to prepare. I am sure by now he knows everything about the teaching system."

"Yes, Lama, he observes everything diligently," the chief attendant affirmed, his voice filled with admiration for Tompo's unwavering commitment to his responsibilities and his spiritual journey.

The lama nodded, as if he were acknowledging Ani Choni and the chief attendant's insights and their advocacy for Tompo, and affirming that the decision to fulfil Tompo's aspiration for dharma teachings had been made.

The chief attendant was about to stand up to take his leave but paused. "Lama and Ani's kindness would undoubtedly benefit him," he said, gratitude written all over his face. "I am confident he will also prove to be deserving of it. Thank you, Lama and Ani." With a bow of deep appreciation, he stood up and left, walking as if buoyed by the air.

"What was that now?" the lama asked the ani, puzzled by the sudden change in the chief attendant's demeanour and his expression of gratitude.

"He never told us or anyone, Lama, but he loves and cares for the orphan like his own brother," explained Ani Choni. "I don't think even Tompo knows it, but I have observed it since his arrival here. I think they have some sort of a karmic connection from their past lives."

The lama, his expression a mix of wry amusement and understanding, nodded in acknowledgement. However, he did not say anything, which in some way added a touch of humour to the moment.

The ani found the situation amusing as well, but uncertain how the lama would react if she sniggered, she held her laughter. Instead, she nodded, stood up, and walked away, breathing a sigh of relief and thinking that she had done right to include the chief attendant in the discussion.

Chapter 21

It was a day off for the monks, and without their early morning buzz, a sense of peace and tranquillity hung in the air.

Some of them were still nestled in their beds, catching up on their sleep or merely resting, but the others had ventured beyond the confines of the campus, some for an outing, some for performing rituals at the invitation of the people from the village, and a few on pilgrimage to the sacred sites nearby.

Amidst this stillness and serenity enveloping the monastery, Tompo had his own plans. Disregarded by everyone, he was embarking on a quiet yet momentous endeavour: preparing for his first day of monastic education.

His hands trembled and his heart raced as he carefully retrieved from beneath his pillow the new set of monk's attire given to him by the chief attendant. These garments were his most valuable possession, which was why he had tucked them where his head did not touch them and damage their newness as he slept.

He held them in his hands and gazed at them, his heart fluttering wildly. He could not believe he was going to be a monk and receive the sacred teachings of Buddha from none other than the great Lama Zangchak. Getting into these garments was what he had prayed for and what he had waited for, for such a long time.

He carefully unfolded each piece and donned it in the customary manner. He first put on the red robe, next slipped into the shirt, and finally draped the shawl over them. Then, he turned and looked around the room, his face beaming, but nobody spared a glance in his direction, not even Kathog, who was occupied opening a text on his bed.

However, it did not matter to Tompo. Carefully picking up his *Chönjuk* text from the ledge above his pillow, he reverently placed it upon the crown of his head, uttered a quick aspiration prayer, then took it back in his hand and stepped outside.

With no one in sight, the campus lay hushed and deserted. In the silence, he could hear the resounding thump of his heart, its volume surpassing the echo of his footsteps as he walked across the courtyard and entered the monastery.

Inside, too, an unusual stillness prevailed, with an empty and tranquil ambience, save for the potent aroma of burning incense that struck his senses.

He strolled across the hallway, paused briefly at the door of the small waiting chamber adjacent to the shrine room, and peeked inside. Even though several years had passed since his arrival, the room evoked memories of that fateful morning when he had been denied access to the lama's audience, piercing his heart with sorrow and pain.

Shrugging off his emotions, Tompo walked on, heading straight to the study room, and settled down in one corner, as he was early. But he was not only early—he was exceptionally early—and it was not until after what seemed a long time that he heard those familiar heavy footsteps approaching through the empty hallway.

His heart racing and his back sweating, Tompo stood and walked to the centre of the room, positioning himself in front of the throne with a deferential posture.

The footsteps drew closer, and soon Lama Zangchak entered the room, looking stern. He walked past Tompo, going straight to the throne, ascended it and took his seat.

Tompo quickly sat down.

The lama stared hard, locking into Tompo's eyes, and spoke, "Even though a good tendrel is a necessary condition for me to take in any pupil, I have agreed to teach you because both the ani and the chief attendant strongly support your case. But you must be very careful not to let anything unmeritorious happen here," he cautioned. "This is a monastery of good tendrel and good fortune. Did you understand?"

"Yes, Lama," replied Tompo, his voice coming out squeaky through a knot in his throat.

Returning a slight nod, barely discernible, the lama proceeded to explain everything that Tompo needed to know in pursuing the path of dharma. Then, he quickly commenced the text, running swiftly through the first few verses, as they principally focused on paying homage to the buddhas and included other introductory matters that were relatively easy to understand.

However, Tompo did not grasp anything concretely, not even a word, for every word was laden with several different meanings. Fortunately, the lama wound up the class shortly afterwards without asking Tompo any questions and left in a hurry to depart for the village to grace a wedding. Even so, having been direly warned in no uncertain terms, Tompo could not help but gravely worry about not understanding what he had been taught and causing something terribly bad to happen.

Anxious and frantic, he went to the quarters and asked Kathog for his help, and Kathog readily assisted, explaining all the verses that had been taught that morning, but it was all the same. Tompo could not comprehend even a word properly, and what little he did understand was tenuous and proved nearly impossible to retain from verse to verse.

Consequently, recalling a monk ardently praying to Jetsun Jampalyang, he fervently prayed to the Buddha of knowledge and wisdom to dispel his ignorance, so that his intelligence could rise to this challenge. Still, no comprehension or awareness came to him, no matter how hard he studied.

Then, becoming gravely worried and upset, he wondered why the text had to be written in compact verse only, rather than in lengthy prose, which he thought could have been easier to understand—and as he stood, gripped with dismay and grumbling, something inside him turned, making him nauseous, much like his first day at the Dungje mansion.

CHAPTER 22

In a short time, Tompo's joy transformed into anxiety and fear, and he didn't know what to do. He desperately wanted to study but was terrified that his inability to understand would cause something unmeritorious to happen, as the lama had warned.

In his earlier excitement, he had pushed aside thoughts of his learning challenges, but now they haunted him with a sense of trepidation, even causing him to question his own sensibility and judgement in deciding to embark on the path of dharma.

When everyone in Tamchu had dissuaded him from pursuing the path and pointed out his lack of intelligence, it had not seemed so important because he thought the effort would be worthwhile, even if he learnt just one word of dharma in his entire life.

However, in his enthusiasm and ignorance, he had only thought about himself and had not accounted for the sacred traditions and conventions of dharma study that he would have to follow, or the undesirable consequences he would bring to the monastery and the lama with his ill-considered actions and bad karma.

A few days later, and still in the throes of this dilemma, Tompo was called for the second class. And, as he had dreaded, the lama caught him struggling to make sense of what was being taught.

But as it happened, the lama mistakenly interpreted Tompo's strained facial expression as a sign of fatigue. "How will you study if you are already so weary this early in the morning?" the lama scolded.

Not realising that his concentration was making him appear drowsy, Tompo put intense effort into listening, straining his nerves that much more, and making him look even more tired.

This began to annoy the lama. "Listen here," he said, raising his voice. "Bodhicitta is a mind of virtue, a mind intent on perfect buddhahood. This verse says that those who wish to be liberated and also wish to help liberate all sentient beings must embrace bodhicitta, not turn their back on it. Did you understand?"

"Yes, Lama," Tompo replied softly, avoiding direct eye contact. But when the lama looked him hard in the eye, he faltered and shied away, sinking his head into his shoulders.

"Did you really understand?" pressed the lama, even angrier now.

"Yes, Lama," Tompo replied in a hushed tone.

"Then tell me, why would anyone aspire to liberate not just oneself but help liberate all sentient beings, when liberating oneself alone seems nearly impossible? Such a pursuit appears reckless, if not foolhardy and impractical, by all measures," the lama said, his voice sounding more like an interrogation, tinged with anger, and his face clouded with doubt about Tompo's understanding.

Tompo was at a loss.

"I asked you a question, Tompo!" The lama's impatience heightened, his face reflecting his frustration.

"I don't know, Lama," Tompo blurted out, his voice trembling.

"What do you mean, you don't know?" the lama thundered, his face red with anger, his eyes blazing. "I told you in our first class that we take a bodhisattva vow to attain buddhahood to liberate all sentient beings from samsara. How can you forget such a basic and simple thing that was taught only a few days ago?"

Tompo sat terrified.

At that moment, the chief attendant came hurrying in. Upon seeing the lama fuming, he froze momentarily, and then bowing at the lama, stepped aside and stood fidgeting at the door.

"What is it, Chief Attendant?" the lama called out.

"The village headman is here to see you, Lama," the chief attendant responded, his voice soft with awkwardness, unsure how to address the situation with the lama's apparent anger making the air around them heavy.

As if recollecting something, the lama scrambled off the throne, but with his frustration getting the better of him, he stopped and glared fiercely at Tompo. "You fool," he uttered sternly. "You had better go back to your quarters and revise everything from first to last. I will ask you again in the next class."

Tompo was too stunned to react.

The lama then turned to the chief attendant. "I forgot about this meeting," he admitted, his expression softening as he shook his head, and then he waddled across the room and out the door.

The chief attendant threw a quick glance at Tompo, concern in his eyes; then he turned and hurried after the lama.

Tompo listened to their receding footsteps with a heavy heart, until they could no longer be heard, and then released a loud sigh, stood up, and left the room.

The hallway was now empty, his footsteps echoing eerily in the silence, adding to his feeling of wretchedness and misery. However, he quickly reminded himself, *No, I must not give in at the first sight of difficulty.*

He steeled himself, determined to face the challenge ahead, and headed to the quarters and diligently studied, recalling everything the lama had taught. But it was the same: he could grasp none of it, deflating his resolve and reigniting his worries.

CHAPTER 23

Tompo went to the next class with his heart in his mouth, his palms sweaty, and a restless energy in his every movement.

However, to his relief, Lama Zangchak was in a jovial mood. He taught in a relaxed manner, explaining everything in detail. The few questions he asked were rhetorical only, intended to make his point, making Tompo feel more at ease.

This atmosphere continued in the next class and the ones after that, bringing immense relief and joy to Tompo, and so he enjoyed every word of the teachings, even though he did not grasp much of it.

But, as always, relief and joy did not last long for Tompo as, one day, shortly thereafter, the lama arrived sullen and angry, much like a summer storm that followed a brief period of tranquillity.

"I have been teaching continually for days, shouting until my throat ran dry," the lama said, with a sombre tone. "But I hope you have been following it. Do not create a bad tendrel for me and my monastery."

With this, he began revising the portion they had covered in the last class, reading quickly through the first verse without pausing for punctuation.

Understand that briefly stated
Bodhicitta has two aspects
The mind aspiring to awaken
And bodhicitta that's enacted

The words were barely intelligible, and Tompo could not catch a single one. He was not even sure from where the lama was reading. Fear gripped him at once, turning his face pale and ashen.

"This one is quite easy," said the lama, looking up from the text and explaining the verse. "There are two kinds of bodhicitta: one that is aspiring to awaken but not yet awakened, and the other that is already awakened. Understand?"

Tompo held his breath, unsure how to respond.

"Now, let us go on to the next verse," the lama went on, but as he looked away from Tompo to glance down at the text, he could not help but notice a shadow of darkness cast upon his pupil's face. There was no doubt that the orphan was confused and worried, yet he decided to continue, and began reading the following verse.

Just as one understands the difference
Between wishing to go and setting out upon actual journey
The wise should understand these two
Recognising their difference and their order

Tompo sat still, listening intently, but he still could not catch a word of it. To make matters worse, his stomach roiled loudly, nauseating him.

The lama looked up from the text. "Just as one understands the difference between wishing to go on a journey and setting out upon an actual journey, the wise should understand the distinction between these two types of bodhicitta and their order. Do you understand?"

Tompo sat dumbly.

Lama Zangchak was about to move on to the next verse, but he sensed that continuing would be purposeless, as Tompo seemed to have not understood. A subtle twitch of frustration touched the corners of his lips, and he shook his head, feeling a growing sense of anger.

"The difference between the mind aspiring to awaken and the mind that is already awakened is that of the sky and the earth." His voice rose in pitch. "It is like the difference between wishing to go on a journey and setting out upon an actual journey. Do you see? We are talking about the two aspects of bodhicitta."

Tompo's face turned grim, and he began to sweat.

The lama leaned forward and his face suddenly contorted. "Did you understand or not?" he thundered, as if the anger of the universe was escaping from his mouth.

"I didn't understand a bit, Lama," Tompo blurted out, a cry in his voice.

"You didn't understand a bit?" repeated the lama, his eyebrows raised, amplifying the mockery in his tone.

"Yes, Lama," muttered Tompo, feeling the weight of fear settle upon him.

"A bit of which part?" the lama pressed, his mocking tone intensifying, as if taunting Tompo for his lack of comprehension.

Tompo's voice quivered as he spoke. "A bit of every part, Lama."

"A bit of every part?" Lama Zangchak repeated again, but this time, his patience giving way: his face flushed, and his earlier mocking tone was replaced with unbridled anger. "What do you mean? Every part of every word, or every part of every line?"

Tompo went pale with fear.

The lama sat up straight, putting effort into calming himself. "Do you even know what you are saying, orphan? You say you don't understand a bit, but you don't even know which bit. How can that be? Unless, of course, you are saying this to try my patience."

Tompo sat stupidly, his mind blank.

"Is that it, orphan?" demanded the lama. "Are you trying my patience?" Once again, Lama Zangchak assumed an aggressive posture, and once again it seemed that a terrible rage was rising from its slumber inside him. "Of course, you are trying my patience," he said between clenched teeth. "You want to test me, is that it?"

"No, Lama."

"No . . . what?"

"No, Lama, I'm not trying to test the lama's patience."

"Then tell me exactly, what did you not understand?"

"Everything, Lama," Tompo blurted out, out of fear. "I did not understand everything."

Lama Zangchak flew into a sudden rage, slamming his hand on the dais. "What did you say, moron? First, you say you did not understand a bit, and now you say did not understand everything." His eyeballs popping out and his fists clenched, he seethed. "You wanted to study dharma from me, but you could not even bring a gift offering! You cause a bad tendrel, and now you do not know a small thing!"

Tompo was stunned.

"Get out of here!" The lama waved his finger furiously across the room and towards the door. "Get out!"

Tompo jumped on his feet and bolted out of the room, running through the corridor and out of the building.

Except for Ani Choni, occupied with something away from her residence at the far side of the campus, the place was quiet and deserted, so Tompo ran across the courtyard, sobbing uncontrollably, without having to worry about anyone seeing him, and disappeared behind the monks' quarters.

Witnessing his flight from the monastery in such a distressed state, Ani Choni hurried after him and found him inconsolable, leaning against the building.

"What happened, Tompo?" she asked, her voice filled with concern.

"The lama is angry with me, Ani," he replied, choking on his emotions. "It is all my fault. I don't have intelligence like the others, and I don't understand anything. Today, I didn't know even the simplest thing, and the lama was mad at me."

Ani Choni's heart went out to Tompo, and she placed a reassuring hand on his shoulder. "It is all right, Tompo, don't cry. Dharma is difficult for everyone, not just you. Everyone gets a scolding from Lama, not just you. You should not take it into your heart and let it hurt you like this."

"No, Ani, it is not like that," he replied quickly, his voice stronger. "It is that I don't understand even the basics. It is my bad karma; nothing can be done about it. The lama is right to become angry."

"Our lama is short-tempered," she told him. "You should know that about him by now. Still, don't worry about it. I will talk to him and appease him on your behalf."

Tompo nodded gratefully, but continued to cry.

Ani Choni, feeling sympathetic, stared at him for a while. When he stopped sobbing, she patted him on the shoulder and hurried back to the residence.

Lama Zangchak was already back home, sitting in the living room, his face still livid with anger. "That foolish orphan, testing my temper," he said as soon as he saw her. "I would have thrashed him for sure if he had not run away."

"Lama, please don't be angry with the orphan," the ani pleaded, quickly removing a wine canister and a wooden cup from the nearby cabinet. "Not everyone is the same, and not everyone has equal capabilities."

Lama Zangchak stared directly into her eyes, his gaze intense. "You don't know what happened today—unthinkable and unimaginable."

Not wanting to provoke him, she shied away from his stare, placing the cup on the choedom and focusing on pouring ara into it.

But the lama would not let it go. "Forget knowing what was taught to him; he doesn't even know what he doesn't know."

"Lama, he may not be blessed with intelligence like others," said Ani Choni, her voice gentle but firm. "People like him need Lama's affection and compassion, even more than the others." She mustered her courage to look up at the lama, hoping to convey the importance of understanding and patience for such unfortunate people.

Lama Zangchak did not see her look. Instead, continuing his thoughts along the same line, he shook his head disapprovingly, but as he did so, he picked up the cup and took a sip—once, twice, thrice—and then his face lit up. "This is a good wine!"

"I distilled it myself a few days ago specifically for Lama," she replied, her voice warm and caring. "I was thinking how Lama was getting exhausted from additional teaching for the orphan these days."

His eyes sparkling, Lama Zangchak drank another sip and held the cup in front of her. Ani Choni, relieved to see him diverted from his anger, cheerily refilled it to the brim.

Lama Zangchak downed the cup at once and then asked for yet another serving. Ani Choni poured more, and then another, and another, until he was thoroughly satisfied and happy.

CHAPTER 24

With his lanky frame drooping and his face so pale it appeared almost grey, Tompo sat on his bed and wondered where his life was going. He had eaten neither lunch nor dinner, and his stomach rumbled. Yet, he was not hungry, as the events of the day weighed heavily on him.

The monks moved about, tending to their own chores, oblivious to his suffering. But when they heard someone greet the chief attendant outside, they scrambled back to their beds and sat properly, a hushed silence descending upon the room.

A moment later, the chief attendant walked in and everyone, including Tompo, stood and assumed the reverential posture. The room filled with an air of respect and solemnity as they acknowledged the presence of their superior.

However, the heavyset monk, waving them to sit, turned straight to Tompo. "You need not worry about what happened today, Tompo," he said, patting the young man on his shoulder while taking a seat. "Ani Choni talked to the lama and appeased him."

"You should not trouble yourself, Teacher." Tompo's voice was low and quivering from emotion.

"No, Tompo, you must not become disheartened like that," the chief attendant persisted. "Our lama is short-tempered, but he is also forgiving. It may take a week or two, but he will call you back to the class."

Tompo's face became brighter and then clouded again just as quickly. "But what good will it be, Teacher? I will not understand anything again, and the lama will only become angrier. I don't have any intelligence."

The chief attendant's brow furrowed and his shoulders rose slightly. He opened his mouth to say something, but the words died down before they were formed.

"It is all right, Teacher," Tompo said, his voice filled with a sense of resignation. "You don't have to feel bad about it. It is my bad karma. I must have done something terribly wrong in my past lives that I not only had a lower human birth, but I would also not be able to practise dharma."

The chief attendant pursed his lips and shifted his body. "I understand how you feel, Tompo. Your situation is one of a rare kind, not heard about before. All you have known in your life are sorrow and pain. Yet I will tell you again, so you will be reassured: karma doesn't work like that."

Tompo remained silent.

"Yes, you are subjected to your karma, like everyone else is," the chief attendant continued. "There is no running away from it. But you are not doomed forever. Your karma will turn around at some point, so you must not give up."

A flicker of light flashed in Tompo's eyes, and his face grew a shade brighter, as he saw some sense in what the chief attendant said. He nodded slowly and a little smile twitched his mouth, but he did not speak, as he still could not see any way forward for himself.

With nothing more to say, the chief attendant nodded back in acknowledgement, and stared at Tompo for a while, twitching his lips. Then he sighed, patted Tompo on the shoulder, stood up, and left.

CHAPTER 25

Lama Zangchak glowed, exuding a cheerful demeanour, as he taught Kathog that afternoon. He openly expressed his feelings of admiration for his favourite pupil, heaping commendation and praise and holding nothing back.

However, Kathog maintained a subdued and solemn countenance, holding back any outward display of emotion, fearful that it might somehow disrupt this sacred moment, or worse, upset the lama.

The lama ended the class a little earlier than usual and began packing the text. "Your progress is truly astounding, Kathog," he said, his fingers deftly arranging the folios into a perfectly ordered bundle. "I have never had a disciple like you. At this rate, you will complete your studies soon."

"It is all because of your blessing, Lama," replied Kathog, watching the lama and being somewhat mesmerised. He knew that the lama was a master of art, craft, and skill, performing all tasks big and small with perfection and dexterity. And even though he was becoming equally good, he still held the lama in great awe.

The lama nodded. "And also, because you are brilliant and hardworking." He now wrapped the text in a silk cloth without a single crease.

Kathog struggled to rein in the pride and joy that felt as if they were bursting out of him. Amidst this overwhelming feeling, a wild thought struck him, causing his face to shine and his eyes to sparkle. *Is the lama intentionally opening up to me?* His mind wobbled, leaving him dizzy for a moment. Then a sensation surged up from deep inside him, as if a fire burned.

"But it is not only your intelligence and hard work," went on the lama, gently placing the text in the centre of the dais. "You also have a remarkably strong karmic connection to dharma. This makes me certain that it was your destiny that brought you here to me, all the way from the foothills."

Kathog held his breath in suspense, anxious to know what the lama was about to say.

"This is very important in dharma," the lama explained, speaking effortlessly, as if the words flowed out on their own. "To make such extraordinary progress, the teacher and the pupil must converge in an auspicious and sacred union." His eyes gleamed with conviction. "It must be nothing short of destiny."

Kathog sat there, quite dazed. What the lama had just said was beyond his wildest expectations, hopes, and dreams. Nothing could have ever prepared him for such a declaration. Amidst the rush of emotions, he could not help but recall his parents and wished they were present to hear such profound words.

"I can't interpret these prophetic signs any other way but as a sacred omen," the lama continued. "An omen heralding greater good things to come; greater progress and further continuance of the lineage of my great lama, Lama Thongsar."

Kathog's heart was again filled with immense joy and happiness, but this time he did not rein in his emotions, but let them flow unchecked, causing his face to radiate an unusual brightness.

"So, it is only fitting that you become my treasured heart-son and carry this great lineage into the future, unveiling its boundless potential for generations to come. I have no doubt that this lineage will grow from strength to strength, and will ascend to an unprecedented height during your time."

"Thank you, Lama. I am truly blessed and honoured to be your devoted pupil."

"As I am to be your lama," the lama nodded, acknowledging the reciprocal nature of their connection.

At that moment, the lama noticed a figure looming at the door. His gaze travelled across the room and lay upon Tompo. "Come in, Tompo," he called out, his voice warm and his expression genial.

Kathog promptly rose from his seat, offering a respectful bow to the lama, and hastened out, as Tompo entered the room.

Tompo was trembling with nervousness and fear. It was almost one month since that unfortunate incident, and the lama had not called him until now. However, seeing the lama in what appeared to be a genial mood relieved some of his fear.

"Your karmic connection to dharma is not strong, Tompo," the lama said right away, but his voice was warm. "Moreover, you have too much negative karma. In this state, it will be challenging for you to grasp the teachings fully. To remedy this, you will chant the guru mantra every morning and evening, starting today."

"Yes, Lama." Tompo bowed as he settled down on his seat.

Lama Zangchak adjusted his body into a comfortable position. "We will revise the text from the very beginning, but before we begin, I will provide you with a general overview, the gist of everything, to help your understanding of the text."

"Thank you, Lama."

"Listen carefully now, Tompo," Lama Zangchak emphasised, his tone carrying a sense of urgency. "The human life form is the most precious gift in the universe, as it grants us the rare opportunity to tread the path of dharma and liberate ourselves from the endless cycle of birth and death. However, obtaining this human life is exceedingly difficult. So, if we misuse this precious existence, acquired through immense effort, we may not get another chance for a very long time."

Tompo tipped his head in response, his gaze falling over the window's periphery in the process and noticing Ani Choni peering in discreetly. Taken by surprise, he paused and stared back, unsure how to react.

Ani Choni swiftly gestured for him to avert his gaze away from the window. "Don't look this way, you fool," she whispered, her expression creasing in unease.

Tompo quickly turned and looked away.

"Like a flash of lightning that lights up the dark cloudy night brightly for a moment," the lama went on, "bodhicitta—or the mind of virtue—arises in us very briefly once in a long time, through the blessings of the buddhas."

Witnessing the lama's pleasant mood, Ani Choni's face relaxed and she breathed a sigh of relief. She felt as though a weight had been lifted off her chest, relieving her of the worry that Lama Zangchak would not teach Tompo, or that, even if he did, he would be harsh on the orphan.

Satisfied, she turned around and walked away. *Bodhicitta must be much like your good mood, arising only briefly once in a while*, she said to herself and broke into a mischievous grin as she sauntered towards her residence.

CHAPTER 26

Lama Zangchak remained in that state of bliss for several months, providing relief and respite from his fierce temper to everyone in the monastery.

Tompo was also able to relax, but there was little teaching for him, and that put him in a predicament. Should he feel happy or sad about it? Happy, because he would not be made to suffer the lama's haranguing; sad, because he was not being taught.

However, when Lama Zangchak proclaimed Kathog his heart-son, throwing the entire monastery into a celebratory mood, Tompo became elated, rejoicing for Kathog.

Thus, as soon as the day for the investiture ceremony was announced, Tompo began cleaning the monastery, diligently preparing for the celebration. He worked tirelessly from dawn to midnight, sleeping only a few hours before resuming his work, until he had singlehandedly cleaned not only the monastery campus, but also the areas around the monastery.

When the chief attendant and Ani Choni, who had been away on some work related to the ceremony, came back to the campus, they saw what Tompo had done and appeared both shocked and alarmed. Then, becoming worried about his well-being, they went looking for him and found him clearing the hillock below the monastery.

"What are you doing, Tompo?" Ani Choni asked, exasperated.

"Who told you to do all this?" the chief attendant asked. "Are you out of your mind?"

"Don't be worried about me, Ani and Teacher," Tompo reassured them, his face radiating joy and happiness. "I am all right and truly very happy. Our Kathog will become the heart-son of our great lama. I guess this is the tendrel you told me about." Tompo put his hands together and stared at the chief attendant in gratitude.

Caught off guard by Tompo's comment, the chief attendant gaped at the orphan.

But Ani Choni quickly gathered herself. "Yes, Tompo, it is the good tendrel that makes good things like these happen, but you must not get carried away. Look, your hands are blistered, and your body strength has weakened."

"It doesn't matter, Ani. I will gain merit." Tompo looked up at the monastery, perched on the hill above. "Do you see? People will look down from this side of the campus and see this pristine little hump by the stream and become happy. I have cleared all the areas around the monastery so that only beautiful scenery will be seen from the monastery during the investiture ceremony."

"Whatever it is, Tompo, if you don't listen to me, at least listen to Ani and take a rest now," begged the chief attendant. "She is worried about you. But understand that we are not telling you not to work. We are only telling you to sleep and eat, for you will need rest and energy to continue your tasks."

Tompo smiled at them. "Ani, nothing will happen to me. I not only have the blessings of our lama, but also that of the good tendrel. You see, it will be the most memorable day of our lives, and everything will be perfect and beautiful, just as we wish and dream."

"I see you cannot be dissuaded, Tompo," said the ani with finality in her voice. "But I think there is also sense in what you say, too. So, yes, carry on, and if you need anything, do let me know. I will also apprise the lama about what you have done."

"Thank you, Ani," said Tompo, putting his hands together. "Even though I possess so much bad karma, I am fortunate to have crossed paths with both Ani and Chief Attendant. So, I sincerely pray that you both continue to grow in every aspect and be able to help more unfortunate people like me in the future."

Ani Choni and the chief attendant stared at Tompo in disbelief for a while, then nodded, turned around and walked away, leaving Tompo staring after them with folded hands.

Chapter 27

Ani Choni sat in her living room, deep in her thoughts, with her butter tea untouched in front of her. She puckered her lips and shook her head.

What has brought this orphan into my life, giving me so much anxiety and fear? What karmic connection could he have with me? Ever since I returned from Jalisili, I have been putting all of my focus and energy into monitoring him, and that is fine with me, as long as he didn't—

The door was flung open, shattering her thoughts, and the chief attendant tripped on the threshold and fell headfirst into the room. He rose instantly and said in between heaves and gasps, "Ani, you should come and see this . . . quickly. There is something strange going on with Tompo."

"What is he up to now?" she demanded in both concern and frustration. "This orphan can't stay idle for a moment. Where is he?" She got up and hurried out, the chief attendant close behind.

"He is up on a hillock above the gate, Ani, but it is nothing to be worried about. It is just that . . . it is a bit weird and abnormal. Birds and butterflies are swarming around him, and he is playing with them."

She stopped so abruptly that he nearly ran into her. "Birds and butterflies?"

"Yes, Ani." With that, he continued to walk.

"Where could they have come from?"

"I don't know, Ani."

"I see what you are saying: he is strange by nature."

The chief attendant and Ani Choni, walking abreast of each other, went around the residence and through the gate. "He is on a hillock beyond that hump," he said, pointing ahead. He ushered her up the trail, and they hiked up the slope of the hump that rose above the gate. "There he is, do you see him? Look, there are birds and butterflies!"

Tompo was atop a grassy hill, singing and playing merrily with colourful butterflies and birds that swarmed around him, their colours and shapes outlined against the sky.

"Where did all these butterflies come from?" she asked, eyes wide, mesmerised. "It is nearly mid-autumn, but butterflies come only in late spring and summer. And those," she added, pointing to a flock of birds overhead. "I have not seen such birds before. They are incredibly colourful and beautiful."

"Yes, Ani, they are," he agreed. "It is as if they are wearing the colours of autumn on their feathers, but I find all this surreal, like in a dream. Even the sky is unusually bright and blue today."

She looked around and saw the nearby forest had turned soft green, with strong shades of yellow, orange, red, purple, and brown. "Nature is out of the ordinary today. It is like summer and autumn are here together."

The chief attendant nodded, his eyes eagerly looking around. "I think Tompo has some sort of a sway over Nature. Ever since he came here and cleaned, the winds have stopped blowing leaves and dust into the campus, and the weeds have stopped growing. And now, recently, after he began to clean for the investiture, leaves have stopped falling altogether."

"That may not be, Chief Attendant. Only the bodhisattvas in the advanced stages will have that kind of power. I think this has something to do with the gods and the deities of the area being pleased. Anyway, let us go and apprise the lama about it."

As they walked back, the ani said, "The monastery looks beautiful with the flagpoles around it. I cannot imagine Tompo alone did all this: bringing the poles from the forest, digging holes and then implanting the poles. There could be over one hundred there."

The chief attendant slowed his pace a bit. "Ani, there are more than two hundred poles there. But if you ask Tompo, he will tell you that this is nothing, because now he wants to put up flagpoles running from the monastery gate to the village centre, and he is quite stubborn about it."

The ani stopped abruptly and turned to face him. "What? He wants to hoist flags all the way to the village centre. This is madness, even by his standards. I have never heard of anything like this . . . anywhere."

"I thought so, too, but he would not listen."

"We must stop him," she declared, turning and striding forward.

"Yes, Ani," he said, his voice low.

When Ani Choni and the chief attendant walked in through the gate, Lama Zangchak was coming out of the monastery and heading towards the residence. They hurried towards him and met him halfway, in the courtyard.

"Lama, something strange is happening with the orphan Tompo up there." Ani Choni turned and pointed beyond the hump. "He is up on the hillock playing with birds and butterflies that I have never seen. They are swarming gaily around him, as if something in him is attracting them. Also, everything in Nature seems to be out of the ordinary today."

"Yes, it is," nodded Lama Zangchak with a rather blissful expression. "The forest, the sky, and everything in Nature has been like this for some time now—beautiful, serene, and pristine. I didn't tell you because I knew you would notice it, too."

"What could it be, Lama?" she enquired, eager and curious.

"What else could it be, Ani? It is the protectors of dharma and the gods and the deities of the territory expressing their joy and happiness for the spiritual union of the lama and the disciple of the lineage of great Lama Thongsar. They are celebrating the proclamation of a dharma prodigy as my heart-son and its lineage holder. This is a momentous time, so even Nature is rejoicing."

"I thought it could be something like this," she said, turning to the chief attendant as if to say, "I told you so," but the man was already turning to Lama Zangchak to state his thought.

"But Lama, what about those birds and butterflies flocking around the orphan? Why would they go to him only, and in such a playful spirit, as if they had known him from before? And he is playing with them, as if he were one of them."

The lama nodded and gave his chief attendant a little smile. "He is one of them, literally in spirit, because he is rejoicing like them. So, they are seeing a kindred spirit in him and flocking around him, and he is responding to them in turn."

The chief attendant looked towards the hillock. "Yes, Lama."

The lama followed the other man's gaze. "We are all part of Nature, Chief Attendant, and at times we can connect with other elements of Nature at a spiritual level, like how we human beings connect with each other. This is said in the dharma."

The chief attendant appeared to be fully convinced. "The orphan wants to put up flagpoles from here to the village centre, Lama, but we thought it was madness even to think of doing this."

"No, no, you should not stop him," said Lama Zangchak, waving his hand. "This is our good tendrel manifesting. So, if he wants to do it, let him do it. Give him the flags. If there are not enough, then make more, or get them from the village. The orphan will gain merit from this."

"Yes, Lama."

The lama nodded and walked away, but the chief attendant and Ani Choni, worried about Tompo's health, stood there, staring at each other, but unable to say anything.

Chapter 28

Although the winter was already setting in, the morning was warm and pleasant, encouraging people of all ages, from all walks of life, and from near and far to dress in their finest costumes and arrive early at the monastery, to ensure that they had a good view of the investiture ceremony.

Since the campus had been prepared for the ceremony grandly, with the gate and the monastery building festooned with silk brocades, and the ceremonial flagpoles erected from the monastery to the village centre, everyone was excited.

Tompo, immensely happy to see the results of his labours, worked in the monastery kitchen, in the lama's residence, and at the courtyard. He was everywhere, doing everything: cooking as well as serving and cleaning.

As such, he missed the investiture proceeding taking place in the shrine room, but he did not mind at all. In fact, it suited him perfectly. The last thing he wanted was to go into the shrine room and have his negative karma defile the sanctity of the sacred investiture ceremony. Yet, hearing everyone talking of Kathog looking so resplendent in his new set of ceremonial costumes, he wanted to have a glimpse of the precious heart-son.

Leaving his work, he went behind the monastery building and peeked through the window into the shrine room. Kathog sat on a beautiful throne in all his magnificence, alongside the majestic Lama Zangchak. This spectacle filled Tompo's heart with great joy and truly buoyed him.

At that instant, the sky became bluer and the sun brighter, and then myriad rainbows filled the sky. Before long, the birds and the butterflies arrived, hovering low in the sky and playing with the colours of the rainbows.

Hearing the sounds of the birds and witnessing a spectacular display of magic, the people poured out of the building and gazed upwards in amazement and fascination.

However, Tompo had no time to stand there and watch, needing to get back to his work, where he remained occupied until the late afternoon, when the ani came into the kitchen.

"Tompo, I was looking for you," she said, as soon as she saw him, her hands waving in the air, her face incredulous. "But you didn't come in, not even once."

"I was busy with work, Ani," replied Tompo, his face showing a hint of awkwardness.

"But you must come and offer a scarf." Her tone became insistent.

"No, Ani, it is fine," he replied softly, becoming more awkward.

"What do you mean it is fine?" she challenged. As she stared at him with her brow creased, a sudden realisation struck her. "Is it that you don't have a scarf? You should have told me, you fool. Come, come, I will give you one. I have several extras."

"No, Ani, I—" His voice trailed off, and he hesitated to continue.

"What now?" she demanded, her curiosity piqued.

"I don't want to offer a scarf," he finally confessed.

"Why not?" she asked, her eyebrows raised.

"I'm—I'm not suited to offer a scarf to him, Ani," he muttered.

"What do you mean not *suited*?" Her eyebrows went even higher.

"Ani, I'm an unfortunate person with so much negative karma, and he is a spiritual prodigy, destined for great things.

I'm not worthy enough to offer him a scarf, and I don't want to go in there and defile the sanctity of the investiture."

"What nonsense, Tompo!" she burst out. "Who said such a thing to you, you fool? Come, come! Come and offer a scarf. Everyone is done, and no one is inside now."

"No, Ani, please don't insist," pleaded Tompo. "I'm a low-born person, and I'm not worthy of such privilege. If I go in there and offer a scarf to Kathog, I will accumulate bad karma."

Ani Choni was stumped, uncertain about what to do or say next, and she did not want to impose on him. "All right then, Tompo, if you feel that so strongly, it is perfectly fine. I will not force you."

Relief flooded his face. "Thank you, Ani. Please don't tell Kathog and the lama about this. With so many people going in, they would not have noticed my absence." He hesitated a bit. "I don't want them to hear about it and then have to think about it. This is a time to celebrate, not to muse about unbecoming things."

"I won't mention it to them, Tompo. But you are wrong to think that way. You are as good as anybody who was there. In fact, you are better than most of us." Seeing that Tompo was about to argue, she quickly added, "I know you will not agree with me, but I have no time to argue with you. At least, not now."

Tompo moved a bit, his mouth partially opening as if to say something, then stopped and stared blankly.

Ani Choni shook her head, sighed loudly, and then turned on her heel and walked out.

Chapter 29

The grand and lavish celebration of the investiture ceremony left the monastery euphoric for months. During this period, Lama Zangchak spent much of his time teaching Kathog, guiding and grooming him in the ways of a lineage-holder lama.

To give his young protégé as many opportunities as possible to learn and grow through real experiences, the lama accepted every invitation that came his way, whether it was to conduct religious rituals or to grace celebrations. But as it was winter, the invitations were primarily to conduct *lochoey,* the annual religious ritual intended to appease a family's deity.

However, as winter came to an end after a festive week of New Year, the people of the village consulted the astrologer for the year's horoscope for their families, and accordingly prepared their *rimdro,* the rituals to avert misfortune and usher in peace and prosperity.

And when the weather warmed and the year was well under way, the headman—in accordance with village tradition that required his family, as the nobility of the village, to conduct his ritual before other families in the village— invited Lama Zangchak and the monks to conduct his ritual for the year on the auspicious fifteenth day of the second lunar month.

Kathog had heard so much about the mansion of the village headman but had never had the opportunity to visit, so he was excited when the invitation arrived.

True to what he had heard, the three-storey mansion was as grand as his father's Dungje mansion, which made him instantly homesick. Memories of his parents came flooding back to him, and he longed to return home and see them. But as soon as the ritual began, Kathog became a part of the rhythm of the ceremony, and he forgot all else, as the chief attendant, in the role of the ritual chant master, led with so much passion and gusto that he became mesmerised.

Even Lama Zangchak, who was seated on a high-rise throne and engaged in silent prayer, enjoyed the enchanting sounds of the ritual instruments. He was a master performer of rituals and he had trained everyone to perfection.

Later in the evening, after the ritual was complete, a bonfire was lit outside the mansion, and the village dancers sang and danced around it. The monks, led by the chief attendant, sat on the courtyard and enjoyed the entertainment, drinking butter tea and eating snacks, but Lama Zangchak and Kathog stayed in the shrine room and watched the programme through the windows.

As Lama Zangchak was about to finish his ara, a woman walked into the room with a wine canister and began to refill his cup. As the woman poured, he looked up and noticed a slight apprehension in her face, which made him wonder if she had evil intentions. However, before he could say anything, she bowed and scurried out of the room.

He stared after her, biting his lips. Then, he picked up the cup and stared at the liquor for some time. *It may not be anything probably, only my mind being unnecessarily suspicious,* he thought and drank one little sip, then two sips, and finally the whole cup. Next, he waited to see if anything happened, but he seemed fine.

With his concerns still hovering over him, he continued to monitor how he was feeling. Then the realisation that it was really nothing filled him with relief. However, before he could castigate himself for being so suspicious, his face twisted with an agony that seized his stomach and then his entire body.

He clenched his teeth, held his breath, and exerted pressure against the constriction of the muscles in his stomach. Large beads of sweat appeared on his brow, and then on his chest and shoulders. He quickly reached for his shoulder bag, dug out a metal box, took out some black balls of medicine, and swallowed several of them.

Kathog, upon hearing some movements, swiftly turned his head to ascertain the cause and was taken aback by the sight of Lama Zangchak, drenched in sweat and writhing in pain.

The village headman, who happened to be entering the room at that moment, rushed towards them, fear etched into his face. "What happened, Lama?" he asked, trying to pull the lama upright, but the pain was too intense.

"It was that poison-giver woman," the lama replied, his teeth clenched in pain as he forced out each word with difficulty. "She came with a wine canister and refilled my cup, but I didn't recognise her."

The headman's eyes were wide with fear. "I will send for the physician!"

The lama shook his head and struggled to stand. "No, Headman, I had medicine, but it alone cannot help. This poison is too powerful. I must go home immediately and perform a *ngag*. Please, the two of you, help me out to the courtyard."

The headman and Kathog carried Lama Zangchak across the room and stumbled out of the door and onto the staircase landing of the second floor. As they manoeuvred the steps, they frantically shouted down, "Come and help! The lama has been poisoned! We have to take him back to the monastery!"

The singing and dancing stopped.

Everyone stared in shock as the headman and Kathog carried the lama, the two men trying to navigate the stone stairs.

When they reached the courtyard, everyone crowded around them, some offering help and others providing suggestions as to how best to carry the lama to the monastery.

One young man bursting with muscled arms and legs pushed through the crowd. Before anyone could argue, he squatted down with his back to the lama, hoisted the lama onto his back, and set out for the monastery.

The chief attendant began to object, insisting that one man could not possibly carry someone that size all the way to the monastery, but the young man was proving him wrong. He carried the lama with ease and continued to do so without stopping, all the way up to the monastery and into the lama's residence. Following close behind were the chief attendant and Kathog.

When Ani Choni saw them, she went pale with fear. "What happened?"

"Lama has been poisoned," the chief attendant replied, as he rushed to help the lama.

"It was that poison-giver woman," said the lama amidst the chaos, as he was set down on his seat in the living room. "I suspected something, but thought it might not be anything."

"Did you have any medicine?" Ani Choni was frantic.

"Yes, I did," replied the lama, his torso bent from the discomfort in his stomach, but his head lifted with a determined gaze when he spoke. "Her poison is too strong for the medicine alone. I must perform a ngag."

A murmur ran through the room.

"Please, don't panic," said the lama. "I will be all right. Just bring my ritual costumes and instruments, along with the silver medicine box."

"Yes, Lama," said Ani Choni, as she ran across the room.

"I must perform a secret ngag," said Lama Zangchak, turning to the chief attendant and others. "All of you must leave the room now, even you, Kathog. It is a powerful ngag to help neutralise the poison, so it is not safe for any of you to be here."

Everyone nodded and hurried out of the room, worried about the lama's health but also hopeful about the ngag, as Ani Choni hastened back into the room with a scary-looking trumpet made from a human femur, along with many other instruments, some ritual costumes and a silver medicine box.

Emerging from the house, the people huddled around the door, their faces grave with worry. However, just as the blaring sound of the trumpet reverberated through the house, a few senior monks, eager to catch a glimpse of the renowned secret tantra ritual, quietly stole away from the group, went around the house and peeped into the room through the gaps between the window shutters.

Chapter 30

Lama Zangchak neutralised the poison in his system by using both medicine and a tantric ngag, but the searing pain persisting in his abdomen would not allow him to sleep. When morning came, he was exhausted and morose. Nevertheless, he dressed and prepared to go and conduct class.

Ani Choni could not bring herself to tell him to stay home and rest, not only out of respect for his position, but also because he was in a foul mood. Both worried and concerned, she sent for the chief attendant, and the big monk came in a hurry, heaving and panting, but upon seeing the lama's mood, he could not bring himself to say anything. Instead, he stood quietly in a corner.

To compound her unease and anxiety, Ani Choni dropped her precious bowl and broke it, giving her an ominous premonition that something bad was going to happen. "Should not Lama stay home and take rest today?" she asked, mustering all her courage. "Perhaps the monks could recite windhorse prayer for Lama, as today is a good day for it. Also, Lama has hardly had any rest lately."

"I am fine," Lama Zangchak responded sombrely, rising from his seat to leave. "I will not be teaching the monks today, so they may choose to recite windhorse prayer or any other prayer, or they can have the day off if they so wish. I will have only a brief session with Kathog."

As someone who set great store by such omens, the ani became even more worried, yet she said nothing, afraid of provoking the lama's ire. Instead, she nodded and watched him leave, with the chief attendant following closely behind.

Lama Zangchak went straight to the study room and sent for Kathog, but his young protégé had fallen suddenly ill that morning.

Subsequently, he summoned Tompo, and the orphan hurriedly appeared, looking visibly concerned and frightened. Adding to this distress, the lama sat there, staring vacantly with bloodshot eyes and audibly sucking on his teeth for some time.

"Before we go to the next verse," the lama then said in a monotone, his voice lacking its usual warmth and authority, "we will recap the gist of the verses that we covered in the last few classes."

"Yes, Lama," Tompo nodded, his voice trembling a bit.

The lama leaned back lethargically into the backrest, his body fatigued and his actions seemingly detached from his thoughts, and began to speak, reciting a verse from memory, without looking at the text on the dais.

A thought such as this—wanting for others
What they do not wish even for themselves—
Is an extraordinary and precious state of mind,
And its occurrence a marvel unlike any other!

As the classes had been conducted irregularly with considerable gaps in between, Tompo did not know which verse the lama was reciting. He frantically flipped the folios but unable to find it, he left the text and looked up at the lama, stretching forward and listening hard, his eyes fixed on the lama's distant expression, trying to catch each word.

"Thinking about the welfare of others, such as the others have not even thought for themselves, is an extraordinarily precious state of mind," explained the lama, his voice flat, and now watching Tompo with a vacant-eyed expression. "The occurrence of such a thought is a marvellous and wonderful thing, unlike any other."

Tompo nodded, but he struggled to listen. The lama appeared ill, and his behaviour seemed strange.

"Why is such a thought a marvel? Why is the occurrence of such a thought important?" asked the lama, as if he was asking Tompo, but the very next moment, he answered himself, "Because it is the bodhicitta mind, the compassionate mind, the seed of enlightenment, the mind intent on perfect buddhahood."

Relief flooding over him, Tompo nodded again but with some sense of hesitation.

This source of joy for all who wander in existence,
This elixir that heals the sufferings of all beings,
This priceless jewel within the mind—
How could such merit ever be evaluated?

Tompo looked down at the text and found the verse on the top folio, so he followed the lines, listening even more intently, fear rising in his chest.

"The source of joy for all who wander in existence, the elixir that heals the sufferings of all beings, the priceless jewel within the mind," the lama repeated the lines of the verse. "How could such merit ever be evaluated? The source of joy, the elixir, and the priceless jewel refer to the bodhicitta mind."

Tompo nodded yet again, but faltered even more.

For if a simple wish to benefit others
Surpasses offerings made before the Buddhas,
What need is there to mention striving
For the welfare of all without exception?

Tompo sat alert, the muscles in his face stretched, maintaining focus.

"If a simple wish to benefit others is more powerful than the offerings made to the buddhas, what need is there to mention the untiring and persistent effort to benefit all sentient beings without exception? How powerful and meritorious would such effort be? Understood?"

Unsure and frightened, Tompo nodded sheepishly.

The lama recognised that look. Yet, he did not react in any way, but just stared at his student with bloodshot eyes and a gloomy expression for some time. Then, he went to the next verse.

Although seeking to avoid the pain,
They run headlong into suffering.
They long for happiness, but foolishly
Destroy it, as if it were their enemy.

Tompo sat tight, fear choking him now.

"Although seeking to avoid the pain, they run headlong into suffering," the lama continued. "They long for happiness, but foolishly destroy it as if it were their enemy. This verse emphasises the contradictions between our desires and the actions we take to achieve them. How is this so?" There was a slight terseness in his question.

Tompo sat gawking, feeling a mix of confusion and fear.

"I am asking you a question, Tompo." The lama came alive, raising his voice, his demeanour turning even more fearsome. "Why would someone looking to escape suffering run headlong into suffering? That doesn't make sense. For whoever is looking to avoid suffering should be running away from suffering, not running headlong into it."

Tompo was totally lost.

"In the same way, why would anyone longing for happiness destroy happiness as if it were an enemy? It doesn't make any sense, but this is what is written here. What does it mean, and how does it happen? I explained this to you thoroughly in one of our last classes."

Tompo thought hard, furrowing his brow, clenching his lips, closing his eyes, and straining the nerves on his neck and face. However, nothing came to his mind, but his expression made him look stupid and infuriated the lama.

"What are you doing, you fool, making a face like that? Are you trying to turn yourself into the mask of a festival clown? If you don't know, you just say so, instead of making a dreadful face like that, as if you are not ugly enough. That would at least be better!"

Tompo went pale with fear.

"I am sick and in pain, and still I am trying hard to teach you something! But you don't know anything!" The lama threw his hands in the air in anger. "For heaven's sake, this is only the first chapter of a foundational text, yet you cannot progress beyond it! Is this even a study of dharma, or is it devilry unfolding to destroy the monastery's good tendrel and good fortune!"

Tompo broke into a cold sweat.

"I warned you about something like this happening from the very beginning, but you did not even admit your lack of intelligence. Instead, you persisted as if you were like any other person, to cause this unmeritorious event to happen, to bring this devilry upon my monastery."

As Tompo stood there stunned, the lama paused momentarily, heaving and panting, with his voice reverberating through the empty hallway, until it eventually dissipated somewhere in the distance.

"Although seeking to avoid the pain," the lama began the next moment, reciting the lines, "they run headlong into suffering!

They long for happiness, but foolishly destroy it as if it were their enemy! Why? Because we ignorant people are deluded into thinking that what gives us suffering gives us joy and happiness! How many times do I have to explain this simple thing to you?"

Tompo trembled, his hands quivering at his sides, his heart pounding.

"I even recited and explained a verse from Chapter Eight that precisely elucidated this verse. But I am sure you don't remember that verse, let alone understand it, do you?" The lama's voice hung in the air as he glared.

Tompo recognised the scornful fury, almost mocking in nature, in Lama Zangchak's eyes, and in that instant his heart nearly stopped. He knew instantly that the lama was going to pose a question and be brutally hard about it. He felt as if he were falling into a bottomless pit, just as he had experienced in one of his nightmares.

"What is that verse?" asked the lama the next moment, his voice seething with rage, just as Tompo had feared. "Recite its lines to me, word for word! Don't say that you don't know, and don't give me a stupid answer! I swear by my lama, I will kill you if you do!"

Tompo thought hard, straining his nerves, but nothing came to his mind. Everything was frozen and blank.

And as he stood there struggling to recall the elusive verse, Lama Zangchak's anger boiled, reached its peak, and then erupted like a furious storm. He picked up the entire stack of the folios of text and hurled them at Tompo. The folios scattered in the air like angry birds, as the lama's voice, reciting the verse at the top of his lungs, thundered across the room.

Whatever joy there is in this world,
All comes from desiring others to be happy,

And whatever suffering there is in this world,
All comes from desiring myself to be happy.

Tompo could neither hear nor see, and as he sat there, the folios came fluttering down and landed all over him, with one gently settling on his head and looping down onto his forehead. His fear, his humiliation, all of it overwhelmed him, leaving him paralysed.

As he stood dazed, the lama, seething with uncontrollable rage, scrambled to climb down from the throne. Tompo was certain the lama was going to strike him. However, at that very moment, he realised that the lama had thrown a sacred text at him. Unable to believe it, he looked around and saw the floor strewn with the folios.

Appalled, he began to pick up whatever he could, placed them on a choedom by the wall along with his text, bowed to the lama, and then ran out of the room. A cry of anguish rose from his chest as he stumbled along the dimly lit corridor and out of the monastery, with the echoes of the lama's voice still reverberating in his mind and tears streaming down his cheeks.

At that very moment, a deafening thunder roared above the monastery, shaking the buildings and rattling the windows. Then, a lightning bolt hit a nearby treetop, large droplets of rain spattered onto the cobblestones, and a strong gust of wind struck the hill, nearly blowing Tompo down. But he ran on, out of the campus and down the hill, almost tumbling down the slope.

The sky darkened and the storm intensified, with lightning flashing across the horizon and thunder roaring through the sky, but he did not slow down. Instead, he ran harder and faster, weeping all the way down to the valley, through the village, and across the farmlands.

The rain pounded with relentless force, and the winds howled with raging fury, as if they carried with them the vengeance of his negative karma, or so he believed. His chest heaved and his legs hurt, yet he did not stop or slow down.

Tompo had no idea where he was going or what lay ahead. He just ran and ran until he reached a large meadow, somewhere far from Tsokar village and the region of Aeling. There, he stopped in the middle, breathless and disorientated, and went down on his knees, crying loudly and beating the ground with his fists in deep anguish and despair.

Then, looking up into the darkened sky and with the raindrops pounding on his face, he shouted, "Why does this always happen to me? Why do I have so much of bad karma? Why am I not able to comprehend even a basic dharma teaching? What have I done to deserve this?"

But no matter how loudly he shouted, his words were devoured by the raging thunderstorm as soon as they were uttered, reducing him to a lone figure sitting on his knees and wailing amidst the vast expanse of green landscape.

Exhausted and defeated, he threw himself onto the ground, resting his forehead against his crossed arms, and wept until his emotions and pain were spent and the storm had abated.

Then, spiritually dead, all emotions drained and his face raw from crying, he stood and began to wander aimlessly into the forest until he reached a small flatland of wild fruit trees, with a rocky cliff on one side and a saddle-shaped hump of a towering mountain on the other.

A faint animal trail wound through this wild orchard, some distance away from the cliffside, but, ignoring this path, he walked past a giant old tree to the cliff, and stood at its edge, ready to jump to his death and end his agony and misery once and for all.

PART THREE

Chapter 31

Tompo remained at the edge of the rocky cliff, gazing blankly at the distant horizon. Below, long tendrils of white fog that rose from the depths of the grey emptiness swayed gently in the breeze like the tongues of a many-headed serpent waiting to devour him.

"If you are considering jumping off that cliff," said a male voice from behind, "understand that your death will neither solve your problem nor end your suffering, but rather compound them." Startled out of his despondency, he pivoted abruptly on his heel in astonishment.

A towering old monk, sporting a long white goatee, stood at a distance. "Your life may end, but your existence will continue," he added with an unmistakable smirk on his face, "first in the bardo, then in the next life form, whatever that may be."

Taken aback, Tompo gaped at the old monk.

"But what could possibly matter more to you than being alive, Monk?" The old monk raised his hands in the air, coming a few steps closer. The way he moved, he appeared sprightly and agile for his age. "The only precious thing that truly matters in this world is human life. Nothing else holds any real value."

"Others' lives may be precious, but not mine, Old Monk," retorted Tompo. His voice was gruff and his tone curt, but he did not care. "My life has no value whatsoever."

"All human lives are equally precious, Monk. A human life is a human life, be that of a king or a peasant, of a wealthy or a poor man. And yes, of a hunter or a monk. No one life is better than the other. They are all the same, without exception."

"How so, Old Monk?" Tompo demanded.

"All sentient beings are trapped in the meaningless existence of suffering, bounced from one life form to the other through the nonstop cycle of birth and death. However, when one attains a human life, one is granted the opportunity to break free from this cycle. For this reason, all human lives are considered equally precious, as they each possess the same human potential to liberate themselves."

"Yes, but you have to practise dharma for that."

"Of course, you do, Monk," the old monk replied, and a grin spread across his face like a ripple on a lake. "Only dharma can liberate us from this aimless drifting through existence. However, you can only practise dharma if you have a human life." He broke into a sardonic smile.

"But a human life alone, even if you are bestowed with a fully able body, is not enough, Old Monk," challenged Tompo. "You also need intelligence to study dharma. And I have none of it. I cannot even grasp the basics of a foundational text."

"So that was why you were going to jump off the cliff," replied the old monk, his grin growing even wider. "I am learning something new today. I have heard of people taking their lives for all kinds of reasons, but not for lacking the intelligence to study dharma."

Tompo felt tears forming in his eyes. "That is because I have great devotion for dharma, and I cannot bear the thought of not being able to pursue its noble path. I would rather die than live and not be able to practise dharma."

"Is that so?"

"Yes, Old Monk, it is."

"It seems that you have a tricky situation here, my friend. You have great devotion for dharma but lack the aptitude for studies," remarked the old monk, his demeanour appearing suddenly pensive, yet continuing to grin. "But still, that is not reason enough for you to end this precious human life."

"That is not the only reason," said Tompo. "All I have ever known in my life is suffering. I was born to a tenant farmer family with no siblings or relatives. And if that were not enough misfortune, my parents died when I was only nine, leaving me in bondage to the village headman. Yet, despite suffering much and having nothing to call my own, I accepted my life with all my heart and lived in contentment."

The monk listened, but remained quiet.

"I didn't desire for anything, and I didn't want anything until I came across a trulku teaching and felt profound devotion for dharma. Then I wanted to pursue the noble path of dharma with all my heart. But as unfortunate as I was with so much negative karma, I didn't get the lama's audience. When the lama finally taught me, I didn't understand a thing, angering the lama so much that he threw the sacred text at me."

The old monk looked away for a moment, and then turned his sharp gaze back to Tompo. "Yours may be a woeful story, but it is no cause for you to end this precious life. In fact, it is a reason for you to be joyous, for you are an *orphan without home* and a *monk without dharma*—a rare life situation that manifested on its own, and one that you must embrace with all your heart."

Tompo's brow furrowed. "What life situation?"

"That of being an orphan without possessions and a monk without dharma. This is a rare treasure, Monk, one that you should not exchange for all the wealth in the world . . . or for all the dharma teaching that exists. Are you listening? You should not trade this situation of your life for anything in the world."

Now Tompo was fully confused. "What are you saying?"

The old man shook his head. "If your life is hard, it is meant to be so for a reason. Sometimes, everything in life is designed to test and prepare us. In the working of karma, it is often not as it seems. A misfortune today may bring a fortune tomorrow, and a fortune today may bring a misfortune tomorrow."

"I can't make any sense of what you are saying, Old Monk."

"Really? Well, if it comforts you, understand that this mundane world has never made any sense to me or to any sensible person. But don't worry, everything will make sense when you lose the sense of the self and the world. For now, continue living this life of an orphan without home and a monk without dharma. In time, a secret treasure will reveal itself on its own."

Thinking the old monk eccentric, Tompo shrugged off what the man had said and directed his thoughts to his decision to kill himself. After a long pause, he said, "I am sorry, I was overwhelmed by immense negative emotions. Otherwise, I would not have even thought about death." He looked into the old man's eyes. "I had no intention of jumping."

"That is all right, Monk."

"And I am sorry for talking to you with impertinence," Tompo said sincerely. "I have never spoken to anyone like that before. It is not who I am."

This time, when the old man smiled, it was kind. "That does not matter as well, but never say anything bad and never do anything foolish when you are being guided by strong emotions. Now," he added, pointing to somewhere in the distance, "if you are heading that way, you had better get going now. The next village is far, and there is nothing along the way."

"Did you know I came from Tsokar?" Tompo asked.

"Does it matter?"

Tompo stared at him for a moment. "Who are you, Old Monk?"

"I am nobody important, no one you would know by name. I am just a plain old monk who wanders around this part of the world. But, if you would like to know something of interest, I call this little flatland the secret garden of the mighty Silver Mountain."

Tompo, not knowing what to say, nodded.

"Everything grows here." The old monk lowered his voice as if whispering a secret. "You can find as many medicinal roots as poisonous leaves, and just as many wild grains and fruits."

Tompo stared, bewildered.

"Both the poison-givers and the physicians come here for their raw materials," the old monk continued to whisper. "As for me, I come here for serenity, and to collect wild grains and fruits. But you, young man, you came here to take your own life."

"I reached this place accidentally," retorted Tompo. "I was wandering with no destination.

"I know, I know."

"And I was not going to jump."

"I know, I know." The old monk nodded again and then said, "Now, if you follow this trail, it will take you to the national pathway going to Kisathang. But I am afraid you will have to travel hard and fast to reach there. This Silver Mountain is one giant of a mountain."

"Thank you," said Tompo, with a slight bow. Having nothing else to say, he slowly turned and walked away.

He walked on for a short distance, then stopped and looked back. The old monk was gone.

With thoughts of life, dharma, and the unexpected twists and turns of the universe, he turned back and continued, following the trail pointed out by the old monk.

Chapter 32

The trail skirted around the secret garden, crossed over the saddle seat, climbed sideways up the pommel, and then met the national mule pathway on the other side of the mountain. From that vantage point, no one could imagine that a flatland existed on the other side.

Tompo walked on with greater determination. However, Silver Mountain was one hell of a giant mountain. The path climbed higher and higher, winding through many undulations, and never seemed to reach the top. Yet, he kept going until, sometime midafternoon, he finally reached the summit.

From there, it was all downhill, making the going easier. But still, the path wound through what felt like a never-ending course of lows and highs. Anxious to get somewhere before dark, he began to run, and eventually arrived at a vantage point overlooking the valley.

It was Kisathang at sundown.

Tompo, drenched in sweat, looked down upon the village and saw that Kisathang was much like any other village he had seen on his way from Tamchu to Tsokar.

Squaring his shoulders, he pressed forward and soon descended into the valley. Then, hastening towards the village, which lay a short distance ahead, he arrived at a large mud house embraced by fruit trees.

By then, the sun had dipped below the horizon, leaving only a streak of vibrant crimson lingering on a patch of clouds.

He walked to the door and knocked, calling out, "Is anybody home?"

He heard some hurried movements inside, followed by what sounded like whispered arguments. Though he could not make out what was being said, it was evident that he was not going to be welcomed.

Soon the door creaked open, revealing five young women crowding the doorway, hesitant and uneasy.

Tompo's eyes scanned their uncertain faces, as he cleared his throat, trying to ease their tension. "I am looking for a place to spend the night," he said, mustering a friendly smile to alleviate their suspicion.

The young women exchanged awkward glances, both with Tompo and with each other. Then the one who appeared to be the eldest stepped onto the threshold. Bowing her head, she said, "We are all girls here, Monk, and our parents are not home."

"That is all right, Sister," he replied, his mind already planning his next move.

"We are sorry, Monk."

Tompo bowed, turned, and left, and after walking for some time reached a dilapidated rammed-earth house with weeds and creepers climbing up the walls. Wondering if there was anyone living there, he cautiously walked to the door and tapped lightly.

"Who is it?" asked a faint male voice from inside the house.

"I am a traveller passing through," Tompo said to the closed door, "and I am looking for a place to spend the night. I don't have any friend or a horse with me, and I assure you, I will be gone at the first light of dawn without inconveniencing you in any way."

From behind the door, the man said, "Both my wife and I are seriously ill, and there is no one else in the house. So, we cannot offer you anything. Please, go on farther and try some other houses. We are very sorry about this."

"And I am sorry for disturbing you," Tompo said.

There was no further response, so Tompo turned and left, continuing until he reached a grand and imposing house. Looking at it, a sense of hesitation came over him. But the daylight was gone and he had nowhere else to go.

He reluctantly made up his mind and climbed the stone steps to the wooden porch on the second floor. The door was wide open, and through it he could see a shadowy figure of a woman seated inside, leaning against the wall, her form barely discernible in the hazy light of dusk and the faint glow from the hearth.

He bowed at her and mumbled a greeting, but for a long, tense moment she did not respond, leaving him in an awkward dilemma about whether he should turn and leave.

"One comes, just as one goes," she said, finally. Her voice was strange, almost surreal to Tompo's ears. "But this one before me is a monk in a robe. But again, what does it matter? Whether one wears a red robe or a black gho, a man is a man inside."

Unsure what the woman meant, Tompo's nerves grew more pronounced. "I'm a monk, a traveller passing through your village, and I need a place to stay for the night. But if you are unwell, or uncomfortable, I will move on."

The woman made no effort to stand and greet him, nor did she acknowledge him properly. Instead, she continued to stare at him, displaying no obvious concern or worry about her impropriety.

Tompo's unease increased, and he did not know how to proceed in this peculiar situation.

"I don't care one bit if you are a monk or a hunter, or if you are travelling or wandering, but if you want, you may come in," she stated. "You may sleep on the floor or in my bed. You may stay for a night or for a life."

Tompo, listening hard, catching every word, found her voice

to be lifeless and flat, without joy or any emotion. He then realised her comments, quite inappropriate to be directed at a monk, were not targeted at him, but at her own sorrowful life.

His anxiety cooled down then, but his own negative emotions from these daylong happenings came surging up from deep inside him, and they seemed to work on him as her emotions worked on her.

"I am not a monk or a hunter, nor even travelling or wandering," he replied, his tone suddenly different. "If I am anything that could have a label, then I am a lump of karmic debt. And if I have reached your doorstep somehow, whether travelling or wandering, then I am drifting through *samsara*."

"I don't hear you saying that, Monk." The woman lifted her head and fixed her gaze on him intently. "No, you are not saying that," she repeated with certainty. "A monk doesn't say such things. Only a person like me makes such lowly claims."

"Yes, I do," he asserted. "There is nobody more miserable than I am, and nobody more unfortunate. I am an orphan without home and a monk without dharma," he said, remembering how the eccentric old monk had called him. "I feel I am better off dead. Sadly, I cannot even die."

"Then we share something in common, Monk." The woman lifted her hand and beckoned him to enter, but without any effort to move from where she sat. "Please, come in. Please, come and share my humble home."

He walked into the house and was stunned to see her at close range. She was an astonishingly beautiful young woman, in his eyes, almost a heavenly being.

"Come and help me to stand up, Monk." She offered her hands to him. "I, too, am a lump of grief, and without any life today. But what a coincidence that two such people should meet at dusk like this."

He observed her tear-stained face, marked by signs of prolonged weeping, and noticed her eyes were without any glimmer of light or joy. In that moment, he felt an inexplicable connection to her, as if their shared experiences of suffering had forged an unspoken bond.

He took her hands and helped her to her feet. Her hands were soft and smooth, and her breath as sweet as a delicate fragrance.

"Come, Monk," she invited, gesturing with both her hand and head. "We have done enough talking to last a lifetime in this short time. Now we will sit by the fire and drink some good ara. A monk without dharma and a woman without virtue, we will make a good twosome tonight."

"A woman without virtue?" Tompo asked, surprised.

"I don't know what kind of a sad story you have, but I am carrying a bastard in my womb from a married man." She pressed her hands against her belly, so he could see the tiny bump. "He wooed me with riches and promises and then left me with a child. He departed from here moments before you arrived."

Uncertain how to respond, he stared at her with a sense of awkwardness. The strong negative emotions that had gripped him earlier were gone now, and in their place he felt hesitant and nervous. Fortunately, she turned and walked towards a cabinet on the far side of the room and could not see his expression.

When she reached the cabinet, she retrieved an elegant wine canister embellished with what appeared to be intricate silver embroidery, along with a pair of burl wooden cups lined with fine silver.

Tompo had only seen such expensive silverware at the Dungje mansion in Tamchu during important occasions, and he had never imagined he would have the opportunity to hold something so fine, much less drink from it.

But the silverware was not the only surprise.

She ushered him onto a rare silk mat that, he thought, must have been laid out for the man who had just left. Then, she fetched and placed a *chentey* in front of him. Made of a beautiful deep-grained wood, the low serving table was unlike anything he had seen and equally as intimidating as the silk mat.

As he sat and watched, gaping in awe, she delicately set one of the elegant cups on the smooth surface of the ivory chentey and gracefully poured to the brim what he presumed to be a specially brewed and distilled ara.

Everything seemed almost dreamlike, yet he lifted the silver cup from the chentey with extreme care. His heart raced, and his hands shook, but he did not spill a drop. Instead, making a silent offering to the gods and the deities of the territory, he slowly drank almost to the bottom and placed the cup down for a customary top-up.

The ara not only smelled good, but it tasted even better.

As she filled his cup, he felt the spirit of the liquor flowing into his veins, and then its warmth spreading through his body until his face became flushed.

"This liquor indeed is for a grieving heart," he said, his voice unintentionally louder than he had intended. "You must drink some too." A mischievous grin spread across his face, catching him off guard with its flirtatiousness.

She nodded, a playful smile dancing on her lips. "But you have to serve me, Monk. Only a desolate woman pours her own drink. Though I may be in pain and sorrow, I am not lacking in self-esteem." Handing him the wine canister, she held up her cup expectantly.

He poured her a full cup, and watched her drink, sip after sip, until her face glowed with a warm rosy colour.

Soon, the evening seamlessly transitioned into night, and they carried on with their eating and drinking, seemingly unfazed by their circumstances, and as they did so, she neither asked for his name nor his story but told hers without any reservation.

Her name was Jadelma, and she was born a bastard to a nun who had died giving birth to her at a nunnery in Zomkhar village. As it happened, nobody knew the nun was pregnant until she could not deliver on her own and had to call for help. By then, she was already dying, and on her deathbed, she claimed her pregnancy to be a mystery, insisting that she remained a maiden who had never been with any man.

Although nobody believed her story, no man came to the nunnery claiming to be the baby's father. Therefore, the head nun adopted the exceptionally beautiful infant and raised her as a recluse in the nunnery, shielding her from the lustful eyes of men.

When the head nun died three years ago, Jadelma, then an elegant young woman, moved to live in the head nun's ancestral house at Kisathang. But the long-abandoned house she now lived in was dilapidated, nearly uninhabitable, and in dire need of major repairs that were beyond her means. Fortunately for her, every man in the village, looking to woo her, showed up to help, but sadly, most of them were either married or betrothed, and their attraction to her caused many problems within their families and relationships.

As a result, many marriages and relationships had been broken by the time the renovation was completed, and Jadelma was labelled a woman without virtue, even though she did not engage with any of the men in any way. She was ostracised and forced to live on the fringes of the society.

With nowhere else to turn to and feeling cast out, Jadelma then gave in to the advances of one wealthy and charming married landlord, who had promised to leave his wife, but had instead left her with a broken heart and a bastard child yet to be born.

When Jadelma ended her story, Tompo found himself in a momentary lull, unsure of what to say. He was quite drunk, but the audacity and the exuberance that he had exhibited earlier were gone.

"You may tell me your story now, Monk," Jadelma said. "You may narrate it briefly, or at length. I will grieve for you either way, for we are two grieving hearts together, consoling and comforting one another tonight."

"Ah," sighed Tompo.

"Is your story that heavy?"

"Yes, I'm afraid it is." He sighed once again. "Such is my story and such are my sorrows that you cannot listen enough and you cannot grieve enough. I have nothing to call mine. No family, no home, no nothing. I don't even have dharma in me. If I ever had anything, it was pain and suffering."

"Then you need not tell me, Monk," she said, her voice soft. "But please do come and sleep with me tonight. Let one grieving heart comfort another grieving heart. You say you are a monk without dharma. Perhaps this is fitting for a woman without virtue, as everyone calls me."

Tompo tipped his head slightly in response, his warm gaze meeting hers. Nodding in acknowledgement, she took the lamp in one hand and Tompo's hand in the other, leading him out of the room and into the hallway towards her bedroom.

The kitchen fell into darkness, and the embers in the hearth hissed and glowed brightly for one last time, as the final remnants of the combustible materials burned and died in the hearth.

CHAPTER 33

Tompo woke up feeling well, his body snug within a thick furry blanket, and saw a long beam of sunlight filtering into the room. For a moment, he did not know where he was. Then he saw the pillow where Jadelma had rested her head.

The memories of the previous night came flooding back, and a surge of panic gripped him, physically jolting him. Aghast at what he had done, he was about to spring off the bed when he remembered the incident at the monastery.

A searing pain sliced through his heart, and he changed his mind and stayed in bed. *What things worse than these could happen to me*? he said to himself, shrugging his shoulders. *Even if they do, I don't care anymore*, he added, clenching his jaw and shaking his head.

But the young woman was genuinely good to me, and she appeared to be in significant distress herself. Thinking about what she had shared, and feeling both compassion and concern, he surveyed the room.

Eight large wooden boxes, all of them carved and painted with the Eight Lucky Signs, were neatly arranged on the wooden floor, flanking the walls on two sides of the bed. Above the head of the bed hung a solitary *thangka* painting of the Four Noble Friends.

Pondering his next course of action, he slowly rose from the bed. What had happened last night was surreal, almost a dream, but now that the morning had come clear and bright, he had to be realistic about his situation and find a way out.

Lost in his thoughts, he walked into the hallway and then into the combined kitchen and living room. There, Jadelma was busy preparing breakfast, looking even more beautiful and graceful in the daylight.

Mesmerised, he stood in the doorway, watching her.

But as if feeling his gaze, she looked up. "There is warm water for you on the porch outside, Monk," she said, without displaying any emotion, either in her expression or in her voice, as if nothing had happened between them. However, the way she called him "Monk" was reminiscent of the events from the last evening.

Uncertain of what to make of it and how to react, he nodded meekly and self-consciously walked the length of the room and out onto the wooden porch.

A dumpy wooden bucket, much like the one used for milking cows, was filled with warm water and sat at the far end of the porch. When he neared it, a curl of hazy white vapour was lazily rising from its surface.

He slowly squatted down and washed himself, taking all the time he needed to sort his thoughts. But nothing fell into place, nothing came to his mind. He had nowhere to go and nothing to do, and he did not know what to make of what she had said the previous night.

Unsure of anything, he went back inside as he had come outside, without a plan for his next course of action.

She had a lavish breakfast ready for them. "I hope you slept well, Monk," she said, ushering him onto a mat. "Even though this house was abandoned for a very long time, I think no evil spirit has ever set foot into it because everyone has good dreams here. Sometimes, I even have dreams so vivid that they are like visions."

"Yes, I slept well, Jadelma," replied Tompo, inadvertently addressing her by her name, and instantly cringing at his slip. For a moment, the ring of her name hung in the air uncomfortably.

Fortunately, she displayed no sign of awkwardness. Instead, she nodded gracefully and began to serve, first him and then herself.

But still feeling uneasy about this, he ate in silence.

And she, too, sensing his discomfort, said nothing until they finished eating and she had cleared everything away.

Then, she settled herself, gazing at Tompo with intent and purpose. "I am sure you know that there are no such things as accidental occurrences in our lives, Monk," she said, her voice soft, yet her tone firm. "Everything, be it good or bad, happens according to our karma."

Unsure of what she had in mind, Tompo held his breath.

"But as much as karma may appear to control our lives, it only determines certain aspects, leaving the decision in our hands. So, even though it is karma that brought you to my doorstep, it is you who must make the choice, consciously and willingly, if you will stay or go."

Tompo was taken aback, yet also filled with a sense of joy.

"Even though we wear the yoke of karma at all times, we live freely by our choices, " she continued. "Therefore, whatever you may decide, you decide freely and willingly. As you can see there," she turned and looked across the room, gesturing with her hand, "I have prepared for both outcomes."

Tompo followed her gaze and noticed a beautiful *kowgum*, readied for a journey with a bedroll strapped onto its top. *She must have filled the cowhide basket with everything I would need on a journey, if I decided to leave*, he thought.

Next to the basket, on a chentey, was a workman's woollen gho with a patang placed on top. The choices were clear, just as she had said.

"If you are going, I have prepared for a departure befitting the companion of solace that you have been," she told him, looking him in the eye. "Inside that kowgum are the wine canister from which you were served and the silver cup from which you drank. If you are staying, I offer you a special place in my life befitting the karmic spouse of destiny you will be."

Tompo pressed his lips together and nodded thoughtfully, taking time to sort his thoughts. "Thank you, Jadelma," he replied, his voice sincere and his expression genuine. "You are being most kind and considerate, beyond anything I have known and heard."

Jadelma listened, her face expectant, yet serene.

"I am the most unfortunate person in the world with nothing to call mine," he continued. "I have no home, no family, and no property. I don't even have the intelligence required to study dharma. Thus, I will not benefit you in any way but will bring ruin and shame into your life."

She studied his face for a moment. "If you want to stay, all you need to do is give me a name, Monk. And, of course, you have to remove your robe and don the garb of a layman. Other things will not matter at all, as everything of our past has ripened into our collective karma."

"Then, I will stay willingly and with all my heart, Jadelma," Tompo declared, his eyes filled with sincerity. "I don't know much about the yoke of karma and the freedom of choice, but I make this decision to stay with utmost joy and happiness." He paused briefly before continuing, with emphasis in his voice. "I am orphan Tompo, and I am a layman by all accounts. I don't have any dharma in me, and wearing this robe alone doesn't make me a monk."

"You redeem my name and reputation today, Tompo," she said, looking at him with a triumphant face. "However, I didn't ask you to stay to redeem my character, but to fill my life with meaning and purpose and my heart with joy and happiness."

"And you redeem my very existence, Jadelma."

They sat there, gazing into each other's eyes, filled with a sense of solace and understanding. Then, Tompo rose from his seat, walked over to the chentey, removed his red robe, donned the woollen gho, and belted the patang, as if finding a new beginning in the midst of their shared pain.

CHAPTER 34

Tompo came out of the house, wearing a bamboo hat and shouldering a spade. He walked to the edge of the porch, surveying the estate, and stood there. The house faced south, overlooking the national pathway. Originally, it had a basic layout and structure, but when it was renovated, it had been greatly improved and expanded with impressive structural and architectural designs.

Even the dome-shaped incense burner in the front lawn had been whitewashed and painted to harmonise with the overall design of the house. On the right-hand side, at the far edge of the lawn, was an old juniper tree that provided incense leaves for smoke offerings. On the left-hand side was a grove of tall willow trees.

With a slight nod of approval, he descended the stone stairs and paused briefly at the landing, then turned right and walked past the incense burner, going beyond the house. As he did, he glanced sideways and noticed that the kitchen gardens and the fruit orchards encircled the house in two layers, seeming to extend until the willow groove on the other side.

Continuing farther, he went past the juniper and arrived at a field that remained untouched from the last harvest season. Despite spring being halfway over, no work had been done there, as if Jadelma had been waiting for him—her companion of solace or, her karmic spouse of destiny, as she called him.

Breaking into a slight grimace at the thought, he spat on his palms and rubbed them together for lubrication. Then, he picked up the spade, swung it high into the air, and brought it down. The soil was soft and moist from yesterday's rain, and the spade cut into the earth effortlessly. It was as if the fierce and unseasonal storm that had marked his departure from Lama Zangchak's monastery had also prepared the way for his arrival at Jadelma's house—almost as if his karma had planned it, just as Jadelma had said.

Convinced that everything had unfolded according to his karma, Tompo set to digging without taking any rest, and soon he finished one-third of the field, leaving behind fresh mounds of dark upturned soil spreading out uniformly from one side to the other.

By then it was lunchtime, and Jadelma came with a stocky, middle-aged woman who wore a look of suspicion. Upon seeing him, she shook her head and spat on the ground.

However, Jadelma's attention was fixated on Tompo as he swung the spade into the air and brought it down again and again, its edge cutting sharply into the soft earth. There was a sense of rhythm and harmony in the movements of his body and the spade.

"It is a work of art on the earth's surface!" Jadelma declared, gesturing towards the fresh mounds of dark soil. "I have not heard of beauty and artistry in digging a field, but even these mounds have a stunning uniformity."

Tompo looked up and smiled. "I didn't even hear you come."

"That is because you were focused on your spade," Jadelma replied. "Not even a top-notch carpenter or mason can show such a level of skill. Tompo, this is sheer artistry. And look at you," she added, gesturing to his clothing. "You are not even soiled!"

He placed the head of the spade in the ground and leaned into its shaft. "I come from a family of tenant farmers, and I have worked in the fields since I was a boy. But look, I took the whole morning to complete just this small stretch. Other strong, hardworking young men would have done much more. This is very good land."

"Yes, everything here is good. I think it is the blessing of the head nun and her ancestors. She said she came from a family of genuine dharma practitioners." Then, picking up on his other point about not completing much, she said, "This is more than enough. You must not work yourself to exhaustion. We are not going to farm much." With this, she turned to the woman. "This is *Aum* Zam."

Tompo smiled and bowed courteously at the woman; however, the woman shrugged and turned her head away.

"She is my only friend in the whole of Kisathang," Jadelma said warmly, not minding the woman's scorn towards Tompo, "but she is better than a hundred friends put together."

"It is important to have such a friend," he concurred.

"Yes, she does everything for me." Jadelma stared gratefully at Aum Zam, but the woman sneered back at her. Jadelma turned to Tompo. "Lunch is ready. If you can stop and come in now, I have everything ready."

With a slight nod, Tompo leaned the spade against a bush and brushed off his hands.

The two women turned and left, as though going ahead of him to ready the lunch. However, as soon as they were out of earshot, Jadelma turned to Aum Zam, her eyes narrowing. "What is wrong with you? Can't you even extend basic courtesy to someone?"

"You ask what is wrong with me?" Aum Zam shot back. "I ask what is wrong with you! You did right to end your affair with Landlord Mikar Drol before his wife came and dragged you naked by your hair. But what have you done now? Married the first man who showed up at your door, and a lowlife monk at that?"

"Please, Aum Zam, don't speak of him that way." Jadelma paused briefly and then walked on. "Tompo is a good person."

"Tompo?" Aum Zam repeated, her expression twisting into a sneer. "What sort of name is that? Who in their right mind would bestow such a name upon their child? I would not even name my lame leper dog Tompo." Aum Zam directed a derisive look at Jadelma.

"Please, Aum Zam, don't pick on everything."

"Don't pick on everything? Are you kidding me? You don't know anything about him! He could be a con man, a thief, or even a killer for all you know, and you have taken him right into your bed."

"Please, Aum Zam, let us set aside such talk for now."

"You are behaving like a child, Jadelma! Don't you understand the whole village of Kisathang has ostracised you? If my family had not been the devoted caretakers for the head nun's dharma family for generations, and if I had not pledged to the head nun to care for you like you were my own daughter, I might have also turned against you."

"Then turn against me."

"Really?"

"Yes."

"What if something were to happen to you? Who will help you?"

"What could possibly happen to me?"

"What could possibly happen to you?" Aum Zam repeated, her expression turning into a mix of mockery and disbelief. "A hundred things could happen to you! He could abscond with your valuables. He could even murder you and make it look like an accident or a suicide, and then take everything, including this house."

"What a dreadful thing to say, Aum Zam!" Jadelma stopped walking, aghast. "You are being purposely wicked now. Why would he do such a thing? Whatever I own will be his, too. We are one and the same."

"Why?" Aum Zam repeated once more, her mouth twisted. "Are you truly that naive, Jadelma? Perhaps he has a lover, his real love, waiting for him to arrive with your riches. He might even have a wife and children awaiting him at home. You don't know anything about him."

"Your thoughts are running wild, Aum Zam!" Jadelma raised her hands in the air in disbelief. "He is nothing like you are imagining. I may not have probed, but last night I saw all that I needed to know about him, with just one glimpse into his heart."

"You set store by such a nonsensical thing?" Aum Zam scoffed, her eyebrows raised in disbelief. "You evaluate someone that you met just once at the devil's dusk by your intuition?" She shook her head. "Wake up, Jadelma, he is nothing more than a charlatan." Her lips curled into a derisive smile. "Changing his garb at the snap of a finger, and digging nearly one field in one morning. It is all trickery."

Jadelma exhaled loudly. "I know how much you feel for me, and I am grateful to you, but your fears are unfounded." She turned and walked away, leaving Aum Zam standing there. "My tea must be getting over-brewed."

"Forget your tea and focus on your life," Aum Zam shouted after Jadelma. "Your tea will only froth more and taste stronger, but your life will be ruined and wasted."

Jadelma did not respond, but kept walking.

Aum Zam, too, not ready to concede and give up on her young friend, hastened after Jadelma, quickening her steps, determined to catch up.

Chapter 35

As if their union were destined and their bond sacred, Tompo's arrival in her life unlocked a profound potential within Jadelma. She discovered joy and happiness that was unbounded, spiritual, and liberating, bringing her complete satisfaction and fulfilment.

She underwent a remarkable transformation, not only on the mental level, with her qualities becoming refined, but also on the physical level, with her appearance attaining the absolute form of beauty. She became the very embodiment of the finest aspects of human nature, qualities, and physical form.

However, the villagers, influenced by Landlord Mikar Drol's wife, were blind to everything good. They would not allow her into their social circle, claiming she was immoral, a woman who had not only broken up marriages and relationships, but also married a monk, desecrating his sacred vow.

Countering the landlord's wife, Aum Zam, who was resolute in clearing her young friend's name and reputation, fought hard for Jadelma, extolling her virtues, and began to affect a few people here and there.

Then the landlord's wife started attacking Tompo, spreading rumours about his parentage and his past. In turn, Aum Zam, who was still suspicious of Tompo, pressured Jadelma to ask Tompo to explain the allegations levelled against him so that everyone in the village would be informed of his character and stop gossiping and judging.

But Jadelma would not hear of it. She neither cared what anyone said about Tompo, nor was she willing to subject him to scrutiny just to satisfy some unreasonable people . . . or allay Aum Zam's unfounded fears.

So Jadelma and Tompo continued to live an ostracised life, except for their contact with Aum Zam. But living in isolation suited them just fine. They were happy, content, and peaceful.

As time flew by, with days turning into weeks and weeks into months and Jadelma's last trimester drawing nearer, Aum Zam gave up her efforts to integrate Jadelma into society. Instead, she channelled her energy into brewing *changkey*, distilling ara, and making other preparations for the birth of the baby.

By then, the autumn was coming to an end, and Tompo was busy harvesting the paddy, reaping the crops from the stalks, bundling them into sheaves, and drying them in the sun. As he moved into the last batch of fields adjacent to the house, the days became shorter and the weather grew chilly.

The winter will be right on time, he thought, cosying up to his long-held idea of spending the cold winter months sitting by the fire, eating, drinking, and chitchatting. What made that notion even more appealing was having Jadelma to share these moments with him.

So, working even harder and faster, hoping to finish work before the winter arrived, he was in the last stretch of the last field, racing to wind down the harvest season over the next few days.

That afternoon, a man carrying a hefty basket on his back and leading several packhorses, arrived at the house. "Is anybody home?" he called out, climbing onto the porch.

Jadelma came waddling out of the door, holding her bulging belly, and courteously bowed. Observing him dusty from a long and hard travel, she remarked, "Wherever you might be bound, you are sure to have come from afar."

"Yes," he said," I have been travelling all around the country trading in spices. This leg of the trip started from Tamchu in the south, bringing nothing other than garlic. But, of course, theirs is the large knob garlic with big cloves," he explained.

"Oh, how unfortunate that I don't consume garlic these days," she said, her head jerking slightly and her eyelids shutting. "I recite the *drolma* mantra, and garlic is said to possess negative energy."

"Yes, indeed," the man agreed. "But that is all right."

She nodded and turned her attention back to his dusty appearance. "You look like you could use a cup of wine. If you are not in a hurry, I could offer you one."

"I would be most grateful." His face lit up. "But I am afraid I would also need a cup, as I lost mine crossing the Tsokarchu. I also nearly slipped and fell trying to retrieve it from the river current."

She nodded and went back into the house.

The man turned and looked around and saw Tompo at work, reaping the stalks from the paddy, bundling them into sheaves, and drying them in the sun. The diligence, meticulousness, and elegance with which the young man performed every action caught his attention, and he soon became so mesmerised that he did not hear Jadelma come back.

"That is my husband," she said.

The man was visibly impressed. "How does he work like that? He is so graceful. I have never seen anyone work like him, so beautifully and with his whole heart."

"He works as if he has magic in his hands." She handed him the cup and poured the ara to the brim, but the man just held the cup and stood thoughtfully. "Please, drink," she said then. "It may not be that strong."

He drank a sip and nodded. "It is quite strong." He drank another sip and held the cup in front of her for a refill.

She refilled his cup. "He is my husband, but he is not the father of the child in my womb. That man left me when I was in my first months. Then he came by, appeared at my door one evening, about six months ago. I think he was a sort of runaway monk. He had no one and nowhere to go. So, I offered him a home, and he stayed on."

The man's face fell and he sighed.

"What is it?" Jadelma asked anxiously.

"So, he is *that* monk," he said sadly, but more to himself. "It has to be him, for no other person would work like that with his whole heart." He spoke as if standing alone.

She nearly dropped the canister. "What do you mean? Have you heard of him?" She felt her heart pounding. "What do you mean by *that monk*? Tell me, please."

"He is from Lama Zangchak's monastery in Tsokar, and he is said to have a pure heart without malice, hatred, greed, jealousy, pride, arrogance, or any other negativity. He is also known to possess an astounding devotion for dharma, and to work with utmost dedication and sincerity."

"Yes, he is all that you say."

"But he was such a dimwit with immense negative karma that he could not make any headway in the dharma study. It was said that he could not grasp even a foundational text, so the lama got angry and threw things at him."

"Oh, my poor Tompo." She sighed sadly as an overwhelming sympathy welled up inside her. She turned and looked at Tompo, and then back at the man.

"He also had a bad tendrel with the lama," the man said. "He didn't have a gift offering. Some say that except for some old clothes to wear and a few sheets for sleeping, he didn't have anything decent enough to offer to the lama. He didn't even have a red robe. So, he was not given the lama's audience for years."

"How long could he have stayed there?"

"I heard that he was there for five years and that he suffered much. Because he thought he possessed so much negative karma, he worked hard, almost killing himself, to purge his bad karma."

"Oh, my poor Tompo," she said again.

"It was then that the ani felt sorry for him and asked the lama to teach him. However, when he was finally given the teachings, he could not understand anything." The man paused. "It must be his bad karma," he remarked, shaking his head. "Then, one day, he ran away and never returned."

Jadelma nodded painfully, her face pale, and her emotions constricting her heart.

The man bowed and walked away, leaving her standing there, numbed by his words. As she stood in pain, everything became clear to her in one instant, giving her an unusual and extraordinary clarity of mind. She knew what she had to do, and she decided to do it, then and there, without any doubt.

With strong resolve forming in her heart, she turned and walked back into the house, where she began to prepare for Tompo's journey to what she thought was the next stage of his life.

CHAPTER 36

Jadelma carefully made her way down the stone stairs, with Tompo close behind, carrying the kowgum on his back with a bag looped over it.

He was leaving the house for the first time since he had arrived six months earlier, and he had no idea where they were going, or what was in the kowgum. She did not tell him, and he did not ask her, because he could see that she was affected by something strange.

She led him up the valley, taking him into Kisathang proper.

The village was not peaceful and harmonious like its name suggested, but rather noisy and chaotic. They passed by a husband and wife raising a ruckus over something, with the husband hurling expletives, and the wife whimpering back in response.

"This village is going through a period of decadence," Jadelma remarked in response to the couple. "The good people have been vanquished, while the bad people run wild."

Shocked, Tompo could only nod.

"I, too, had fallen into that pit of decadence once," she said, admitting her own mistake. "Fortunately you came along and rescued me."

Again, Tompo did not respond, and so they walked on in silence.

The village was not prosperous either. Most of the houses they passed were dilapidated, the orchards around them dying, and the cattle, horses, pigs and chicken—the few that still remained—were scrawny and looked diseased.

In a little while, Tompo and Jadelma arrived at the village centre and came upon a large crowd. Not wishing to have anything to do with these people, they kept to the periphery; they even avoided looking towards the crowd.

The people also seemed to mind their own business. But that was only until one young man shouted something obscene at them. Then everyone broke into an uproarious laughter, with some men even whistling and catcalling after them.

Still, they paid no heed, but continued walking, with Jadelma heaving and panting under the weight of her large belly, until they arrived at a three-way junction, with a giant prayer flag fluttering high in the sky.

Jadelma rested for a while, then circled the prayer flag three times and led the way up to a small hillock, resting at the base of the southwest side mountain of the valley of Kisathang.

Wondering where the path was leading them, Tompo followed her to the top and stood frozen in utter surprise. Before him lay a magnificent monastery with a cobblestone courtyard in the front and a large green campus behind it. His surprise turned to suspicion as he spun and stared at his wife, presuming that she had brought him to be enrolled in the monastery.

She was still heaving and panting from the climb, but before he could say anything, she nodded at him with an encouraging look, as if to convey that all was fine. Then she placed her hands on his shoulders and looked him squarely in the eyes, but just as she was about to speak, she was overcome by her emotions and could barely utter a word.

Tompo watched her with a mix of emotions, his mouth open and his eyebrows raised.

"This is Lama Jamsempa's monastery," Jadelma finally said,

bobbing her head as she fought her emotions. "You will study here from today on. You are not a poor orphan anymore, and you also have a gift offering for the lama."

Tompo's heart melted, eyes moistened, and his face contorted all at once, making it difficult for him to say anything.

She squeezed his shoulders, conveying to him that all was well, but her eyelids batted as she struggled with her own emotions.

After a long moment, Tompo's emotions subsided enough for him to be able to speak. "I don't know if I should feel happy or sad," he said in a wobbly voice, "but I'm feeling them both now: happy because I'm being given another opportunity to pursue the path of dharma, and sad because I'm intellectually incapable of studying it."

"No, Tompo," Jadelma disagreed, shaking her head. "There is no such thing as being capable or incapable in pursuing the path of dharma. Intelligence, devotion, faith, and perseverance are equally important."

"No, Jadelma," persisted Tompo, his voice gentle. "My intelligence is below that of the average person. I can't understand even a foundational text. So, my faith, devotion, and perseverance are of no use. There is no way for me in dharma. I believe this is due to my bad karma."

"You are wrong here, Tompo," she insisted, her voice equally polite, yet firm. "How can your faith and devotion be of no use? No person's faith and devotion will be useless in the pursuit of the path of dharma. If that is so, then it will not be dharma."

"Yes, it is, but—"

"And as for karma," she went on, catching on to his point about bad karma. "Yes, karma is an unavoidable factor that determines the course of our life, but it is not a set thing. It changes all the time, according to our actions."

Tompo nodded, beginning to feel encouraged.

"Your bad karma will exhaust one day, just as your good karma will," she added, lowering her voice. "You will then find your way forward. You are not doomed. No one should be doomed. There should be a path for everyone. This is Lord Buddha's dharma."

He looked at her and saw kindness and honesty. He was moved that she believed in him, in his possibilities. "Thank you, Jadelma, but who will look after you and the baby? How will you get by without anyone by your side? It is only a matter of days or a week before you give birth." As he spoke, he heard his own words, and his concerns for her suddenly grew.

"You should not worry about me, Tompo. It was my good karma that brought you to me. I have found a purpose and a goal in you. You have strengthened my will. All these are happening according to our collective karma. Come now," she said, leading him through the courtyard and up the flight of stairs, and then into the monastery building.

The chief disciple met them in the hallway and took them straightaway into the shrine room, where Lama Jamsempa, a tall and lean man with a soft and kind face, sat on a throne.

Tompo prostrated three times, walked to the throne and offered a ceremonial scarf and a gold statue of Buddha to the lama, who took the scarf and placed it around Tompo's neck and placed the statue on his dais.

As Tompo slowly retreated backwards from the throne, the chief disciple readied to brief the lama about Tompo. However, Jadelma cleared her throat and turned to the chief disciple, saying in a thick emotional voice, "Please, allow me to apprise the lama myself, Chief Disciple."

Surprised, the chief disciple nodded.

Jadelma turned to the lama and respectfully submitted, "Lama, he is my Tompo. He possesses great devotion for dharma but lacks intelligence. He was with Lama Zangchak in Tsokar. Unfortunately, he had to leave because his inability to grasp even a fundamental teaching angered the lama."

"Lama Zangchak has a fierce temper," acknowledged Lama Jamsempa in a gentle voice. "But he is a great scholar and teacher. We studied together under the same lama. We were two different people—he was fiery and hot-tempered, and I was soft and tolerant—but we got along well. We are still close; we write to each other regularly."

Surprised and alarmed, Tompo quickly said, "The lama tried his best to teach me, but I was useless. I could not understand anything. Any lama could have become angry."

"If you are not bright enough to study text, you should chant the guru mantra. Not only will you gain merit, but it will also create a favourable karmic condition for you to pursue the path of dharma in your next life. And if your devotion is as strong as she says, you may even attain enlightenment in this life."

"Lama, please let him study," Jadelma said, folding her hands in a plea. "I am not undermining the merit of chanting the guru mantra, but Tompo wants to study. He will work hard, Lama. I can promise you that."

The man looked at Tompo's eager face. "He can sit in the foundation group."

"Lama, the foundation group must be ahead of him," replied Jadelma. "Even if it is not, he will not be able to keep up with them. Lama, please teach him separately. I beseech you on his behalf."

The lama bestowed her with a kind smile. "I will see."

Jadelma was about to insist, but this time the chief disciple looked at her with a stern expression, causing her to stop and bow reluctantly to the lama. Then, without even letting Tompo prostrate to the lama, the chief disciple ushered them out of the room and out of the building.

"I am sorry, Chief Disciple," apologised Jadelma.

The chief disciple nodded tersely and led them around the monastery building and through a large spread of lawn to the monks' quarters, located at the end of the campus. This was a long rectangular building, much like the one in the monastery of Lama Zangchak, but unattached to the kitchen.

The area was quiet and deserted, with no one in sight, much like the rest of the campus, and Tompo and Jadelma wondered where the monks were, as they did not see them in the monastery building either.

They wanted to ask the chief disciple, but the man was still acting annoyed and surly, and although he seemed to be aware of their thoughts and the questions they wanted to ask, he did not offer to tell them anything.

In fact, he did not say a word to them but simply pushed open the door and walked in. Tompo and Jadelma followed him inside and found the quarters well arranged and orderly, with the floor shining brightly in the sunbeams coming in through the door.

The chief disciple saw them impressed with the quarters, and his face softened. "You can choose whichever spot you like," he said then, pointing to the empty spaces between the bedrolls that were neatly rolled up along the walls.

"Thank you, Chief Disciple." Tompo bowed.

The chief disciple nodded and turned to leave, then stopped. "The monks have gone to the forest to gather firewood. If you go out, please pull the door shut; there are stray dogs wandering around."

"I will do that, Chief Disciple," said Tompo, bowing again.

The man nodded and walked out.

Then, Tompo and Jadelma, alone on their own, became aware of their impending separation. However, unable to speak about it right away, they looked around the room, giving a cursory glance at everything, without paying attention to anything in particular.

"All right then," said Jadelma finally, trying to sound normal, but her voice coming out wobbly. "You have everything you need in the kowgum. I even bought two new red robes from the five sisters."

"Thank you, Jadelma," Tompo replied, his voice trembling slightly. "I will walk you to the gate," he offered.

Jadelma nodded, trying to maintain her composure.

Tompo dropped his kowgum and shoulder bag in one corner, and they walked out of the room, being sure to pull the door closed behind them.

They traversed the lawn, passed the monastery, and continued through the large courtyard. No words were spoken, as they were both lost in their own thoughts, until they stopped at the gate, turning and facing each other.

"You need not worry about me, Tompo," said Jadelma, emotions rising in her voice. "Aum Zam will help with the work and the baby. You just focus on your studies. I will come to visit you with the baby when I am well and strong. This could be some weeks after the delivery."

Tompo could only nod, his teeth clenched.

As if unable to bear this any longer, Jadelma patted Tompo's shoulder several times and then walked away.

Tompo stared after her, fighting to keep his emotions under control and expecting her to stop and say something.

But Jadelma walked on without looking back once, and she soon disappeared in the foliage surrounding the campus.

Tompo rushed to the edge of the hill and looked down. By then, Jadelma was already far below, walking past a group of monks, all of them staring at her.

"She looks like a princess from a heavenly realm," said one monk who, judging by his facial expression, appeared to be an eccentric individual, when Jadelma was out of earshot. "I believe she truly bears the mark of a dakini. I have never seen anyone so beautiful and celestial."

Surprised, Tompo wiped away the tears and redirected his gaze downwards attentively. Two mischievous-looking monks, one fair and lanky and the other swarthy and weighty, exchanged grins. Then, as if pretending to be deeply religious, they both turned and faced the eccentric monk.

"Yes, I think so too," nodded the fair and lanky one. "I have also not seen anyone as celestial as her. I hear she has her mark on the most sacred of places on her body. That is the sign of a true dakini."

"Where could that be?" asked the eccentric monk, his mouth wide open.

"Below her navel," answered the swarthy one.

Ptooey! The eccentric monk spat at the two, glaring fiercely, as everyone burst into hysterical laughter. "The likes of the two of you will disrespect even the bodhisattvas and the buddhas!" He swore, spat again, and then marched away.

"Carrying a bastard in her womb, and married to a homeless wandering runaway monk, she surely must have a dakini mark," said one monk, his face marked with cynicism. He, too, then left the group, following after the eccentric monk up the hill.

The others also walked on, laughing and teasing each other.

But Tompo could only stare at them, feeling lost and confused. He took a deep breath, released it slowly, and then hurried in the direction of his new quarters, trying not to think about the vulgarities he had just heard.

CHAPTER 37

Tompo bedded next to the eccentric monk who took an instant liking to him, as if they were kindred spirits. In truth, the monk really was much like him, friendly and accommodating and good at heart. And like Tompo, he too had an unusual name, Pentsa.

What they did not share was their heritage: Pentsa, unlike Tompo, came from a landed family, and despite being regarded as eccentric, he was surprisingly good in dharma study. He was also short-tempered, a volatile man who could be aggressive, flaring up when he was teased.

Yet no matter how fiercely his anger flared up, the two mischievous monks—of whom the fair and lanky one was Thogarp and the swarthy and weighty was Nagpo—teased him endlessly.

Known as the unlikely pair due to differences in their features, they were always together, often engaged in some mischief or another, but since Tompo's arrival, they had begun to shift their attention to him, mostly teasing about Jadelma and her dakini sign.

However, no matter who the two monks were teasing, whether it was Pentsa or Tompo, Pentsa would fiercely defend—glaring, swearing, cursing and even spitting. He would not allow even one slight to go unanswered.

"I apologise about Thogarp and Nagpo," Pentsa said one time, after he fought off the two monks. "They are like that by nature. They have nothing good to say about anyone or anything. If they were not in the monastery, they would probably be sitting in the village centre, teasing everyone passing through there."

"That doesn't matter, Pentsa," Tompo replied, pacifying his friend.

"It does matter, Tompo," Pentsa countered. "Teasing us is one thing, but making fun of your wife's dakini sign, whether she has it or not, is sacrilegious. The term *dakini sign* itself is sacred, not something to be mentioned lightly. And definitely not to be made fun of. They are so inappropriate."

Tompo was uncertain what to say.

"I am sure they don't know her story," Pentsa continued, "but are merely parroting what that landlord's wife and her friends are saying. Nagpo is distantly related to the landlord's wife, and Thogarp is the landlord's beneficiary, receiving everything from innerwear to outerwear."

Tompo was surprised to know of the monks' connection to the infamous landlord and his wife.

"They were gossiping about your wife even before you came to the monastery, or for that matter, before you came to this depraved village. So, the teasing has nothing to do with you but everything to do with the landlord's wife and her friends, who have the whole village in their rumour bag."

Tompo remained silent, again unsure how to respond.

"But whatever they may say, those who believe will believe. That does not go for me: nothing they say will influence me. Even the chief disciple can say all he wants, but I will not be swayed."

"The chief disciple?" Tompo's eyes widened in surprise.

"Yes." Pentsa lowered his voice and looked around to see if anyone was listening. "When I asked him about your wife's dakini sign, he didn't even let me finish speaking, but straightaway trashed it as rubbish, not worthy for discussion. He might be more learned than I, but he is wrong here."

"No, Pentsa, he is right," replied Tompo. "Jadelma didn't tell me anything about it. I think this is a baseless rumour started by the landlord's wife and her friends as a way to insult and embarrass her."

"She might not have told you because everyone was making fun of it, or perhaps out of her humility," Pentsa persisted. "She seems to be modest, even about her beauty. You tell me, Tompo, what woman in this day and age would not feel pride in possessing such celestial beauty?"

Tompo was not happy with the direction this was taking. Yet, he could not bring himself to say it to his new friend.

"It is also likely that your wife doesn't know if she has a dakini sign. The head nun who raised her might not have told her, for some reason, or perhaps didn't know about it herself. But look at your wife: she is like a dakini, even in her nature and essence, a true form of enlightened energy!"

"Yes, she is, but—"

"Also," said Pentsa, cutting him off, "look at the story of her birth. Her mother was an orphan nun who swore on her deathbed she had never been with a man. Why would she lie and hide the father of her child when she was dying? Don't you think she would have felt pity for her child and revealed the father? That is, if she had actually been with a man and had not conceived the child so mysteriously."

"I don't know, Pentsa," said Tompo, struggling to understand how to interpret this situation, let alone how to respond. "She didn't tell me anything about it, and I don't know what to make of it. However, I am not saying that you are wrong. Maybe she doesn't know it herself, like you say, or is not prepared to reveal what she knows. But whatever it is, you are a good monk, Pentsa, and you believe that something sacred does exist."

"Thank you, Tompo, and I hope you don't mind my speaking like this. If it were someone else, I would not have said it, but you are a good person and a good monk, deserving of someone like her to help you on the path of dharma."

A darkness fell over Tompo's face. "I am not a good person, much less a good monk, and I am not deserving of her, but she is helping me. I am here only because of her. I told you about my stay at Lama Zangchak's monastery, and how I fled and came to Kisathang. My wife took me in, she gave me a home, and now she has sent me on the path of dharma again. But to be honest, Pentsa, I don't know what to make of all this."

"All you need to do is believe it, Tompo."

"No, I am talking about my life and my pursuit of the path of dharma," Tompo corrected. "I can't make any sense of it. To be frank, I was too preoccupied by all that had happened to give any thought to other things. And that includes Jadelma's dakini mark. It has been too much, and far beyond my comprehension."

"Oh, my friend," lamented Pentsa, now realising Tompo's state of mind. But before he could respond further, Tompo was speaking again.

"I had thought the path of dharma was closed to me forever. I had even abandoned the idea fully and wholeheartedly accepted my new life with Jadelma. Then, out of nowhere, she gave me another opportunity to pursue the path. Is this my destiny unfurling, or my unexhausted negative karma dragging me back to the world of suffering and pain? I wish I knew."

"Forgive me, my friend," said Pentsa. "I didn't know what you were going through, and so I blabbered about what was on my mind. I should have known better than to pester you, but I have a one-track mind. I cannot think beyond my present thoughts."

"That is all right, Pentsa." Tompo nodded, yet his thoughts raced on. He could not help but wonder if the situation would be the same here, or if it would be different with Lama Jamsempa.

Unsure of what the future held for him, Tompo became anxious, restless and impatient. He thought that the only way to gain clarity was to attend class. Perhaps then he would discover what path his life was destined to take.

CHAPTER 38

Tompo walked through the dimly lit corridor and entered the study room, clutching the *Chonjük* text, nervousness gripping him. Wondering how the class would unfold and uncertain of what his true path might be, he felt a mix of excitement and anxiety.

Lama Jamsempa sat on a throne with a shade of uneasiness clouding his face, as though he might be questioning his decision to instruct Tompo individually and pondering the value of such a time-consuming, one-on-one teaching.

His nerves gripped him tighter, and the weight of trepidation hung in the air, as Tompo settled onto a seat, preparing to face the unfolding of another pivotal moment in his journey on the path of dharma.

"You will study the *Jangchub Sempe Chopa la Jukpa* only," the lama declared with a ring of sternness in his voice. "This is an important Mahayana text taught to all monks everywhere." When Tompo nodded meekly in response, he continued, "You must also continue to practise your vows, as they form the foundation of all dharma practices."

"Yes, Lama," Tompo replied.

Lama Jamsempa commenced teaching then, but no matter how he phrased each sentence, Tompo could not grasp anything . . . as he had dreaded. Nevertheless, concentrating as hard as he could, he followed the teaching, word after word, and line after line.

The lama went on from the first verse to the second, and then to the third, and on and on, all the time asking question after question, urging and pressing Tompo to think hard, to grasp the referenced and out-of-the-text meaning, and to keep track of the throughline of this meaning from one verse to the next.

Tompo put all his effort into comprehending until the muscles in his shoulders ached, the nerves along his neck emitted painful jolts, and his hands nearly bled from his fingers being clenched into fists. However, nothing got into his head, as if his mind were a blank sheet determined to remain blank.

After a while, the rhythm and flow of Lama Jamsempa's teaching began to falter, his expression growing grimmer, until he finally stopped. "There is no point in continuing if you cannot grasp anything," he said. "It seems the harder you try, the more confused you become. From today onwards, we will just do one verse in one day. It may take many months, or even years, to complete just one chapter, but I see no other choice."

Tompo felt shame flood his face. "Thank you, Lama," was all he could say.

"But if you don't make any progress after that, we will have to stop teaching altogether, as it will not only be a waste of time and resources, but also improper. For those who cannot learn the texts must recite prayers and chant mantras."

Tompo felt sweat on his brow, a few beads already running onto his cheek. "Yes, Lama," he muttered.

"All right then," said the lama, giving Tompo a dismissive wave.

Tompo nodded with a bow, stood up and left, his heart heavy and his spirits perhaps the lowest they had ever been. Lost in his sadness and sense of failure, he didn't see Pentsa sitting on the bed when he entered the quarters.

"What happened, Tompo?" Pentsa asked, looking concerned.

Tompo sat on his bed. "I knew there was no hope, but still I hoped that my lesson would magically turn out differently. Well, it didn't. In fact, the lama's emphasis on meanings outside the text is even more difficult. When I cannot understand what is written in the text, how can I grasp what is meant *outside* the text?"

Pentsa shook his head, clearly stumped.

"Being here is a waste of Jadelma's resources and the lama's time. But, what good can I do, an unfortunate person with unpurged negative karma? My very existence is a burden to everyone, but I can't even end it. I'm that useless and hopeless."

There was both concern and alarm in Pentsa's face. "End it? What do you mean?" he asked. "I know you have been through a lot, but you should not think like that. The study of dharma is difficult for everyone, not only you. If it were that easy, everyone would excel and become enlightened in no time. Sadly, that is not the case. The path of dharma is difficult, which is why few people pursue it."

Tompo buried his face in his hands. "That is exactly what is wrong with me, Pentsa. I don't have the intelligence required to study dharma. I am a dimwit who should not be among those pursuing this path. But here I am. So, you see that my case is different; I am not meant to be here." He turned to face Pentsa and repeated, "But, here I am."

Pentsa remained silent.

"I don't understand why this is happening to me," said Tompo. "I don't have any intelligence for studying dharma, yet I have such a strong yearning for it. These two contradictory aspects are tormenting me and destroying my life. Not having any intelligence is all right; it is my bad karma. But why do I have this strong yearning for it? To make me suffer?"

"Whatever it might be," said Pentsa, emphatically, "you must not worry so much."

They heard the floorboards creaking from the doorway, announcing someone's entrance into the room. Then, a familiar voice, intoning the declaration of a prophecy to a saint in a vision, said, "Oh, glorious Tompo." They turned and saw Nagpo. "Why do you even need to study dharma when you have such a beautiful heavenly-being-like wife with a mark of dakini?" he continued, the sarcasm in his words matching the smirk on his face.

"Yes, do hear us, great saint," added Thogarp, stepping into the room, "our renowned Tompo of Tsokar of Aeling." He raised his hands in the air. "The path to enlightenment lies in her alone. If you still cannot find it, you must seek your new good friend, Pentsa, for he knows all about it."

Pentsa went livid with rage. He turned and glared at Thogarp and Nagpo, as everyone in the room burst into laughter.

However, Tompo just ignored them. Nevertheless, the mention of his wife by Thogarp and Nagpo brought memories of Jadelma to the forefront of his mind. *She will deliver the child any time now*, he thought. *I wonder if it will be a boy or a girl.*

These thoughts about her filled him with a sense of longing, and he earnestly hoped that she would come to meet him soon, as she had said she would. Yet, he knew that Aum Zam would strongly object to Jadelma's plan to visit him, and would do everything possible to stop her from coming.

Aum Zam must be pleased that I have left the house, even though it was only to study, he thought ruefully. *The woman doesn't like me one bit and desperately wants me gone from Jadelma's life for good. But then, she is merely protecting Jadelma*, he reasoned.

Thus, he did not mind her interference in their relationship. Instead, he felt grateful for her constant support for Jadelma, and sincerely prayed that she accrued no negative karma for thinking ill of him.

Chapter 39

Through the endless rumours and gossip spread by villagers and monks alike, Tompo heard that Jadelma had given birth to a beautiful baby girl, and that she resembled her father, Landlord Mikar Drol.

Tompo had not seen the infamous landlord in person, and he did not care whether the baby resembled the father, but he was relieved that Jadelma had delivered the baby safely.

He looked forward to Jadelma regaining her strength and bringing the baby for a visit. That thought brightened his mood, filling him with joy and happiness for the first time in a very long time.

But she did not come.

Days turned into weeks, and weeks into months.

Then, Tompo knew that she was not going to come, but not for any other reason than to avoid disturbing him in his monastic life and to spare them both from experiencing a painful parting like the last one.

Amidst these thoughts, the idea of going home and paying her a short visit crossed his mind. However, he quickly dismissed it, realising that this would only burden her with work and expenses, and also displease Aum Zam.

Consequently, diverting his mind from the thought of seeing her, he plunged headlong into his studies, but still unable to make any progress, he fell into a state of depression, misery, hopelessness, and sorrow.

And it was while in this dire state that he remembered once again, after so many years, what his father had said about merit and became certain that he did not have enough merit to pursue the path of dharma and learn something, no matter how much effort he put in, or how anyone tried to teach him.

"Maybe I should just quit and go home," he muttered to himself one morning, as he came out of the monastery and walked down the stone stairs. He was about to continue this inner conversation when he noticed Aum Zam at the gate. She was handing a large shoulder bag to a little monk boy.

His face brightening with joy, he hurried down the flight of stone stairs, calling her name. But Aum Zam feigned not to hear him, exchanged some words with the monk boy, and hastened away.

Utterly disheartened, Tompo stopped halfway through the courtyard and stared after her. Even though Aum Zam detested him, he had desperately wanted to talk to her.

Taken aback by what had just happened, the little monk boy handed the bag to Tompo. "The woman said to give it to you," he said, his voice faltering.

"What else did she say?" Tompo asked, hoping to glean some information.

"She mentioned," the boy faltered again, "that there are roasted rice puffs, clarified butter, dried beef, and packed lunch in here."

"Anything else?" Tompo pressed.

"No," the boy said, shaking his head.

"She didn't even say who it was from?"

The boy shook his head again.

Tompo took the bag and walked away, thinking Aum Zam had intentionally avoided divulging any information about

Jadelma to make him disheartened, discouraged, and ultimately inclined to go away from Jadelma's life for good.

The thought made him even more depressed and miserable, yet he insisted on telling himself that she was only doing it for Jadelma's good. He also consoled himself that Jadelma herself cared for him truly, as evident from the parcel.

To add to this positivity, he dreamt of Jadelma that night. She said that she could not come to see him, as she had been ill for months, and that it was better if she did not come, as her visit would not only disturb his studies but also make their parting even more difficult than the last time, as he had thought.

Even though it was a dream, it gave him the joy and the strength to go on and not give up on the path of dharma. Thus, he mustered even greater devotion, prayed more fervently, and studied harder. However, despite his continuing efforts, he could not make any progress.

CHAPTER 40

Lama Jamsempa grew increasingly intolerant of Tompo's inability to grasp and retain even the most basic thing over time, until one day he suddenly stopped halfway through a verse in frustration, declaring that he could not continue.

Tompo turned grave, tears forming in his eyes.

"What am I supposed to do?" The lama's hands went in the air in exasperation, responding to Tompo's tears. Then, he softened almost immediately, his head shaking gently, and stood in silence for a while. "In all fairness to your devotion," he finally said, "I will teach you until the end of this chapter, Tompo." He paused, unsure what more to say. "Then I will see," he added vaguely.

Tompo was overcome with sudden relief and joy. He put his hands together into one. "Thank you, Lama. Even though I am an unfortunate person of great unpurged karma, I am fortunate to have met Lama. I will never forget Lama's kindness."

"Tompo, you must not think like that." Lama Jamsempa shook his head, expressing strong disapproval. "Your inability to grasp the teaching is due to your lack of intelligence. But, of course, that is because of your karma. But it does not necessarily mean that you are an unfortunate person of great unpurged karma. No one is like that."

"Yes, Lama, I understand."

"Do you?" the lama replied. "You have an astounding devotion, which is as important as understanding the dharma texts. If you chant the guru mantra or any other mantras with devotion, you will gain immense merit, or perhaps achieve enlightenment in this lifetime only."

"Lama is correct," said Tompo. "I not only lack the intelligence for dharma study, but my devotion is better suited for mantra chanting." He paused briefly. "Unfortunately, I also have a great and inexplicable yearning for dharma teaching, and this comes from deep within me, making me want to listen to dharma and understand it."

"Making you want to listen and understand?" asked the lama, his brow creased in surprise.

"Yes, Lama. Even if I don't understand, I want to listen to the dharma teaching, because just hearing the words of Buddha's dharma gives me great joy. But there are times when I also feel deeply sorrowful."

"You are one of a unique kind, Tompo," Lama Jamsempa said slowly, his head bobbing in disbelief. "I have heard countless stories of devotion for dharma, some feeling great devotion for dharma and those not feeling anything at all, but I have not heard anything like yours."

"Yes, Lama," Tompo replied. "My case is different. I believe it is my unexhausted bad karma meant to bring more suffering into my life. There is no other explanation; it simply doesn't make sense. I yearn for dharma teachings, but I lack the capacity to understand them."

The lama pondered over this for a moment. "I don't know, Tompo. In conventional dharma path, there is a blessing that purposely invokes obstacles. It goes something like this: *may you encounter appropriate obstacles*. So, you see, obstacles are not necessarily bad, but in your case—"

"Yes, Lama, mine is not an obstacle like that."

The lama nodded. "Yes, of course. Typically, obstacles to dharma are such things as falling ill, death, or other misfortunes in the family that prevent one from pursuing the path of dharma, but which can be overcome at an appropriate time. But yours? Your situation is different. How can you overcome your lack of intelligence? That is something unchangeable."

"You are right, Lama," said Tompo, sadness in his voice.

"But, of course," the lama continued, "your uncontrollable and irresistible yearning for dharma teaching could become controllable and resistible, or even go away completely. When that happens, you may even want to chant mantras and recite prayers."

"Lama, it is not that I don't want to chant mantras and recite prayers," replied Tompo, a wave of emotion overcoming him, prompting him to put his hands together. "In fact, I am ready to commit myself to chanting any mantra the lama commands for the rest of my life. I can start right now."

"Tompo, don't let your emotions take control of you," Lama Jamsempa said, raising his hand. "Remember that there is only a thin line between devotion and emotion. If you are not strong, rational, and objective, you could easily slip into an abyss of emotions."

"I am sorry, Lama."

"Remember that there is what we call *the skilful means* in the study and the practice of dharma. You should be skilful every step of the way. That is why I am telling you to recite prayers and chant mantras, because doing this will create good karma and open the path for you in this life or the next."

"I will do as you say, Lama."

Lama Jamsempa nodded his head meekly and then said, "We will leave it here for today."

"Thank you, Lama." Tompo quickly wrapped his text, stood up, and departed, leaving Lama Jamsempa staring after him with a concerned look.

As he turned away from the door and walked through the hallway, he heard the lama sigh heavily and mutter something. But he could only make out the word *dimwit.* The other words were unintelligible.

CHAPTER 41

With their thoughts swaying between the resolve to go on and the temptation to stop right then and there, Tompo and Lama Jamsempa stayed the course, covering verse by verse. Whenever the lama became overtly frustrated by what felt like a waste of time and resources, he pushed Tompo even harder, sometimes to the point of despair.

In these moments, Tompo accepted his fate, a pitiful expression on his face, and agreed to retire, where he would recite prayers and chant mantras. This, in turn, evoked some sympathy in the lama, and he continued to teach, telling himself that they would at least complete the first chapter, as he had said earlier.

But every class was a challenge, always with an unsatisfying end, and the man's patience was wearing thinner with each failed verse. Nevertheless, he dragged on with every bit of patience he had and every ounce of energy he could muster, and one morning, they finally completed the chapter.

Then, locking eyes with Tompo, he said, "Whether you understood or not, this brings us to the end of the chapter, Tompo." A subtle hint of relief graced his expression. "I will decide if we should continue to the next chapter or not, based on how much you have understood."

"Yes, Lama," Tompo replied, his face falling.

"This is because, if you have not understood anything, there is no point in going forward. It will be not only a waste of time and resources, but also bad for both of us. This is dharma, Tompo, not some worldly day-to-day activity that can be done as we please. With dharma, there are set protocols, traditions to be followed."

"You are right, Lama," Tompo replied, unable to argue the point.

"You say that hearing the words of dharma gives you joy, even if you don't understand them. Well, I suppose this is good, but it is not enough for Buddha's dharma, because it is not only meant for hearing, but also for understanding, analysing and, of course, practising."

Tompo nodded, a sick feeling running through him.

"To see if you have understood anything, I will ask you two questions. If you get one of them correct, even partially, then you have proven that you have understood and retained at least something. This will be good enough for us to go to the next chapter. But if you get both the answers wrong, with no right parts, then we will stop it here. You may then chant the mantras and recite the prayers of your choice. This is a fair way to decide, Tompo, for both you and me."

"I understand, Lama."

"All right then, here is your first question: when bodhisattvas suffer greatly, they don't generate negativity but increase their virtues. Why? Why does the bodhisattvas' suffering generate no negativity but increase their virtues? Did you get it? Write it down."

"Yes, Lama," answered Tompo, writing furiously.

"And here is the second question: how do bodhisattvas come into being? Did you understand? How are bodhisattvas born? Write it down. You can't discuss these questions with anyone. You have to find the answers on your own. Read the chapter, remember the teaching, and refer to your notes, but you cannot discuss it with anyone. Understood?"

"Yes, Lama, thank you."

"Well, then, that is it," Lama Jamsempa said, concluding the class.

Tompo nodded with a bow, stood up, and left, trying to hide his pain-marked face from the lama.

Lama Jamsempa stared after his pupil, feeling guilty for putting him through such an unpleasant ordeal. *But what choice do I have?* he thought, raising his hands in the air. *There is nothing I or, for that matter, any other lama, can do about it.*

CHAPTER 42

Tompo read the first chapter, word by word, line by line, and verse by verse, remembering everything that Lama Zangchak and Lama Jamsempa had taught him that entire afternoon, but he could not find the answer, not even a part, to either of the questions.

Becoming frustrated and angry, he raved and ranted, chiding and cursing himself for his stupidity. However, giving a free rein to his emotions only made everything worse for him, as he became more worked up and impassioned.

Soon, the sun went down behind the mountains, and daylight faded into whitened lavender dusk, making him frantic and restless. As the daylight dimmed further, and its soft hue thickened into a darker shade of oncoming evening, he became more agitated and uneasy. It seemed the darker the sky, the more disheartened he felt.

So, he finally gave up on finding the answers. Accepting his fate, he decided with a heavy heart to recite the prayers and chant the mantras that the lama would command. As there was no way he could ever overcome his lack of intelligence and study dharma, the best he could hope for was that the merit he accrued from reciting the prayers and chanting the mantras would eventually destroy his yearning for dharma.

He sat on his bed, nursing his sadness, too upset to even consider dinner, when Pentsa came back from his outing to the village

"What happened, Tompo?" Pentsa asked, concerned.

"The chapter ended this morning."

"Oh." Pentsa's face fell further.

"The lama has given me two questions to assess my understanding. I only have to get one of them partially right. Unfortunately, I don't have the slightest clue as to what the answers are."

Pentsa opened his mouth to say something, but nothing would come out.

"This is the end of the dharma teaching for me." He paused for a moment, tasting those words on his tongue. "I guess it is better in a way. Now, I can forget dharma teaching for good and concentrate instead on chanting the mantras."

Pentsa thought about this for a moment. "Maybe the lama said that only to make you study harder, or to get you so angry that you would put everything into learning. He will not stop teaching, not just like that. You do know, don't you, that deep down he is a sympathetic and kindhearted person? I am sure he will reconsider his position."

"No, Pentsa, he is serious about this, I am sure."

Just then, they heard the sound of someone running across the courtyard in the direction of the monks' quarters. Tompo and Pentsa looked at each other, as voices suddenly rose, permeated with urgency. The commotion outside got closer, and then the door was flung open and a young monk raced in, heaving and panting.

Before they could question him, the young monk announced, "The lama has fallen ill. He cannot move! Come to the residence immediately! Only Ani Pema and the chief disciple are there!" With that, he ran out, leaving Tompo and Pentsa standing there stunned.

In seconds, Tompo and Pentsa were running after the young monk, following him at full speed across the campus and straight into Lama Jamsempa's residence. There was a gathering of monks at the door. Tompo and Pentsa pushed their way through and saw Ani Pema and the chief disciple standing over the lama.

"Move this side, Lama," Ani Pema said, her voice heard through the growing number of monks pressed together at the doorway.

"I can't," came the lama's reply.

Tompo and Pentsa pushed farther through the crowd and came to the fore. The lama was on the raised seat and Ani Pema and the chief disciple were trying to help him move parts of his body.

"Then see if you can move this side," she told him, touching his arm.

There was a strain on the lama's face as he struggled to comply, and then a look of defeat. "I can't move this side either."

Thogarp and Nagpo entered, heaving and panting from having run across the campus. They pushed through, shoved Tompo and Pentsa aside, and stood in the front, just as Ani Pema turned and faced the monks.

"I don't know what it is," she said, her expression turning grimmer as she spoke, "but our lama seems to be seriously ill. Someone will have to go and fetch the physician quickly. If we wait until tomorrow, it may be too late."

"Nagpo and I will go, Ani," offered Thogarp.

"Yes, Ani, we will go," agreed Nagpo.

"Thank you," she responded. "If he is not at home, go look for him, wherever he may be."

Thogarp and Nagpo turned and raced out.

Ani Pema shifted her gaze to the assembly of monks. "I don't know what this is," she uttered, her voice hushed and filled with worry. "It just happened without any warning. The lama was quite normal, eating and drinking, and all of a sudden he could not move his right arm and leg. It is very strange."

The monks, one by one, inched closer to the lama. They studied his face, his extremities, and seemed as confused as Ani Pema.

But Tompo remained where he was, unable to either grasp or accept how the lama could fall gravely ill like that, unable to move his body.

The village physician, residing just down the valley, arrived in a hurry, entering the room with a sense of urgency. To everyone's relief, he conducted a thorough examination of the lama, and to everyone's surprise and elation declared that there was nothing wrong with him. Then, giving some medicine and assuring the lama would soon recover, he left.

Only then did Tompo move from the spot, wanting to see the lama and talk to the ani.

CHAPTER 43

Lama Jamsempa's condition did not improve the following day or the next. Instead, his illness gradually worsened, with his right hand and leg remaining partially paralysed, despite the constant attention from the village's physicians and healers.

This alarmed everyone in the monastery and in the village, and so all monastic activities were suspended, and everyone's focus and attention were directed towards nursing the lama back to health.

Ani Pema, fearing that the local physicians and healers might be missing something, sent for physicians and healers from neighbouring villages, but even they could not reverse the lama's condition.

In fact, it began to deteriorate even further, so she sent for famous physicians and healers from the far-off places. Unfortunately, nothing could stop his condition from worsening, and soon his arms and legs were fully paralysed.

All joy and happiness disappeared from the monastery, and everyone fell into a state of gloom and grief.

As there was no teaching, soon the majority of monks went home on leave and never came back. Thus, the monastery, once so vital and an important part of the village, became deserted. This desolation stirred fears not only about the future of the monks, but also the future of the monastery.

However, some monks refused to leave, preferring to remain with their lama and the ani, hoisting prayer flags, performing rituals, chanting mantras, reciting prayers, and helping in every way possible.

Among them were Tompo and Pentsa, Thogarp and Nagpo, four devotees of the lama who became handy with all the work and stayed in the lama's residence from early morning to late evening.

One afternoon, Thogarp and Nagpo, along with Tompo and Pentsa, were seated on one side of the living room, awaiting the moment when they would be needed. Suddenly, Ani Pema hurried out of the lama's chamber, causing Thogarp and Nagpo to scramble quickly to their feet.

"The lama had a loose motion and soiled his bed," she informed them. "It must be because of that new medicine sent by the physician from Ta Zarong. He had warned about it causing loose motion, but I forgot . . . until now."

Thogarp and Nagpo, their heads turning away in revulsion, fell back into their seats instantly. Observing their reaction, Ani Pema was both surprised and dismayed, but before she could react, Tompo, without the slightest hesitation, and with genuine love and care, stood and came over to her.

"I will clean it, Ani," Tompo said.

"No, no, Tompo," she said, horrified at the thought of him cleaning the soiled lama.

"It is all right, Ani," Tompo reassured, waving away her concerns. "You please, take a rest. You didn't have any proper sleep. If you go on like this, you will become sick as well." Tompo gently took her hands and led her to a seat. "I will go and get water."

Ani Pema, surprised and touched, stared after Tompo as he hurried out.

Just then, the strong odour of the loose motion wafted into the room, and Thogarp and Nagpo instantly turned their heads away from the smell and shielded their noses in discomfort.

"What to do now?" murmured Ani Pema, dismayed about the situation, looking at Thogarp and Nagpo. "The odour is strong and permeating everything. Why don't the two of you go out for a while until I finish cleaning?" She scrambled to stand.

Thogarp and Nagpo, suddenly feeling caught in the act, uncovered their noses and pretended not to be affected by the unpleasant odour. "No, Ani," they replied in unison, as if rehearsed. "It is not that strong."

Before the ani could respond, Tompo walked in with a large pot of water, seemingly impervious to the foul odour pervading the atmosphere. Without a change in his expression, he walked across the room and disappeared into the lama's chamber, leaving Ani Pema staring after him, her heart moved by his unconditional devotion.

Then, Ani Pema suddenly remembered how Lama Jamsempa complained to her about Tompo, saying how stupid he was, and the lama's words rushed into her mind. *Where on earth could he have come from, bearing a peculiar name like that? What could have brought him here, bringing so much negative karma to my monastery? And what could have set him on the path of dharma with no intelligence?*

After a while, spurred by her thought, she went into the lama's chamber and saw that Tompo had already cleaned him up, and the lama was staring at him with something like guilt . . . or perhaps embarrassment.

Standing in the doorway and seeing them like this, the ani felt a sharp pain slice through her heart, and then a tear formed in her eye. Unable to bear the sight any longer, she left the chamber and went into her bedroom.

She closed the door behind her, shutting off the world falling apart only a short distance away in the lama's chamber, put her face in her hands, and began to weep.

CHAPTER 44

A haggard, dishevelled, and gravely sick Lama Jamsempa sat on his bed, leaning on the wall, in the room that had become his bedroom since falling ill. Ani Pema and the chief disciple sat facing him, both wearing sombre expressions.

"I am sure, by now, the two of you know that I will not recover," Lama Jamsempa said, sharing his thoughts. "But, please, don't feel sad about it. This is my karma, and I must go through it. One who is born must die, whether today or tomorrow; there is no other way out. Even for the buddhas and the bodhisattvas."

"Lama must not think like that," pleaded Ani Pema. "This is a small obstacle on your path of dharma. You will not only recover and regain your full health, but you will also go on to live a long, healthy, and prosperous life. This is clearly mentioned in your horoscope, Lama."

"Yes, Ani, it is," agreed the lama. "But even the prophecies made by great saints are sometimes unable to be revealed, due to the severity of the obstacles. However, mine is only a small horoscope, one that was prepared at my birth by a village astrologer, so we should not set much store by it."

"Whatever it may be, Lama must not feel that way," said the chief disciple, putting his hands together as a supplication to the lama. "Even though it might be to a better place that Lama will be going, Lama must not think about leaving us and going so soon. For what would we do without Lama?"

"You must not lose hope and speak that way, Chief Disciple," the lama said, his voice slightly stern. "The ani is a woman, and the monks are young and inexperienced. You must stay strong and take charge of everything. My death is not in my hands or in yours, and there is nothing we can do to avert it. It is all karma. If my time has come, it has come."

"Yes, of course, Lama," said the chief disciple with a nod.

The lama tried to shift his position on the bed, but he was hardly able to move. "So, instead of pointlessly dwelling on my death and wasting the precious time that is left," he continued, "we must focus on the time after I am gone and ensuring that the monastery continues to flourish and doesn't go to ruin and decay. This monastery must not cease to exist, because I am not here."

The chief disciple nodded again, his face filled with emotion.

The lama looked first at the man and then at the ani, and back to the chief disciple. "I have been thinking. Even though you have completed your studies, you are not yet fully ready to teach. However, we need someone who will not only teach, but will also lead this monastery. This is a big responsibility, one that is not given lightly, but one that is thrust upon someone by destiny, as this is a monastery with a great lineage."

"You are right, Lama," the chief disciple replied.

"I have given a lot of thought to this, and I have come to a decision. I intend to write to Lama Zangchak and ask him to send us someone of that calibre, someone who can take over the monastery immediately, since he has a qualified chief attendant and a highly acclaimed heart-son who has been trained in the ways of a lineage-holder lama."

The chief disciple lowered his head, as if not wishing the lama to see his emotions. "Even at a time like this, instead of thinking of yourself, Lama has been thinking about us and the monastery. This is truly the *great one hundred good thoughts* that only the compassionate and magnanimous ones such as yourself can have. So, Lama need not have any misgivings about it: be assured that this will benefit all of us . . . not just now, but in the future as well."

"Thank you for thinking the same, Chief Disciple," said the lama.

"Thank you, Lama. Thank you for showing me the way to the right thought. All the monks and I are truly blessed to be your pupils. Even if Lama should not be here with us because of our lack of good merit, Lama's blessings will be always here to benefit us."

"My prayers will be always here for you, Chief Disciple, but this tragedy of mine may not be due to your lack of good merit. We should not attribute every bad thing happening to us to our bad karma. We don't know how karma manifests. We don't know what each incident in our lives, whether it is good or bad, is designed to achieve in the larger scheme of things."

There was a quiet in the room as three people, with a long history together, were absorbed in their private thoughts.

"We will draft the letter now," said the lama.

The lama's writing table was at its place, along with all the writing materials. The chief disciple pushed the lama's seat aside, sat squatting on the floor, and began to write as Lama Jamsempa dictated his message word by word. When the letter was completed, he pressed the lama's official seal onto it, folded it, and sealed it with wax.

CHAPTER 45

Lama Zangchak wore a grave expression as he looked up from the letter, his eyes moving first to Ani Choni and then to the chief attendant.

Seeing the look on his face, Ani Choni's face grew grim, and her hands went to her mouth, as if suppressing a cry.

"Lama Jamsempa's condition has deteriorated further," said Lama Zangchak. "Except for being able to talk, hear, see, and move his head, he is completely paralysed. And as nothing seems to help him, he has given up all hope of recovering. Therefore, according to this letter, he is requesting someone from here to teach and head the monastery."

"This is so distressing and painful, Lama," said Ani Choni. "Why does illness and death always strike the good people first? This is not fair, Lama." Unable to control her emotions, she broke into sobs. "Life is not fair."

"It is his karma, Ani," replied Lama Zangchak, his voice becoming heavier. "It is his karma ripening. We are all subject to karma. Again, it is not only his karma, but everyone's who is connected to him, one way or the other. For we exist in a web of karma."

"I know we are all responsible for what happens to us, Lama, but I sometimes feel karma is so cruel and unjust . . . and it is out there to punish anyone it doesn't like without reason. I feel that karma is not the result of our actions, but a scheme plotted by someone biased... up there." To emphasise her point, she pointed her finger upwards, her gaze following it.

"Yes, it does feel that way at times," agreed Lama Zangchak. He started to say more, but remained silent, allowing the ani to vent her emotions. "But as scheming and punishing as karma may seem, nothing undeserved happens to anyone in this world," he continued, picking up on his earlier point, when she had regained her composure. "From our birth to our death, everything happens according to our karma, according to what we do. Our actions determine everything, Ani."

Ani Choni nodded; she didn't say anything.

They all sat quietly for some time.

Then, Lama Zangchak took a long deep breath and turned towards the chief attendant with a purposeful gaze. "Lama Jamsempa has asked for someone exceptionally good, someone who can not only teach and head the monastery, but also become a lineage lama, and strengthen and propagate the lineage of our great Lama Thongsar." He glanced at the ani briefly and then at the chief attendant. "Someone of Kathog's calibre and capacity."

The chief attendant and Ani Choni nodded in agreement, but did not say anything in response.

"Since I made Kathog my heart-son," Lama Zangchak went on, "I should be sending you when such a request comes, Chief Attendant, but the destiny is decidedly that of Kathog: it is predestined for him."

"This is a matter of dharma that Lama knows better than all of us," replied the chief attendant, without any resentment. "So, I am all right with anything that Lama decides. For in the matter of dharma, nothing should fall short."

"Yes, Chief Attendant, nothing must fall short of anything in dharma. So, viewing it in that light, it is his destiny deciding,

Chief Attendant, not me. For like I said earlier, this is not Lama Jamsempa's karma alone that we are dealing with, but that of everyone who is connected to him."

"That is true, Lama. Kathog excelled beyond our expectations with dharma coming to him naturally and without much effort. And just as he completed his study, Lama Jamsempa made this thinly cloaked request, asking for him only. Everything fell into place for him. This is his destiny, Lama."

The ani saw a direct correlation between Lama Jamsempa's illness and Kathog's destiny and became convinced that everything happened for a reason as determined by the individuals' merit and demerit. Everything had a cause; nothing happened by chance. This caused her to nod her head decisively.

Lama Zangchak, observing her expression and reading her thoughts, stared at her triumphantly. "I made a big plan for Kathog, but he is destined for even bigger things," he said, raising his hands to stress his point. "To fill in Lama Jamsempa's place at such a young age is no small feat. His future is far beyond us, and we should not meddle with his destiny."

"Yes, Lama is absolutely right here," the chief attendant replied. "When destiny is on his side, who are we, unenlightened beings, to get in his way? Lama should not have any misgivings about it. Please send him. This is the fortune of dharma shining, not only on him but also on us and our monastery."

Lama Zangchak bobbed his head in relief and joy, and as he did so, the guilt and the awkwardness that had marred his face disappeared.

Announcing that it was a good tendrel, not only for Kathog but for all of them, he recited a quick aspiration prayer.

Chapter 46

Kathog could have completed his studies a few years earlier, but the lama dragged them out for some unknown reason. However, now that he had completed them, he was offered this rare opportunity that seemed to arise from nowhere, surpassing his wildest hopes and dreams.

At first, he could not believe his ears, and then he could not believe his good fortune. But the lama assured him that this was his destiny unfurling, and because he had been trained in the traditions of the lineage-holder lama, he was more than ready to fulfil his purpose.

After receiving the sacred scarf and the title of teacher from Lama Zangchak, Kathog departed for Kisathang astride a beautiful mare, leading a caravan of attendant monks, porters, and packhorses, and with the people of Tsokar lining along the way, their ceremonial scarves fluttering in the breeze.

It was a splendid fanfare, a heartfelt farewell, and a pompous entourage befitting his stature of a dharma prodigy en route to meet his destiny. But with the horrifying experience of his travel from Tamchu still fresh in his mind, he led his caravan with ease and comfort, halting one night on the way, and then timing their arrival at the monastery on the afternoon of the following day.

However, the news of his arrival had spread throughout Kisathang, and the people of the village were waiting to receive him along the way with welcome drinks and burning incense. Stopping to grace the receptions and interact with the people, the entourage got delayed, and they could not arrive at the monastery until sundown.

A small group of monks, led by the chief disciple, was waiting at the gate with tea and snacks to receive Kathog and his entourage.

"We apologise for not being able to arrange a formal reception for you, Teacher Kathog," submitted the chief disciple. "All of us have been engaged in a major rimdro for the lama for the last few days. Otherwise, we would have been able to arrange at least a modest reception."

"No, Chief Disciple, such a reception is not important, and considering the circumstances, not proper," Kathog responded. "How can we even think of having a reception when the lama is lying ill? Actually, even this small gathering was not necessary," he added, indicating the modest reception with a gesture.

"Yes, Teacher Kathog, we also thought likewise," agreed the chief disciple, "but the lama wanted a proper reception held, not only to welcome you, but also to create a good tendrel for your coming to our monastery."

"Yes," acknowledged Kathog, "a good tendrel is important for my arrival, but for the lama to even think of it while lying gravely ill is sheer magnanimity, capable of creating far better tendrel than any grand reception ever would. So, as someone who sets great store by good tendrel, I cannot help but feel fortunate to have come here."

The chief disciple nodded in agreement. "You are right: a good tendrel, in the end, is created by good energy, good intentions, and good thoughts. A ceremony is merely a ritual to evoke these virtues. I thank you for this valuable wisdom."

"And I thank you for everything, Chief Disciple," said Kathog.

The chief disciple nodded again. "Please come, Teacher Kathog." He ushered Kathog towards the path paved with cobblestones that took them alongside the building. "You must be exhausted and longing to take a rest. I will show you to your quarter."

Kathog and the chief disciple went ahead, with the others following behind. They crossed the large spread of green lawn, but halfway through, they turned towards the lama's residence on the hillside, walked past it, and reached a small wooden cabin at the far end of the campus.

Although the cabin appeared modest from outside, it was spacious and cosy inside, instantly making Kathog feel at home. He was also overcome with emotion at the thought of having a private home of his own, after living in the monks' quarters for so long. But more than anything, everything had been readied for him, much like at the Dungje mansion.

Feeling a unique sense of freedom and happiness, he washed up at his own pace and liking and then rested until the chief disciple returned to accompany him to see Lama Jamsempa. By then, night had fallen, and the moon shone brightly in the sky.

The chief disciple led him back the way they had come to the lama's residence, where he was greeted by Ani Pema and right away shown into the lama's chamber.

Lama Jamsempa was a dishevelled and sickly figure, sitting on his bed and leaning on the wall. However, Kathog's eyes were straightaway drawn to Tompo, a fatigued attendant monk crouching by the lama's bedside.

Kathog was surprised to see Tompo there. He had thought that he had seen the last of his bondservant, antithesis, and dharma colleague in Tsokar. Yet, there the man was, crossing his path once again, as if their destinies were intertwined.

Kathog was lost in his thoughts for a moment, and when he came around, everyone was staring at him. He quickly turned back to the lama and prepared to prostrate.

"No need to prostrate, Teacher Kathog," said Lama Jamsempa, his voice frail and sickly.

Kathog proceeded to prostrate nevertheless, and after this he offered a statue of Medicine Buddha, which the lama received with Tompo's help.

"I can't thank you enough for coming here, Teacher Kathog," Lama Jamsempa said as soon as Kathog had settled into a seat. His expression was a mix of admiration and gratitude, yet his voice was filled with emotion. "I have been sick for a long time, and my monks have wasted their precious time."

"Lama need not feel that way," Kathog replied, bowing his head in respect. "I am honoured to be here."

"I have heard many good things about you, Teacher Kathog. Lama Zangchak writes highly and fondly of you." Lama Jamsempa's eyes lit up, and his voice steadied, becoming warm and sincere. "My disciples are fortunate to have someone of such extraordinary calibre as you."

"Thank you for your kind words, Lama. I am fortunate to be given this sacred opportunity." Kathog lowered his head again, expressing his appreciation. "I have heard many great things about Lama and the monastery, and I am truly happy to be here. But I cannot describe the pain I feel seeing Lama in this condition."

"This is my karma, Teacher Kathog, and I must face it whether I like it or not, whether I accept it or not, and whether I agree with it or not. There is nothing that I can do to evade it, or to make it go away and leave me alone." Lama Jamsempa looked firm in his conviction, but at the same time resigned to his fate.

"I agree, Lama, there is no other way around karma. But as Lama has been beneficial to all sentient beings in this samsara in numerous ways, this could only be another way to do better for all sentient beings: *to selflessly suffer on behalf of all sentient beings.*

So, I am certain Lama will recover as soon as the greater good is accomplished."

"On the aspiration level, that is always there, Teacher Kathog, whether it materialises or not," replied the lama. "I am deeply grateful to you for presenting my situation in a positive light. For even I cling onto one small last hope. This is actually quite pitiable and pathetic, to hope when there are no grounds for it. But then, this is how we unenlightened beings are. We cannot accept the truth in front of us if it is not to our liking, but embrace a far-fetched lie if it suits our purpose."

"Lama must not think like that," Kathog replied. "For even if Lama's situation is not entirely a dharmic means of bodhisattva suffering, but rather a karmic result instead, Lama's condition is not that dire. People in far worse condition have recovered, so Lama must not lose hope and give rein to such negative thoughts."

Lama Jamsempa managed a nod before his face contorted in pain from a sudden muscle spasm.

Tompo climbed onto the bed to help the lama stretch his limbs and body, and then assisted him into a more comfortable position.

Kathog rose gracefully and offered a respectful bow to Lama Jamsempa, then acknowledged Tompo with a nod of his head, his expression once again transforming into one of surprise, and took his leave.

CHAPTER 47

Kathog commenced the regular classes within a week and resumed all other activities shortly thereafter. Even the monks who had gone home came back, and soon the monastery was as lively and jubilant as before, as if nothing had happened.

Kathog taught with great passion and gusto, unleashing his brilliance and enthralling and captivating the monks, which made him popular with everyone, not just in the monastery, but also in the village of Kisathang. The excitement around his presence aroused in Tompo an interest in the young man's teaching.

But Tompo had no opportunity to participate in any of the teachings, as he was attending to the lama day and night. Since none of the other monks would come and relieve him, not even for a short time, he was doing everything from nursing the unsightly bedsores to cleaning the soiled bed. But he did not mind at all. In fact, he was happy for the opportunity to serve his lama.

Late one afternoon, Tompo went outside to gather the herbs that had been dried. While he was at it, he wanted to take a walk and get some fresh air, leaving the ani to have time alone with the lama.

He walked past Kathog's quarter and saw him, through the window, teaching a group of monks with great enthusiasm.

Since the shoot is not other than the seed,
No obliteration of the seed occurs in the sprout.
Since they are also not one and the same,
The seed cannot persist within the sprout.

Tompo had seen and heard Kathog explain the shoot and the seed thing so many times, so although he didn't understand anything that was said, he knew that Kathog was teaching the *Uma la Jukpa* text. This was a text that fascinated him greatly, so he stopped and listened with ecstatic joy, as if he were hearing it for the first time, forgetting everything around him, until the ani's frantic voice called out for him.

First startled and then hit hard with a jolt of self-reproach, he ran back to the residence, grabbed a handful of herbs from the drying stand outside, and dashed straight into the house and the lama's chamber. His chest heaving from the exertion, he found the lama shrieking in pain and the ani pressing down on his stomach.

"Make the potion fast, Tompo!" she cried out. Flustered and sweating profusely, her hair matted in ugly sheaves, a panic-stricken Ani Pema glared fiercely at him. "The lama is having another attack of stomach pain!"

Tompo quickly put the herbs into a cup, poured in water, and stirred. The moment the potion frothed and turned greenish, he fed it to the lama, who was by now covered in sweat, his body writhing in pain.

As the medicine was absorbed into his system with its effect slowly reaching the intended areas, Lama Jamsempa began to relax.

Ani Pema stood up, using her sleeve to wipe the sweat from her brow.

Tompo, however, was so overcome by self-reproach that his face was almost grey.

Ani Pema looked at the young assistant. "It is all right now, Tompo," she assured him. "There is no need to feel bad, but you must not disappear like that without telling me." She looked closely into his face. "I thought you were outside and nearby, but there was no response when I called, no matter how much I shouted."

"It seemed a good time to stretch my legs and get some fresh air, when Ani was with the lama," replied Tompo, his face downcast. "But as I went past Teacher Kathog's quarter, I saw him teaching some monks, and I became lost in his words, as I listened at the window."

Ani Pema, quite baffled by the situation, shook her head and turned away to tend to something.

However, despite his pain, Lama Jamsempa was instantly reminded of Tompo's insatiable yearning for dharma teaching. He also recognised the young man's profound sense of guilt for having failed in his duty, driven by his unwavering devotion to the lama.

This evoked a strong emotional response deep within Lama Jamsempa. Recalling his treatment of Tompo, especially his thoughts of not teaching him, Lama Jamsempa pondered over what bad karma could have brought about this strange and cruel turn of events. A heavy sigh escaped him as his body shuddered, and a tear rolled down his cheek.

Ani Pema, who did not see the lama's reaction, shook her head again and mumbled something, but Tompo's attention was on the lama's face, and that little tear now streaming down his face. He was keenly aware of the pain in the lama's eyes, and he wondered what emotional suffering afflicted the lama. But this was the great lama, so he did not ask.

CHAPTER 48

Lama Jamsempa was suddenly awakened by footsteps outside his window. He heard their voices and knew they were two monks on their way to the prayer hall in the monastery building. He wondered if they had slept at Teacher Kathog's quarter, for this was not their regular path.

"Teacher Kathog is truly brilliant," remarked one monk, his voice unusually animated for so early in the morning, "and it is undoubtedly why people call him a dharma prodigy destined for great things. To be taught by a person of his stature makes us no less than any monk."

"Yes, it is said that dharma comes naturally to him," replied the second one. "I heard that he learnt the *Uma la Jukpa* text all by himself, and in just his second year. Then he began to teach everyone who had difficulty understanding it."

The first monk said something in response, but the lama could not make out the words, their voices fading in the distance. In the stillness of the early morning darkness, he listened to their departing footsteps and faint voices.

Soon, the darkness dissolved and daylight filled the room. Lama Jamsempa gazed across the room and saw that Tompo had fallen asleep, sitting on the floor and leaning against the wall. As he observed Tompo in such a vulnerable state, his heart ached, seeing the innocence in his face, and he could not help but recall how cruelly the events had unfolded between them.

Even though he knew very well how Tompo yearned to learn, he was about to stop teaching the young man without consideration, all because, unlike other monks, he was not bright enough to understand the teachings.

But when the lama fell ill, it was Tompo who had stood by his side, caring for him with utmost dedication, cleaning his ugly sores and soiled clothing without any reluctance. When no one else offered even a supporting hand to help him sit up, it was Tompo, and only Tompo, who provided unwavering support and care.

Tompo stirred a bit, interrupting Lama Jamsempa's thoughts, and then woke up with a start, realising he had slept past the lama's wake-up time. He quickly turned his head, looked at the lama, and saw the concern and emotion on his face.

"Did you know the answers, Tompo?" Lama Jamsempa asked.

Tompo was taken aback as much by the question as the way the lama looked at him, and it took one full moment for him to gather himself and realise that the lama was asking him about the two questions the lama had given him.

"No, Lama," he answered falteringly.

"I was not going to teach you if you didn't know the answers, as I told you," said the lama, his voice harsh, but directed not at Tompo for not knowing the answers, but at himself for having made such a bad decision not to teach him further. "I had decided strongly, and I was not going to change my mind."

"That was all right, Lama, I understood."

"Yes, of course you did, Tompo, but it doesn't matter anymore. You would not have gotten the teaching anyway, as I became sick. We are talking about this in hindsight, when the time for doing the right thing had gone past me, when I am useless and helpless, and when I can't do anything."

"Please, don't say that, Lama," Tompo implored, his eyes suddenly welling up with emotion.

"Tompo, I was wrong," the lama continued, his voice filled with remorse and pain. "But again, I guess it was our karma. I was not going to teach you further, treating you like you were not my disciple. But look now, it is you who are doing everything for me. Even my blood son or heart-son, should I happen to have one, would not have done as much."

"Please, don't harbour such thoughts, Lama," Tompo said earnestly, his voice filled with deep respect. "I am fortunate to have this opportunity to serve you. I don't know if this is our karma or not, but being by your side, my root teacher, is everything to me. I will treasure this as a true blessing, my Lama."

Lama Jamsempa bobbed his head a bit, as a way of nodding, but didn't respond. Instead, he lay there with a blank stare, making Tompo worry. After a while, his head slowly turned towards Tompo. "Please, come and help me, Tompo. I want to sit today."

Tompo was taken aback by this request, but he arose quickly and helped Lama Jamsempa to sit up, moving the man's body so he could lean against the wall.

Beads of sweat from this exertion appeared on the lama's face and neck, which Tompo immediately wiped away with a dampened cloth.

"Now, come here," said the lama, "and put your forehead against mine."

Tompo was surprised at this rare invitation, but again he said nothing, nor did he hesitate in any way, but instead stepped forward and slowly placed his forehead against the lama's forehead.

"I could not give you any teaching, Tompo, but you have my most sincere aspiration prayer for receiving the highest of the dharma teachings in this lifetime." Lama Jamsempa then closed his eyes and, while slipping into a deep concentration, mumbled a long prayer for Tompo.

When Lama Jamsempa finally ended his prayer and opened his eyes, Tompo moved his head away, deeply touched and feeling so devotional that he sobbed gently, bringing tears to Lama Jamsempa's eyes as well.

Later that morning, the sun paled and a shade of yellow turned the sky to a sickly and ominous hue. Lama Jamsempa's condition suddenly worsened, and towards the late afternoon, while seated cross-legged and leaning on the wall in a state of meditation, he peacefully passed away.

Ani Pema went down on the floor, sobbing profusely, but Tompo remained by the lama's bedside, the numbness of grief overtaking him.

CHAPTER 49

Since Ani Pema was too distraught with grief to assume any responsibility, everyone turned to Teacher Kathog to take charge of the affairs around Lama Jamsempa's death, even though he was only a young man, no older than some of the monks he taught.

But, as he was thoroughly trained as a lineage-holder lama, he promptly organised everything methodically and efficiently, and since Lama Jamsempa had been gravely ill for a long time, with his health deteriorating critically in recent times, no one other than Ani Pema and Tompo took his demise hard.

Thus, everyone at the monastery sprang into action right away, and soon the lama's residence was swarming with activity. But no matter what happened around him, Tompo would not come out of his shock, nor could he come to terms with the lama's death.

Unable to bear the overwhelming grief that felt like a weight crushing his chest, he went out and cried inconsolably in a quiet corner until his stomach and chest hurt. But nobody, not even Pentsa, came looking for him, as if he were no longer needed.

When Tompo finally returned to the house, it was late at night, and the monks were reciting prayers. He went into the lama's chamber, sat beside Ani Pema near the silk brocade enclosure that had been erected around the lama's body, and fervently prayed for the lama's swift rebirth in the Buddha realm of Dewachen Zhingkham.

The night wore on and morning came, but neither Tompo nor the ani moved. Without them noticing, day turned into night, and then night into day, and on it went, but still they did not move, except to go briefly to eat and to visit the outhouse.

This continued until the day before the cremation, when the silk brocade enclosure was dismantled to prepare the lama's body for the funeral rite.

By then, it was almost nearing the forty-ninth-day ritual, and everyone had been impatiently waiting for Lama Zangchak to come, not only to pay his last respects to his dharma friend, but also to preside over the cremation. But, owing to a sudden sickness, the lama could not make the journey.

Thus, it fell on Kathog to preside over the cremation that was attended by one and all from the village of Kisathang, except Jadelma. However, Tompo was too grief-stricken to notice who came and who did not, as he sat by the burning pyre and prayed.

Ani Pema was also too devastated to care about anything or anyone. She sat in one secluded area and prayed. Nothing and no one mattered to her anymore. The partner of her life, her revered and beloved dharma teacher, was gone. And with him, her joy in living.

CHAPTER 50

Immediately after the forty-ninth-day ritual, Ani Pema packed a few of her personal belongings in a kowgum and prepared to depart from the monastery. Before she left, she called Tompo to the late lama's chamber, and gave him a magnificent gold statue of Chenrezig.

"This is our late lama's treasured possession," she explained. "It is very old and sacred and was given to him by Tamar Rinpoche, the root teacher of his root teacher, Lama Thongsar. Our late lama regretted that he could not give you any teaching. He said that, in hindsight, if he should have wished for anything, it would have been for you to have received all his teachings, and perhaps even become his heart-son."

"But I could never have learnt anything, Ani," said Tompo.

"I know, Tompo, and so did the lama, but this was his wish."

Tompo felt both sadness and joy, knowing that the lama thought of him like this. "The lama need not have felt that way."

"Why not, Tompo? You offered him the most unconditional love, such dedication from a disciple to a lama. So yes, you deserved it, even if it was only the wishful thinking of a dying lama."

"Thank you, Ani, but you should keep the statue."

"No, Tompo, you deserve it more than I do."

"Ani, how can I possibly deserve it more than you?"

"This is not to be argued, Tompo. Keep it and always remember the lama."

Tompo held the statue, finding its surface comforting. Just then, they heard voices in the living room. Tompo and the ani left the lama's chamber and saw Kathog and the chief disciple walking towards them.

"Teacher Kathog and Chief Disciple," the ani said. "I have called the two of you here to inform you that I am leaving, and of course, to hand over the residence." Seeing a look of utter surprise on their faces, she quickly added, "I am going on a pilgrimage. I am sorry I didn't tell you before, but we were all so busy."

Kathog stood quietly, knowing it was not his place to speak, but the chief disciple's face told a different story. He appeared awkward and embarrassed, as if he might have failed in his duty. "With whom are you travelling, Ani?" he asked.

"I am going alone, Chief Disciple."

His face grew grimmer, showing both surprise and concern. "Which places do you intend to visit, Ani?"

"I don't know. I will travel and see where this takes me."

"But how can you get by on your own, Ani? I hope you don't intend to travel far."

She did not respond, as if intentionally holding back information about her pilgrimage.

The chief disciple's face changed suddenly, the realisation striking him. "Ani, are you intending never to return here?" He was almost in tears.

"Yes, Chief Disciple," Ani Pema nodded. "I intend to travel far, visit sacred sites and monasteries, receive blessings and teachings, offer butter lamps and incense, recite prayers and chant mantras, and do circumambulations and prostrations. So, no, I don't know if I will come back. Perhaps if I don't die during my journeys, I will come back to spend my last days here."

The chief disciple seemed unable to find words.

"You need not feel bad about it, Chief Disciple," she said. "I am leaving not out of sorrow, but with the realisation that this dreamlike life, in the end, has no substance. Fleeting and illusory, it is all meaningless and empty. This is why I want to spend the rest of my days on pilgrimage."

The man nodded. "Forgive me for not being much help to you, Ani."

"That is fine, Chief Disciple," the ani responded gently. Then, addressing Kathog, she continued. "Teacher Kathog, I leave everything here, including our personal possessions, to the monastery, to be dispensed as you see fit at your convenience. The lama's religious items may be put in the main shrine room."

"I will see to this, Ani," Kathog replied.

"Well, then," she said, looking around her. "If I don't die on my travels, and if I come back here someday, I hope to see all of you in good health." She then turned to Tompo, bent down and placed her forehead against his. "Tompo, you have my aspiration prayer that you receive the teachings that will liberate you in one lifetime and one body." She then closed her eyes and quickly mumbled a short aspiration prayer.

"Thank you, Ani," Tompo said, his voice barely above a whisper.

"If we don't meet again in this life, I pray that we meet again in our next life." She patted him on the shoulder and turned away. Then, picking up the kowgum from the corner, she swung it onto her back and walked out, leaving everyone in the room unable to speak, and the chief disciple appearing not only grave but remorseful.

Like the others, Tompo had not been told about Ani Pema's decision to go on a lifelong pilgrimage, leaving everything behind. At first, he felt surprised, and then he was struck by an overwhelming sense of life's meaninglessness, which made him feel empty.

He left the residence and headed straight to the monks' quarters, and as he walked in, he remembered the first time he and Jadelma had entered the rectangular hall. And then he suddenly realised that this was the last time he would walk into that room, and that his path of dharma had once again come to an end.

Tompo felt empty and lifeless. He had nothing more in him, not even enough sorrow to shed another tear. There was nothing left for him here, in the monastery, so he packed his belongings into the kowgum, changed into the gho that he had worn when he first arrived, and left quietly, without saying goodbye to anyone, not even to Pentsa.

PART FOUR

CHAPTER 51

Lachem Dema, a charming young girl, was singing a jubilant festival song while swinging on a rope from the old juniper tree outside Jadelma's house when Tompo arrived, carrying a kowgum on his back and gripping a shoulder bag by its strap.

Seeing him approaching the house, the little girl stopped singing and stared at him curiously. Tompo stared back, thinking how much she had grown and how fast the time had passed. But before he could speak, Jadelma came bursting out the door and dashed down the flight of stairs and across the lawn with such speed that her feet hardly seemed to touch the ground. As she came upon him, her expression changed from one of joy to concern as she noticed the look of emptiness on his face.

"Oh, my poor Tompo," she lamented, her heart instantly melting. "I didn't know that it had been this difficult for you. The very sense of emptiness has set in your heart. It is not just grief, but also despair. You have not only lost your lama, but also a part of you." She tenderly caressed his face. "Tompo, you should not take it so hard, but how deaf I must have been not to have heard about it."

"I am sorry, Jadelma, I failed you."

"Oh, my poor Tompo," she lamented once more, her gaze lingering on his clothing, noting that he had swapped his red robe for a gho. "Don't let such thoughts enter your mind, let alone dwell on them," she said firmly. "You did not fail. This setback is a minor bump on your journey, due to Lama Jamsempa's untimely demise. Even so, you fulfilled your responsibility to your lama, and this is also a part of the path of dharma."

"I don't know, Jadelma," he responded, his head lowered.

"You are too affected to think clearly, Tompo," she said, her head tilting in sadness. "Come, let us go inside." She guided him across the lawn, up the stairs, and into the house. After helping him set down his kowgum in one corner, she led him onto a new mat that she had recently acquired in a barter with a trader from Lhasa.

Lachem Dema followed them and stared at Tompo curiously from the door, but when Tompo turned to look at her, she quickly averted her eyes and left. He wanted to call after her, but in that state of mind, he did not feel up to it.

Jadelma set him a chentey and served him ara in a silver cup.

Even though he was in grief and despair, it felt good to be back home with her. Sitting there, drinking and talking, he began to feel lighter. "Thank you for all you have done, Jadelma," he said, his voice soft and melancholic. "You went out of your way. You sacrificed so much." He paused for a moment. "Yet it all ended once again."

She did not agree with what he said, but as he was not finished, she nodded meekly and waited for him to speak at his own pace.

"Ani Pema gave up everything and went on a lifelong pilgrimage. She said that she might come back some day, if she does not die. But I doubt she will ever come back."

"I know how you must be feeling, Tompo, but you must not lose hope. It may have ended again, but it is not the end. In fact, it could very well be another beginning, the start of something new because you can always begin again," she said, fixing him with a look of encouragement.

Tompo stiffened, surprise looming on his face.

"After Lama Jamsempa's illness became critical," she added, "I started saving everything I could to prepare for your journey. Now, you must also travel very far, like Ani Pema. I am sure you will meet a great rinpoche somewhere who will give you all the teaching you need."

Tompo jerked, his head shaking. "No, no, no! No, Jadelma! I cannot put you through this again. Dharma is not in my destiny. I have neither the intelligence nor the merit to study dharma. I will stay home and recite prayers and chant mantras. This is the only way for me."

"Tompo, you must not think like that. Dharma is very much in your destiny, as much as it is in others. And as your spouse, I must help you fulfil it the best way I can. For that is our collective destiny, our collective karma."

He shook his head quite forcefully. "Jadelma, I discussed this issue with the lama in great length before he fell ill. The path of dharma is fraught with so many obstacles, but these are only temporary and can be overcome with the right remedial measures someday, when the condition is ripe."

Jadelma listened.

"However, my case is different, not like the others. I am a dimwit, and my lack of intelligence is permanent. It is something that is inside me, that is inherent in me, and it cannot be overcome by any measure, or changed by anything. The only way out of this is to die and come back in another human life."

"What the lama said may be true," she replied. "Still, you must not give up easily like that. At least take this journey and see, for me, for you . . . and for our collective destiny. You never know what lies ahead. The path of dharma may not be fraught only with obstacles that can be cleared away in time, but it may also be filled with miracles that can overcome anything."

"I don't know, Jadelma." Tompo shook his head.

"I know you have been through a lot, Tompo, but this is not the time to give up. This is the time to have an even stronger faith. Do you not see? If you are not normal, you may not need to follow a normal way. If you are different, there may be a different path laid out for you."

"That path is the path of prayers and mantras, Jadelma."

"No, that is the path that the lama had shown you. It is not something so different. In truth, it is a normal path that many people take for many reasons. You don't belong in that category. You are a monk who doesn't want to take that path, but who is desperately yearning for dharma teaching."

"I know you are trying to encourage me, Jadelma, but there is simply no way that I can learn anything worthwhile. It will be the same all over again. I will waste your money and disappoint you in the end, not to mention the inconveniences that I will impose on many people, like Lama Jamsempa, in the process."

"Money is immaterial here, Tompo, and so is my emotional reaction to the outcome, be it disappointment or satisfaction. Whatever it may be, what is important is that you take the journey and look for the path. So long as you do that, finding or not finding will not matter, for you will have tried it, doing everything that you can. Unless, of course, you have lost interest."

"No, of course, no, Jadelma."

"Then you should go, Tompo."

"Oh, my poor Jadelma." He sighed and stared, uncertainty and confusion in his eyes.

"Yes, my dear Tompo." She nodded in encouragement. "You have brought a purpose into my life and given me a will to live for something as noble as Buddha dharma. I consider this not only my good karma, but also my destiny. You see, after I delivered the baby, that man came back to me, but I sent him away, telling him that he had no part in my life."

He stared at her, his eyes wide.

"I told him that he had come into my life only briefly, to prepare me to meet you, and that I had nothing for which to thank him or forgive him. So, you see, dear Tompo, this is our karma, this is our destiny. You must go and seek your path again. You will find it. Even if you don't, you can recite prayers and chant mantras as you desire, because out there, in those sacred places, it will be different."

With strong and newfound courage rising in his heart, he nodded with conviction. "Thank you, my Jadelma. Though I bear a suffering like the unrelenting pains of *narmé* hell, even one small moment like this with you makes me the most fortunate person in the world. As of now, my happiness knows no bounds."

Her face lit up. "Neither does mine, my Tompo. I feel almost weak and faint with joy. Come now, drink, for celebrate we must."

"Yes, Jadelma," he said, picking up the cup from the chentey. He drank a sip, and his brow furrowed, realising something important. Then he took another sip, carefully assessing the taste, and his expression froze, his eyes gleaming with recognition. "Isn't this the same ara from last time, Jadelma?"

Jadelma's eyes sparkled with delight as she responded, "Not the same ara, Tompo, but the same kind in every aspect." Her voice was filled with joy and excitement. "I brewed and distilled this with extreme care to replicate the taste and potency, all for a moment like this." She paused, before adding, "I was not sure if you would remember it, but you did. How wonderful!"

"Of course, I remember it, Jadelma," Tompo replied with a childlike enthusiasm. "Everything about that night is etched on my mind like a painting on a thangka. But you must also drink. Pass me the canister, please. Let me serve you like the last time."

"It would be like last time," Jadelma reminisced, her head tilting slightly, and her eyes squinting as if lost in fond memories.

"I also remember everything about that night so clearly and vividly, as if it were only yesterday."

She took out the second silver cup and held it in front of him, and he poured the ara until it nearly spilt over its brim.

"I have not had anything to drink in a long, long time, Tompo." She dipped her finger into the cup and sprinkled a few droplets into the air, her offering to the gods and the deities, and slowly drank it, sip after sip, until her face glowed with a warm and rosy colour.

The daylight quickly faded into dusk and the dusk thickened into darkness. As the night wore on, little Lachem was put to bed. But Tompo and Jadelma continued eating and drinking, much like the night they first met, and when the last embers in the hearth hissed and died, she took his hand and led him into the bedroom, very much like that first night together.

CHAPTER 52

As the sun rose from behind the eastern mountain, setting the horizon ablaze, Tompo walked out of the house wearing his red robe and carrying the kowgum on his back. Jadelma followed closely, with his shoulder bag in her hand.

They climbed down the stairs and walked across the lawn in silence, stopped near the pathway, and turned and faced each other with overwhelming emotions gripping them and tears filling Jadelma's eyes.

Tompo gently wiped her tears away with his robe and took the bag from her, all the while fighting his own emotions. "Don't cry, my Jadelma," he said, nearly choking on his emotion.

"I will cry now, Tompo," Jadelma replied, her head tilting and her lips clenched, "but when you return after many years, I will rejoice and host a grand celebration in your honour. I will sing a song of praise for you so loudly that *dakas* and dakinis everywhere will hear and know what you have accomplished, and rejoice for you."

Tompo touched her cheek. "Thank you, my Jadelma."

"And this may sound crazy, Tompo, but I will cook and ferment a nine-grain mixture. I don't know for what reason, but I prepared this mixture from the first batch of the harvests last year, even though I had not prepared for any rimdro."

Tompo stared, his brow creased in confusion.

"Aum Zam asked it for her rimdro, but I didn't give it," Jadelma added. "At that time, I thought I was being strange, for I didn't know the reason. But now that I know, I am happy for it— it was meant to be fermented for your spiritual attainment!"

The look on his face expressed surprise.

"I know you must be thinking that I am insane, for no such nine-grain mixture had ever been cooked and fermented, but I am not. It was kept in the shrine room all this while for a reason, do you see? This is our destiny, Tompo."

With a strong belief rising in him, Tompo nodded.

"I will lay down the grain mash in the shrine room and make the most powerful aspiration prayer that I can muster, asking that it ferment only when you have received the highest dharma teaching, and you have achieved the greatest accomplishment. I will not even touch it until then."

His face softened with pleasure. "Thank you, my Jadelma."

Jadelma put her hands together and closed her eyes while making an aspiration prayer. "If my dakini sign is real, may it in all earnestness help my Tompo to receive the highest dharma teaching and to achieve the most supreme accomplishment in this lifetime."

Tompo stared at her wide-eyed. *She does have the dakini sign*, he thought. But before he could say anything, she put her hand on his arm. "Go now. Go, before I break down again. Lingering here is only making it more difficult."

Tompo nodded, emotions rising in him.

"May the country's guardian deities protect you from all harm and misfortune," she told him, her voice tender. "And may the buddhas bless you with the greatest accomplishments."

Struggling to keep the pain from his face, he nodded again, but his lips quivered, and his jaw contorted. Turning around, he walked away from her, following the path he had taken when he arrived from Tsokar, without even once looking back.

Although nothing seemed to have changed since he had come this way, everything along the path looked different from this reverse view. This reminded him of his journey from Tsokar to Kisathang and triggered the memories of that day so vividly that he felt the emotional pain as if it had just happened.

Literally shaking off his thoughts, Tompo walked on, his steps steady and determined, and soon arrived at that same tiny hilltop at the foot of the mountain from where he had first looked down at the valley of Kisathang. A quick glance told him that Kisathang was as it had been before.

However, as he scanned the village, without looking for anything in particular, he saw Jadelma's house and felt a stab of pain in his heart, and a wave of emotion surging through him. *How had it not occurred to me to look for her house in the first place?* he asked himself, a scowl marking his face.

As he stood there battling his emotions, he thought about how he had been in this very spot five years ago. *I was a homeless orphan and a runaway monk with nowhere to go, and with no idea of what the future held for me. But here I am now, with a wife and a home, setting off on the sacred pilgrimage of a lifetime.* Reminding himself of this, he felt better.

But I still don't have any dharma in me, he mused, shaking his head sadly. Then, wondering whether Kisathang would be the same when he returned years later, he turned and walked away.

He had taken only a few steps when a corresponding thought occurred to him. *Kisathang might be the same, but what about myself? Would I be the same person years later? Would I have changed in some . . . or many . . . ways?*

Of course, I would, without any doubt, still be the same man, a monk without dharma. What more could a dimwit expect? I was fortunate to have met Jadelma and to have been taken in as her spouse. But as for dharma? Even if she is a dakini woman, even if I should meet a great rinpoche and be given the most sacred teaching, I would not be able to understand it. So, how could I possibly change?

The path wound higher up the mountain and then began to incline towards the east. Walking at a steady pace, he soon reached a Y-junction where the path diverged into two. The one going to Tsokar went up and around the mountain eastwards, but the other path descended westwards into the valley.

I did not even notice this particular path when I passed here before, he thought, as he made his choice and began descending towards the west, without even thinking about going back towards Tsokar.

Tompo walked on without stopping to drink or eat, but having not walked anywhere since Lama Jamsempa had fallen sick, he realised that he had missed being out in the wilderness.

Unleashing his pent-up energy and enthusiasm, he walked hard and fast, covering a great distance, but as he had not been beyond that junction, he had no idea where he was headed.

The path wended its way around the mountain, descending gradually. As it neared the base of the mountain, it became woodsier, and the rushing sounds of a river were heard, but the path soon veered northwest, and these sounds slowly died down.

Towards midday, Tompo emerged from the woods and arrived at what was not actually the base of the mountain, but a small U-shaped valley boasting a lush green meadow with a towering rocky mountain on the other side.

He stood there, taking in its beauty and its calm. There was something mystical about this place.

He was neither hungry nor thirsty, but he felt it wise to stop for a rest. Sitting in the middle of the meadow, he poured a cup of ara, dipped his finger into it, and sprinkled a few drops into the air, his offering to the gods and the deities of the area. However, before he could drink even one sip from the cup, a tall figure clad in a monk's robe came down the rocky mountain, following a small trail that ended in the meadow.

There was something familiar about the monk, but Tompo could not make him out from such a distance. He stared hard, straining his eyes, trying to identify this man coming towards him, sauntering with a gait that was even more familiar to Tompo. Then, he recognised the old monk from the Silver Mountain.

"It is you again, Old Monk!" Tompo exclaimed, as he stood, feeling both disbelief and joy. "I can't believe we are meeting in the forest again after all these years! What are you doing here?"

The old man first smiled, and then he laughed. "Look who is here, the orphan without home and the monk without dharma!" He still wore that same old grin that bordered on a smirk.

"*Monk without dharma*, yes. But *orphan without home*, not really," Tompo replied, grinning back. "Not anymore," he repeated. "You see, Old Monk, I may still be an orphan—for there is no way I can change that—but I am no longer without a home. Some things have changed in the last five years, I'm happy to say."

"I would still consider you an orphan without a home," said the old man. "I heard everything about you, how the woman offered you hospitality, but only on your journey from one place to another. Nothing more. In my mind, that is not enough to call it your home, at least not in the conventional sense of having a home and a family."

Tompo felt anger rising in his chest. "How can you say such a thing, Old Monk?"

"She is only helping you so you can make progress on your spiritual journey, Monk. Consider her your benefactor, and if you must associate with her in terms of relationship, as you seem bent on doing, then think of her as your spiritual muse dakini. Trust me, you are better off as an orphan without a home."

Tompo's eyes grew wide.

The old man gestured towards the ara Tompo was holding. "Now, will you not offer me some wine, orphan-without-home and monk-without-dharma?" he teased. "Many say that liquor brings good luck and good fortune, so let us see if we can forge some of that for ourselves."

"I apologise, I forgot to offer it to you." Tompo took out his silver cup from the kowgum and handed it to the old monk, and then poured ara to the brim.

"Thank you." The old monk dipped his finger into the cup, sprinkled a few drops in the air, took a gulp, and held out the cup for a refill. "This is a good liquor, good enough to forge our good fortune." He downed the ara in one big gulp, wiped the cup on his robe and returned it to Tompo. Then he stood up to leave, and stopped as if having a second thought.

Tompo remained there, saying nothing.

"Since you offered me your best liquor in your fine silver cup, I will tell you a secret before I leave, orphan-without-home and monk-without-dharma." The old monk grinned almost impishly. "Now, listen to me carefully, because this might turn out to be important to you someday."

Tompo remained silent, curious to know where this conversation was going.

"Dharma is only a path. Studying the texts, practising the vows, and doing all such stuff are just you—yes, you—journeying on that path. But what you are after is not the path or the journey. It is the destination. Of course, without the path, how would you journey, and without the journey, how would you arrive at the destination? It is an enigma, to be sure, but sometimes the destination is reached."

Tompo felt perplexed, evident by the way his eyebrows were drawn together.

"Sometimes, in a rare and extraordinary situation,"

continued the man, "you could have already reached that destination—in essence, through living your life without having taken the journey through the path of dharma. In such a case, you may not need the path or the journey. This is outrageously bizarre, right? Yes, I believe it is, but all within the realm of possibility. Reflect on that, and see for yourself." With that, he turned to leave, and then turned back. "Farewell to you again, my friend."

"Please, wait a bit, Old Monk," called out Tompo.

The old monk stopped and stared at him, grinning.

"Who are you really?" asked Tompo. "And what do you mean when you say that dharma is only a path? What rare and extraordinary situation are you talking about?"

"That dharma is only a path, you will understand one day. But for now, you hang onto being the orphan without home and the monk without dharma. Who knows, this might turn out to be your rare and extraordinary situation."

Tompo stiffened in surprise.

"And as for me, I am just an old monk who wanders around these areas. The place where we met last time is on the other side of this mountain, and I remember telling you that it was called Silver Mountain. Well, here is a twist for you: from this side, we call it Gold Mountain. Funny, isn't it?"

Tompo nodded to concur.

"I find it funny because the mountain doesn't have silver or gold from any side, nor does it even appear silvery or golden. These are names, and with little meaning. Likewise, that giant rocky mountain, which has neither copper nor looks coppery, is called Copper Mountain. But then, what is in a name? It is merely a label, yes? Unfortunately, who you are outside by label is exactly what you are inside in essence is the most fundamental thing in dharma."

Tompo stared, lost.

"But, of course, even that will change as you advance further. Then you will see that nothing is as it seems. Far from it, in truth, the day will come when you find that nothing is even as it is." He paused briefly and spoke with emphasis. "Sometimes, happiness has a tail, and sometimes happiness has no tail. It all depends on the one pursuing it. In tantra, nothing is definitive, but everything is fluid. Even reality is not real, but that is quite complicated for you to grasp right now."

Tompo, totally lost, stood with his mouth hanging open.

The old man stared across the meadow, as if seeing answers. "For now, look into yourself and reflect on who you are outside by situation or by label, and what you are inside in essence, and then see if the two correspond well, for that may determine your future from today onwards." He smiled at Tompo. "Farewell to you, my friend," he said, and then turned and walked away, heading back the way he had come and disappearing below the edge of the valley at the base of the rocky mountain.

Tompo downed his cup of ara in one gulp and then, replacing the canister and the cups in his shoulder bag, he stood and resumed his walk.

When he reached the base of the rocky mountain, he saw a trail going down into a deep gorge. But there was no sign of the old monk. Still, he stared at it for some time, then turned and went on his journey.

The path wound precariously around the naked face of the rocky mountain, but Tompo became oblivious to his surroundings, as he delved deeply into what the old monk had said and reflected on who he was outside by label and what he was inside in essence.

CHAPTER 53

Tompo journeyed from one place to another, scaling hills and mountains, crossing rivers and streams, walking in the sun and the rain, braving storms and snowfalls, and surviving on salt and flour. Days turned into weeks, weeks into months, and months into years. Yet, he never stopped, but went on and on.

He visited monasteries, chortens, and sacred sites; attended *duchens* and *drupchens;* performed *chagbums* and *korbums*, received *wangs* and *lüngs;* offered butter lamps and incense; and met trulkus and rinpoches—all the while reflecting on what the old monk had said.

He recited prayers and chanted mantras days and nights. As the time went by, helping to make water offering and clean butter lamp cups wherever he went, Tompo slowly became aware of the clinking sounds of the offering bowls, the butter lamp cups, and the water kettle, and he began to love how they sounded. He also soon began to hear and love the sound of water being poured into bowls.

In time, he stopped reciting prayers and chanting mantras, and instead he listened to the sounds when he was making a water offering, or when he made and offered butter lamps.

Then he began to hear all other sounds, see everything within his vision, smell everything that left an odour in the air, and feel with increased sensitivity everything his body came in contact with, as if his senses had been dramatically enhanced.

Thus, he stopped reciting prayers and chanting mantras altogether and lived in the present: hearing, seeing, smelling, and feeling everything around him. After a while, he felt as if he were a part of the environment, and he could hear, see, smell, and feel his surroundings without consciously calling up his senses.

Zigzagging north and south, but heading westwards little by little, Tompo crossed into the Kingdom of Denzong, and from there to the Kingdom of Balyul. Continuing even farther, he arrived at the Kingdom of Ladakh, the westernmost region of the lands of *the dharma of the insiders*. From there, he turned northwards and finally headed to Bod, the great motherland of *the dharma of the insiders*.

His journey became extremely difficult and harsh from then on. Despite ascending the snow-clad mountains for days, he did not come upon any human settlement, and his meagre rations were soon depleted.

Nevertheless, he pressed on, sustaining himself only with salt and water. He crossed one snow-clad mountain after another and finally, in a delirious state, arrived at an isolated monastery perched atop a pinnacle, with a sheer cliff on one side and a gentle slope that appeared to descend into a valley on the other.

In this dreamlike state, he climbed the stone stairway and reached a landing in front of the entrance, which dizzyingly looked down the cliff. Quickly averting his gaze, he walked in through the door and arrived in the inner courtyard.

The area was quiet and deserted. Glancing around to see if anyone was there, he slowly walked across it.

As he reached the other side, he heard a faint murmur from one of the rooms that ran alongside a hallway going into the inner sanctum of the monastery and a stairway ascending to the upper floors.

He walked towards the room and entered through the open door. About fifteen monks were seated on the floor with their backs towards the door, and an aged lama, a man he instinctively understood to be a great teacher, was teaching.

He stood in the doorway and listened to the teaching for a while, and then turned and walked out. He strolled back across the courtyard and found two elderly monks and a little monk boy waiting at the entrance. They ushered him out and accompanied him down the slope, in the same delirious state.

Halfway down the slope, the two elderly monks bade him goodbye, and returned to the monastery. But the little monk boy continued with him until they could see a green patch of orchard on the landing below. From there, the slope angled in a different direction, like a stairway.

"The orchard belongs to the monastery," the child said, his face bearing an innocent yet radiant expression. "Feel free to pick and enjoy any fruit you desire." When Tompo stared at him with a doubtful expression, he gazed back at Tompo reassuringly, nodded, turned on his heel, and walked away.

Tompo continued downwards and approached the orchard hesitantly, wondering if it really belonged to the monastery while casting furtive glances in all directions to see if anyone was watching it or coming towards it.

Lost in his vigilant scrutiny, he failed to notice the large and healthy fruits growing uniformly and in abundant clusters, until he was right inside the orchard. Then, he observed everything in its profound state, and their magnificence overwhelmed him.

He slowly cast his gaze around without even seeming to feel his hunger, and a sense of admiration for existence began to grow within him. But as he was in a rather delirious state, he didn't know if what he was feeling was from his conscious mind or a product of his delirium. He didn't even know if the orchard was real.

Unsure of anything, he left without picking any fruit, hastened down the gentle slope, and soon reached the first house in the valley, where he was immediately taken in, given food and water, and put to bed.

Totally worn out from the journey, he slept through the night and the following morning. But when he woke up at noon, fully rested and conscious, he still observed everything in its profound state and admired the magnificence of existence.

He then began to feel connected to everything around him, as if he shared the same source of existence, enabling him to live in the present, not only conscious of his environment by sight, sound, smell, and touch, but also feeling connected to everything around him.

CHAPTER 54

After traversing the vast expanse of Bod for nearly a year, Tompo arrived at a provincial centre with a magnificent monastery sitting high on a hillock. By this time, he had undergone a significant transformation. He had become calm and acutely aware of everything around him.

His devotion for dharma had also taken on a noticeable and palpable form on his appearance, which became more apparent as he stood in the valley, studying the monastery. Soon, a farmer and his wife who were passing by, stopped and stared at him.

"What monastery could that be?" Tompo asked them. "It is the most magnificent structure I have seen in all my travels."

"Ah, that is the renowned Namodara Monastery, Monk," responded the farmer. His voice held a trace of uncertainty, as though he were gauging the level of respect to offer the pilgrim monk who, judging by the appearance, did not seem to be anyone of importance. "You must have heard about it," the man added. "Or perhaps about Thokmay Jatso Rinpoche. He is the greatest *dzogchenpa* of our time and the twelfth reincarnation of Garzang Thokmay Jatso."

Tompo felt a surge of devotion well up from deep inside him. A ripple of energy ran through him, and he shuddered. "Thokmay Jatso Rinpoche," he said, almost as if in a trance-like state. "Just hearing his name is raising the hair all over my body."

The farmer was impressed. "That is good, Monk. You must have a karmic connection with the rinpoche from your past lives. Many lamas, *khenpos*, trulkus, and even rinpoches come to receive teachings and empowerments from the rinpoche. Some wait for years just to get inducted."

Tompo did not respond, as if he had not heard the farmer, but in that same trance-like state, he placed his kowgum on the ground and prostrated three times towards the monastery while saying his prayer, oblivious of the farmer and his wife staring at him, astonished.

"Your devotion is astounding," said the farmer, inching closer, bending down slightly in reverence. "It can be seen all over your face, as if you are wearing it. Who might you be, Monk, for no ordinary monk can muster devotion like that?"

"I am only a pilgrim monk, nobody important, certainly no one you would have heard about." Tompo picked up his kowgum and swung it onto his back. "Thank you for giving me this valuable information. I will seek an audience with the rinpoche. Is this the way?" He pointed to the path going up towards the hillock.

"Yes, it takes you up to the monastery."

Tompo nodded with a slight bow, turned, and left, following the path. After a short climb, he arrived at the monastery, straddling the hillock in all its magnificence and architectural grandeur. Around it, hundreds of people were engaged in circumambulation, reciting prayers and chanting mantras.

Tompo was struck by the wonder, faith, and devotion he saw before him, and he stared for some time before leaving his kowgum in one corner of the courtyard and walking through the entrance.

He reached a large inner courtyard with hallways leading to different parts of the monastery and stairways ascending to the upper floor. Monks in vibrant red robes and visitors in attires of various countries went about their destinations and tasks.

After surveying the area and getting the feel of it, he approached a monk rushing through a hallway towards him. "Is it possible to receive an audience with the rinpoche?" he asked. "I don't have any specific purpose or reason; I only want to be in the rinpoche's presence once and receive a blessing. So, perhaps I can join a group that is going in."

"There are about four hundred people waiting in line for an audience with the rinpoche," the monk responded, his brow furrowed. "So no, you can't tag along with others; you must wait your turn, which could take as much as a week. At this time of the year, we have many pilgrims and visitors, not only from Bod, but also from all over the southern countries."

Tompo offered a friendly smile. "I will wait."

"Then you will have to meet the rinpoche's attendant and put your name on the list, but he is in the rinpoche's chamber now. You can meet him later this afternoon. For now, you go and meet the monk in charge of the guests. He might give you something to eat and find a place for you to sleep." With this, the monk turned on his heel and took off.

Tompo bowed slightly after the monk. Then, content with the course of events thus far, he strolled around, visiting the shrine rooms, engaging in prostration and prayers, and receiving blessings. Following this, he went back into the outer courtyard and commenced circumambulation around the wish-fulfilling chorten situated in the distant corner.

There, all by himself, lost in his prayers, he failed to notice a magnificent rainbow with extraordinary luminance and radiance that appeared arching above the monastery shortly thereafter.

Soon word of this sacred sign spread through the monastery, and everyone came out the door, gazing skywards. As they observed, the clouds sailed away beyond the horizon, the sky turned cerulean blue, and a bright halo formed around the sun.

A little later, Thokmay Jatso Rinpoche himself emerged, accompanied by the attendant monk and a few close aides. He gazed upwards, pondering the cause behind the manifestation of these uncommon sacred signs. But even as he watched, a papery translucent image of a dakini materialised in the sky, invoking immense faith and devotion among all who witnessed it.

As if certain that something auspicious was causing these signs, the rinpoche looked around, and his gaze fell on Tompo, an isolated figure in the far corner of the courtyard, prostrating and circumambulating around the wish-fulfilling chorten with great devotion, oblivious to everything that was happening. Stretching his neck forward, the rinpoche stared hard at Tompo. "Who is that pilgrim monk?"

"We have not seen him before, Rinpoche," replied the attendant monk. "He must have arrived last night or early today. I have not had the opportunity to meet anyone today. Should I enquire about him, Rinpoche?"

"Yes, bring him to my chamber."

The attendant monk nodded and hurried away.

The rinpoche glanced skywards once more, observing that the image of the dakini was fading, while the rainbow over the monastery and the halo encircling the sun were intensifying. Folding his hands and offering a swift supplication to the image of the dakini, he made his way back into the monastery.

Chapter 55

Hearing the sound of hurried footsteps, Tompo turned and noticed the attendant monk rushing towards him, with a large crowd of people staring at the man from the other end of the courtyard. Puzzled by the scene unfolding before him, Tompo shifted his gaze from the crowd to the important-looking monk.

"The rinpoche has asked me to fetch you," said the attendant monk, quite short of breath. "Please come, follow me." He gestured, turned around, and rushed away, heading towards the entrance.

With no time to process his thoughts, Tompo took to his heels, following the man across the courtyard, through the door, along the corridor, up the stairway, and all the way into the rinpoche's chamber, tucked away somewhere high up in a secluded part of the monastery.

Tompo stood transfixed, utterly awestruck by the moment as soon as he walked in. Thokmay Jatso Rinpoche sat on a throne more majestic and imposing than he had ever seen, and the chamber was grander than any place he had ever visited.

Yet, he remained serene and aware of everything around him. He prostrated to the rinpoche and then sat on a fine silk mat on the floor, as directed by the attendant monk.

As soon as Tompo was settled, sitting perfectly still, the rinpoche looked at him and noticed a profound and pervasive devotion in his serene demeanour.

"Who are you, Monk?" asked the rinpoche. "And what brings you here?"

"I am Tompo, Rinpoche," Tompo replied, his voice soft, yet distinct and clear. "And I am seeking a dharma teaching that can provide a path to liberation from this samsara—in one body and one lifetime." He paused momentarily before continuing. "I have travelled far and wide for weeks, months, seasons, and years on end in search of a teacher who could impart to me this teaching."

"What is your level of study and practice?"

"I have nothing in the way of achieving level, Rinpoche, but I have looked into myself, reflected, and contemplated who I was outside by label, and what I was inside in essence, and to see if who I was outside was what I was inside, Rinpoche."

Feeling both the depth and the absurdity of what the strange young pilgrim monk had said, the rinpoche broke into a slight snigger. "So, who are you outside and what are you inside?"

"I am an orphan without home and a monk without dharma by label, Rinpoche. Orphan without home because I lost my parents and home and have had nothing to call mine since I was a little boy; and a monk without dharma because, despite studying under two good lamas, I could never learn, owing to my lack of intelligence."

"I see," the rinpoche said. "And what are you inside . . . in essence?"

"I am that same orphan without home and that same monk without dharma in essence, too, to a large extent, Rinpoche, for I have not only wholeheartedly accepted and embraced the life that was laid out for me by karma, but also lived it as truthfully as I could."

"Really, how so?"

"My parents died owing money to the village nobleman. So, right after their death, I was taken to the nobleman's mansion to work as a servant. At first, I was lonely without my parents and wished they were not dead. I was also worried about their rebirth, for I could neither conduct proper ritual rites nor carry out any *gewa*."

The rinpoche nodded but said nothing.

"Then one night I dreamt about them. They told me not to worry about them because they were through the intermediate state and had been reborn in the zhingkham of Dewachen. Even though it was only a dream, it made me happy that they had left the human world of suffering for the buddha realm of guaranteed enlightenment."

The rinpoche gave Tompo an approving look. "Yes, that was the right way of thinking."

"From then on," continued Tompo, "there was nothing to restrain me from living the life of an orphan without home truthfully, without wishing for anything else. I was not only content and satisfied, but also appreciative of and grateful for everything. So, I worked hard day and night without any complaints."

The rinpoche's eyebrow rose. "But tell me, how could you have had such clarity of thought and purpose at that age? Even reincarnated rinpoches cannot be so virtuous and saintly at that young age. It was as if you had conquered all your human vices and evils. Unless, of course, you never had any immorality in your nature, for some reason."

"I was without any immorality by nature, due to my family's unique way of living, Rinpoche," Tompo submitted. "I come from an ancient family of tenant farmers who, despite toiling for their landlords, were wholeheartedly devoted and dedicated and profoundly sincere and truthful in their work. So much so that the gods and the deities became pleased with them and blessed them."

"Blessed them?" repeated the rinpoche, curiosity in his voice. "How?"

"By getting Nature to reciprocate to them," Tompo replied. When the rinpoche stared at him, he added, "The soil on their fields became moist and soft, the weather in the area grew pleasant, and the rain came on time, all the while the pests and the wild animals stayed away from their fields and crops, giving them bountiful harvests, year in and year out."

"That is incredible. Go on." The rinpoche leaned forward, eager to hear more.

"Over a period of time, that manner of working became a way of life for them, making them capable of living truthfully and feeling great devotion, among other things. But, of course, their decision to live in such a way was not driven by any spiritual clarity of thought and purpose, as Rinpoche put it. I think they were just that way because of their situation."

"What makes you say that?"

"My father seized the first opportunity that came his way to become a landed man. But just then he fell gravely ill and could not keep his end of the deal. This made him realise that he could not change the life that he was born into without exhausting his negative karma. So, he told me to live my life virtuously and exhaust my negative karma, so that I may have a better rebirth in my next life."

"And that changed you?"

"Yes, but not right away, Rinpoche," Tompo responded. "The nobleman, thinking I was bright and intelligent, offered to educate me so that I could be his son's study companion and become someone in future. I accepted his offer willingly, although I had little choice. In any case, I turned out to be a dimwit, and I could not learn anything, no matter how much I prayed to the gods and the deities."

"But were they blessing you in other ways?"

"Yes, Rinpoche. Even my body and my clothes were responding to me. I had become graceful in my physicality and pure in my thinking, and my clothes stayed in place as I wore them. But my brain and intelligence would not respond to me. And then, thinking it was my bad karma blocking my way, I gave up and went back to living a contented life."

"I see," the rinpoche said, nodding.

"Then, one day, a trulku passed through our village, kindling a great devotion for dharma in me. It was only then that I wanted something, but not in the worldly way of possessing things or becoming somebody. I just yearned for dharma teaching, and I only wanted to pursue the path of dharma. But as I was a dimwit, I could not learn anything, angering my lama greatly. So, I ran away from the monastery."

"Then what happened?"

"And then, with nowhere to go, I gave up on the path and got married, but in a strange turn of events my spouse became my spiritual muse dakini and sent me back on the path—although I had no intelligence to study dharma."

The rinpoche nodded, taking a moment to contemplate before speaking. "You have lived a virtuous life, and you have also reflected on it and realised that you were *inside* in essence what you were *outside* by situation," the rinpoche said, repeating what Tompo had told him, but with a hint of scepticism in his voice, mingled with curiosity. Then, unsure of how to interpret this, he enquired, "But what is the point? What does it make you?"

"The point is that dharma is only a path, not the destination, Rinpoche. A means to free us from the grasp of the samsaric world and prepare us for whatever is beyond it." He paused for a moment and stared at the rinpoche. "But," he stressed, "if you are already freed, you may not need the path."

"You mean you are freed from the grasp of samsara?" the rinpoche asked, his eyes wide in surprise. "That is a tall claim to make, even for someone like you. You know that it is not so simple and easy. Yes, dharma is only a path, but it is a necessary path, something that you cannot do away with. In any case, how did you gain this level of understanding? This is a very high-level concept."

"An old monk who wanders around the Gold Mountain area in Druk Yul told it to me, Rinpoche. I met him twice. The first time, he said that I was an orphan without home and a monk without dharma, a situation he would not trade for all the dharma teaching in the world. The second time we met, he told me all of this that I have submitted to Rinpoche now."

The rinpoche put his hands together in supplication and mumbled a short invocation prayer. "He was the great *Tokdenpa* Gyal Raypadmë, the lone, lion-like mountain wanderer whose untrammelled vision, in just one glimpse, cuts through duality and all its confusion," he said. "He is my root teacher, and he came to me in my vision one month ago."

Tompo was initially taken aback and then felt a mix of surprise and regret. "I am sorry, I didn't know, Rinpoche."

"How could you have possibly known? Anyway, he said that an unconventional monk very much like you, seeking to cross the sea of samsara without even a boat, was headed my way, and that should he arrive here at Namodara, I should take it as my destiny to prepare him to make this great unorthodox journey, for if he was the one, he was destined to become the first of his kind, the traveller without the path."

Tompo's face brightened for a brief moment, and then he humbly bowed, as a profound sense of gratitude washed over him.

"And looking at the great auspicious signs manifested today, and from what you have told me, I am certain you are the one. But to ensure that it is you, let me ask you if anything in the way of spiritual development has happened to you over the course of this time."

"I don't know if it can be considered spiritual development," replied Tompo, "but many things have happened during the last few years that have made me capable of not only living in the present—hearing, seeing, smelling, and feeling everything—but also seeing everything in its profound state and feeling inherently connected to them, as if I am a part of them. But I still don't understand any dharma teaching that I receive, Rinpoche."

"You will now."

"I will understand the dharma teaching, Rinpoche?" Tompo's face lit up once again.

"Yes, you will understand not just any dharma teaching, but the highest dharma teaching that there is in tantra. In fact, you will understand and know all there is to understand and know in this universe."

"How, Rinpoche?"

"You will see in a little while."

"Thank you, Rinpoche, I am truly blessed."

The rinpoche nodded and turned to the attendant monk and the aides standing silently. "All of you may leave the room now. Close the door and don't let anyone in until I call you myself. And you are not to tell anyone about this."

The attendant monk and the aides bowed and walked out of the room, pulling the door shut after them.

CHAPTER 56

Thokmay Jatso Rinpoche quickly recited a mandrel prayer, shut his eyes, and made an aspiration prayer for the success of the secret teaching he was about to impart. Then, he cast his gaze downwards at Tompo, seated on the floor.

"We will begin your teaching from what you told me about Nature and existence." The rinpoche's voice was clear and distinct. "This way, we can begin your teaching from what has happened to you and what you have achieved, in terms of the stages of the path of dharma, whether you take the path or not."

"Thank you, Rinpoche."

The rinpoche leaned slightly forward, locking his eyes with Tompo's. "All phenomena are empty of intrinsic existence. That is to say that they did not originate independently on their own, but in dependence on other factors. Therefore, all phenomena are empty of inherent nature, in that they lack the very essence of the identity imputed by their labels. In other words, all phenomena exist merely in name, as they are labelled in our mind, and they are not truly existent, as we think they are."

Tompo closed his eyes for a moment, trying to absorb this. "Yes, Rinpoche."

"What appears real to our eyes is only an illusion, not the true nature of reality. This room is an illusion, you are an illusion, and even your mind will turn out to be an illusion in the end.

But then, what is the ultimate, true nature of reality? We will discuss that later. For now, we will say that the true nature of all phenomena is the emptiness of independent origination."

Tompo sensed a sudden opening within his mind, accompanied by a radiant and luminous influx into his brain. It felt akin to the unlocking of a door or the removal of a blockage in his vision. Startled by the sensation, he visibly tensed, attracting the rinpoche's attention.

"What is it, Tompo? What just happened?"

"It was something like a door being thrown wide open in my head, Rinpoche," Tompo replied, looking for words to describe his experience. "Now I have more clarity, I am more aware of everything, more connected to everything, but this awareness and feeling are not felt by my physical senses, but come from inside me. I also feel an unusual level of tranquillity."

"It is the spiritual awakening of your wisdom and knowledge, or the third eye," the rinpoche explained. "This will enable you to understand everything and even see a reality beyond ordinary human vision. This means you are on the right track, and that everything you have told me is true." He paused, then raised his hands in the air. "But, of course, the great tokdenpa would have never gotten it wrong."

"I see, Rinpoche. But how did it happen?"

"Normally, this is achieved only through intense meditation and inner transformation, where one purifies the mind, cultivates insight into the true nature of reality, and develops heightened awareness. However, in your case, it is different. You have achieved much of this outside of the traditional path, as you narrated."

"I thank Tokdenpa for it," Tompo said, bowing in gratitude.

The rinpoche nodded. "Let's move on," he said. "All things in the universe are made up of five basic elements: earth, water, fire, wind, and vacuum or space. And of these five basic elements, space in its particulate form is the most important one, responsible for the origination of the universe itself. This particulate form is the central force of all phenomena. The universe evolved from this particulate form, and it will eventually dissolve in this particulate form."

Tompo listened attentively, and understanding came to him easily. He understood everything that the rinpoche said, without any vagueness in his comprehension. The clarity was so crisp and well-defined that he felt he could literally lay a finger on it.

"This is how everything, including the universe itself, comes into existence, materially, through the interplay of the five elements. Now, since all things are made up of these five elements, everything, including sentient beings and Nature, is connected at an elemental level. Did you understand? This will be one of the bases on which I will explain how Nature and everything around you had responded to you later."

"Yes, Rinpoche."

"When we say that all things in the universe are made up of the five basic elements, we are referring to the material composition of their bodies. However, in the case of sentient beings, there are also internal elements existing within them, and these elements vary in their form, from one to the other. Some are glaring, while others are subtle, and there are those elements that are even subtler."

Tompo straightened up, his face shining with amazement.

"Of these inner elements, the consciousness is the innermost and the most important one in the sphere of dependent origination. It is a subtle element that is further composed of five basic elements in their subtlest forms. These subtlest forms of elements serve as the conditions for producing the other internal elements that constitute sentient beings. And sentient beings, in turn, cause the existence of the external environment they inhabit. This is the law of dependent origination, in your context."

Tompo tilted his head towards the rinpoche, increasing his concentration, more out of habit than necessity.

"So, it is not only that sentient beings and the environment they inhabit are materially connected at an elemental level, but they are also causally linked through the chain of dependent origination. This means, everything has elemental connection and causal linkage to the consciousness."

Tompo nodded, feeling the familiar eagerness of his old listening habit mildly pulsating amidst his newfound calmness.

"That was how Nature and everything else has responded to you, when you reached your innermost element through living your life truthfully. Because when you reached your consciousness—your innermost element—you connected with everything around you, and your intent got transmitted to them."

"So, it was not the gods and the deities, Rinpoche?"

"Maybe up to a certain extent, but not to that level. The gods and the deities could have gotten Nature to reciprocate to you in the beginning, but after some time, when you had lived your life truthfully, accepting who you were, and most importantly, free of clinging to anything and therefore free of delusion, your mind was at its subtlest elemental state. As such, it reached the elements of your consciousness and of Nature . . . and everything."

"But why would not my brain and intelligence respond, Rinpoche?"

"Because of your karma. You were still not free of it."

"I see, Rinpoche." A pensive look crossed Tompo's face.

"That was also how you observed everything in its profound state and felt connected to it, as if you were a part of it," the rinpoche added. "Of course, you were a part of it. We all are, at the elemental level. However, although all of that was astonishing, it was still an experience of duality and dependent existence."

"Of course, Rinpoche."

"This explains the occurrences of your spiritual experience in a nutshell," the rinpoche concluded the segment. "Now, to delve a little deeper into this matter," he continued, "in interdependence, things depend for their existence upon causes and conditions, their own parts, or the conceptual mind, which is our focus here. This is to expand on the role that sentient beings play in the creation and perception of reality in dependent existence and explain your path forward in the process."

"Yes, Rinpoche."

"Now, to again explain this aspect of dependence upon the conceptual mind within our context," the rinpoche said, "everything exists because our conceptual mind perceives it . . . and labels it. This means the existence of the universe, including ourselves, is entirely dependent on us. It is as if, if we were not here, the universe would not be here either. This is the fundamental principle of dependent existence."

Tompo nodded, feeling almost lightheaded from this new comprehension. "This is fascinating, Rinpoche."

"There is more to this too, but we will leave it here, and go into your life's situations—an orphan without home, and a monk without dharma—as the tokdenpa has defined them, in equivalence to the essence of dharma. That is, a determination of what you have achieved and how far you have reached in terms of the stages of the path of dharma." The rinpoche paused and then stared at Tompo, as if awaiting his response.

Tompo nodded in acknowledgement and leaned forward, his face eager.

"When you lived the state of an orphan without home," the rinpoche said slowly and with emphasis, "profoundly and truthfully, without desiring or wishing for anything, you reached the primordial state of being in essence, free from the grasp of samsara. Therefore, the state of an orphan without home is a great achievement, beyond even what many diligent practitioners achieve in their entire lives."

"Yes, Rinpoche."

"So, in terms of the stages of the path of dharma, you are all set to free yourself from clinging to duality and abandon the notion of the *self* and the *I*. That means you are prepared to transcend the conceptual mind and discover that everything you perceive is only a projection of the mind and that nothing truly exists. This is how you will realise the emptiness inherent in all phenomena, the true nature of reality."

Tompo's astonishment overtook him, and he gaped in wonder.

"In this manner, you have directly reached the secret path of *dzogpachenpo*, the final and ultimate teaching, at an advanced level where one must abandon dharma to progress further. For like you said, dharma, in the end, is only a path, and just as you have to leave the path behind upon reaching the destination, you have to discard dharma to attain the state of emptiness because, ultimately, dharma itself doesn't exist."

"I see, Rinpoche."

"But, unfortunately, even after reaching this most advanced stage, many get stuck here, clinging to dharma. The state of a monk without dharma, therefore, is even a greater achievement. However, having never comprehended any dharma teachings and engaged in practices, this concept may seem empty. Nevertheless, the essence of this state that you have attained will truly manifest its power and potential when you begin practising, after I impart the instructions to you."

"I understand, Rinpoche."

Thokmay Jatso Rinpoche continued explaining, as well as pointing out the instruction through the afternoon and into the evening, and then through the night and into the early hours of the morning, and Tompo absorbed it all in, grasping everything, without any vagueness.

Later that day, three clarion birds flew in from beyond the mountains and hovered in the sky, circling the monastery. Soon word spread among monks and visitors alike of a pilgrim monk receiving secret teachings from the rinpoche. Yet, shrouded in mystery, no one knew for certain who he was, or what teaching he was receiving.

As the days unfolded, more auspicious signs appeared, and the whispers of those who bore witness to these events traversed distant corners, beckoning one and all from far and wide. Yet, despite the growing curiosity and the influx of pilgrims and visitors, the veil of secrecy held firm, and no one knew what exactly was transpiring inside the rinpoche's chamber.

Soon it was time for Tompo to leave, and he left quietly one early morning while everyone was still sleeping.

He headed south, traversing mountains, valleys, and enduring all manner of weather until he reached the narrow U-shaped valley nestled between the peaks of Gold Mountain and Copper Mountain.

There, he settled upon the very spot where he had encountered the old monk amidst the verdant grass, and filled a cup with ara. However, this time, the great Tokdenpa Gyal Raypadmë did not appear from anywhere.

Thus, gulping down his drink and returning the cup to his bag, he went to the base of Copper Mountain and began ascending it, following the same dim trail by which the old monk had come down before.

The way was rocky, narrow, and steep, and after what seemed to be a long and arduous climb, he arrived at a cave high up on the mountaintop.

Setting his kowgum aside on the ground, he surveyed the expanse of the mountaintop and observed tiers of rugged ridges forming an almost circular enclosure around him, stretching into the vast distance.

Satisfied with his inspection of the area, he ventured into the cave and found it to be quite spacious. However, except for a thick scroll of parchment wedged within a crevice of the rocky wall, it was empty, as if it had been vacated recently.

He carefully removed the parchment, unrolled it and read the text inscribed on the outermost sheet.

> *For the orphan without home, the monk without dharma, the traveller without path, and now the dweller without companion; to the greatest of the tokdenpas to journey without following the traditional path of dharma. These instructions are left for you in case you need to validate your initial results as you commence the practice of dzogpachenpo. For, as you progress in the later stage, you will traverse into the realm where even I myself have not yet ventured.*

Tompo methodically flipped through the sheets one by one, glanced briefly at the writings, carefully rolled it all into a scroll, and tucked it back into the crevice of the wall.

PART FIVE

CHAPTER 57

Jadelma dreamt of Tompo arriving at Kisathang carrying his kowgum. He was completely transformed, with a white circular spot on his hair above his forehead, and a distinct eye-like mark between his eyebrows. The dream was so vivid that she took it as an omen of him arriving after receiving the highest dharma teaching.

In anticipation, she acquired a beautifully crafted new throne with a dais for Tompo and arranged a modest reception on the front lawn. Then, donning a new patterned silk kira and a silk brocade tego, she waited there every day, ready to receive him with a ceremonial scarf, which amused the people of the village.

However, Tompo did not arrive, much to the delight of the people. The days turned into weeks, and the weeks stretched into months, but still there was no sign of Tompo.

Initially, those who gathered in front of Jadelma's house laughed and teased her, but they soon began to ridicule her, with some even growing raucous and directing lewd comments both at her and her daughter, Lachem Dema, who was now a young girl.

Even though Lachem Dema was neither embarrassed nor annoyed at her mother for what she was doing, and so staunchly remained by her mother's side, Aum Zam had had enough of the drama.

The stocky and now ageing woman approached Jadelma one afternoon. "Jadelma, you have to stop this nonsense immediately," she said, keeping her voice low so that villagers milling about could not hear her. "It has been going on for months now. Don't you see he is not coming back? He has been gone for ten long years. Who knows if he is even alive?"

"He will come, Aum Zam, he will come," Jadelma replied with conviction. "If he doesn't come today, he will come tomorrow. If not tomorrow, then the day after tomorrow. Or the day after that, but he will come. It is not a matter of *if*, but *when*."

Aum Zam gave her a sceptical look. "Dreams have no substance and significance for people like you and me, Jadelma. Omen and prophecy are for trulkus and rinpoches. Come to your senses and stop this nonsense right away. You cannot afford to have everyone mocking you. You have to think about Lachem's reputation and her future."

Jadelma grew quiet, but she was still resolute.

"Even your nine-grain brew mash has not fermented despite your aspiration prayer. Isn't this a clear sign that you are no dakini woman, and that he is no destiny monk? Things just don't happen like that, Jadelma."

Jadelma released a loud sigh. "Aum Zam, you are right to be angry at me. But please, don't say such a thing. I may or may not be a dakini woman, but you must never underestimate anyone's aspiration prayer. My brew mash may not have fermented, but it has not gone stale either."

"You don't know if it has gone stale or not, Jadelma, because you have not unwrapped the blankets. It could be stinking inside, or all dried up and hardened. Anything could have happened with that mash, except fermentation."

Just at that moment, Jadelma saw a figure appear from a far-off distance. It seemed to be a man, and he was carrying a kowgum on his back. *Can this be Tompo?* she thought. *Isn't this just like I dreamt?*

Someone in the small crowd pointed and called out, "Do you see? It is Tompo!"

The noises and the heckling stopped suddenly. Jadelma, beaming with joy, prepared her scarf into folds to welcome Tompo, whose beaming face could now be recognised.

He sported an eye-like mark between his eyebrows and a circular white spot on his hair, just above his forehead—the same Tompo who had appeared in her dream. Filled with great joy, she unfurled the ceremonial scarf and offered it to him. This sight left everyone not only astonished but also in utter silence.

"You have returned, my Tompo," Jadelma exclaimed, her face expressing a blend of joy and vindication. "I knew my dream would not deceive me. I saw you precisely as you appear now, just like this."

"Oh, my poor Jadelma," sighed Tompo. "You saw me in your dream exactly as I am? It must have been my longing for you that manifested into your dream, for I have kept you in my thoughts, even when my mind was dissolving and holding any thought was difficult."

"Oh, Tompo," she sighed. "How kind to remember me even when you were in such a sublime state. I will never ever forget this. Please, come now, come and sit on this throne that I had made for you as my offering. It may not be as beautiful, but it has my aspiration prayer."

Tompo's face filled with emotion. "My Jadelma, my spiritual muse dakini woman, I cannot thank you enough for all you have done. But we are in this together; you will come where I go. While for others, for the lives lived together, the karma generated will be different for each of them. For us, the karma generated will be the same for each of us. For that was my aspiration prayer."

Becoming even more joyous, she ushered him onto the throne. Offering him a cup of ceremonial ara, she knelt in front of him, her hands outstretched forward and lifted in the air, in the gesture of offering, and sang the verses of praise, triumph, and celebration in his honour.

Everyone watching fell into a mesmerising silence, but a rowdy couple known to be spiteful of Jadelma came by and broke the spell. Then, suddenly, everyone began to make noise, and soon some people started to shout and hurl jokes and insults at her, all of this disrupting the reception.

But Jadelma and Tompo did not pay attention to these people. Instead, they went on with the ceremony until the very end, after which Jadelma ushered Tompo into the house and offered a welcome feast, one in which Aum Zam participated begrudgingly.

"Teacher Kathog went into *losum choesum* retreat some years after you left, leaving the monastery in the care of the chief disciple," Jadelma said, updating Tompo on the affairs of the monastery. "And as soon as he came out, he was enthroned as the lama of the monastery. Now, he has taken Uma Dolma from your village as his spouse."

"That is good news, Jadelma."

"Yes, it is," Jadelma nodded. "Lama Kathog has now become highly acclaimed and renowned. People from all corners of the region seek his audience and blessings. Also, most of the monks who were there with you are still here, even though they have completed their studies. They want to stay on, serve the lama, learn more, and perfect their skills. Our village is truly blessed now."

"Yes, indeed, my Jadelma."

Jadelma nodded with a slight bow, and Tompo reciprocated the gesture in acknowledgement. Then he drank a sip of ara from the silver cup and held the cup in front of her, and she refilled it, using the silver canister, much like before.

Chapter 58

Ani Uma Dolma was standing by the gate, seeing off the villagers who had come to offer food grains, vegetables, cheese, butter, and tea leaves to the lama and the monastery, when Headman Thodak Zamba and Amala Nangsa Dolkar emerged on horseback from below the rim of the hill, leading a caravan of dusty men and packhorses.

The ani stared at her parents-in-law in disbelief, as if she were seeing their ghosts. "Where are you two coming from, appearing as if in a dream? Not even a word about coming."

"We left in a hurry," said the headman as he dismounted. "There was no time to send word." The headman clenched his teeth and groaned in pain. "Never travelled this hard and fast."

"Yes, we travelled like we were chased by a devil," added the amala, her voice carrying a sharp edge of anger, as her horseman helped her down. "But it was the work of a devil," she continued, and paused upon noticing the villagers watching. "I hope all is well here," she said then, changing the subject and softening her tone.

"We are all fine," Ani Uma Dolma replied, her expression composed, although she noticed that her in-laws appeared troubled, even fearful. Their eyes appeared to be sunken in their sockets and their expressions were grim. All of this worried her, but she refrained from asking in front of the villagers. "Come and rest then." She ushered them towards the residence.

"Where is Kathog?" asked the headman. "We need to see him right away, as we have an urgent matter to discuss."

"In the shrine room," the ani replied, indicating the monastery.

The headman and the amala nodded and walked across the courtyard and into the building, with the ani following closely behind.

Lama Kathog sat on a throne, administering *kago* to a group of people. In a red hat and a maroon robe, he looked so majestic that both the headman and the amala felt proud of him, momentarily forgetting their trouble.

"Our old man Orop expired suddenly without any obvious illness, about one month ago," the headman began as soon as the people had left and they had settled down. "We cremated him and conducted all the rituals and rites properly, but he has been haunting and terrorising everyone in the village since the night he died."

"That miserable old man always said he would haunt us after death," said the amala, curling her lips with disdain. "His thoughts were so evil that the moment he died, his consciousness turned into a malevolent spirit. And he is so nasty that he is moving things physically, even touching people in their sleep. Everyone is so frightened now that they are petrified of going to bed."

"I am sorry to hear about this, Father and Mother," said Lama Kathog, his voice filled with empathy. "Agay Orop was angry and bitter by nature, with a deep and inexplicable rage inside him, consuming him alive. To be honest, I am surprised he lived this long."

The headman nodded his agreement. "He may have lived a long time, but he could not come to terms with his karma and accept his life. I am sure he carried that anguish in his consciousness to the bardo, confusing and stopping him from learning about his death."

"Yes, it is likely, Father," said Lama Kathog. "But you and Mother need not worry: I will conduct a ritual tomorrow. Wherever his consciousness may be wandering, I will summon it here and chant guidance and wisdom to it."

His father seemed relieved. "We came for this purpose only."

"Father, I just heard that Tompo was back today."

"Another wretch who will haunt us when he dies," the amala interjected with frustration. "We provide for them, and yet they think ill of us when they are alive and haunt us when they are dead. What to do with the likes of them?"

But the headman's face lit up. "That is a remarkable coincidence. You should ask him to come here tomorrow and offer an earnest aspiration prayer for the old man. Since they were close, like father and son, the old man may finally find his peace."

"Yes, Father," promised the lama. "I will send someone to inform him."

The headman nodded, a sense of relief washing over him. As his body eased, and the weight on his heart lifted, the exhaustion from the arduous journey and the tormenting nights suddenly descended upon him, and his eyes slowly closed.

CHAPTER 59

A thick curl of dark smoke rose from the spent incense and lingered in the air of the shrine room as Tompo concluded his morning prayer. He made his aspiration prayer and stared at Jadelma's nine-grain brew mash sitting on a raised bed at the side of the altar, concealed beneath a thick layer of cloths.

As he began to rise, he heard a muffled conversation from the porch. It was Jadelma, and she was talking to a man. He walked across the room, went through the door, and met her in the hallway looking quite sorrowful, as if something unfortunate had happened.

"What is it, Jadelma?" Tompo asked, his voice soft.

"Lama Kathog's parents came yesterday. The old man, Orop, died suddenly without any sickness, and although all the rituals and rites were performed, he is haunting and terrorising everyone in the village."

A tear came to Tompo's eye, but his face remained calm. "Agay Orop was like a real father to me, Jadelma, and I owe him so much. When we parted ways, I offered an aspiration prayer that we meet again in this lifetime, even if it is in death, so that I would be able to do something for him and fulfil my duty as a son."

Jadelma nodded. "Lama Kathog is conducting a ritual today to summon his consciousness and chant guidance on his way through the bardo to his next life. So, Lama Kathog and his parents are asking you to come and pray for him, so that he can leave in peace."

Tompo nodded meekly.

She touched his shoulder. "I will go with you, Tompo."

After a quick breakfast, Tompo and Jadelma set off for the monastery, but they were not the only ones en route. As the news of the ritual had spread through the village, many were going to offer their prayers and contribute something to it.

This made Tompo and Jadelma's journey unpleasant, as every person they met along the way cast curious glances their way or enjoyed suppressed laughter at their expense. Yet, they carried on undeterred, keeping to themselves and refraining from engaging with anyone.

When they reached the monastery, the ritual had begun in the shrine room, and the monks and the villagers assigned to help with the logistics were busy outside the makeshift outdoor kitchen built on the side of the courtyard.

Unsure to whom they should hand over the bags of grains and vegetables that they had brought for the ritual, they walked to the outdoor kitchen, glancing around. As they stood there, Amala Nangsa Dolkar and Ani Uma Dolma emerged from inside and stopped, clearly surprised to see Tompo, completely transformed, and Jadelma, dazzlingly beautiful. In fact, the two women seemed to be at a loss for words.

"Amala and Ani," Tompo greeted with a respectful bow.

"Oh, it is you, Tompo," the amala responded, regaining her composure. "I didn't recognise you. How have you been?"

"I am well, Amala."

The amala glanced at Jadelma and then turned back to him. "It is good that you came for the ritual, Tompo. I don't know what happened. We performed all the rituals properly, but the old man is still wandering in the bardo. Please, go inside and make your aspiration prayer for him. It might help him find his way out of this state of suffering."

"Yes, I will, Amala."

Tompo and Jadelma handed the bags to Ani Uma Dolma and went inside the monastery building and into the shrine room, just in time for a recess. The ritual instruments stopped, leaving behind a deafening silence and causing everyone to turn and stare in surprise.

Thogarp and Nagpo, the two ritual masters standing at the far side of the shrine, broke into a grimace, whispering to one another and giggling.

But Pentsa, seated among the row of monks engaged in the ritual, swiftly rose to his feet, his robe and shawl swishing, and hastened across the room to greet Tompo. "You really have returned, Tompo!" he exclaimed, his eyes wide and his face beaming. "Where did you disappear for such a long time?"

Tompo was equally thrilled to meet his old friend. "I was wandering from place to place, visiting monasteries and sacred sites. You know how quickly time flies when you travel."

"But what changed you so much?" Pentsa stared at Tompo from head to toe. "You look so different."

"Nothing really, Pentsa. Perhaps, just the way I see things."

"Just the way you see things?" came Thogarp's taunting voice from behind him.

Tompo and Jadelma turned around and saw Thogarp and Nagpo approaching.

"How so, Tompo?" continued Thogarp, a smirk playing on his face. "That sounds quite high-level and esoteric."

"Yes, Tompo," said Nagpo, feigning solemnity. "That went right above my head. Is it an advanced secret teaching that you received from some rinpoches somewhere? I am sure you must have met many great masters and received many secret teachings on a journey this long."

Pentsa became furious, but with everyone watching, he knew to say nothing.

In a voice both calm and cool, Tompo responded, "Not really like you put it, Nagpo. But yes, as it happens, I did meet some great rinpoches, and also received some advanced teaching on achieving liberation without the path."

"Liberation without the path," exclaimed Thogarp, sarcasm in his voice. "That is awesome, Tompo. You must tell us about it, but first, prostrate to Lama Kathog, " he pointed to the middle of the floor, "and make your aspiration prayer for the dead."

Unable to control his laughter, Nagpo turned his head away.

Tompo nodded submissively, and then he and Jadelma turned towards Lama Kathog and prostrated three times, and turned towards the altar and repeated the same number of prostrations, all the while offering their aspiration prayer for Agay Orop's swift rebirth.

By the time Tompo and Jadelma had completed their prayer, Pentsa and the others were back in their seats, ready to resume the ritual, so they quietly turned and left the shrine room, returning to the courtyard.

The ani and the amala were busy receiving the guests and overseeing the work, but the monk serving one group of guests took them aside and served them butter tea and snacks.

Shortly after tea, Jadelma departed for home, leaving Tompo behind at the monastery to spend the day reciting prayers and chanting mantras for his dear old friend. However, not wishing to go back into the shrine room, he found solace in the monastery's outdoor butter lamp shed, located on the lawn at the side of the monastery.

The spacious rectangular lawn overlooking the valley, his favourite spot on the campus, appeared as it did when he was last there. Away from the courtyard and the shrine room, it was relatively quiet and deserted.

As no one in particular seemed to be looking after the task of preparing the butter lamps, he took charge of it, tending to the extinguished lamps, making new ones, and lighting them, all the while reciting prayers and chanting mantras.

CHAPTER 60

The ritual for Orop was over, but instead of finding relief, Headman Thodak Zamba and Amala Nangsa Dolkar became more worried. Not sure whether the old man's consciousness had been reached and guided through the process of rebirth or not, they wondered if they had made a mistake by coming to Kisathang. If the ritual was not successful, it would damage their son's reputation.

"What should we do?" asked the headman. "If we ask Kathog, it might appear as though we doubt his capability."

"We cannot ask him," the amala asserted. "Nor can we bring this up with Uma Dolma."

"But if we sit down together for dinner, we will have to say something about it," remarked the headman. "Perhaps we should eat something and retire to bed early."

"I don't feel like eating anything," replied the amala. "I just had a large snack with the monks."

"In that case, I too will not eat; I have had my fill for the day as well."

In agreement, they went to their room and retired for the night, but they had trouble falling asleep, fearful of the old man haunting and tormenting them in their dreams, as he had done every night, even after they had left the village.

However, when they finally fell asleep, late into the night, their sleep was so light that when they woke up in the morning, their transition from sleep to wakefulness was seamless.

"Did I fall asleep?" the amala asked, sitting up and looking at the headman. "I feel as though I had not slept a wink. How can this be?"

"Ah, yes," the headman replied, his brow furrowing in confusion. "Even I am not certain."

She raised an eyebrow, her expression mirroring his puzzlement. "You too? This is quite strange."

The headman's face illuminated with a spark of understanding. "Perhaps we were so terrified of having a nightmare about Orop that we didn't know if we slept or not. This sort of thing happens at times, especially when keeping watch over a dead body. We drift off into sleep, wake up with a start, and then wonder if we even slept at all."

"Are you saying that we actually slept?" she asked, a puzzled expression on her face.

"Yes, I am quite certain we did," he affirmed. "I dozed off for some time, but not long enough to have a nightmare. And I am confident you slept, because you were snoring when I woke up one time. I nudged you a bit, and you turned on your side and stopped snoring."

"I remember it now," she exclaimed, a flicker of recollection crossing her face, but no sooner did she utter that than her expression froze, and her brow furrowed. "But how could Orop have gone to Dewachen Zhingkham? He neither prayed to Buddha Yoedpame, nor did he have any religious inclinations." Noting the headman's puzzled expression, she added, "I dreamt of the old man being ushered into Dewachen Zhingkham."

"Really? That is good then."

"Yes, but how could he—"

"It was not his merit," the headman remarked quickly, his face beaming with joy, "but the power of the ritual officiant that enabled him to be reborn in a buddha realm. It is said that the officiating lama, if he is highly accomplished, can transfer the consciousness of the dead straight to a buddha realm through *phowa*."

"That means our Kathog is highly accomplished already," the amala said, her eyes wide. "No wonder he has gained such fame. He is a great lama. And he is only thirty-five." Her face beamed even more, recalling something. "He was right when he said he would achieve greatness, like that of Riwang Trulku."

"Yes, he did well to pursue the path of dharma."

"And we did well to support him wholeheartedly."

The headman nodded. "It is such a relief. Our porters and attendants and everyone in the village must have had a peaceful night for the first time in over a month." He pushed his pillow onto the wall and leaned back.

The amala also pushed her pillow onto the wall and leaned back. And as they sighed with relief, one after another, their bodies relaxed and they felt peace slowly descend into their hearts. It was then they knew for certain that the old man's consciousness was finally through the bardo and had been reborn or was being reborn somewhere better.

"But Tompo is wasting his life," she said, returning to her thoughts about Lama Kathog's achievement and greatness. "He should have listened to Lama Jamsempa and chanted mantras, but I believe he insisted on receiving teachings. Looking down on mantras will only bring him more bad karma."

"That is bound to happen," said the headman. "He didn't heed his lama's advice, and he also wasted his wife's wealth travelling around for ten years. If he did not recite prayers and chant mantras, he could not have done anything worthwhile, even if he had been on a pilgrimage."

"I agree: he would not have achieved anything."

"If he is to save himself from karmic consequences before it is too late, he should completely forget this dharma nonsense and lead a good, meaningful life. If he carries on like this, he will squander her resources and accrue more negative karma in return."

"I don't think he will quit on his dharma, not in this lifetime. In fact, I think he will double down on it. Did you hear that his wife had a throne made for him, and he sat on it? I can't believe that he did that, sitting on a throne like a lama. Who in his right mind would do such a thing?"

"Tompo will not listen to anyone if he sets his mind to something," the headman commented, as he got up from his bed and began to dress.

The amala also stood, shaking her head. "A dimwit with bad karma is one unfortunate person," she remarked.

Relieved and happy, they went out to the patio chitchatting, washed with the pot of warm water left there by an attendant monk, and joined their son and daughter-in-law for breakfast in the living room.

"Father and Mother," said Lama Kathog, looking confused and sounding a bit dismayed. "What happened to you last night? I had just gone to wash up, but you had already gone to bed. Were you able to fall asleep that early?"

"We were utterly worn out," the headman replied, but his tone carried a hint of guilt. "The journey took its toll, coupled with over a month of sleepless nights. And, naturally, our concerns for the people back in the village added to the strain."

"That is exactly what I told him," said Ani Uma Dolma. "Anyway, I am certain you had a good night's sleep. I dreamt of the old man going to Dewachen Zhingkham. He looked so serene and peaceful."

"I also dreamt about him being reborn there!" said the amala.

"Really?" the ani asked, her face lighting up with surprise. "Then he certainly has been reborn in Dewachen."

"Yes," said the headman. "The ritual was successful."

"You didn't have the nightmare then?" asked Lama Kathog, appearing surprised. "Uma Dolma told me that the porters and attendants didn't have the nightmare either."

"No, I didn't have it," the headman replied, "and I am certain everyone back in the village also had a peaceful night. You have done well, Kathog. We will let the villagers know about it as soon as we are home."

"I thought two of you would stay here for a while, Father," said Lama Kathog, his expression becoming sombre. "You rushed back home after my enthronement, and also after our wedding."

Not wanting to remain, yet unable to immediately decline his son's request, the headman appeared remorseful.

Observing his reluctance, the amala flew into a sudden rage. "I am not rushing back home after this gruelling journey and weeks of sleepless nights! I am going to stay put for months and recover my energy and peace of mind."

"But I have some pressing matters to attend to," the headman lamented.

"Nothing that the clerk cannot handle!" she retorted.

"But . . . I didn't authorise him."

A scowl crossed her face. "Seriously? You can send a letter through the porters and the attendants!"

The headman looked sceptical. He did need to return for his work, but he also wanted to placate his wife.

"Please, stay for some time, Father," entreated Lama Kathog. "Once you go home, you will not be able to come again unless something unfortunate like this happens. And when such a thing happens, we cannot spend any quality time together in peace."

Mulling over his son's words, the headman stroked the stubble on his chin, holding the others in anticipation. Then, his expression suddenly changed, and he nodded, eliciting a collective sigh of relief from everyone present.

CHAPTER 61

Jadelma stood on the porch, her gaze fixed on the setting sun, as she held the yarn ball in her left hand, took the drop spindle with her right hand, slightly lifted her right leg, and rolled the shaft on her thigh and sent the spindle spinning in the air.

As the spindle, suspended from her left hand, spun in the air, a lone traveller, weary and dusty from a long and hard journey, halted in front of her house and turned to her with a haunting look.

She was not sure why, but it touched her deeply, piercing her heart.

"I am from Mendrelgang village," said the stranger, his voice trembling. "My son teeters on the precipice of life and death, as his life force was ensnared by the spirit of a woman who died a few years ago."

Jadelma nodded, her expression filled with sympathy.

"We did everything we could," the man continued, his tone bearing the anguish of a father, "but he didn't recover. Then, in this darkest hour, whispers of hope reached us. We heard that Lama Kathog, a sage said to possess great hidden abilities, had transferred the consciousness of an old man who had been haunting the village to a zhingkham."

"Yes, that is true, the old man was the servant of Lama Kathog's parents," Jadelma replied in one breath, her words carrying a sense of assurance. "You did right to come to Lama Kathog. He will free the consciousness of the woman from whatever spirit she was born into, and this will release your son's life force." Her voice held a gentle understanding, as if she could empathise with the traveller's situation. "You need not worry; this can be done."

"Thank you," he replied, relief passing across his face. "How far is the lama's monastery?"

"Not very far," she replied, shaking her head. "It is at the end of the valley, atop a hillock. If you keep to this main path, you will reach a three-way junction with a giant prayer flag. From there, take the path going up the hill."

"Thank you so much." The man nodded gratefully, his demeanour now infused with a renewed sense of hope and his eyes moistened with tears.

Jadelma nodded back and noted his relief.

He turned and walked away, leaving her staring after him.

"Poor fellow," she muttered to herself, lifting her spindle to spin, but as she did so, she turned slightly and noticed Tompo standing at the door, staring after the man. "He was so worried that even a little hope brought him to tears," she said.

"You did well to give him hope, Jadelma," Tompo replied.

"But I hope his son's life force can really be freed."

"The woman must have been reborn as a malevolent spirit," said Tompo with confidence. "Her consciousness can be freed from it and guided to her next rebirth. This will release his son's life force. So, you need not worry, my Jadelma. I will also go and help with the ritual."

"Please, do so," she replied. "The agony this man endures is deep and profound. Also, take something along. As he is a stranger to this village, anyone coming to his ritual with some things to help will give him strength and hope."

"Yes, Jadelma."

Jadelma readied a bag of grains and vegetables that evening, and Tompo left for the monastery early morning the following day and arrived before the ritual had even begun.

He handed the bag to the man from Mendrelgang, saying it was from his wife, whom the man had met yesterday. Just as she had said, the man was deeply touched and filled with gratitude and hope.

Then making his prostrations, as directed by the two ritual masters, Thogarp and Nagpo, Tompo went out and worked in the outdoor butter lamp house.

"Are you here to help, Tompo?" said a man behind him. He turned and noticed the headman and the amala walking towards him. "It is good of you to have come to help," he continued, bobbing his head. "Making butter lamps has great merit. You will surely be born intelligent in your next life. You may then pursue the path of dharma without any difficulty."

"Thank you, Headman."

"Yes, Tompo," added the amala, her tone carrying a note of sincerity. "For this lifetime, you forget this nonsense of receiving dharma teachings. You have a beautiful wife, a house, lands, and basically everything a man needs. Lead a good life, recite prayers, chant mantras, and accrue merit. It is still not too late for you."

"I will, Amala."

"Don't go wandering again," she said, almost as an admonishment.

"I won't, Amala."

The amala and the headman extended a synchronised nod towards Tompo. With their message conveyed without further words, they lingered in the area for a while and eventually departed, leaving Tompo to his tasks.

CHAPTER 62

The ritual for the son of the man from Mendrelgang was so successful that even before the man departed for his home the following day, the news of his son's immediate recovery reached Kisathang through a night traveller.

With such a miraculous recovery, Lama Kathog's name and fame spread throughout the country, and people began to flock to the monastery to conduct rituals for the sick and the deceased, to receive kago and blessings, and for many other purposes.

Tompo also frequented the monastery and helped with the butter lamp work whenever there was a ritual for the sick and the deceased. However, it was not long before both the villagers and the monks, believing that he was doing this work at the monastery to avoid his duties at home, began to criticise and mock him.

But it didn't matter to him.

Neither did it matter to Jadelma. She continued to treat him with the utmost respect, arranging an elevated seat with brocade covering, and serving him the finest wine in a silver cup, poured from a silver canister, on all occasions, whether big or small.

But it was not the same for Aum Zam. She had had enough of Tompo's behaviour and decided to confront him directly, instead of expressing it through Jadelma, because she was certain that her good-hearted friend had been taken in by his bag of trickery and would never say a word against him, much less do anything.

Determined not to let Tompo ruin Jadelma's life, she swore she would act as she and Lachem returned home one evening after a strenuous day in the fields. But even more, she had decided that she was not going to feed Tompo with the food she grew with her hard work and sweat. Just thinking about this prompted her to spit on the ground.

As expected, Tompo had arrived, and Jadelma was serving him wine. "Ah, our Lama Tompo is home," Aum Zam remarked, her voice dripping with heavy sarcasm.

Jadelma's body tensed, Aum Zam's confrontational tone and words sending both shock and anger coursing through her. "Aum Zam," she responded, her voice sharp with reprimand.

Tompo, however, remained nonchalant. "Yes, Aum Zam, I just arrived a moment ago," he replied calmly.

"I am sure you will go tomorrow, too," Aum Zam persisted, her words piercing the air once again with a cutting tone.

"Yes, Aum Zam," replied Tompo politely, ignoring her nasty tone of voice. "A group came from the far east to conduct the forty-ninth-day ritual for their deceased, who is not only terrorising the entire village but also bringing sicknesses and death. I thought I would go and help with the ritual."

"A group will be arriving tomorrow as well, Tompo." Aum Zam's anger was now fully ignited. "And then another group will come the day after that. In fact, groups will keep coming every day because Lama Kathog's fame has reached far and wide. But you have no such fame, so why do you feel you have a reason to go there every day? There is work here, Tompo. We need you to do your part for your family."

"Stop it, Aum Zam, stop it!" insisted Jadelma, her voice shrill, and her face red with anger.

"I will not stop without speaking my mind today, Jadelma!" Aum Zam retorted. "Is Tompo working in the fields? No! We are doing all the work there, as well as at home, while he idles away his days in the monastery, doing absolutely nothing."

"He doesn't just sit there, Aum Zam!" persisted Jadelma.

"Yes, he does, Jadelma! He sits there and makes butter lamps, as if he doesn't have any work at home! Why does he have to go every day, as if he is the lama officiating the rituals and guiding the dead to zhingkham, or freeing the life force of the sick from the evil spirits?"

Jadelma's eyes were wide with disbelief. "How can you say such a thing, Aum Zam?"

"Why can't I say it, Jadelma?" Aum Zam's exasperation grew more palpable. "I am sweating in the field for you and Lachem, not for him to indulge in pleasures as he wishes! How long will you let him go on like this?"

"Oh, you unfortunate woman," lamented Jadelma. "If only you would listen to me, but I guess this is your bad karma and nothing can be done about it. You don't know what merit you can gain by keeping quiet and, by the same token, what demerit you can accumulate by speaking evil."

"It is fine, Jadelma," interjected Tompo, seeking to ease the tension. "Aum Zam is not at fault, not truly. She is merely repeating what others are saying. You must not blame her, and not let her accrue negative karma on our account."

"I hear what you are saying, my Tompo," Jadelma replied, mellowing a bit.

Tompo's face took on a more serious expression. "If Aum Zam accrues any bad karma on your account, it would not be right or fair, for she genuinely feels for you. As for me, I have always prayed from the beginning that she gathers no negative karma on my account, and she would not for certain."

Jadelma nodded.

"But as for the people of the village wilfully slandering me for no reason, there is nothing I can do," he added, shaking his head. Then turning to Aum Zam, he said, "I know people say all sorts of things about me, but it doesn't matter to me. Nothing they say or do will affect me in any way, but their words and actions will have grave karmic consequences on them."

Aum Zam was quite stumped and a little frightened. She could not fathom Tompo's intentions, speaking with an air of authority, as if he were a lama, trulku, or rinpoche. Whichever it was, she liked none of it. Her demeanour grew dark, and she ate in silence, refusing to utter a single word throughout the evening.

CHAPTER 63

The monastery's makeshift outdoor kitchen slowly settled down as the lunchtime flurry and the hustle from serving the monks and guests subsided.

When they completed their tasks, those working in the kitchen to cook, help with the culinary tasks, and serve food and drinks, as well as those assisting with logistics to provide external support for the ritual and handle other errands, came to eat.

Ani Uma Dolma, with Amala Nangsa Dolkar by her side, monitoring and overseeing every detail, served them. "We need a plate for Tompo," she shouted into the kitchen, as Tompo appeared from the corner of the building, wiping away the grease stains on his hands from the butter lamps.

"Tompo never carries his plate and cup," remarked someone from inside, sounding annoyed.

"Serve him on that lid," the amala suggested, pointing to the aluminium lid of a vessel resting on the ground. "It doesn't matter to him. He grew up eating off things like that. Where would he have found a proper plate?"

The ani released a loud sigh. "Get that lid, Tompo."

Tompo picked it up and held it in front of the ani, just as Thogarp hurried out of the monastery, carrying Lama Kathog's gleaming wooden bowl and cup filled with his leftover meal.

"Wait, Ani," Thogarp called out, running down the steps. "Don't serve him."

Ani Uma Dolma paused and watched as Thogarp came and overturned the bowl and cup onto Tompo's aluminium lid, causing the food to slop over its rim. "Here, Tompo," he announced. "Lama Kathog's blessing. It will dispel your ignorance, enhance your intelligence, and clear your path for dharma."

"Thank you," Tompo acknowledged with a nonchalant nod, ignoring Thogarp's insult, and strolled over to Pentsa, who was standing on the side of the courtyard after finishing his lunch. "What has gotten you so riled up now?" he asked, observing Pentsa's face flushed with anger.

Pentsa threw up his arms. "How can you even ask, Tompo? That monster Thogarp has not an ounce of respect for anyone who is not someone important or someone useful to him. He is an evil spirit in the body of a person and a devil in the robe of a monk, and he will die a horrible death for doing that to you."

"What a dreadful thing to say for so trifling a matter, Pentsa. You should not take everything to heart. Truly, there is nothing significant about it. But if you make a big fuss about it and spew such strong hatred, it will harm you more than his actions will harm him."

"When it comes to Thogarp and Nagpo, I don't care."

Tompo's face softened, and his expression was almost benign. "See, Pentsa, whatever others say and do to you are perceived from your point of view. These words and actions don't reflect them, but yourself. For whatever happens to you, whether caused by humans or nature, is brought about by your karma."

"But what about them?" Pentsa retorted.

"They, too, will gather karma equivalent to their actions; there is no doubt about it. Except for the buddhas and the bodhisattvas at an advanced stage, no one is free from karma. But that is for them, from their standpoint. For you, however, and from your point of view, it is about you and your karma."

Pentsa was surprised by the wisdom in Tompo's words, and his face turned pensive. As he reflected on them, he nodded slowly, and with each nod his anger gradually dissipated. "You are right, Tompo," he replied. "I never considered it that way. As much as it is about them from their perspective, it is about me from my perspective, even though they are the ones performing the actions."

Tompo looked very pleased. "Yes, Pentsa, that is how karma works."

"Thank you, Tompo," Pentsa replied, his voice sincere. "I am grateful to you for opening my eyes. From now onwards, I will not respond to their actions, regardless of what they say and do. I will not stoop to their level. I will not let my anger get the better of me."

"That is good," said Tompo.

Pentsa thought about this for a long moment, and then said, "I see now how a clear perspective changes everything."

"It all depends on our view, Pentsa," Tompo affirmed. "Having the right view is crucial. I am not talking about the right view of dharma, but the right view of general things in our daily lives."

Pentsa nodded. "Yes, I see it now. The wrong view deludes us."

"It does," Tompo agreed. "And delusion, as you very well know, is one of the defilements, according to dharma."

The conch blared from inside the monastery, summoning the monks conducting the ritual back from the recess, but Pentsa stood there and made no effort to move. "You are truly a good person, Tompo," he said. "You always were."

"You are as well, Pentsa."

"Yes, but you are the one with the pure heart, a man without vices, like that of a bodhisattva. And now, having been on the holy pilgrimage of a lifetime, you have also become learned and wise, not only in the ways of the world, but also in the ways of dharma." He placed his hand on his chest. "Tompo, I am saying this from deep inside my heart."

"I know you are, Pentsa, and I thank you for it."

"I don't know where you have been, whom you met, or what teaching you received, but you have now acquired the wisdom and knowledge of a bodhisattva. I know this because what you have just told me has enlightened me more than all the texts I have studied. So yes, you have become a true bodhisattva, my friend." With that, Pentsa turned and walked away.

"And you will become one yourself, my friend, in a not-so-distant future," murmured Tompo, his voice barely audible. "By feeling this genuinely, and saying it aloud, you have sown the seed of bodhisattva in yourself. This was all that was needed to bring our friendship to a spiritual fruition."

A clarion bird flew over the monastery, its call resonating through the air.

Tompo looked up into the sky and then down at the aluminium lid, a smile playing on his lips. "You have fulfilled your part. Now, let me fulfil mine." He dug into the food and ate joyously, without spilling a morsel. Then he washed the lid clean and placed it back atop the vessel that sat in the corner. "May you continue to nourish countless hungry stomachs and shape numerous destinies," he said quietly.

Tompo heard more clarion birds as he walked back to the butter lamp house. He gazed upwards and said, "Here they come, the messengers of the buddhas and the bodhisattvas, to connect the mundane to the divine."

The birds continued to soar over the monastery until the ritual ended towards sundown. Then, they followed Tompo home, soaring high above him, their melodies echoing through the valley.

When Tompo reached home, it was dusk and Jadelma was outside making an evening smoke offering at the incense burner. Hearing his footsteps on the grass behind her, she turned. "You are a bit late, my dear," she said, her voice gentle. "I hope all went well, as it should have."

He smiled, his face radiant as usual. "Yes, my Jadelma."

However, despite his smile and the radiance on his face, she discerned a fleeting trace of sadness in his eyes, yet she chose not to mention this. Instead, she said, "That is good then, as it should be."

"Yes, my Jadelma," he repeated. An atmosphere of solemnity grew between them.

She took his hand and led him across the lawn, up the stone stairs, onto the wooden porch, and into the house. Then she paused suddenly at the doorway and sniffed the air. A strong scent of sweet alcohol wafted into her nostrils. "My brew mash has fermented," she said.

In her excitement, she forgot the solemnity of the moment. Releasing Tompo's hand, she hurried across the living room and disappeared through the inner door. "Yes, it has fermented!" she exclaimed from inside the shrine room. "What a sweet aroma, like heaven's nectar has dripped into it!"

When Tompo joined her in the shrine room moments later, she had already peeled the blankets off the brew mash and was poring over it. "You were right to tell me to leave it as it was," she told him, turning towards him.

"Yes, my Jadelma, as you should have."

She was about to concur when she detected that same undercurrent of sadness once more. Her smile disappeared. "You appear somewhat sad today, my dear Tompo. I observed it then, and I observe it now. This is not as it should be."

"No, Jadelma, this is not as it should be," Tompo responded. "There is no cause for sorrow here, only cause for celebration.

Nevertheless, this is where our journey ends, where we part our ways, even if it is only for a time, until we meet again. So, I permit myself to be a little sorrowful on your account."

"Oh, my Tompo," Jadelma breathed, her hands instinctively clasping her chest. "You continue to regard me, to treasure this mundane part of me, even in this sublime state."

"Yes, I do, my Jadelma," Tompo nodded. "As illusory as it may be, it is what has rendered this ultimate reality possible."

"Yes, certainly, my Tompo."

Tompo nodded, and they stood for a while in silence. "Then, everything will be just as I have told you," he said.

"Yes, I comprehend the nature of the phenomenon that is to transpire and also grasp the depth of its teaching, as you have elucidated to me, time and again, both in person and in my vision. I have also made all preparations to receive the three dakini women to arrive here from the three directions of north, south, and east."

Tompo nodded.

"I have also briefed Lachem about everything."

Tompo nodded once more. "The brew mash will require no distillation," he said. "You merely place it in a vessel and let it sit overnight. By tomorrow, it will have transformed into a pure wine of heavenly nectar. You offer this wine to the buddhas of the past, present, and future in the cave of Copper Mountain."

Jadelma nodded, rose, and walked away to fetch the vessel.

Tompo turned and gazed out of the window and noticed the moon peeking over the mountains, its gentle glow casting a silvery veil on the landscape lining the sky and bathing the valley in a serene, ethereal light.

CHAPTER 64

Amidst the flurry of activities, with everyone bustling around to fulfil their tasks, one monk boy paused in the centre of the courtyard and looked up.

The sky displayed an extraordinary shade of blue, almost mystical and transcendental, and a distinct golden halo encircled the sun. As the young monk observed, enchantment evident in his face, everything gradually took on an even more magical appearance.

Noticing his gaze skywards, another young monk joined him, also lifting his gaze in astonishment. Upon witnessing this, another monk halted and directed his attention upwards. And soon, a group of them had gathered, all fixated on the sky with a sense of wonder.

"What are you fools searching for in the sky in broad daylight?" a stern voice admonished from behind. They turned and found themselves facing Amala Nangsa Dolkar, holding a cake of butter wrapped in a leaf. "Don't any of you have tasks to attend to?"

"Yes, Amala," they chorused and scattered in different directions.

"Monks or layfolk, children are still children." The amala shook her head as she went around the corner of the building to the butter lamp house.

All the butter lamps were freshly lit, and Tompo was sitting on the ground and chanting mantras with his eyes shut.

Not wishing to disturb him, she quietly left the cake of butter on an old choedom by the side of the building and turned to leave. At that moment, Jadelma and three young women, all dressed in dakini costumes, appeared from around the corner of the building.

The amala was so taken aback by their presence that she nearly slipped and fell. Then, as much embarrassed by her clumsiness as offended by the absurdity of their attire, her face shifted into an expression of rage.

However, Jadelma and the three dakini women did not even cast a glance in the amala's direction, let alone become unsettled by her expression.

"I will make sure to have a talk about this with Uma Dolma," the amala said, as she stomped away. She rounded the corner of the building and hastened towards the courtyard. But just as she arrived at the stairs, a farmer came running through the gate.

All tasks came to a halt as everyone's gaze fixed on the man who was heading towards Ani Uma Dolma, gasping for breath.

"Khennor Jaden Rinpoche is coming, Ani," he announced.

"Khennor Jaden Rinpoche?" Ani Uma Dolma repeated, surprised.

"Yes, with his entourage," the farmer replied, his words coming amidst heaves and gasps.

"From where, and what for?" she wanted to know.

"I'm not sure, Ani, but there is a retinue of monks, disciples, attendants, and followers accompanying the rinpoche. They have also asked everyone from the village to join them, and now a large crowd is arriving. It appears as if they are in some sort of urgency. They are travelling swiftly and vigorously. They will reach here shortly."

"We must organise a reception," she exclaimed, before turning to address everyone. "Drop whatever you are doing and clear this area immediately. We must arrange a reception for the rinpoche. I will inform the lama."

There were comments all around, but everyone understood the importance of this and began their work.

The ani dashed across the courtyard towards the monastery. As she went up the stone stairs, she could hear the amala barking orders to both monks and farmers left and right. *Trust the amala to get everybody working*, she mused, as she rushed into the monastery.

She raced down the long corridor and burst into the shrine room, startling Lama Kathog and his monks and disrupting the rhythm of their ritual instruments and the flow of their chanting.

"Khennor Jaden Rinpoche is coming!" she announced.

"What?" exclaimed Lama Kathog, setting aside his *damaru* and *drilbu*.

"Khennor Jaden Rinpoche is coming!"

In that instant, all instruments fell silent, and her voice bellowed through the hushed room. "He has a large retinue of monks, disciples, and attendants. He will be here any moment now."

"Where is he coming from?" asked the lama, scrambling to his feet.

"No idea, Lama, but he is nearly up the hill."

"Then we need to prepare a reception."

"I have already told the people outside, but what about in here?"

Lama Kathog turned to his disciples. "Quick, clear everything and sweep the room clean. One of you go and fetch a new silk brocade for the throne!"

In a flash, the monks were on their feet and in action.

Lama Kathog descended the throne and followed his wife out of the room, along the corridor, and onto the landing above the stone stairs. From there, he beheld a scene of frantic activity. Everyone was working swiftly to clear the courtyard and arrange a ceremonial throne. But before he could exhale a sigh of relief, the sound of the rinpoche's arriving caravan reached his ears.

Everyone worked even faster and managed to set up a modest reception by the time Khennor Jaden Rinpoche appeared on horseback atop the hill's crest, leading a caravan of monks, disciples, attendants, porters, ponies, and the people of Kisathang. And as the rinpoche dismounted and entered through the gate, they swiftly organised themselves into two lines, facing each other, on either side of the gate, standing ready to receive him.

"No need to prostrate," the rinpoche announced. "Don't prostrate!" he repeated, waving his hand when Lama Kathog and Ani Uma Dolma put their hands together. "I didn't come here for a visit."

Lama Kathog and Ani Uma Dolma, positioned at the forefront of the line, paused, and others followed suit, confusion in their expressions.

"You need not have made these arrangements," the rinpoche said, looking at the throne and everything done to welcome him.

"I regret that we didn't do more, Rinpoche," offered Lama Kathog.

The rinpoche tipped his head to acknowledge the effort. "There was hardly time to send someone ahead and inform you of our coming," he said. "We have travelled hard and fast for days and weeks, and most of us are very tired."

Lama Kathog nodded, unsure of what to say.

The rinpoche surveyed the campus around him. "I saw your monastery in my visions and dreams exactly as it is. I have also seen you, your spouse and parents, and all your monks, Lama Kathog. You may be wondering how I know your name, but I know all your monks by face and name."

Everyone, including Lama Kathog, was greatly surprised and pleased.

Observing their expressions, the rinpoche remarked, "You all may not be aware of this, but there is a great tokdenpa among you. He is perhaps the greatest dzogchenpa ever to come."

Everyone looked around, hoping to recognise this tokdenpa, this great master who had transcended duality, the notion of *self* and *other*, the root of suffering and ignorance.

"He has attained enlightenment, complete liberation from samsara," the rinpoche continued, "and he did so without following the traditional path of dharma, the path of intense study and practice. This is astounding, a feat never accomplished before. So, we are fortunate to be here today."

Lama Kathog's surprise and joy transformed into uncertainty.

The rinpoche then, motioning for everyone to join him, proceeded across the courtyard, and the others, led by Lama Kathog, followed in his wake. He went past the stone stairs, rounded the corner of the building, and reached the outdoor butter lamp house.

Tompo sat there cross-legged, his eyes closed, immersed in the recitation of an arcane mantra, and Jadelma and the three dakini women, now wearing headdresses in addition to their ritual attire, stood in the four directions around him, each holding a damaru in one hand and a drilbu in the other.

The rinpoche put his hands together and lowered himself to the ground in prostration before Tompo. Following his lead, every one of his monks, disciples, and attendants prostrated.

However, Lama Kathog, his monks, his wife, his parents, and the people of Kisathang remained frozen in disbelief, their faces mirroring confusion and uncertainty. Amidst the crowd, Aum Zam pushed her way to the front, and what she saw evoked utter shock and disbelief.

Subsequently, the rinpoche and his followers seated themselves on the ground, their hands clasped together in a gesture of supplication and obeisance to Tompo.

Once again, Lama Kathog, accompanied by his spouse, parents, monks, and the inhabitants of Kisathang, stood and stared. Eventually, feeling awkward to continue standing and unsure about what to do, they gradually sat down in ones and twos.

When everyone was seated, Tompo concluded his chanting, and calmly opened his eyes, taking in his surroundings with a grace and dignity that the people of Kisathang had not seen from him before. "Khennor Jaden Rinpoche, you made it on time," he remarked nonchalantly, with a hint of sarcasm directed at Lama Kathog and the others.

"Yes, Tokdenpa," submitted the rinpoche with a bow. "We travelled hard and fast to be here with you."

Tompo nodded his acknowledgement. "I am afraid Rinpoche will have to wait a little longer, as a forty-ninth-day ritual is underway," Tompo said. "I have transferred the consciousness of the dead to a zhingkham. Now, I have to transfer the consciousness of the pig, whose meat we consumed today, to the pure land as well." With that, he closed his eyes and went back to chanting.

Everyone stood there, stunned by what they were hearing.

Lama Kathog did not know if he should sit there and cry, or stand and run. His parents and his wife, seated beside him, were likewise frozen in place, unsure of how to respond.

Aum Zam gasped, her heart racing and her mind flooded with the harsh words she had hurled at Tompo.

Thogarp and Nagpo stared in disbelief, pondering how this could possibly be. Was this the same Tompo they had once ridiculed?

Even Pentsa sat there gaping.

Tompo concluded the chanting of the mantra and stared directly at Lama Kathog and the monks. "Lama Kathog, you and your monks need not feel bad about the way you have behaved towards me. It was not your fault; you didn't know. But, of course, the way you treated me is not how we treat anyone, whoever he is."

Lama Kathog's expression changed from embarrassment to shame, an overwhelming remorse rising from deep inside him that contorted his face and twisted his mouth.

Tompo observed the lama's shame and then spoke. "Lama Kathog, we began our spiritual journey together, from our encounter with the great Riwang Trulku. But as great as he was, it was not his power that brought about those rare auspicious signs that day. While he was undoubtedly a great master, he didn't possess such abilities."

Utterly surprised, Lama Kathog turned to his parents and saw that they were equally taken aback.

"Nobody had told me about Riwang Trulku passing through our village that day," Tompo continued. "So, when I came upon the crowd at the riverbank and heard his sweet melodious voice uttering the words of Buddha's dharma, it was so sudden and unexpected that I felt my hair stand on end."

The headman and the amala looked at each other, remembering that day vividly.

"Then, after manoeuvring through the crowd, I saw him, appearing like a celestial being, sitting regally on a lofty throne, and I heard the crowd chanting the guru mantra at that precise moment, electrifying the atmosphere and sending shivers down my spine."

Ani Uma Dolma remembered the day and her heart wept.

"Then, I felt devotion for dharma so great that it caused my body to rock with such intensity that I felt something erupt within me in one moment and overwhelm me in the next. But most importantly, that devotion was so powerful that the dakinis felt it from the pure lands. That was why those rare and auspicious signs manifested, and a dakini appeared in the sky."

Thogarp and Nagpo exchanged glances, the weight of realisation settling upon them as they recalled every wrongdoing they had committed against Tompo.

Similarly, Aum Zam's heart grew heavy as she yearned for Jadelma to glance her way, if only once. But she did not.

"Of course, I didn't know it then," Tompo admitted. "No one knew, not even the trulku himself. But now I do. I know everything there is to know in the universe. I can see a reality beyond the normal human vision, for I have attained the spiritual awakening of knowledge and wisdom—I have attained the third eye. I have realised the primordial nature of mind, which is absolute knowing."

The headman and the amala's expressions turned grave, feeling not only remorse but also fear of karmic consequences, as the gravity of their negative actions towards Tompo weighed heavily in their hearts.

Tompo adjusted himself into a more comfortable position. "Now, Rinpoche, monks, and all others who have assembled here today," he said, addressing them in a formal tone, as if about to deliver a sermon.

"If Tokdenpa wishes to go to the courtyard," Khennor Jaden Rinpoche interjected, "there is a throne arranged there."

"Rinpoche, that throne is too high for me," Tompo replied. "Even when I sat on the modest throne my wife made for me, after my return from years of wandering, the people of the village expressed dismay and disapproval. Some of them were appalled that I would have the audacity to sit on a throne at all."

"They are ignorant, Tokdenpa," said the rinpoche.

"Yes, that they are, Rinpoche," Tompo replied. "However, I have no need for a throne, as I am not going to give any teaching.

For me, that time has passed. As Rinpoche is well aware, a teaching such as this rests entirely upon destiny and, of course, on people's merit. But again, there is no reason to lose hope. My Jadelma will elucidate the whole teaching later, and the merit of hearing it from her will be as much as hearing it from me."

"Thank you, Tokdenpa," said the rinpoche.

Overcome with remorse, Thogarp and Nagpo, along with those monks and villagers who had in some ways mistreated Tompo, wept openly.

Pentsa put his hands together in supplication and obeisance to his dear friend, and Tompo acknowledged him with a nod, and then turned to Aum Zam. "You need not fear your karma, Aum Zam," Tompo said. "But you must engage in the practice of dharma to free yourself from this samsara. I have left a simple practice for you with Lachem. Follow it diligently for the rest of your life, and you will be liberated in this lifetime . . . or the next."

With tears streaming down her face and a sense of profound relief enveloping her, Aum Zam bowed her head. As she lifted it, she saw Jadelma gazing at her, a gentle and reassuring smile gracing her lips.

Jadelma nodded at her once and turned away, just in time to meet Tompo's gaze.

"Now, my dear Jadelma, my dakini consort, and my spiritual companion and benefactor," Tompo said, addressing her, "the time has come for me to depart. Therefore, perform this last task for me with a heart full of joy, for we will meet again in a buddha realm."

Jadelma nodded, though a hint of sadness lingered in her eyes. "Yes, my dear Tompo, this is what I have lived for."

"Thank you, my dear Jadelma," Tompo replied, settling into a meditation posture, and then he nodded.

Jadelma and the three dakini women chanted the praise of Kuntuzangpo in melodic and poignant voices, playing their damaru and drilbu, infusing the air with electrifying energy.

The midday sun shone brightly from behind the monastery, yet Tompo's shadow gradually faded until it vanished completely. Subsequently, he closed his eyes and entered a state of tranquillity. Then, his countenance grew serene and his skin glowed with a youthful luminosity.

As everyone watched in astonishment, a symphony of melodious voices and the enchanting tones of damaru and drilbu resonated from the sky. They raised their gaze upwards and witnessed dakinis, each wielding a damaru and a drilbu, forming a circle around the sun and singing the praise of the primordial Buddha in harmony with the dakini women.

The sun's fiery rays were also gradually waning and its brilliance dimming, and this continued until the sun transformed into a white circular presence against the backdrop of the vast blue sky.

When their attention returned to Tompo, his skin was glowing even more brilliantly, and as they watched, his body began to emit radiant beams that intensified gradually, growing brighter and brighter, until his entire being exploded into myriad colours of rainbow light.

Jaws dropped, eyes widened, and gasps of astonishment echoed through the crowd, as Tompo's explosion of rainbow light filled the air with a brilliance that left them in awe.

These myriad colours of rainbow light then coalesced into a swirling motion, forming a human figure of pristine white radiance that shot up into the white circular sun, leaving a trail of white radiance behind, and exploded into a light so brilliant that it eclipsed the entire blueness of the sky.

In that breathtaking moment, fervent voices from the assembly joined the dakinis and the dakini women in prayer, embracing a profound state of reverence.

As they prayed in impassioned voices, the white light gradually disappeared, and the white circular sun, with a human figure of luminous white light seated cross-legged inside it, appeared in the blueness of the sky.

The dakinis turned and faced the human figure within the sun, and as they did, the white sun transformed into a rainbow-coloured circle of the primordial Buddha, Kuntuzangpo, and the human figure inside the sun turned into Tompo.

At that instant, innumerable rainbows filled the sky, and everyone rose to their feet en masse to offer prostrations to Tompo, their fervent voices reaching a crescendo.

But even as they revered him, the rainbow-coloured circle metamorphosed back into the pale white circular sun, and Tompo dissolved back into the luminous white light figure that slowly dimmed and disappeared into the whiteness of the sun.

Simultaneously, the rainbows disappeared from the sky, and the dakinis also gradually faded, with their voices and instruments growing fainter. This continued until they were no longer seen or heard.

Then the four dakini women concluded their praise of Kuntuzangpo, and the sun and the sky returned to their natural state.

Still, everyone continued to gaze upwards, until sweet heavenly fragrances wafted through the air, capturing their senses. They shifted their attention downwards and beheld the four dakini women radiating an extraordinary luminosity, the rare and sacred pundarika and udumbara flowers blooming amidst them, and the holy jangchub tree sprouting, all emitting a mixture of celestial aromas.

As they stood reeling, Jadelma stepped forward and knelt in front of Khennor Jaden Rinpoche, taking the posture of offering a song of praise, and recited the teaching on liberation without the path in verses, exactly as Tompo had instructed her to do.

Then, leading her cohort of three dakini women, Jadelma left for Copper Mountain to begin her lifelong retreat.

Chapter 65

Khennor Jaden Rinpoche turned around and faced the assembly. Everyone stood dazed, still reeling from the spectacle they had just witnessed and feeling an emotion akin to experiencing the ecstasies of both life and death at once.

"The tokdenpa achieved a rainbow body without undergoing the process of death," he explained, his words carrying a sense of both solemnity and transcendence. "He has left the human world and departed for a zhingkham. This attainment of the pure light body is the highest realisation possible, a pinnacle reached only by the greatest of the great masters."

No one said anything, or reacted in any way. Instead, everyone stood in a state of wide-eyed wonder.

"Let us sit down, and I will tell you about it." The rinpoche's words carried an inviting tone, beckoning the assembly to gather for a sacred exchange of knowledge and wisdom.

This time, everyone slowly took their seats.

"Who was Tokdenpa Tompo, Rinpoche?" Pentsa asked, his brows knitted in earnest contemplation and his eyes gleaming with astonishment, as soon as he was settled down. "Was he a buddha living among us incognito? I am sure he was no ordinary person, or even an ordinary rinpoche. To be capable of such a feat, he must have been a buddha." As he spoke, his gaze remained fixed on the rinpoche, awaiting his wisdom and insight.

"He was no incarnation of any master," the rinpoche responded, his wise gaze meeting Pentsa's questioning eyes. "Nor was he an average, ordinary human being, for he lacked the intelligence to grasp and retain even the basics of dharma teaching. But he possessed such purity of heart and mind that he was able to live his life most truthfully and reach an advanced stage of dzogpachenpo."

Pentsa gaped, perplexed, much like everyone else.

"Of course, it didn't unfold simply like that, but with a clever guidance of one great dzogchen master, whom he was fortunate to encounter," the rinpoche quickly clarified, his voice carrying a note of reassurance and a sense of reverence for the role of the dzogchen master.

Everyone stared at him, their confusion deepening further.

"Dzogpachenpo or dzogchen," the rinpoche went on to explain, "as most of you know, is the secret path of tantra that is inherently fluid and flexible. Within this approach, nothing is rigidly set or fixed; rather, everything is open and versatile. This approach enabled them to find an almost impossible way into something truly extraordinary."

A resounding hum echoed through the gathering, as everyone seemed to resonate with this explanation. But as they struggled to fathom the magnitude of Tokdenpa Tompo's accomplishment, the crowd fell into contemplative silence.

Amidst this hushed atmosphere, Lama Kathog cleared his throat and spoke. "Rinpoche, we—all of us here—may have, in some manner, mistreated Tokdenpa Tompo." His voice was gruff, and his tone heavy with remorse and fear. "I cannot imagine the karmic consequences due us."

Lama Kathog's words hung in the air, carrying the weight of collective accountability for everyone involved, as Khennor Jaden Rinpoche pursed his lips and thought this over.

"If you have planted rice, rice will grow without any doubt," the rinpoche responded. His expression was calm and reassuring, but his voice carried a gentle admonition. "Likewise, in karma, you will reap what you have sown. There is not an inkling of doubt: you cannot escape the consequences of your actions. There is no running away from your karma."

A stunned silence, echoing the unspoken truth, hung in the air, as Lama Kathog nodded gravely.

"However, you are not doomed," the rinpoche clarified. "You can always offer a repentance and make amends, and if your remorse is sincere and potent, your negative karma can be exhausted in this lifetime. If you then pursue the path of dharma genuinely and wholeheartedly, you may also be liberated from samsara within this very lifetime."

The rinpoche's words had no reassuring effect on the crowd, thus another silence hung in the air, this one heavy with a sense of impending doom.

"This is because, no matter what you did, you were fortunate to have had some association with the tokdenpa and to have been in his presence," continued the rinpoche. He paused briefly before lifting his finger to emphasise his point. "Even more significantly, you have borne witness to today's most sacred event of dharma. This means you have acquired great merit, merit capable of propelling your practice with immense power."

Lama Kathog nodded with a slight bow, a glimmer of hope reflected in the depths of his expression. "Thank you, Rinpoche."

"Rinpoche," a farmer spoke up from behind, his voice trembling. "We have also greatly mistreated his spouse, dakini woman Jadelma. We were told of her dakini sign, but we regrettably dismissed it and even ridiculed her."

A ripple of unease coursed through the assembly, as everyone collectively realised the consequences of their shared actions.

Thus, the duo of Thogarp and Nagpo, with their hands clasped together in a gesture of contrition, and with remorse and pain etched visibly on their faces, rose to their knees before the rinpoche could respond.

"Of all, we have sinned the most, Rinpoche," submitted Thogarp, his voice heavy, and eyes downcast. "We said and did everything that was bad to both the tokdenpa and the dakini woman. We even helped turn the community of Kisathang against them."

The rinpoche's expression remained impassive, his wise eyes resting on Thogarp, acknowledging his admission, yet feeling a slight sense of disapproval for a monk engaging in such immoral deeds.

"Like the tokdenpa, dakini woman Jadelma is bound for one pure land or another," the rinpoche replied, casting a contemplative glance towards the distance, as if envisioning the spiritual journey ahead. "Hence, any misdeed directed at her will yield unimaginable negative karma. Nonetheless, as I said earlier, you have a pathway to correction through repentance."

The rinpoche's gaze turned back to the assembly, his eyes seeking those of each individual present. Too ashamed to meet his eyes, most cast their gaze downwards.

"You see," the rinpoche said, his voice carrying a note of emphasis, "the good merit you have gained today will equal any amount of negative karma you would have accrued from your past interactions with them. This is because the tokdenpa didn't just leave for a pure land, having attained a rainbow body, but he displayed the process for us to witness in person and be blessed."

A heavy silence persisted in the air, as no one uttered a word.

"Merely witnessing a *thongdrol* is said to free us from samsara one day," the rinpoche continued. "But today? Today we witnessed the actual happening of one of the most sacred events in dharma. So, you see, you are more fortunate than unfortunate. But, of course, you will have to repent truly, which means you must carry out a penance to purge your demerit."

Everyone sat silently, some dazed by his words and others fearful.

Finally, Pentsa cleared his throat and spoke. "Rinpoche, even though we may not comprehend anything, please tell us how a rainbow body is achieved, so that we gain some merit from hearing it." Pentsa paused, as if unsure he should continue, and then added, "It is a thing of great wonder that one can turn oneself into rainbow light and leave for a zhingkham without dying."

"Yes, it is," answered the rinpoche. "But it is neither magic nor trickery, but a case of exercising complete mastery over the true nature of existence." He paused, and gazed intently to make a point. "Now, listen carefully," he ordered, his eyes sweeping from face to face. "Everything in the universe, including we human beings, is made up of five basic elements whose true nature is energy or pure light existing in perpetual motion."

Pentsa nodded.

"Of these five elements, space in its particulate form is the central force from which the universe originated and into which it will ultimately dissolve. Now, how did the universe evolve? Better yet, how does everything manifest and evolve? For, if we delve deeper, we will see that evolution is ongoing. There is no beginning and no end. The universe is made and unmade every moment."

Pentsa sat upright, his attention fully focused on the rinpoche.

"But that is a discussion for another day. For now, to comprehend how a rainbow body is attained, let us go directly into the process of cosmic evolution. Pay attention to this. The space or the cosmos is translucent and open, allowing free movement of the other four basic elements. First, the element of air stirs up and creates wind. This wind in turn swings rapidly into fire. The element of fire then gives rise to water, and from water emerges the solidity of the earth."

Everyone listened, absorbed in the explanation, momentarily forgetting their concerns.

"So, you see, it is through this cosmic evolutionary process, where the high vibratory state of pure light gradually slows down to form dense matter, that the physical world consisting of you and your environment is created," the rinpoche concluded. "This is what the dzogchen practitioners realise when they gain mastery over the true nature of existence."

"Rinpoche," Pentsa interjected, his voice soft, yet brimming with eagerness, "I have heard that the dzogchen masters have the ability to see everything in the form of light energy."

"Yes, these masters not only understand the cosmic evolutionary process of the universe and perceive its true nature in essence, but they also possess the extraordinary ability to visually discern everything as light particles that appear like spinning dots or wheels or, at times, like squiggles or moving shafts of light."

"This is amazing, Rinpoche," came a voice from the assembly.

"Indeed, it is," the rinpoche affirmed with a nod at the person, and then continued. "But those who are highly accomplished can go beyond to reverse the cosmic evolutionary process and transform the solidity of their bodies back into pure light. This phenomenon, as you are aware, is known as attaining the *rainbow body*. Again, there are varying levels of this ability. While most shrink their bodies a bit after death, some have their bodies disappear entirely, leaving behind only hair and nails."

Pentsa nodded, leaning forward.

"However," the rinpoche continued, his eyes gleaming and his voice rising in pitch, "some of the great ones don't even leave their nails and hair behind. And still, the greatest of the great transmute their bodies into pure light at will, without undergoing the process of death, and depart for a zhingkham effortlessly."

"Like our Tompo, Rinpoche?" asked Pentsa.

"Yes, like Tokdenpa Tompo."

Many nodded strongly, their faith and devotion, their hopes and optimism, all welling up from deep inside their hearts.

But a few sat in solemn silence, gripped by fear, hopelessness, and cowardice from deep within.

CHAPTER 66

With a grim face, Lama Kathog packed his kowgum, his movements deliberate as his mind churned with purpose. His spouse and parents stood watching, their faces even grimmer.

"I am not going to remain here, not even for one night," Lama Kathog said, his voice filled with pain. "I will go on a life-long pilgrimage to offer repentance to Tokdenpa Tompo and to carry out penance. If I can purge this seemingly unpurgeable negative karma in this life, then I will seek a teaching that could liberate me in one lifetime and one body."

"Kathog," said his parents in unison, but when he turned to them, their voices trailed off into painful silence.

"Father and Mother, you will also have to leave everything behind and take the path of repentance and penance," he said, his face showing resolve and his voice carrying conviction. "There is no other way, and there is not much time left."

The headman and the amala stood in fearful silence, their expressions frozen.

"Uma Dolma," Lama Kathog said, turning to his wife. "I am afraid even you must go on this path to save yourself. All those words that you uttered and all those deeds that you performed, no matter how insignificant, will haunt you in the bardo when the *great impermanence* has taken over you."

His wife and parents stared blankly, their faces filled with worry and uncertainty, and in that poignant moment, Lama Kathog realised that they had been relying on him for every little thing when it came to matters of dharma, and now he was casting them adrift to navigate on their own.

As he watched their distress, his expression softened. But there was nothing he could do to help. "No matter what binds us together in life," he explained, "we must part ways and go on our own in death: you to your making and I to mine. For even in the lives lived together and the things done together in companionship, the karma generated by each of us is different."

His family appeared even more frightened.

"Father, Mother, Uma Dolma," he said then, addressing them with distinct emphasis. "Heed my words: there is no other way out of this. Even though we are a family, none of us can help the other in this circumstance. Each of us must go on our own, find our own way, and save ourselves on our own."

Neither his parents nor his spouse could find words to speak.

"Father, you must pull yourself together now," he urged, his brow creased, and his hand raised. "You must also tell Mother and Uma Dolma to muster their courage and prepare to take the path of repentance and penance. You cannot afford to remain like this. You will have to offer repentance and carry out penance if you are to save yourself from this negative karma."

"We cannot just take off as you can," the headman finally replied, his tone almost curt, imbued with a trace of anguish and helplessness. "We need initiations and empowerments to embark on such a path."

"Yes, you do, Father," Lama Kathog nodded. "I am only urging you to make up your mind and do what you must."

"I cannot imagine how Tompo achieved such a great feat," the amala said, her voice gruff and her face blank.

"Not Tompo, Mother. He is Tokdenpa Tompo," Lama Kathog corrected.

"It is his destiny, and our bad karma," the headman remarked.

"The destiny that he carved for himself out of nothing," Lama Kathog replied, "and the bad karma that we dug for ourselves for no good reason."

The headman nodded meekly.

Lama Kathog lifted the kowgum and slung it over his back. "I will take my leave," he announced. "Father, Mother, Uma Dolma, I make this aspiration prayer that everything goes well for all of us, and that our paths cross once more in this lifetime." With this, he closed his eyes and mumbled his aspiration prayer, and then turned around and walked away.

The monks and villagers, still enveloped in a state of astonishment, drifted through the monastery campus, basking in the golden glow of the setting sun. As Lama Kathog strode across the campus, they threw fleeting glances his way, and then went about their ways.

Lama Kathog, likewise, exchanged glances with those in proximity before continuing beyond the monastery building, across the cobblestone courtyard, and through the wooden gate.

When he reached the edge of the hillock, he stopped, turned around, and cast one last gaze upon the monastery, before turning back and venturing forward, beyond the crest of the hill.

However, Lama Kathog was not the only one leaving the monastery. His two disciples, Thogarp and Nagpo, were already on the path ahead of him, performing penitential prostrations along the way, their first steps in their lifelong repentance pilgrimage.

As Lama Kathog caught up with them shortly, he did not pause to converse with them, nor did they stand to greet him. But as he walked past the two prostrating men, he caught a fleeting glimpse of sombre expressions etched on their faces.

He sighed and shook his head, his thoughts returning to the journey he and Tompo had undertaken from Tamchu. He was a brilliant scholar and the heir of Dungje nobility, astride a horse heading towards his destiny, and Tompo but a humble servant trudging along, bearing a basket on his back that was as heavy as the weight of his perceived bad karma.

Now, twenty years later, in a twist of destiny, a change of fortune, here he was, embarking on a lifelong pilgrimage of repentance and penance, while Tompo had transformed into rainbow light and departed for a zhingkham, a buddha's abode, alive and unburdened by the process of death.

Author's Note

The Monk Without Dharma was first written as a screenplay for film for international markets. Therefore, it was set in a fictional country in the eastern Himalayas and intended for production in the English language. This imaginary land was also the setting for all my other stories.

However, when I expanded the screenplay into a novel, I chose to place the story loosely within the historical context of Bhutan, sometime during the eighteenth and nineteenth centuries, even though this timeframe is not explicitly mentioned or referenced anywhere in the story.

Yet, despite this historical grounding, much of the story remains generic to the Buddhist cultures and traditions of the Himalayas in general, owing to its dominant content and themes of dharma. This universality is exemplified by the hero's seamless journey across the region.

The novel had secured a publishing deal with Harper-Collins in India, but due to the unforeseen delay caused by the pandemic, the contract was terminated. Nevertheless, this set-back was used as an opportunity to take the publication to the United States of America and introduce the book to a wider global audience.

Glossary

(For story understanding only)

Agay—Grandfather, or a term reserved for all old men

Amala—Respectful title for elderly women, mostly those with social stature

Aum—Respectful title for elderly women

Ani—Lama's spouse, or nun

Ara—Traditional alcoholic beverage

Bardo—Intermediate state between death and rebirth, lasting for forty-nine days

Bodhisattva—Someone who has taken a vow to attain full enlightenment for the benefit of all sentient beings and to help all sentient beings attain that same state

Changkey—Traditional alcoholic beverage brewed during the birth of a newborn baby

Chagbum—One hundred thousand prostrations

Chentey—Small, low table for serving food and drinks to a person of social stature

Choedom—Intricately carved and beautifully painted table for a raised seat

Chokë—Language of dharma

Chorten—Stupa, a Himalayan Buddhist monument, mostly built on strategic natural spots such as pathway junctions, mountain passes, river confluences, and hilltops

Dangrim Chorten—A long rectangular chorten

Daka—male equivalent of dakini

Dakini—Female emanation of wisdom, or female embodiment of enlightened energy

Damaru—Small hand drum used in Himalayan tantric Buddhist rituals

Dharma—Buddhist teachings and principles

Drilbu—Ritual bell used in Himalayan tantric Buddhist rituals

Drolma—Jetsun Drolma or Tara is a powerful female Buddha and meditation deity in Vajrayana Buddhism. She is known as the mother of liberation

Duchen—Important sacred day in Himalayan Buddhism, such as the Descending Day of Lord Buddha

Drupchen—Sacred intensive group practice accomplishment ritual

Dzogchenpa—Practitioner of Dzogchen

Dzogpachenpo—Dzogpachenpo or Dzogchen, translated as Great Perfection, is the final and ultimate teaching, the heart of the teachings of all the Buddhas

Gewa—Activities such as distributing foods and drinks to people, lighting butter lamps, and hoisting prayer flags, done to benefit the deceased in the bardo and in the next life

Gho—Traditional dress for men

Guru Mantra—Sacred chant or incantation of Guru Rinpoche

Khenpo—Scholarly title for monastic scholar

Kira—Traditional dress for women

Korbum—One hundred thousand circumambulations

Kowgum—Basket made of cowhide

Lama—Spiritual teacher in Himalayan Buddhism

Lochoey—Annual religious festival or ritual for a family to appease the family's deity

Losum Choesum—Meditation retreat for three years, three months, and three days

Lüng—Oral transmission of sacred texts

Mandrel—Prayer

Mantra—Sacred syllables chanted in Vajrayana Buddhist practice to invoke the buddhas, bodhisattvas, and deities

Narmé—Vajra hell or the lowest of the Eight Hot Hells, translated as the Hell of Unrelenting Pain or the Hell of Ultimate Torment

Ngag—Mantra or spell with spiritual power

Palang—Long large bamboo used for carrying water

Patang—Short sword handy for all sorts of work

Phowa—Consciousness transference at the moment of death

Rimdro—Himalayan Buddhist ritual for extending life, averting misfortune, overcoming illness and obstacles, accumulating wealth, and such other purposes

Rinpoche—Rinpoche, translated as precious one, is an honorific term for notable reincarnate masters in Himalayan Buddhism

Samsara—Cycle of conditioned existence, birth, and death, characterized by suffering, in which one is continually reborn until attaining enlightenment

Tantra—Esoteric form of dharma and its practice in Vajrayana Buddhism

Tego—Traditional Bhutanese jacket for women

Tendrel—Ceremony to create auspiciousness, or auspiciousness created by the alignment of causes and conditions, interdependence, or dependent arising

Thangka—Sacred Himalayan Buddhist scroll painting of buddhas, bodhisattvas, deities, and mandala

Thongdrol—Thongdrol, translated as liberation on seeing, is a large scroll painting of buddhas, bodhisattvas, and deities

Tokdenpa—Tokdenpa, translated as realized one, is someone who has transcended duality

Trulku—Trulku, translated as incarnation, is a reincarnate bodhisattva in Himalayan Buddhism

Tshongpon—Trader
Wang—Life-empowering blessing bestowed upon people by trulkus and rinpoches
Zhingkham—Pure land of a buddha

Made in the USA
Monee, IL
30 March 2025